A New York Times Notable Book of the Year

"Smashing and satisfying . . . After finishing *Glitz*, I went out and bought everything by Elmore Leonard I could find. . . . [Leonard] moves from low comedy to high action to a couple of surprisingly tender love scenes with a pro's unobtrusive ease and the impeccable rhythms of a born entertainer."

Stephen King, *New York Times Book Review*

"Very good indeed . . . No one else working the suspense genre quite so fleshes out each and every character, and no one else is such a master of street dialogue."

Chicago Tribune

"Leonard's cinematic grasp of scene and setting, his ability to arouse within us a helpless sympathy for even the lowest of his characters, his quirky pacing and plot twists, and his sly humor and artfully oddball prose sear our eyeballs and keep the pages turning."

Miami Herald

"A giant among writers of crime fiction."
Columbus Dispatch

Books by Elmore Leonard

ELMORE LEONARD

GLITZ

HarperTorch

An Imprint of HarperCollinsPublishers

This is a work of fiction. Names, characters, places, and incidents are products of the author's imagination or are used fictitiously and are not to be construed as real. Any resemblance to actual events, locales, organizations, or persons, living or dead, is entirely coincidental.

HARPERTORCH
An Imprint of HarperCollins*Publishers*
10 East 53rd Street
New York, New York 10022-5299

Copyright © 1985 by Elmore Leonard
Back cover author photo © Linda Solomon
Excerpt from *Tishomingo Blues* copyright © 2002 by Elmore Leonard, Inc.
ISBN: 0-06-008953-9

First HarperTorch paperback printing: October 2002
First HarperCollins trade paperback printing: May 1998
First William Morrow hardcover printing: March 1983

HarperCollins ®, HarperTorch™, and ❤™ are trademarks of Harper-Collins Publishers Inc.

Printed in the United States of America

Visit HarperTorch on the World Wide Web at www.harpercollins.com

10 9 8 7 6 5 4 3

1

THE NIGHT VINCENT WAS SHOT he saw it coming. The guy approached out of the streetlight on the corner of Meridian and Sixteenth, South Beach, and reached Vincent as he was walking from his car to his apartment building. It was early, a few minutes past nine.

Vincent turned his head to look at the guy and there was a moment when he could have taken him and did consider it, hit the guy as hard as he could. But Vincent was carrying a sack of groceries. He wasn't going to drop a half gallon of Gallo Hearty Burgundy, a bottle of prune juice and a jar of Ragú spaghetti sauce on the sidewalk. Not even when the guy showed his gun, called him a motherfucker through his teeth and said he wanted Vincent's wallet and all the money he had on him. The guy was not big, he was scruffy, wore a tank top and biker boots and smelled. Vincent believed he had seen him before, in the detective bureau holding cell. It wouldn't surprise him. Muggers were repeaters in their strungout state, often dumb, always desperate. They came on with adrenaline pumping, hoping to hit and get out. Vincent's hope was to give the guy pause.

He said, "You see that car? Standard Plymouth, nothing on it, not even wheel covers?" It was a pale gray. "You think I'd go out and buy a car like that?" The guy was wired or not paying attention. Vincent had to tell him, "It's a *police* car, asshole. Now gimme the gun and go lean against it."

What he should have done, either put the groceries down and given the guy his wallet or screamed in the guy's face to hit the deck, *now*, or he was fucking dead. Instead of trying to be clever and getting shot for it.

This guy wasn't going to lay himself out against any police car, he had done it too many times before—as it turned out—and it didn't pay. He shot from the hip and that was where Vincent took the first one, in his own right hip, through and through. The .38 slug chipped bone, nicked the ilium, missed the socket by a couple of centimeters but raised other hell in its deflected course: tore through his gluteus maximus, taking out his back pocket and wallet containing seventeen dollars and punched his gun out of the waistband of his pants, where it rode just behind his hip. The guy's second shot went through the Hearty Burgundy, passing between Vincent's right arm and his rib cage. At this point Vincent dropped the groceries and went for his piece, yelling at the guy, who was running now, to halt or he'd fire. Here again was a lesson to be learned. When you say it, mean it. The guy halted all right, he half-turned and started shooting again. By now Vincent was on the ground feeling for a Model 39 Smith & Wesson nine-millimeter automatic among broken glass and spaghetti sauce. He found it and fired, he believed, four rounds, three of them entering the guy's body just under his right arm and passing through both lungs.

The Sinai Emergency staff tore Vincent's shirt off looking for a chest wound until one of them sniffed him and said, Christ, it's wine. They x-rayed him, closed the exit wound in surgery, attached some plastic tubes and cleaned glass out of both of his hands.

He was in Intensive Care for the night, wheeled the next morning to a private room as somebody special. The nurse who came in said, "Well, you look just fine to me." Vincent said, thank you, he was. Except for a terrible pain, down there. Pointed and said, "In my penis." He had never called it that before. The nurse took it in her hand, gently removed the catheter and he fell in love with her, her perky cap, her perfect teeth, her healthy body in that starched white uniform. At night she rubbed hospital lotion over his back, his shoulders, soothed that raw gluteus muscle in his right buttock and he called her Miss Magic Hands. Her name was Ginny. Deeply in love he told her the front of his hip hurt too, awful, right there where the leg met the body. Ginny gave him a sly smile and the plastic bottle of lotion. He asked her if she'd like to go to Puerto Rico.

He was going. He'd been once and loved the food. Went down to pick up a wanted felon and waited over a long weekend for a judge to sign the release. He got to visit with a friend of his on the Puerto Rico Police, but didn't get out to Roosevelt Roads that trip. His dad had shipped out of there and was killed at Anzio, taking in an LCVP during the invasion of Italy. Vincent wanted to see Roosevelt Roads. He had a picture of his dad at home taken at El Yunque, up in the rain forest: the picture of a salty young guy, a coxswain, his white cover one finger over his eyebrows, grinning, nothing but clouds behind him up there on the mountain: a young man Vincent had never known but who looked familiar. He was twenty years older than his dad now. How would that work if they ever did meet? His mother said rosaries in the hope they would.

The guy he killed was running on speed and trailing a lifetime of priors, destined—they told Vincent—to crash and burn or die in jail.

"I didn't scare him enough," Vincent said.

He told this to his closest friend on the Miami Beach Police, Buck Torres.

Torres said, "Scare him? That what you suppose to do?"

Vincent said, "You know what I mean. I didn't handle it right, I let it go too far."

Torres said, "What are you, a doctor? You want to talk to the asshole? You know how long the line would be, all the assholes out there? You didn't kill him somebody else would have to, sooner or later."

"Don't you know what I'm talking about?" Vincent said. "If I'd scared him enough he'd still be alive. I mean scare the guy so bad he stops and thinks, he says, man, no more of this shit."

Torres said, "Yeah? How do you know when you scared him enough or you have to shoot him to save your own life? Right in there, that moment, how do you know?"

That was the question.

He'd take it with him to Puerto Rico on his medical leave. Maybe think about it while he healed, maybe not. Lieutenant Vincent Mora was at a point, he wasn't sure he wanted to be a cop anymore. Until that night he had never killed anyone. It made him think about his own life.

2

ISIDRO LOVED THIS GUY TEDDY. He was Mr. Tourist, every taxi driver's dream. The kind not only wants to see everything in the guide book, he wants the same driver every day because he trusts him and believes whatever the driver tells him. Like he wants the driver to approve of him.

This Teddy bought souvenirs he sent to his mother in New Jersey. He wrote postcards and sent them to a guy in Florida, an address with a lot of numbers. He sat in the front seat of the taxi saying, "What's that? What's that?" His camera ready. Isidro would tell him, that's La Perla. Yes, people live down there in those little houses . . . That's San Cristóbal, that's Fortaleza, Plaza de Colón . . .

"What's that? With the bars on the windows?"

"Tha' was the old jail of the city, call La Princesa. But now the jail is in Bayamón." Isidro had to stop so Teddy could take pictures of the entrance, like it was an historical place.

"That used to be the jail, 'ey?"

He always said that, not "hey," he said, " 'ey." He was interested in everything he saw. "The policia drive black and whites, 'ey? Most towns in the States I think our policia drive black and whites too." He took pictures along the narrow streets of Old San Juan. He took pictures of the Caribe Hilton and pictures of the liquor store that was in a building down the street. Strange? A liquor store. He took pictures of the old Normandie Hotel, nearby, that once looked like a ship but was closed now, decaying. A block from this hotel was the Escambron public beach. As soon as the tourist saw it it became his favorite place in San Juan.

It wasn't a tourist place. Isidro said, "You want the most beautiful beach we go to Isla Verde." No, he liked this one. Okay. Isidro believed it was because of the young girls in their bathing suits. The tourist would fix a long lens to his camera and photograph the girls discreetly, without calling attention to himself. Isidro loved this guy.

He kept his money—listen to this, Isidro told his wife—in a money belt made of blue cloth beneath his shirt. He would take money out of it only in the taxi, next to me, Isidro said. He goes in a shop and buys something for his mother in New Jersey, he returns to the taxi before he puts the change in his money belt. He trusts me, Isidro said. Isidro had lived in New York City nine years in a basement and was relieved to be back. His wife, who had never left Puerto Rico, didn't say anything.

Every morning pick him up on Ashford Avenue by the DuPont Plaza, he's ready to go. Ask him how he slept. Oh, he slept like a baby with the breeze that comes from the ocean.

This ocean was different, the tourist believed, than the ocean up in New Jersey. Though it must be the same water because the oceans were all connected and the water would get to different places.

"You know what?" the tourist said. "I might've pissed in that same water when it was up in New Jersey a long time ago, 'ey? I mean back when I was a teenager. I liked to piss on things then. Or be pissing in an alley when a girl comes along? Pretend you don't see her and give her a flash? . . . You go up in the mountains there and take a piss in a stream, where does it go? It goes out'n the ocean. People have been doing it, they been taking leaks, millions and millions of people for thousands of years they been doing it, but it don't change the ocean any, does it? You ever thought of that?"

What Isidro thought was, maybe this guy was a little strange. Innocent, but abnormal in his interests. He's still a prize though, Isidro told his wife. His wife didn't say anything.

The third day at the beach the tourist went swimming. It was easy to find him in the ocean, the sun reflecting on the dark glasses he always wore. He splashed out there, cupping his hands and hitting the water. Man, he was white—holding his arms as though to protect himself or trying to hide his body as he came out of the water in his red trunks. It was interesting to see a body this white, to see veins clearly and the shape of bones. Isidro, originally from Loíza, a town where they made West African masks, was Negro and showed no trace of Taino or Hispanic blood.

"It was when he came for his towel," Isidro told his wife, "I saw the name on his arm, here." Isidro touched the curve of his arm below his right shoulder. "You know what name is on there? MR MAGIC. It's black, black letters with a faint outline that I think was red at one time but now is pink and almost not there. My Mr. Magic."

His wife said, "Be careful of him."

Isidro said, "He's my prize. Look what he gives me," and showed his wife several twenty-dollar bills. He didn't tell her everything; it was difficult to talk with the washing machine and the television in the same room and she didn't seem interested. But that night his wife said again, "Be careful of him."

There were whores on Calle de la Tranca in Old San Juan, different places for anyone to notice. In Condado the whores stood in front of La Concha, another empty hotel that had closed. But none had approached Teddy because Isidro was with him, taking care of him, and the whores knew Isidro in his black Chevrolet taxi. He believed, from the way Teddy looked at the whores displaying themselves, his tourist desired one but was timid about saying it. So Isidro didn't roll his eyes and ask how would you like some of that, 'ey? He wanted to offer him the pleasure of a woman without presenting it as a business transaction. He cared for his tourist.

On that third day at the beach he began to see a way he might do it.

With his tourist wandering about taking pictures, Isidro had time to look at the girls and study them. They seemed to him girls who were lazy and yet restless, moving idly even as they moved to the music of their radios. They seemed to be looking not for something to do but for something to happen, to entertain them.

One in particular he believed he recognized and searched his mind for a name. A girl who had come out of the Caribe Hilton late one night, tired, going home to Calle del Parque. She had given him her name and telephone number saying, "But only men who stay at the Hilton, the Condado Beach, the DuPont Plaza and the Holiday Inn."

Light brown hair with that dark gold skin, and what a body. It was her hair that helped him recognize her, the way it hung down and nearly covered one of her eyes. She held the hair back with the tips of her fingers, like peeking out of a curtain, when she looked at somebody closely. As she did talking to the man with the cane.

Iris Ruiz.

That was her name. He had phoned several times with customers but never reached her. Iris Ruiz.

Talking to the man with the cane.

He remembered now she had been with him yesterday and the day before. The man in the same aluminum chair, reading a book, the cane hooked to the back of the chair. The girl, Iris, kneeling in the sand to talk to him, earnest in what she was saying. The man looking up from his book to nod, to say something, a few words, though most of the time he seemed to read his book as he listened.

His skin was dark from the sun. His hair and his beard, not cared for though not unattractive, were dark enough for him to be Puerto Rican. An artist perhaps, an actor, someone from the Institute of Culture, a member of the party for independence. But this was only his look, his type. Isidro knew, without having to hear him speak, the man was from the States.

The man pushed up on the arms of his chair to rise. He was slender, a lean body in tan trousers that had been cut off to make shorts. No, he wasn't Puerto Rican. The girl Iris took his arm, to be close rather than to support him. He limped somewhat, using the cane, favoring his right leg, but seemed near the end of his injury, whatever it was. He wasn't a cripple. Something in the hip, Isidro believed. Sure, he was okay, he played with the cane more than he used it. He liked that cane. They approached a vendor who was selling pineapples.

Isidro waited a few moments, enjoying the sight of the girl's buttocks as they walked past him, before following them to the cart where the vendor was trimming a pineapple with quick strokes, handing them slices. Isidro saw the girl's eyes as she glanced at him and away, indifferent, without a sign of recognition. He heard the man who wasn't Puerto Rican, it was proved now, say quietly:

"People up there, you know what they do?"

The girl, Iris, said, "Here we go again."

"They work their ass off all year." The guy with the beard ate pineapple as he spoke, in no hurry. "Save their money so they can come down here for a week, take their clothes off. Now they have to hurry to get tan, so they can go back home and look healthy for a few days."

Iris said, "Vincent, I was born with a tan, I got a tan wherever I go. Wha's that? I want to be where people *are*, where they doing things, not where they go to for a week." They were walking away now, Iris saying, "Miami Beach is okay, tha's where you work. I think I like Miami Beach fine."

Isidro followed them to the edge of the sand.

"But you never tell me nothing, what you think. Listen, I got an offer right now, Vincent. A man I know owns a hotel, *two* hotels, wants me to go to the States and work for him. Wear nice clothes, be with people in business—"

"Doing what?"

"Oh, now you want to know things."

The tourist was coming back with his camera. Isidro walked over to the taxi to wait, ready to smile.

Before returning to the DuPont Plaza they stopped at the Fast Foto place on Ashford Avenue—perfect— where the tourist left his rolls of film overnight. Perfect because now they drove past La Concha where a couple of afternoon whores who could be college girls in shiny pants, blond hair like *gringas*, stood by the street.

"Oh, my," Isidro said. "Is okay to look at them, but if a man wish to have a woman he has to be careful. Know the ones are safe so you can avoid disease."

The tourist said, "I imagine you know some, 'ey? Being a cab driver."

"All kinds," Isidro said.

"I don't go for hoors," the tourist said. "I don't want any parts of 'em."

"No, of course not. *These* girls you pay and then you do it. There are other girls, you don't pay them but you leave a gift."

"What kind of gift?"

"Well, you could leave money, is okay."

"Then what's the difference?"

"One is a payment," Isidro said. "The other, is for her to buy her own gift. Save the man the trouble."

The tourist said, "What about, you know of any that aren't hoors but like to, you know, do it?"

"Let me see," Isidro said. "A girl who's very pretty? Has light skin, nice perfume on?"

The tourist said, " 'Ey, sounds good. But don't bother."

"Please, is no trouble."

The tourist said, "No, see, I'm not gonna need you no more. I know my way around now. I'm gonna rent a car."

Isidro's wife was no help. He asked her how this could happen to him, losing his prize, his dream tourist. His wife told him to pray to Saint Barbara, thank her for sending him away, this Mr. Magic.

The next morning Isidro said, "An idea came to me. I believe I can talk to him and make him see he needs me." His wife didn't say anything. But as he drove away in his black Chevrolet taxi that had traveled 170,000 miles and always returned to this home, he saw her standing in the doorway with their four children, watching him leave. Something she had never done before.

* * *

Here was the plan. Pick up the tourist's prints at the Fast Foto place, deliver them to him and refuse to accept payment. A risk, but look at it as an investment. No, please, it's my gift for the pleasure of driving you and for your generosity. Something like that. Then . . . It's too bad you haven't been out on the island, have the pleasure of the drive to Luquillo. Or . . . Oh, what a fine day to go to El Yunque, the rain forest. Or Utuado to see the pottery.

The goddamn prints cost him more than twenty-seven dollars.

He sat in his taxi outside the Fast Foto, still thinking, getting the words in his mind. He opened one of the envelopes of prints, not curious, but to be doing something. They were pictures the tourist had taken of the beach during the past three days. Twenty-four prints—Isidro began to go through them—all in beautiful color.

Less than halfway through he stopped and started over, already feeling an excitement. He looked at the first prints again quickly before continuing on, wanting to be sure the subject of nearly all these pictures was the same and not there by accident. Isidro felt himself becoming inspired but nervous and laughed out loud. He became calm again looking at pictures from the second envelope, taken in the Old City. Fortaleza, Casa del Callejón, those places . . .

But in the third envelope he was back at the beach of Escambron. Here was an ice-cream vendor, here was a man displaying jewelry on a straw mat. Girls, yes, pictures of girls and a number of shots that were so bright they showed almost nothing. But of the forty-two prints in the two envelopes of beach pictures—count them—twenty were of Iris Ruiz. It seemed more than that, one after another, so many views of her in different poses. Wherever the tourist went on that beach he must have been watching Iris, taking pictures of her through his long lens.

Iris talking to the man with the cane, Vincent. Gesturing, posing. Iris lying next to him on a towel. Standing behind him, her hands in his hair as he tried to read his book. Kissing him. Walking with him . . .

Oh, man. Isidro saw those pictures and had the best idea of his life. He drove to Iris Ruiz's house on Calle del Parque and knocked on the door to her upstairs flat.

She was dressed to leave, white purse under her arm, a scowl on her face. He believed at first she scowled because she didn't recognize him and was annoyed, but soon found it was her nature to scowl. When he explained who he was and reminded her of a few things she shook her head and said in English, "I think you have the wrong person."

Isidro said, "It's okay with me," following her down the stairs. "But let me tell you about this guy who's too good to be true. One in at least a million . . . Listen, where you going? Come on, I drive you, free." Like that, getting her in the taxi, the steps of his plan falling into place. Until he handed her the pictures—letting her open the envelope herself, curious now, sure—because everyone liked to look at pictures. She looked at five or six of them, scowling again, said in English, "Why you showing me these? I never want to see him again!" And threw the pictures at the windshield.

Isidro had to stop the taxi, reach down to gather some that were on the floor, wipe them on his leg, look to see if any were damaged. He could scowl too, saying, "What's wrong with you? I'm not showing you *him*, your frien', whoever he is—"

"He's *not* my frien' no more."

"That's okay—who cares who he is? I'm showing you pictures of *you*." He made his voice soft, with an effort, and said in English, "Every one of them, you look good enough to eat." Offering her the prints again. "This guy I mention, Teddy, I never saw a guy with the look he has in his eyes. I think he adores you."

"Yeah?"

"Listen, he's my prize. He's polite. He smells good.

He cleans his fingernails. I believe he'll take you to Howard Johnson for dinner."

"I'm going to the States pretty soon. Couple of days."

"He keeps his hundred-dollar bills in a money belt, under his shirt."

Iris said, "Oh? Where's he stay?"

At the DuPont Plaza. But he wasn't there. The doorman said oh, that guy, he went out with his camera. For the next minute Isidro crept his taxi along Ashford Avenue, suffering anxiety, trying to concentrate on the tourists, Iris scowling, telling him she was late for her appointment . . . And there he was, the flowered shirt, the camera bag— thank you, Jesus—coming out of Walgreen's. Look what a nice guy he was.

Iris said, "He looks like the kind who's afraid of the dark."

Isidro said, "You'll love him, as I do."

"You believe it?" Isidro said to Teddy. "She saw you at the beach and would like to meet you." The two of them standing in front of Walgreen's, tourists walking past them, Isidro's own tourist adjusting his sunglasses as he glanced at the taxi, shy.

"How'd you run into her?"

"At the Foto place. It was lucky, uh? She recognize me because of you. I tole her, sure, I know him. I think he would like to meet you also."

"What'd she say exactly?"

"Ask me if I drive for the photographer. I say, sure. Maybe he like to take your picture." Isidro took a chance, a liberty, and winked at the tourist. "She's a very nice girl. She has an appointment in Isla Verde, but I think she can be free this evening."

Like that, getting him in the taxi.

What was disappointing—Iris remained in front, to show she was a nice girl, and didn't turn all the way around, rest her chin on the back of the seat and give the tourist the business with her eyes and her tongue. Isidro hoped she knew what she was doing. They were so polite he couldn't believe it.

Are you enjoying your vacation? Very much. Do you like Puerto Rico? Yeah, it's really nice. Is a nice climate, uh? Perfect.

Jesus Christ. Isidro wanted to say to the rearview mirror, You got twenty pictures of this whore. You desire her or not? But he kept quiet. At least the tourist was in his taxi again. Now she was telling him she was going to the States pretty soon. Atlantic City. "I have a position offered me with the company I'm going to see."

And she knows all the positions, Isidro was thinking—when the tourist surprised him.

He said, "Yeah? I'm from right near there. Born in Camden, New Jersey. My mom lives in Margate now, that's practically right next door to Atlantic City. You ever been there?"

Iris said no, but she had been to Miami once and didn't like it very much.

The tourist said, "You walk down the Boardwalk from Atlantic City you come to Ventnor and then Margate, but it's like all one. You know what I mean? One city. I lived in Miami a while, I didn't like it either."

"I was going to live in Miami Beach," Iris said, "but I change my mind. I prefer Atlantic City."

"There's way more to do there," the tourist said.

Tell her what you want to do to *her*, Isidro said to the mirror.

"They want me to work as a hostess for the company," Iris said. "They have many social functions."

"A hostess," the tourist said. "They got a few of those in Atlantic City, all right."

"The position was offer to me by the boss himself, Mr. Tommy Donovan. He owns the big hotel in Isla Verde I'm going to. He's crazy for me to work for him. He tole me that."

Hurry, Isidro thought, *some*one. He was helpless.

They turned off the highway and soon came to the beach, to the casino hotel that resembled a mosque among palm trees. Part of it did. Three stories of arched Moorish Modern topped with a dome the shape of a spade, an inverted heart pointing to heaven. Signs in all sizes, everywhere, said *Spade's Isla Verde Resort*. The tourist said, "Jeez, what a place, 'ey?" The hotel, tan cement and dark glass, rose fifteen stories above the east end of the casino complex.

Iris said, "Is nothing compare to the much bigger hotel in Atlantic City, where I'm going to be a hostess." Telling the tourist she was too good for him. She left the taxi, not even saying thank you.

"I can tell you where she lives," Isidro said. "Number five two Calle del Parque. Close by your hotel."

The tourist watched her go inside the casino before he moved into the front seat. He opened one of the envelopes, looked at the prints for a moment and said, "Let's go for a ride."

Isidro had his tourist again and felt so good that he could admit, "I pick up the pictures to give you so I could speak to you again and hope to be of service." The tourist seemed content, gazing out at the countryside from the highway as they drove toward Carolina. "There is so much to see out on the island," Isidro said. "All this use to be sugar cane here. Now, look, use car places. Way over there, apartment buildings."

The tourist would look out his side window, turn his head slowly and Isidro would see his sunglasses, his serious expression. Interested, but not amazed at anything today. Not asking what's that? . . . what's that? Instead he said:

"Why'd you think I wanted to meet her?"

"Well, she's a nice girl, very nice looking, I believe educated . . . We can go north to Loiza, my home where I was born. If you like to buy a famous *vejigante* mask, for your mother." The tourist didn't say anything. "Or we can go to El Yunque. You hear of it? The rain forest on the mountain, very beautiful . . ."

"Let's go up there," the tourist said, and Isidro relaxed; he had his tourist for at least the rest of the day and could show him the sights, show him some excitement on the way up there, some expert driving.

Blowing his horn, leaning on it through blind mountain curves, climbing through dark caverns of tabonuco trees a thousand years old, gunning it past the diesel noise of tour buses—everybody going to El Yunque, the showplace of the island. Look, what forests were like before men were born. Where frogs live in trees and flower plants grow on the branches. The tourist didn't raise his camera.

"You don't want pictures?"

"I can get postcards of this."

Not in a good mood. He didn't want to go in the Rain Forest Restaurant, he wasn't hungry today. At the Visitor Center he said, "Let's get away from these goddamn buses." Isidro removed a barrier where the road was closed because of a landslide. It was slippery in places but no trouble to get through. Nobody working to clear the mud. This was more like it, not running into people everywhere. A jungle in the clouds. The tourist said, "Let's get out and walk." Okay—once Isidro found a place to put the taxi, off the road deep into a side trail, in case a park service guy came along. Park service guys liked to be important, Isidro said, yell at drivers.

The tourist led them along a footpath, following a sign that said *El Yunque Trail*. They left it behind, following side trails, and came to an open place that ended, fell away hundreds of feet to a sight of clouds like fog over the treetops below. Beautiful. It gave Isidro the feeling he could dive off and land down there in that soft green sponge. Now he saw the tourist bring his camera case in front of him and open it, take out the camera and hang it from his neck. The tourist looked out at the view, then at Isidro, then stepped away from the edge, raising his camera.

"Smile."

Isidro posed, nothing behind him but clouds, trying hard to smile. He believed it was the first picture the tourist had taken of him.

"You want me to take one of you?"

"No, stay there." The tourist snapped another picture and said, "Tell me what you're up to."

Isidro said, "Please?"

Something was wrong. It was in the tourist's expression. Not a serious one but not a nice one either. He wasn't happy, he wasn't angry, he wasn't anything. The tourist took off his sunglasses and slipped them into his shirt pocket as he said, "They ask you a lot of questions about me?"

It was as though a disguise was removed and Isidro was seeing him for the first time, seeing the man's eyes as tiny nail points holding him, telling him he had made a mistake, failed to observe something. For a moment his wife was in his mind, his wife speaking to him with the sound of the washing machine and the television. He was confused and it made him angry.

"*Who?* Nobody ask me anything."

"No? They didn't pay you?"

"Mister, I don't know what you talking about." The only thing he knew for sure, the man was no longer his prize.

"Tell me the truth. Say the girl approached you?"

"Yes, she want to meet you."

"Go on."

"I said okay. See, I thought you like her, a lot."

"You did, 'ey? Why?"

"Man, all the pictures you took of her." He

watched the tourist stare at him, then begin to smile, then shake his head back and forth and heard the tourist say:

"Oh, shit. You looked at the prints you picked up this morning. Didn't you?"

Isidro nodded. Why not? The tourist didn't seem angry now. "But I didn' hurt them, I jus' look at them."

The tourist said, "Jesus, you thought I liked Iris, so you were gonna fix me up. All this was your idea."

Isidro said, "Is up to you. It doesn' matter."

The tourist was still smiling, just a little. He said, "You dumb fuck, I wasn't taking pictures of *her*."

Isidro saw the tourist's hand go into the camera case and come out holding a gun, an automatic pistol, a big heavy one. The tourist—what was this?—he would have film and suntan lotion in there, not a pistol. If there was something wrong with him, if he was abnormal—it was okay to be abnormal, sure, act crazy for fun, wear masks . . . when it made sense to act crazy, want to scare people. *This* trying to scare him made no sense . . .

And he yelled at the tourist, "But she's in the pictures!"

The tourist said, "So's the guy with her."

Isidro paused, still not understanding, then saw it, what was going to happen, and yelled out again, "*Momento!*"

The tourist shot him in the head, almost between the eyes. He listened to the echo and shot him again, on the ground, before rolling him over the edge of the mud bluff, into the clouds.

Teddy had a frosted Rain Forest Julep at the restaurant. It wasn't bad. He bought a handicraft hand-painted parrot for his mom, wandered out to a Gray Line charter bus with a bunch of sightseers and was back in San Juan by six o'clock: in time for the evening traffic on Ashford Avenue. Jesus, but PRs liked to play their radios loud. This day had been a kick in the ass. It woke him up, told him to quit creeping around acting like a fool. Get it done and get out.

3

THE RESTAURANT CALLED EL CIDREÑO offered Creole
cooking and was popular with the Criminal Affairs
investigators who worked out of Puerto Rico Police
headquarters on Roosevelt Avenue, Hato Rey.

They would come in here or look over from their
tables and see the bearded guy with Lorendo Paz
and make the guy as an informer. Look at him. The
hair, the work shirt they gave him in Bayamón.
Caught in a drug bust and fell out a window—the
reason for the cane—and after a month in the hole
willing to make a plea deal. Except that Lorendo
Paz, always properly attired, wearing the cream-
colored suit today, would touch his napkin to his
trimmed mustache, take the napkin away and be
smiling, talking to the guy like they were good
friends. So then the cops who came in El Cidreño or
looked over from their tables would think, sure, the
guy was a narc, DEA, and had to dress like that, the
junkie shirt with the jeans and rubber sandals . . .
But if he was undercover or he was an informer,

what was he doing out in the open talking to a Criminal Affairs investigator? Finally a cop known for his determination got up from his chicken and plantains, went over to the table where Lorendo sat with the bearded guy and said, "Lorendo, I need to talk to you later today." Lorendo said, "Of course," and then said, "Oh, I want you to meet Vincent Mora. With the Miami Beach Police, Detective Bureau. We know each other a long time, since the FBI school. Yes, Vincent has been here, almost two months, on a medical leave. A robber shot him in the hip."

Oh.

After that the investigators would look over and wonder if the bearded guy, Vincent, was any good. A robber had shot him, uh? What happened to the robber? If they say he got away maybe it wasn't a robber who shot him but a woman's husband. The investigators, eating their black beans and rice, their fried pork and bananas, enjoyed that idea and suggested different ways the shooting might have occurred. Their favorite one was Vincent going out the window naked—*bam*.

Vincent Mora. The guy didn't look Puerto Rican, though his name could be. All the money that cops in the States got paid—why didn't he buy some sharp clothes with style? What was he talking about to Lorendo so intently?

* * *

He was talking about Iris Ruiz.

Lorendo made his face look tired, without effort, and told Vincent he was making a career of Iris Ruiz because he needed something to do that was important to him and concerned a person's life, not because Iris was a special case. There were a thousand Iris Ruizes in San Juan.

Vincent narrowed his eyes at him.

And Lorendo raised Iris's rating. All right, there was no one like her. Okay? Fantastic girl. Her looks could stop your breathing. She had style, class, personality and she made sure a doctor looked up her every week without fail.

Vincent shook his head.

And Lorendo said, "What you're doing we've both seen, how many times? The cop who has a feeling for a whore. He wants to be her savior, change her, make her like she used to be, uh? Before she found out that little fuzzy thing she sits on can make her money."

"That's not nice," Vincent said.

"Oh, is that so? What is it attracts you to her, her mind? Her intelligence?"

"I don't know what happened," Vincent said. "Ever since I got shot I've been horny. It started, lying in the hospital looking at the nurses. What is it about nurses? Almost every woman I look at now I take her clothes off. Not all women, but more than you'd think."

"Who doesn't?" Lorendo said. "Man, you don't have to get shot."

"It's like I'm starting over again, looking at girls."

"It's your age. How old are you, forty?"

Vincent said yes, and then said, "Forty-one."

"Sure, it's your age. Maybe getting shot, too. You see you aren't going to live forever, you don't want to miss anything."

"Maybe . . . You ever been shot?"

"No, I've been lucky."

"It can happen," Vincent said, "when you least expect. I was off duty, walking home . . ." He said, "You know, I could retire with fifteen years in. I could stay right here and draw three-quarters of my pay for life." It would buy a lot of cod fries and crab turnovers, get him a nice place near the beach. He could live here. Why not? He said, "I could stand to get married again. It's what people do, they get married. But not to Iris. That's never entered my mind."

"Good. There's hope for you."

"You know what she has for breakfast? Toast and a Coke."

"You need to go back to work," Lorendo said. "You think she has a problem. You're the one with the problem. You nice to a girl like that, give her what she wants, oh, everything's fine. You don't give in to her, what happens?"

"She whines, she breaks things . . ."

"Vincent," Lorendo said, amazed, "this little girl, she's leading you around by your *bicho*. You know that?"

"All she talks about is going to the States."

"Of course. It's the dream, marry some rich guy. They all want that. Man, you stick your nose in there, you bring all this on yourself. I love it."

"Well, now she's going. This guy Donovan that owns the hotel, she says offered her a job as a hostess. In Atlantic City."

"Ah, Mr. Tommy Donovan," Lorendo said. "Now we're getting to something."

"Not here, Atlantic City."

"I heard you. They built a place there last year, cost a hundred million dollars."

"I want to talk to him."

"Go out to the hotel. You take the T-One bus."

"He's never in his office," Vincent said, "or he's in conference. And his home phone's unlisted."

"So that's why you take me to lunch. You want me to get you his private number."

"And his address. I want to look him in the eye."

"I don't believe this," Lorendo said. "You going to see this guy, head of one of the biggest private companies in Puerto Rico, he's in land development, man, he's in hotel casinos, to ask him about *Iris?*"

"You just put your finger on it," Vincent said. He pushed his plate of crab shells away from him to lean on the table. "Tell me why a guy like that wants to take a girl like Iris all the way to Atlantic City? As a hostess—whatever a hostess is."

"Because," Lorendo said, "he can do anything he wants. That's the thing that gets you, isn't it? Man, it's becoming more clear to me. You resent this guy Tommy Donovan. It doesn't matter you don't want Iris, you don't want him to have her. Vincent," Lorendo said, "she's a whore. What whores do, if they can, they go where the action is."

"She quit."

"Oh, you believe that?"

"Get me the guy's address," Vincent said. "Would you do that for me?"

He paid the check. Lorendo, waiting for him outside, was talking to the investigator who had approached their table. The investigator nodded to Vincent as he came out, looking at his rattan cane, his rubber sandals, and Lorendo said, "Vincent, my associate was asking, he would like to know what happened to the man who shot you."

"He died on the way to the hospital," Vincent said, looking directly at Lorendo's associate, straightfaced. "I think he lost his will to live."

* * *

Calle del Parque, Number Fifty-two, upstairs.

Teddy knocked on the door and knocked and knocked until it opened a few inches and there was a pretty sleepy girl looking at him over the chain. Her eyes puffy, what he could see of them in all that hair.

"Hi. You remember me?"

Iris said, "I'm still sleeping."

"We met in the taxicab yesterday. How'd your business appointment work out? I remember you said you were going to Atlantic City. I thought, hey, maybe you'd do me a favor."

"Listen, why don't you come back—"

Teddy held up the crisp hundred-dollar bill, folded twice, between the tips of two fingers, laid it on the chain right in front of her nose. "I got something I need delivered. That is, if you're going."

She seemed to wake up, staring at that C-note. "I don't know for sure. I think tomorrow or the day after."

"That'd be perfect. See, my mom's birthday's pretty soon. I got something special for her"—he patted the camera case hanging at his side—"but she won't get it in time if I send it by mail. I was thinking—see, it's only a few miles from Atlantic City down to Margate. You ever play Monopoly? She lives in Marvin Gardens."

"What?" She frowned at him.

"Hop in a cab, you're there."

"For that money?" Iris said.

"It's worth it to me. My mom's gonna be seventy."

It surprised him that a Puerto Rican girl would be so cautious. He usually got into apartments with the old survey routine. "Hi, I'm with International Surveys Incorporated"—show the phony card—"We're conducting a study to learn what young ladies such as yourself think of current trends in . . ." the price of bullshit. You could tell them almost anything.

He palmed the C-note as she closed the door to release the chain and that was that. It was dim and quiet inside, the way he liked it. With just faint sounds out on the street. It smelled a little of incense, or perfume. She held her silky green robe closed, then relaxed, yawning, and let the robe slip open before pulling it together again, though not in any hurry. She was wearing little white panties under there, no bra. He sat down in a sticky plastic chair without waiting to be asked. Shit, he was in now. Reaching into the camera case he almost began to recite his International Surveys routine. ("If I might ask what your husband does . . . He's at work, is he?") Taking out the handicraft parrot wrapped in tissue paper he said, "I don't have a box or anything to mail it in, either." Fool around for a minute, make sure they were alone. One time a big hairy son of a bitch had come walking out of the bedroom in his undershirt . . .

She was yawning again, hair hanging in her face. He liked that sleepy look. She stretched, arching her back. The robe came open to give him a peek at a brown nipple, a big one. He liked that, too.

"How's your boyfriend?"

"My boyfrien', who's that?"

"Guy you're with at the beach every day."

"He's not even a frien' of mine no more. Listen, when you going to pay me?"

"Guess I was wrong. I met him one time. His name Vincent Mora?"

"Yea, Vincent."

"He live here with you?"

"Man, are you crazy?"

"I thought you two were pretty tight."

"What happen to the money you had in your hand?"

"I got it." Teddy showed her the C-note. "Right here."

"Yeah, what do I have to take to your mother?"

"This." He showed her the package. "It's a parrot. Mom loves parrots. She's got a real one sits on a perch outside the cage. You know what it says?"

Iris shook her head.

Teddy constricted his throat to imitate the parrot. "It says, 'Hello, May! Hello, May! Want a drink?' That's how it sounds. The parrot's name is

Buddy. She's got parrot dishes and cups, parrot ash-
trays, parrots made out of china sitting on the mantel. Let's see, she's got a satin parrot pillow. She
loves parrots . . . Yeah, I thought you and Vincent
might be living together."

Iris said, "No way, José."

Teddy grinned. "That's cute . . . Let me ask you,
Vincent lives—I was told he lives over by the Hilton
on that street runs next to it? In the Carmen Apartments? That's what they said at his office when I
called there."

"Yes, the Carmen Apartments."

"Is that the place there's a liquor store in it? I
didn't see a sign or nothing, I wasn't sure."

"Yes, in the downstairs." She kept looking at his
hundred-dollar bill.

"Handy to the beach," Teddy said. He glanced
around the room. "You live here alone, 'ey?"

"Till I move to the States. I can't wait."

"You bring guys here?"

She began to frown now and looked mad. Got up
on the wrong side of the bed, his mom used to say.

"What do you ask me questions for? You want
me to take that thing? Okay, give me the money."

Teddy folded the hundred-dollar bill between his
thumb and two fingers, then folded it again into a
tight square. He said, "Catch," and threw it at her.

Iris let go of her robe and caught it, showing
good reflexes for a crabby girl. She had probably

had money given to her in some interesting ways. He watched her slip the C-note into the band of her panties. She said, "I be back," and walked out of the room.

Teddy waited a few moments and followed her, into a little hall, then left a few feet to the bedroom. He watched her from the doorway, her back to him, taking the money out of her panties and slipping it into the top drawer of her dresser. There were clothes on the floor. The bed was a mess, the sheet all tangled up. But it was a bed, and there she was next to it.

So easy.

Iris turned, raising her eyes to Teddy, not at all surprised to see him. "Will you excuse me so I can go to bed?"

Should he whip it out?

No, too easy.

The best part, always, was seeing that shit-scared gleam of terror in their eyes, the woman realizing this wasn't any survey of current trends, what housewives liked or didn't . . .

This one was different. Now that he hesitated and thought about it, this one *was* a survey. Find out exactly where the guy lived. Now he knew. Now, if he watched himself, didn't get carried away, he could fool around with this girl. Play with the cop's girl. See what it was like.

Teddy said, "Why don't I get in there with you?"

"Please, I'm very tired."

Teddy raised his sport shirt hanging out of his pants to show her the money belt that was like a blue nylon cummerbund around his middle. "You know what this is?"

Her expression seemed different now, her mouth open a little like she was thinking, about to make a guess. She said, "Is it a life preserver you wear for swimming?"

Teddy grinned. "You're pretty cute, Iris. You know it?"

She said, "It's not *I*-ris, like your eyes. It's *Eer*-es."

"Like your ears?" Teddy said. He thought she'd laugh, but she didn't. She was staring at his money belt.

"What do you keep in that?"

Teddy said, "Let's see," and put his chin on his chest as he zipped open the flat pouch. "I got a comb. I got a little penknife I use to clean my fingernails. A pack of Certs, breath mints. Let's see, I got rubbers. My mom must've put 'em in there." He looked up and winked at her as he said it. She didn't laugh or even smile. He continued the inventory and got a note of surprise in his voice as he said, "What's this? Why, it looks like a bunch a money."

Iris said, "I hope you don't think you can give me money and go to bed with me."

Teddy said, "No way, José," grinning. Shit. "I'm gonna go to bed with you, sweetheart, then leave you a present, a gift. If you know what I mean."

Iris said, "Because you adore me."

"Not only that," Teddy said, "it'll be my first time in over seven years."

Iris frowned at him. "Since you did it?"

"With a woman," Teddy said. "I been away."

Vincent took a shower that afternoon after the lunch with Lorendo Paz, thinking about what he had said outside the restaurant. "He died." The guy who had shot him. "Lost his will to live." Talking cop to cop, offhand, nothing to it. It was all right; maybe cops needed to do that. Play it down. Though he might have asked them about scaring guys to keep them alive, what they thought of it. In his mind, not paying attention, he slipped getting out of the shower, caught himself but banged his hip against the tile wall, hard. God *damn* it hurt. He had to sit on the bed to pull his pants on: khakis fresh from the laundry. With a blue shirt, he decided, dark blue tie and the linen sportcoat that cost ninety bucks on Ashford Avenue and almost matched the khakis but was lighter: his suit, his best outfit. Dressing up to go see Mr. Donovan.

He looked at himself in the bathroom mirror. Moved closer, picked up the scissors and snipped at his beard, attempting to weed the thin streaks of gray, aware of himself in the silence, look, getting older. He would have to shave off the beard to get rid of the gray. But he liked the beard, so keeping it was a compromise. Living here would be the same thing, if he decided to stay. He didn't know what he wanted. If he quit the police and stayed would it be because the guy shot him or because he shot the guy? Was he going to see Donovan because he was concerned about Iris? Or to get back into it, to be doing something, practice his trade? Analyze that.

His hip still hurt as he hobbled out on his cane through the courtyard of the Carmen Apartments that was like a small parking lot for the liquor store. People parked on the sidewalk in San Juan; they parked everywhere. He tested himself moving through the cars: walk all the way over to Fernandez Juncos, in some pain, to hop a T-1 bus, or get a cab at the Hilton for the ride to Isla Verde? This was no way to live—without the city providing a car. Even a gray Plymouth Reliant with nothing on it.

The guy in the straw hat and sunglasses was studying a map spread open on the roof of his car. The guy looked up and said, "Excuse me?" As though he weren't sure if he should be excused or not.

Vincent recognized him from the beach: the tourist who came in the black Chevy cab and took pictures.

"I think I'm lost."

Vincent thought of saying to him, No, you're

not. His cop mind telling him the tourist had been waiting for him. Which could mean the tourist had followed him or knew beforehand where he lived. The tourist didn't act lost. He didn't have the proper lost expression, helpless or annoyed. The tourist was grinning, the grin saying, Look what a nice guy I am. And Vincent thought, bullshit; the guy was trying too hard. Guys like that made him nervous.

"I came over from Condado Beach," the tourist said, "the traffic across the bridge was going both ways. Now it's one way and I can't figure out how to get back."

The guy had come up with a good one. Maybe he was all right. Vincent said he'd show him and got in the car. Then was sorry. The guy was a terrible driver. Vincent would feel the guy looking at him, see the rear ends of cars lighting up in the traffic and have to brace against the dash as the guy hit the brakes.

The tourist said, "The PRs sure play their radios loud. You notice?" He said, "They can't drive for shit." He said, "I think I've seen you someplace. I know I saw you on the beach, I mean before that."

Vincent waited.

"Was it in Miami?"

Vincent said, "I don't know. It might've been."

"That's where you're from, 'ey?"

"Miami Beach."

The tourist took his time. "You're a cop. Huh?"

Vincent glanced at him to make sure he had the guy in his mind, then looked back at the traffic. "If we've met before, tell me about it."

"I understand you got shot."

Vincent didn't like this guy at all, the feeling he was getting. He said nothing and listened to the guy's voice, his unhurried delivery, the words rehearsed.

"I bet it hurts to get shot, 'ey?" The tourist wearing sunglasses and a straw hat, props, with the sun gone for the day, off behind them somewhere. The tourist said, "You don't have no idea who I am, do you?"

Vincent would be willing to make a guess now, in a general area, and bet money on it. But he said, "I'm afraid not. Help me out."

"It was seven and a half years ago."

"What was?"

"When we met."

"Take a left at the next light. It goes straight through to Ashford, if you want the beach."

"We first met I didn't get a good look at you," the tourist said. "But after that I had time." He paused, making the turn, before he said, "Four days in a row."

"Dade County Court," Vincent said.

"That your guess?"

Vincent said, "You can let me off at the corner there'll be fine. I appreciate the ride."

The tourist kept going. He said, "Do I make you nervous?"

Vincent said, "Your driving does. Jesus."

The light at Ashford was red and the tourist stopped on the left side of the one-way street, so Vincent would have to get out in the traffic. The tourist said, "I'm gonna let you think about it, Vince. Till we see each other again." He took off his straw hat and sunglasses, giving Vincent one more chance to make him.

Vincent got his left leg out of the car before pushing himself up to stand in the street. The light changed. Horns went off close behind him. He hunched over in the doorway, his back to the noise. "You know why I don't recognize you?"

"Why?" the tourist said.

"Because all of you shifty ex-con assholes look alike," Vincent said. He slammed the door, limped around behind the car and into Walgreen's drugstore.

Vincent reversed the charges on his call to Buck Torres, Miami Beach Police. Torres came on with, "What's the matter? Is anything wrong?" Vincent asked him how it was going and Torres said, same old thing, trying to stay ahead of the assholes. They talked for a minute, Vincent watching the traffic, the young Puerto Rican guys in their cars, turning onto Ashford to make a slow loop through the Candado tourist section, playing their radios. Vincent said:

"What I need, check with Hertz for me. Find out who's driving a white Datsun, PR license number Twenty Baker Two-Eighty and where he told them he's staying. Okay? Now close your eyes and look at a male Caucasian, mid-thirties, five-nine, a hundred and forty, dishwater straight hair, long thin nose, mole under his right cheekbone. Creepy guy, we sent him up about seven and a half years ago."

Torres said, "I don't see anybody."

"Get the name from Hertz and run it. Okay? I think he was released in the past couple of weeks, he looks like shit."

"He just got out," Torres said, "how'd he get a credit card?"

"I don't know," Vincent said, "but he's driving a rental. If he stole the I.D. all the better. Comes to Puerto Rico and does five to ten. But I'd have to canvas all the hotels to find him, wouldn't I? And my leg hurts."

"You saw him and you think you know him, or what?"

"He knows *me*," Vincent said. "He knows where I live, he knows I was shot . . . I think I'm the reason he's here. Because I fucked up his life."

"Sure, it's your fault, Vincent."

"Can you do it now, call me right back?"

"Everybody's on the street but me. Why don't I call you later, at your place?"

"Where do you think I'm staying? I don't have a phone." He watched polished Japanese cars turning onto Ashford. The bus stop was three blocks away. The ride out to Isla Verde could take a half hour. He said, "Wait, I got a number you can use," and took a slip of notepaper out of his coat pocket. "But you have to call within the next hour. Okay?"

Torres said, "You miss work, Vincent—is that it?"

4

THE MAID WAS NERVOUS because she had worked in this house only ten days, taking the place of her sister, and she didn't want to do something bad and be fired. But she was so nervous she was afraid she was going to cry and not hear anything the man was saying.

She wished Mr. Donovan would be quiet.

She was talking on the telephone—the white one on the wall in the kitchen—to a man who had called and was telling her in Spanish to write something in English. She had finished high school last year, but she couldn't think and spell the words fast enough to keep up with the man's voice. Then she wouldn't hear something he said, with Mr. Donovan talking at the same time.

Mr. Donovan sat at the kitchen table eating a bowl of chili made with beans, a fence of green bottles in front of him; he wore only tennis shorts and appeared naked at the table. Before, when he began eating, he drank down an entire glass of beer and said, "Oh Jesus," his eyes wet, as though he was crying, drank a second glass without stopping and said, "Honey, you know what? I'm going to live." He asked her to get him two more bottles of beer from the refrigerator. Eating the hot chili his eyes watered even more and he said, "Oh Christ, Oh Jesus," using this blasphemy to show his pleasure, using the good linen napkin to blow his nose. His eyes were so strange, appearing wet with emotion but at the same time drugged, staring without seeing. His body, too, was strange. A giant man made with parts and tones of color that didn't go together. Waves of silver hair. His face colored red and brown. A handsome man if you didn't stand close to him and see he must be fifty years old. Suntanned neck and arms. But narrow shoulders of bone and a body so pale and softly round it could belong to a fat woman from the States with very small breasts. She had seen such women.

When the phone rang and she began to talk to the man calling from Florida, she could hear Mr. Donovan saying, "I'm not here. Christ, I'm not anywhere yet . . . Tell whoever it is I moved and left no forwarding address . . . Honey, tell 'em you're busy . . . The hell are you writing?" Never shutting up as she tried to listen to the voice on the phone and write the information, the voice telling her a name she thought was *mágico*, then spelling it for her and it wasn't like *mágico* at all. She was saying to the voice, *"Despacio,"* repeating it every moment, and Mr. Donovan was saying, "Tell them they've got the wrong *número*." She was feeling her tears coming, not wanting to lose this job that had been her sister's, but thinking she was going to have to run out of here . . .

When the door opened and Mrs. Donovan came in from the garage to save her.

Mrs. Donovan, beautiful in her straw hat, her white dress that was tied about the waist but loose and showed her body as she moved. A saint coming in that soft dress, saying to her husband, "You look lovely."

Mr. Donovan said, "Sit down and have one. It's cocktail time."

Please, the maid thought, not having to say it because she could see Mrs. Donovan's eyes, shaded by the straight line of the hat brim, so calm, and knew she was saved.

In her quiet voice: "Who is it?"

"I don't know what he's telling me I'm suppose to write." She believed she could let her tears come now and it would be all right.

Mrs. Donovan removed one of her earrings. She took the phone, covering it with her hand. "Someone's at the front door." Almost as she said it the maid's eyes widened with the sound of the chimes and Mrs. Donovan smiled with her kind eyes. "I saw him as I drove in." As the maid walked off she heard Mrs. Donovan say, "Yes, can I help you?"

She wished she could stay and listen to Mrs. Donovan talk to the man on the telephone. Her sister had told her she could learn amazing things working in this house and the house up north in New Jersey, where they lived most of the year.

Watch the way Mrs. Donovan treats the great Mr. Donovan, her sister said. It's better than the television. They're both married for the second time, to each other less than three years. Does she love him? See if you can tell. They sleep in different bedrooms. She's more intelligent than he is, but he doesn't know it. Watch out for him when he's drinking, which is every day. Watch out for him late at night. He believes all women are in love with him. Her sister, who left this house to be married and live in New York, said, Never lie to Mrs. Donovan. Never tell anyone what you see and hear. Some of it you won't believe.

The maid's name was Dominga. As she reached the front door the bell chimed again.

Vincent said, "Hi, how you doing?" He told her he'd like to see Mr. Donovan.

Dominga paused a moment. "Can I say to him who you are?"

"I want to surprise him."

"Yes, but I'm suppose to ask your name."

He could use his shield and I.D., but it could complicate matters once he was in. "Okay. Tell him Vincent Mora."

The maid came to life. She said, "Mr. Mora— yes, please, come in."

He waited in a sitting room he believed no one had ever sat in: wondered about the Taino Indian bowl on the marble table, the primitive displayed in the formal setting; wondered why the maid had looked so surprised; wondered if this piece of pottery was more authentic than the ten-buck Taino stuff and if it was, how could you tell. He heard the sound of narrow heels in the tiled hall that was big enough to hold the rooms he lived in. The sound coming, echoing. Not the maid . . .

The woman in the Mercedes who had turned into the drive as he approached the house. Not wearing the wide-brimmed straw now . . . He liked her hair. Sun-streaked, natural looking, sort of parted and almost to her shoulder. Mid-thirties, five-five, slim, one-ten—his cop mind filing it away—movie star teeth, brown eyes that were calm, quietly aware, measuring him, maybe curious, maybe not.

"Mr. Mora?"

She came from the doorway onto the oriental rug, but only so far, a piece of plain white notepaper in one hand, the other closed around a small object that made the hand a delicate fist.

"I'm Nancy Donovan . . . your answering service."

Vincent said, "Let me explain that, okay? It took me longer to get here than I thought it would."

Nancy Donovan waited.

"I don't have a phone."

She said, "Oh, I see."

"I thought, if I'm here and I get the call you wouldn't mind. Except I didn't make it in time. I had to take a bus from Candado."

She said, "You don't have a phone, you don't have a car either." She was looking at his cane now. "I'm sorry—here, let's sit down." Coming over to the marble table. "I'll give you your message, if I can read my own writing. What's your friend's name, Torres?"

"Buck Torres."

He liked her. He liked her quiet tone, her eyes. He liked her a lot. They sat across from each other at the marble table, cool to the touch. A conference in a room at the Institute of Culture. He watched as she opened her hand to place a pearl earring on the table, then move the Taino centerpiece out of the way, carefully. Maybe he should ask her about it; learn something. He watched her place the sheet of notepaper between them, turning it to him. He caught the scent of her perfume, saw her straight-up-and-down handwriting, saw the name on the first line jump out at him, printed in capital letters.

TEDDY MAGYK.

"Teddy," Vincent said. He sat back and seemed relieved. "It's funny, on the bus that name went through my mind, Teddy Magyk, but I didn't recognize him. I don't know why." He had to think about that for a moment, seeing Teddy again in the Datsun—something different about him, more grown up.

Nancy Donovan looked up and Vincent saw those eyes again. Confident, not the least self-conscious. He hunched over the table as her gaze returned to the note.

"This word—I forgot what Mr. Torres said. Is it Ranford?"

"Raiford. The Florida state penitentiary."

She said, "Yeah, Raiford. Teddy Magyk—I love the name—was sentenced to ten-to-twenty years and released after seven and a half. For first-degree sexual battery?"

"Rape," Vincent said. "The first time he went up, also for rape, I think he did a couple years in Yardville. That name comes to mind."

"I know about Yardville," Nancy Donovan said, "it's in New Jersey." Looking at him again. "I assume you're with the police. In Florida?"

"Miami Beach."

"And you came here after Teddy?"

"I think it's the other way around," Vincent said. "He wants me to know he's here, worry about him, what he's up to."

She was looking right at him again, those brown eyes patient, waiting.

"They come out of Raiford, quite a few of them, they think they're pretty tough guys. After all, they made it. Or they learn how to survive as snakes. Never confront a problem, someone giving you a hard time, if you can stick him in the back. Which I think is Teddy's classification. He's the kind of guy, he'll do time, never lay the blame on himself for being there. Or any trouble he was in, it was always somebody else's fault. The guy who stuck the gun in his ear and put the cuffs on him."

She said, "And you were the arresting officer."

"The Nemo Hotel in South Beach, a room on the third floor. I pulled him out of bed—" Vincent paused. "I almost threw him out the window. Teddy raped a seventy-year-old woman. Beat her up, she was in the hospital I think nine weeks." He saw Nancy Donovan staring at him in silence, into his eyes. "You look at him you think he's harmless. Kind of guy, you can see him riding a three-wheel bike selling ice cream. But he's nasty and I don't think he's been rehabilitated. Not after two falls. Sooner or later he's gonna try for three."

She said, "How do you know?"

And Vincent said, "It's the way it is."

They stared at one another across the marble table and he felt she was going to ask him about himself, something about his personal life. But after a moment she looked at the note again. "He's staying at the DuPont Plaza." Her eyes raised. "That's a pretty expensive hotel. If he just got out of prison . . ."

Vincent was nodding.

She said, "Wait," and looked at the note again. "He put down a cash deposit for the car."

"So he's got money," Vincent said, "but hasn't had time to earn any, at a job."

She was giving him a funny look. It surprised him because it was so intent. Wanting to ask a question but not wanting to. Finally she said, "This is getting close to home."

He didn't know what she meant.

"Are we coming to my husband now? I've been trying to figure out how he could be involved with Teddy."

Vincent had to smile. "No, no—this has nothing to do with your husband."

She said, "Are you sure?"

He would remember that. *Are you sure?* And the look in her eyes. "No—I came to see him about something else."

She said, "Well, I'm glad to hear that."

He would keep that one, too. A dry offhand remark, not trying to be funny. He said, "Is your husband around?"

She hesitated now. "I'm afraid not."

Vincent didn't believe her. "All I want to do is ask him something. He hires a girl as a hostess, what exactly does that mean?"

"A hostess . . . This is a friend of yours?"

"Her name's Iris Ruiz. She's twenty years old," Vincent said, "she's been out of the country once, spent two weeks in Miami and thinks she knows everything."

"But basically she's a decent girl," Nancy Donovan said, "and you don't want to see her get into something she can't handle."

Vincent said, "Let's just say a young, very pretty girl who has her heart set on going to the States, but isn't really experienced enough—"

"Wait. I thought she was offered a job here."

"No, Atlantic City. Spade's Boardwalk."

"Oh, she's something special."

"Ask her, she'll tell you," Vincent said. "She's not going to New York and live with her cousins and she knows she's not going with me, if I ever go back to Miami Beach"—he saw the lady's eyebrows raise at that—"because I won't take her. You have to understand, there's nothing between us. So, she's going to Atlantic City."

"Out of spite."

"Out of dying to dress up and be a hostess. What

I'd like to know, is if a hostess does what I think she does."

"Tell you the truth," Nancy Donovan said, "I'm not sure myself what a hostess is. Unless you're using the term loosely."

"That's what I'm afraid of."

"We have *hosts*, all of them men who know the business inside and out. Their job is to bring in the elite customers, the high rollers, and take care of them, keep them happy. Arrange transportation, tickets for shows, introduce them to celebrities, entertainers, maybe throw a cocktail party . . . Now there are girls at the parties you might consider hostesses, some who work at the hotel. They're more decorative than anything else. They mingle, smile a lot."

"If one of the special customers," Vincent said, "the high roller, invites the girl up to his room, then what?"

"You mean his suite. Well, she can always say no."

"And keep her job?"

Nancy Donovan hesitated. "Do you know anything about casino gambling?"

"The first week I was here," Vincent said, "I lost sixty dollars playing the slots."

"Well, when you're willing to play with five thousand or more the hotel will comp you for just about anything you want. Your room, your food, your drinks are all complimentary, as long as you gamble. You can win, everything is still on the house. We want you to keep coming back. Because if you do, in the long run we'll take about twenty percent of whatever your line of credit is, or the amount you deposit with us."

"So the hostess," Vincent said, "is there for any crapshooter you want to keep happy."

Nancy Donovan said, "You're very serious about this, aren't you? But whatever the girl does, it's still her choice. No one forces her to dress up and smile and be charming. Some girls love it."

"No one's forcing her," Vincent said, "but to me, you know what it is? Take a girl like Iris, born in Mayaguez in a barrio? Dress her up, dazzle her with all that glitzy bullshit? It's entrapment, the same thing, and entrapment's against the law."

Nancy shrugged. "What can I say? Her choices may be limited, but it's still a choice. Unless there's something you'd like me to do, speak to my husband."

"No, you're right," Vincent said, "it's up to her. She's like a little kid, but I can't force her."

Nancy Donovan seemed relaxed, her gaze lingering on him, almost but not quite amused. "Teddy and now Iris," she said. "You keep pretty busy, don't you?"

"I'm not even working," Vincent said. "I mean I'm not supposed to be. I'm on a medical leave."

Her gaze moved to his hand on the curved end of the cane. "What happened to you?"

"I got shot."

She said, "You did? Where?"

"In Miami Beach," Vincent said, and saw a glow in those brown eyes, the lady of the house, Mrs. Donovan, looking at him the same way he was looking at her.

She said, "And what happened to the man who shot you?"

Nancy sat on the patio deck, in the glow of a citronella candle. She watched Tommy swimming lengths of the illuminated pool, his flesh shining in the pale green oval. She could hear his wet breathing, his labored slapping strokes. Beyond the pool and the amber insect lights in the garden, beyond the hedge of hibiscus and the row of palm trees and the chainlink fence, the beach stretched flat to the Atlantic and the Atlantic reached into the night. She could hear her husband but not the ocean.

She watched him rise out of the pool, naked, lumber over to the umbrella table to his towel and can of beer. She would cast him as a politician, or a New York City judge, on the take. His favorite line, looking over his domain: "Who would've ever thought a Mick from Columbus Avenue would someday own a layout like this?" At either of the hotels he might recite the line looking over the casino floor. She had the feeling he couldn't believe it himself, that it all had to do with luck.

What he did believe, with his jock attitude, he could swim every evening, jog a mile now and then and drink all the beer he wanted, it was okay, and nip at stronger stuff. Tommy would say, "Look at Paul Newman, he drinks beer all the time." He would say, "I might not look it but I'm in shape, guy my age," and slap his belly with both hands. "Go on, hit me as hard as you can," arms extended, offering himself. "Sock it to me." Tommy was easy to cast. Vincent Mora . . .

She saw Vincent as an artist, a sculptor who worked with scrap iron. Or painted murals on barrio walls. Or the wrong man, with his sinister look, falsely accused. But in close shots you know he's innocent. Look at those eyes. She asked what happened and he said, "I got shot." Not giving it much, a nice sense of timing. He could be an actor. She liked his smile, his sorta-wild dark look with the jacket and tie. "I got shot." Where? "In Miami Beach." That was all right, he could get away with it. Fifteen years a policeman, playing cops and robbers. She asked him if he was good at it and he nodded, yes. She asked him if he was afraid now that'd been shot and knew it could happen to him and he nodded again and said yes, it was different now. She asked him if he had ever entrapped anyone and he said, "Not that you'd notice."

She asked questions easily and got answers. She had gone from her home in Narberth, Pennsylvania, to Emerson College in Boston to become an actress, but couldn't get out of her head long enough to manufacture emotions. Since she rarely if ever cried, even in movies, it wasn't something she could do on cue. She joined a casting service in New York and worked with film actors and got them good parts. She liked actors, thought she enjoyed the work—but wait a minute. She was putting all her energy into pushing *their* careers. What about her own? . . . She was home for Christmas when she met a tweedy martini drinker named Kip Burkette at the Merion Cricket Club. Sweet guy, prematurely gray, properly good looking, major shareholder of Burkette Investments, Philadephia. She married Kip and moved to Bryn Mawr, became rich and was used to it long before Tommy arrived . . .

Tommy coming up the steps now to the deck, dripping on the blue tile . . .

At the wrong time, too soon after, she had compared Donovan the deal-maker, the closer, to Kip, the ivy-covered gentleman, listened to Donovan's breezy style after ten years of Kip's monotone, his Main Line lockjaw . . .

Tommy coming into candlelight with his can of beer, towel stretched low about his hips.

"We gonna eat in or go out?"

"I heard a scream," Nancy said, "I think Dominga saw you coming out of the pool and ran."

"'Aiii, that Señor Donovan,'" Tommy said, "telling her girlfriends all about it. 'Ees hong like a *caballo*.'"

"Dominga say that, or was it Iris?"

"Iris? Who in the hell's Iris?"

"You're sending her to Atlantic City."

"Is that right? Iris, huh?"

"Is she for you or customers? Or maybe Jackie."

"Come on—I don't know any Iris. Wouldn't I remember a broad named *Iris?*"

"Especially this one," Nancy said. "I hear she's a knockout. Twenty years old, gorgeous."

"You mean Eer-es? Yeah, that's Iris. I didn't know who you were talking about. Yeah, she isn't bad looking at all. Blond hair with the dark skin."

"Where're you going to use her?"

"I don't know, the lounge. Cocktail waitress maybe. Who told you about her?"

"Her boyfriend. He came to see you, wanted to know what a hostess does."

"Jesus, gonna defend her honor. Those guys kill me, get very dramatic about it."

"He's a cop," Nancy said.

"You serious? That's what I need, a hot-blooded, pissed-off Puerto Rican cop. With a gun."

He said this was the kind of thing, another example, it wasn't Gaming Enforcement or the Casino Control Commission causing him problems. It was always little guys with fucked-up personalities. Guys like this cop could turn out to be. They had loose wiring or some fucking thing, like they weren't plugged into the real world. Guys at the top, Tommy said, you didn't have any trouble with. You could always deal with guys at the top. But little guys with wild hairs up their ass, there was no book on guys like that.

There were times when Nancy listened to him, fascinated.

She thought of clarifying one point. The cop was from Miami Beach, not Puerto Rico. But Tommy kept talking and later, when she thought of it again, she decided why bother? Two weeks from now she would remember, she had not prepared her husband for Vincent Mora.

5

TEDDY PLAYED WITH VINCENT the next day. That was his plan, the way it started out.

He parked the Datsun at the beach so Vincent would be sure to see him. Not too close but sitting by itself in the shade of Australian pines. What a day—bright and fair as usual at the postcard beach. If Vincent came over he would take off: he didn't want to talk to him, he wanted to worry him, get him worked up. But Vincent didn't come over. He was alone sitting in his chair. Some of the girls would stop by and talk to him, but they didn't stay long.

Next, later that afternoon, Teddy parked near the old Normandie Hotel and watched Vincent walk past with his cane and his chair on the other side of the street, not limping as much as he had the day before. Vincent looked over, was all he did. Teddy felt like yelling at him, " 'Ey, where's your girlfriend? You go for that PR pussy, 'ey? So do I, man, so do I." But he didn't.

Next, he trailed Vincent to the Carmen Apartments and parked across the street, near the entrance to the Hilton. He could sit out here as long as it might take, easy, after living in a Florida cellblock with the heat and smell of that place, the smell of cons. Different cons smelled different. The ones that put cologne on over their smell were the worst. Jesus, enough to make you gag. There were others smelled pretty good. He saw Vincent appear and go in the liquor store. He would've had trouble recognizing him from that time before, over seven years ago, with the beard he wore now. Though once he'd studied the pictures he took he knew he had his man. He'd learned at Raiford, just before he got his release, that Vincent had been shot. There were some happy boys in the yard that day, feeling they should have ice cream and cake. Cons at Raiford knew everything and liked to gossip. They said he got capped by a junkie; shit, but didn't die. Teddy got out and learned on the streets of Miami Beach where Vincent lived, that he had once been married—a guy who sold dope out of the hospital saw Vincent there when his wife died—and so on. It was no problem to call the Detective Bureau and say he'd checked Vincent's apartment, he wasn't home; ask after him, how was he doing?, sounding like a friend of Vincent's, sincere. Cops were dumb.

When Vincent came out of the liquor store he looked over and Teddy was ready to get out of there. But Vincent didn't come over, he went back up to his apartment.

Next, Teddy thought he might have a refreshment himself. So he went over to the liquor store, bought a pint of light rum, a few cans of Fresca and some paper cups. When he got back to the car two PRs were standing there. Skinny guys, taller than most, taller than Teddy, with little thin mustaches. They looked like twin PRs, both wearing those PR shirts with pleats and pockets that hung outside the pants. They looked familiar.

One of them opened his wallet to show his I.D. and said, "*Policia.*" They were cops. They looked familiar because Teddy believed, from his observations, all PR cops looked alike. Skinny guys with little mustaches.

He said, "Officer, I parked in the wrong spot, 'ey? I'll move it right out."

But one of the cops opened the door on the passenger side, pulled the seat up and motioned for him to get in, in back, while the other one went around to the driver's side. As that one got in Teddy saw the bulge and the tip of the black holster sticking out from under his shirt. He said, " 'Ey, wait a minute. Where we going?" The one behind the wheel motioned for the key, asking for it, Teddy believed, in Spanish. "The hell you guys doing? I parked in the wrong spot, gimme a ticket, 'ey? Christ, you take people in for illegal parking? Listen, why don't I just pay the fine right now? Save us some time." He pulled his shirt up to show his money belt, but they weren't looking, both of them in the car now, in front. He tapped one of them on the shoulder and the guy looked around. "Officer, how about I give you guys some dollares? How much you need?"

No dice. They drove off and didn't look back at him again, though the two chattered at each other in that machine-gun PR Spanish, clickety-clicking away as they drove through traffic east out of San Juan, Teddy thinking, Jesus Christ, thinking of that cab driver dead up in the rain forest. Had somebody found him? Except—wait a minute—it sure as hell didn't look like they were going to a police station. And then he began to think, Are these birds really cops?

They drove along a beach road with no other cars in sight, empty beaches and the ocean seen through palm trees off to the left, beautiful, though the road was a bitch, full of potholes that had Teddy's head bouncing off the roof. "Take it easy, asshole!" The driver looked hard at the rearview mirror. He knew what asshole meant. They drove, it must have been twenty miles out of San Juan, the light getting flat, dusk approaching, when they came to the end of the road.

Teddy looked through the windshield at the rear end of a gray car waiting. Beyond it was an inlet or the mouth of a river, mangrove along the banks, about a hundred yards across. All he could see over there was vegetation and a few shacks. They could be in Africa.

The gray car in front of them moved ahead and now Teddy saw the metal barge at the end of the road: a dirty flatbed raft, handrails on two sides, rusting out. The gray car eased aboard and they followed, creeping, bumping over the metal ramp and onto the barge that might hold six cars, but only the two today. A black guy stood on the outside of the rail holding onto a pair of thin ropes. Another black guy appeared from behind Teddy's car to join the first black guy. The barge was moving now, drifting, Teddy could feel it, pushing through the mangrove leaves thick in the water. Now the two black guys began to pull on the pair of ropes and this jungle ferryboat eased out into clear water at about a half mile an hour. Jesus. He could see that not far upstream the river or inlet took a bend out of sight . . . toward those cloudy mountains where a cab driver lay dead.

The two PRs got out; the one pulled his seat forward and Teddy got out. He stood by the side of the car watching the two black guys pulling on the ropes, in unison, in no hurry—shit, not going anywhere. He watched them because he couldn't believe it, these guys actually pulling on *ropes*, hauling *cars* that could roll off this thing and go close to a hundred miles an hour. When they were out in the middle of the stream the two rope pullers quit and lit up cigarettes, though they held onto the ropes. Teddy believed they were taking their break. Sure, they had been working at least ten minutes. The ferry began to drift a little toward the ocean. It was quiet out here. One of the PRs came over then and began talking to him.

Teddy squinted, watching the guy's mouth, looking for a familiar word in that clickety-click Spanish, trying at least to catch the guy's tone. Was he pissed off or what? Teddy looked over at one of the rope pullers. "You know what he's saying?" The rope puller didn't answer him.

Now the other PR started on him, sounding like he was asking questions. Teddy had forgot about the gray car ahead of them on the barge, some kind of Chevy. Until he noticed, looking past the PR talking to him, the door open.

Vincent Mora got out.

Teddy said, "Jesus Christ!" Experiencing a revelation. He saw Vincent look at him a moment, then come around to stand between the two cars. "Mr.

Magic," Vincent said to him. "How you doing, Teddy?" Then looked off, taking in the sights. Pretending to.

What were they pulling here? So he'd been made. Okay. The guy had finally remembered him or somehow had him checked out. Cops had all kinds of computer shit they used now . . . One of the PRs started talking to him again, asking a question, but Teddy kept his sunglasses on the bearded American English-speaking son of a bitch who had once put him away.

"You mind telling me what you're doing?"

"I'm not doing anything." Vincent motioned with his cane. "Looks like you're in the hands of the Puerto Rican Police."

"Okay." Patient. "You mind telling me what *they're* doing?"

"They're harassing you. They're giving you a hard time. What'd you think they were doing?"

"What for? I haven't done nothing."

"Yeah, well, they know about you. They want to ask you something."

"Get me all the way out here, uh-huh, and what're you, the interpreter?"

"That's right."

"Bullshit."

One of the Puerto Rican cops said something to Teddy.

He saw Vincent listen, then begin to nod. "He says you should be careful where you go. Come out to a place like this . . ."

"Cut the shit, 'ey? You think I asked to come here?"

The Puerto Rican cop spoke again, no expression on his face, reciting something.

Now Vincent said to him, "They want to know if you've ever been to Caguas."

"The hell's Caguas?"

"Take the freeway south out of San Juan through Hato Rey, it goes to Caguas."

"Yeah? So?"

The Puerto Rican cop spoke again.

Vincent said to Teddy, "He says, on the way to Caguas you see Oso Blanco."

"Is that right?" Teddy said. "The fuck's Oso Blanco?"

"The joint," Vincent said to him. "They call it the White Bear. You see it off to the left when you're on Number One. It isn't white, it's sorta tan. Big place, twenty-foot double fences with barbed wire on top, gun towers all the way around. You can't miss it."

The Puerto Rican cop spoke again.

Vincent said to Teddy, "He says, you do time in Oso Blanco, it would make Raiford seem like Disneyworld."

"Bullshit," Teddy said. Guy was putting him on and he knew it.

"That's what he said," Vincent said to him.

"You bring me all the way out here to give me this shit?"

"They want you on a plane tomorrow."

"Come on, 'ey?"

"They know all about you and they don't like you." Vincent walked up to him now to stand face to face, less than a couple of feet separating them. "I don't like you either. I can't stand to look at you. They say they don't want to see you again after four-thirty tomorrow."

Teddy felt restless, wanting to hit him, give him a shove. He said, "Bullshit. I can stay here long as I want."

"They say if you're still here they'll find some smack in your bag and you'll stay ten to twenty. That long enough?"

"You guys, you cop assholes," Teddy said, "you're all alike, aren't you?"

"No," Vincent said to him, "we're not. These guys see you again they'll bring you up on something, dope, assault with intent, and throw you in the can. I see you again, well, that's a different story."

Teddy had to squint at that bearded face, stare hard through his sunglasses to read the guy's cop eyes. He said, "Bullshit." Because the guy's eyes didn't look mean, they looked sad, or tired. They were not the eyes he remembered from seven and a half years ago.

Vincent said to him, "Teddy, I know where you've been, what you learned in there, how to make a shiv, how you settle your differences. I know what a sly little back-sticking motherfucker you are and I know what you feel like doing."

"You know everything, 'ey?"

"I know I'm not gonna walk backwards the rest of my life," Vincent said to him, "worry about a freak who wants to get even. You understand what I'm saying? Nod your head, I don't want to hear any more from you."

Teddy was about to speak, but the curved end of the cop's cane came up to rest against the bridge of his nose.

"Don't say it," Vincent said to him.

Teddy didn't move. Those eyes were different now. They still weren't mean, they were calm. But they stared into him the way they had stared once before—when he had opened his own eyes to see the gun in his face in the hotel room in South Beach and the cop's eyes staring. He wanted to say, Jesus, loud as he could, *You don't know anything!* Yell it out. *You don't know shit!* Scream it in that cop face.

But he clenched his jaw shut to keep from making even a sound and when the cop told him to nod his head, yes, he was leaving and would never come back, he nodded his head down and up, once. Because the cop's eyes told him the cop was ready to kill him if he didn't.

6

IRIS SAT IN THE EASTERN BOARDING LOUNGE waiting for the flight to someplace in Florida where she would get on another flight to Atlantic City. "Follow me," Tommy Donovan had said, "when we change in Tampa-St. Pete," and winked at her and said he didn't want to lose her. "But don't talk to me. You understand? I'm going to be with someone."

Sure, he was with his wife. His wife was attractive, beautifully dressed—sitting over there by herself reading a magazine—but she was old. She was perhaps forty, or close to it. Sitting with her legs crossed, nothing to worry about. Not with her money. Tommy was standing in line at the Duty Free counter. He had said to her, "Have you got a coat? It's going to be cold up there for a while."

She had a pink sweater with sequins in her shopping bag and a black raincoat like rubber across her lap for the weather. She had a *Mademoiselle* magazine also in the shopping bag to read on the plane, select a wardrobe to buy in Atlantic City. She could hardly wait now. She didn't care if it was cold up there, she'd buy a fur coat, a long white one. Wear a green silk scarf with it, look nice. Tommy would buy her whatever she wanted.

Two months ago she had met Vincent at the beach and her life began to change and then stopped changing.

One month ago she had met Tommy Donovan and her life began to change again and was still changing.

She would remember standing in the lobby of Spade's Isla Verde Resort, the casino part, near the entrance to the Sultan's Lounge. A group in there, dressed in orange satin shirts, was playing salsa, calypso, mambo, making a lot of noise. It was late. There were no tourist guys to be seen anywhere except in the casino and they told her if she went in there, no standing around, she had to spend money.

Suddenly he came up to her, taking her by the arm into the Sultan's Lounge, not saying a word. This big American guy with a red face and silver-white hair. He seated her before going over to converse with the barman for a moment. He wore a black silk suit—she could see it shining in the dark. Very soon a bottle of champagne was presented to them by one of the girls wearing the harem costume—they called it that—a bra and panties, gold necklaces with a glowing jewel stuck in the girl's navel. The guy sipped his champagne staring at her, still not saying a word. He was old, but not old enough to have white hair. He was too big to ever let him be on top. She sipped her champagne. It was good. He sipped his, his eyes never leaving her. Finally he said, "I'm gonna take you to Atlantic City with me." She had heard of it, of course. The Miss America on TV. He said to her then, "Little girl with your looks, you must work your ass off during the season." At this time Iris was catching glimpses of a fashionable apartment in the Candado section, this big silver-haired rich guy coming in with his key. In the next blink of an eye she would see them together on a sailing boat. It could happen to her. She didn't need any Miami Beach cop. This guy could be sent from heaven. Except he was assuming she was a whore and it was offensive to her.

Iris said, "Oh, thank you very much for thinking I'm a person like that. Escuse me." She took a small risk and got up to leave. He surprised her by getting up also.

He said, "I want to talk to you. We'll go upstairs, have some privacy."

She said, "Oh, you mean to your room?"

He said, "Rooms, honey, rooms."

"Oh, you still think I'm that kind of person?"

He said, "Look, I'm your friend, Tommy. Say my name. Go on. Tommy."

He sounded crazy. She said, "Tommy?"

"Not like that, like you're not sure." He grinned. "Hi, Tommy. Like that."

Wow, crazy. She said, "Hi, Tommy," and had to smile. It sounded okay, like they were friends.

He said, "Hi, Iris." Even pronouncing it correctly.

She said, "Hey, how do you know my name?"

He said to her, "Honey, I even know your future."

It gave her that strange feeling like someone was blowing on the back of her neck, making her shiver. But it felt nice, too, because she could tell by Tommy's look he saw only good things in there. The waitress said, "Goodnight, Mr. Donovan," flirting with him a little as they left. The barman hurried to the end of the bar to say goodnight. The guys in the group, in the orange shirts making noise, waved to him. A couple of casino employees, in the lobby, said his name, bowing to him.

Iris said, "They certainly treat you with respect."

That was when he said they better, since he owned the fucking joint—and Iris knew her life from now on would never be the same.

He was buying cartons of cigarettes at the Duty Free, waiting for the girl to bring him his change. Iris watched him look across the lounge toward his wife, checking, then look this way—Iris pulling her hair aside so he could see her good—and wink before turning back to the counter. He liked to wink, meaning by it there was a secret between them. Though she was sure everyone in the hotel knew he was taking her to bed. Through his office into a study with a white sectional sofa you could make a square bed out of and he called his playpen. He made her put a towel under her. Then he would get on and do it to her, arms stiff to hold up his weight and so he could look down, trying to hold his stomach in, and watch himself doing it. He didn't want to try any new ways to do it that had been discovered since Rae Dawn Chong showed that cave guy in the movie how to make fire and do it face to face. Being an important man Tommy was always in a hurry.

He had given her the plane ticket but no money, no paycheck, because she hadn't yet started to work. He would have to give her money for hostess dresses, too, a red one, a bright green one . . .

She had worn her black cocktail dress, nice one but old, last night when she went to Tommy's hotel to get her ticket. Waited forever and then sat in a booth in the Sultan's Lounge between Tommy and a fat guy with curly hair named Jackie Garbo. The

Caribbean group, La Tuna, was gone. The picture out in the lobby for the past two weeks was of a girl named Linda Moon. She was playing the piano and singing slow songs.

Tommy called to her, "Do 'Here's That Rainy Day' again."

The girl looked at him for several moments across the piano before she began to play it, for the third time.

Iris tried to sit closer to Tommy than to Jackie Garbo, so Tommy wouldn't get jealous. Jackie Garbo's leg was against her, the way they were squeezed into the curved booth looking from this dark part of the room to the girl playing in a pink spotlight. The girl, Linda Moon, sang in a low voice without trying very hard.

Tommy said to Jackie Garbo, "What do you think?"

Iris felt Jackie Garbo's hand come to rest on her thigh and pat it lightly, keeping time with the music. It was okay, he was being friendly. Jackie Garbo worked for Tommy in Atlantic City. He was in charge of the casino up there.

He said to Tommy, "You want a cocktail piano in the lounge?"

"She's good," Tommy said. "She did six weeks at the Candado Beach. They wanted to renew and I swung with her."

"She's good," Jackie Garbo said, "but she'll put the fucking people to sleep. Couple of sets like that, they go beddy-bye."

"She can do up-tempo, anything."

"I hope so," Jackie Garbo said. "You don't have chairs in the lobby you don't want people to sit down and fall asleep. Same thing. Lounge act, man, you gotta keep 'em alive. Rest a set, get back in that casino."

"I like her," Tommy said. "She's good."

"You like her, take her," Jackie Garbo said. "Play her noon to four, nobody's in there anyway." He snapped his fingers and said, "What about, hey, put her in with that jig group, what's their name, they got all the fucking drums, the washtub—"

Tommy said, "You mean La Tuna?"

"La Tuna. Why not? Those guys—you sit and listen to those cats you can't sleep for two days, your fucking head's ringing. You want to do this broad a favor put her up there in front of La Tuna, featured. Get rid of the piano, give her some maracas, some fucking thing, you know, make some noise, shake her ass. They need a broad."

"It's an idea," Tommy said, "but I don't think she'll buy it. She's a tough lady."

"You mean, she won't buy it. *Tell* her, for Christ sake."

Iris could feel Jackie Garbo's hand trying to squeeze her leg. The hand down there the same as

the little fat hand pinching the stem of his champagne glass on the table. When the hand down
there couldn't get a good grip it moved up her leg,
exploring, wanting to know if she was wearing
panties. Iris hoped a casino manager was an important guy. He was asking Tommy if Linda Moon
wanted to go big time or stay here among the fucking natives. Tommy said he wasn't going to spring
La Tuna on her yet. He'd ease her into the idea.
Jackie Garbo said, "You know how many cocktail
piano players there are on the circuit?"

Iris didn't like Jackie Garbo, his hand or the way
he spoke. She couldn't understand how he could
talk this way to his boss, the man who owned the
hotels. Or speak about *her*, in front of her, as
though his hand knew she was at the table but the
rest of Jackie Garbo didn't. Saying, "Iris's gonna do
all right, lemme tell you. You know who's gonna
flip when he sees her?" Tommy nodding, winking
at her—yes, but what was the secret of that wink?
It was a different kind of wink than before. Winked
at her but meant for Jackie Garbo.

When Linda Moon finished her set she came to
the booth and sat in a chair across from them. She
folded her hands saying she didn't care for anything
to drink. Tommy told her he loved her and then
said, "I want you to think about something, rather
than doing straight cocktail piano . . ."

Linda said, "I don't play cocktail piano, Mr.

Donovan, when I have a choice. When I don't have requests coming at me."

Tommy said, "Hey, knock off that Mr. Donovan. You know my name. I want you to think about maybe a group, getting some backup."

Linda said, "I *am* a group, Mr. Donovan. I've got a keyboard, synthesizers, two guys in New York I can get in a minute, guitar and drums. Or I can go with the guitar and a rhythm box if you want. I've got charts on pop, top forty, some original stuff . . . You have to hear us, Mr. Donovan."

"You mean Tommy," Tommy said. "What's the name of the group?"

Linda said, "Moon. You like it? Just Moon."

Tommy said, "I can dig it. Yeah, I like it."

Jackie Garbo said, "I want to see your rhythm box. You play loud?"

Iris watched Linda, sitting with her hands folded, turn her eyes on him and say, "Jackie, we drive. You want, we'll blow 'em right out of the fucking lounge into the casino. Would you go for that? Give me eight weeks guaranteed and you're going to want eight more."

Iris watched Linda because she was so calm and didn't seem afraid of these guys. Tommy said to her, "Lady?" and sounded serious. Then smiled and said, "Let's see what we can put together." Right after that Tommy and Jackie Garbo left the table.

Iris continued to watch Linda as she poured a little champagne now and sipped it.

Iris said, "They don't have to hire you they don't want to." She saw Linda look up from her glass. "I mean, you work for them," Iris said, "but you don't act, you know, ascared of how they can treat you."

Linda said, "What's the worst thing they can do, make me play 'Shake, Rattle and Roll' every set? I know the lounge audience, what's expected. Who's working the main room? Tom Jones? Liberace? That gives you an idea. I'll do three golden oldies for every *one* I want to play, and if that doesn't work, well, I can always break my fingers. Right? Draw workmen's comp. I have to go back to work."

Iris sat there trying to figure out what Linda said. Then Vincent came in the Sultan's Lounge and she had something else to think about.

Now Tommy was walking away from the Duty Free counter with his cigarettes, going to his wife to sit down next to her, the wife still looking at the magazine. Iris watched. She'd try to see if there was love between them. She didn't think so. Then she couldn't see them. There was a shirt with flowers coming to stand close in front of her. She looked up as Teddy said:

"Well, I'll be." Smiling at her, holding his camera case and a ticket envelope. "I thought you'd already gone."

What Iris thought in that moment, he was going to ask her to give him back the souvenir parrot and the hundred-dollar bill. But he didn't. He seemed very happy to see her. Maybe he wouldn't think of the money.

The fifty he had paid to go to bed with her wasn't in question. She had earned it. When they were in the bed he asked her if she could cry and look afraid. She told him if she could cry whenever she wanted she wouldn't have to do this, she'd be a movie star. That made him angry. He took the little knife he used to clean his fingernails from his money belt—wearing the money belt naked—put the tip of the knife in her nose and said, "You want me to shove it all the way up?" She said, okay, okay, and gave him an Oscar performance. It wasn't hard to be afraid with the knife blade in her nose. It took a minute, less than that, and he was smiling again to show he was really a nice guy. But he wasn't. He was the creepiest guy she ever met.

He was smiling at her now as he said, " 'Ey, what seat are you in? Maybe we can sit together."

Iris hesitated, looking away from him to think as quickly as she could—saw Linda Moon in the Duty Free line, the piano player buying cigarettes, and felt instant relief. She said, "Oh, I'm sorry. I'm sitting with a good friend of mine name Linda."

Teddy still smiled. He said, "Maybe some other time then, 'ey?"

7

THE POLICEMAN who came to Vincent's apartment was one of the pair who had brought Teddy to the Loíza ferry and pretended to speak only Spanish. His name was Herbey Maldonado, nice guy, a Criminal Affairs investigator who worked for Lorendo Paz. It was Lorendo's idea to use the ferry when Vincent told him what he wanted to do. They let Teddy have his rental car on the other side of the inlet, lost for sure, and Vincent rode back with the two cops. Near Isla Verde they stopped at a place on the highway to relax and drink a few beers. Herbey said, man, that was fun, scaring the shit out of a guy like that.

Vincent wanted to be sure and asked them if they believed Teddy was scared enough to leave. Both cops were certain they would never see him again. They didn't believe Teddy was much to worry about, he didn't look to them like a killer. After a couple of hours Vincent was feeling pretty good,

his hip didn't hurt him at all; he invited the two
cops to dinner. They ordered dishes like *alcapurrias*
and *pastales, piononos*, and Vincent tried to guess
what he was eating—meat with bananas or mixed
with some kind of root, *yautía*, he'd never heard of.
It didn't matter, he liked it.

Vincent told the cops he'd take a bus or a taxi
home, he had a stop to make, and walked from the
highway toward the beach, finally coming out of
the trees to see green neon written in the sky:

Spade's Isla Verde Resort

Lorendo said the name was an acronym for the syn-
dicate that held ownership. Seashore Properties
and Donovan Enterprises. Tommy Donovan presi-
dent, chairman of the board. But a figurehead more
than he was an administrator.

Or a potentate, Vincent thought. Did he sit on
cushions and smoke a water pipe, clap once for
whatever he wanted? In there somewhere, beneath
that spade-shaped sultan's dome lighting up the
night. Jesus Christ, Vincent thought. He wondered
what all this meant and who had thought it up.
What the Muslim look had to do with gambling . . .
the Puerto Rican Arab doorman having to wear
that cape and turban. People handing him a buck
getting in their cars, not even cracking a smile or

looking twice—*he* was smiling, the doorman, saying yeah, they serious, but I get paid for this shit. All the people inside were serious, too, trying to make money or trying not to lose it. Vincent walked past the casino floor into the Sultan's Lounge.

He sat in the booth with Iris. She asked him if he wanted a glass of champagne that cost eighty dollars a bottle but was free. He ordered scotch; it was only four dollars. The music was all right, it was pleasant, played by a dark-haired girl in a soft blue spot. Iris told him he should wear a coat to come in here. He said, or a cape and a turban. And had to smile. This couldn't be serious. How could she get in trouble in a place like this?

"I'm leaving tomorrow," Iris said. "So I tell you good-bye now."

He thought a moment and said, "Can I give you one word of advice? . . . Don't. You know what you're gonna be?"

"Yes, of course, a hostess."

"You're gonna be a comp."

"Yeah? Wha's that, Vincent, a comp?"

"Like the champagne, a gift. You're gonna get handed out, passed around. You're gonna have to learn how to smile."

"I know how, Vincent. I smile when I'm not with you."

"You're gonna have to be nice to assholes."

"I'm nice to everybody."

"You're gonna get handed out."

"You already tole me that."

"You're gonna get treated like shit."

"Oh, is that so? I'm tole a very important guy in business is going to flip over me."

Vincent said, "It's too late, huh?" He stared at her and said, tired if not sad, "Iris, you're the best-looking girl I've ever seen in my life."

"Thank you, but is pronounce Eer-es."

"And probably the dumbest."

"Goodnight, Vincent."

"Good-bye, Iris."

Two weeks had gone by.

He thought of Iris once in a while, he also thought of Nancy Donovan. From one extreme to the other, and realized he could go either way. Still horny.

Herbey Maldonado came to Vincent's apartment to tell him Lorendo wanted to talk to him. Call him this afternoon or, if he could, meet him for lunch at the Cidreño. Herbey was a quiet person, but seemed more than quiet today. Vincent asked him what was up. Something the matter? Herbey said he didn't know what it was about. He offered to drive Vincent to the restaurant. Fine. It was almost time. On the way there Herbey said they had been out to El Yunque all morning investigating a homicide that looked like it would be a difficult one. Lorendo's squad had it. Lorendo, he said, should be back by the time they got to the Cidreño. Herbey dropped him off.

Vincent drank beer as he waited, getting hungry, deciding he'd have the *asopao de pollo*, sort of a chicken stew with rice. He could taste it already. With the beer and fresh crusty bread and hard butter. Jesus. Lorendo Paz came in and sat down, worn out, his cream-colored suit smudged with dirt.

"You've got a tough one, uh?"

"Guy is dead a couple weeks or more." Lorendo touched his forehead. "One in here." He touched his temple, the left side. "Another one here, to make sure."

"Two weeks out there?"

"At least. They been insects and things, animals, eating him, plants growing on him. His face isn't much left. A week ago they found a taxi out there, but we don't know if it belongs to the guy. He didn't have a wallet, any I.D. on him."

"How about Missing Persons?"

"We got to talk to them, see who they looking for."

"If he's the cab driver, maybe there's a record, where he picked up his fare."

"I'm going to see about that too, Vincent."

"Who found him?"

"Some hikers, by luck. He wasn't near a trail. This guy whoever it was, shot him and then pushed him off a place, you know, where you go see the view. So, we still looking for the wallet out there. Meanwhile they do a post on him at the medical center, look for a bullet. We get some prints of the guy and see if they match prints in the taxi. Then where are we, uh?"

"Just getting started," Vincent said. "What's different about this one?"

"They all different," Lorendo said, "aren't they? Once you see how they came to happen, the reason. Maybe this one is robbery. But we don't know the same person shot him took his wallet, do we?"

Vincent said, "You asking for an opinion?"

Lorendo shrugged. "You want to give it, sure. This point, I listen to everybody." Smiling a little.

Vincent said, "You feel like buying lunch today? Is that why we're here?"

"Well, it's my turn," Lorendo said. He looked off to find a waiter and said, "There is something else," still looking off. "I received a phone call this morning . . ."

Vincent watched Lorendo straighten and glance at him, only a glance, taking something from his inside coat pocket—a folded sheet from a legal pad—opening it now as though he didn't want to.

Vincent eased upright, wary. He said, "You've

got my full attention." Sounding like he was kidding with Lorendo but serious. "Who was it called you?"

Lorendo was studying the sheet of yellow paper. "Guy from Atlantic County, in New Jersey. A captain name Davies, with the Major Crime Squad. They're in the prosecutor's office."

Vincent sat back in his chair. He said, "Oh, shit. Iris, huh? They pick her up?"

"They found her—"

"What'd she do, solicit a cop?" "She didn't do nothing, Vincent. She died."

8

THE OLD MAN, MR. BERTOIA, said to Vincent, no, it didn't have to be closed. He breathed and sighed through his nose. He said, the poor girl. Fifty years on Oriental Avenue, it broke his heart every time, see a young girl like this taken from us. He said, yes, of course it should be open, glancing at his middle-aged son. Friends, love ones, they want to see the departed, they don't want to look at the coffin.

The younger Mr. Bertoia said it wasn't a coffin, it was a casket. Saying this to his father in front of Vincent. The terrain of the old man's face was weathered and creased; Vincent thought of him as a stonemason or a mountain guide, a man who spent his life outdoors. The son was balding, sallow; he stood with his hands behind him in the pose of a minor official, always right, the assistant principal whose literal mind lies in wait. He made his statement now, saying, "Let me remind you, the pelvis, the spine, the hips, you could say they were pulverized. You could say she literally broke every bone in her body."

The old man said, "Yes, but her face is good."

"Her face is, well, it's *okay*." The younger Mr. Bertoia shrugged. "You could show it. The rest of her though, I wouldn't show to her worst enemy."

The old man's eyes flared and he whipped his son with a burst of words in Italian.

The younger Mr. Bertoia straightened. "I'm only trying to explain the condition of the deceased. You want me to fill her out? Fine. I'll pad her, make up her face for viewing. But it's going to take some work, and it isn't specified in the contract."

"This gentleman," the old man said, "is requesting this. You don't understand it?"

"Fine. I'm only saying we have a contract," the younger Mr. Bertoia said, "and the girl that brought her in is paying the bill." He thought for a moment and said, "Linda Moon. If that's her real name. She still owes us money."

Vincent said, "You think you can get it open today?"

The old man said, "Sure, of course. Right now."

But the younger Mr. Bertoia didn't move. "The appearance of the deceased is only one consideration. There's also the cost. This person Linda Moon signed a contract for our minimum plan, including cremation. She has not yet selected an urn." He looked at the bare casket made of wood-grained, high-gloss plastic shining in fluorescent light. "What she's getting is exactly what she hasn't paid for yet."

Vincent listened, aware of the casket, the worn linoleum floor, the empty rows of metal folding chairs, the closed venetian blinds. It was cold in the room. He motioned to the younger Mr. Bertoia to follow him as he turned to the door. The younger Mr. Bertoia said, "Yeah? What is it you want?" and Vincent motioned to him again, finally bringing him out to the hall to stand between gold-framed paintings of the Good Shepherd on one side and the Sacred Heart of Jesus on the other. Over the younger Mr. Bertoia's shoulder Vincent could see the old man watching from the doorway to the parlor, where Iris waited in that plastic box.

Vincent said to the younger Mr. Bertoia, "Nothing's free, is it? Anything you have to do I expect to pay for. Anything that's owed you I'll take care of that too. I'll give you a check before I leave. But right now, what I'd like you to do if you would please, is go in there and open the fucking coffin. You think you could do that for me?"

Vincent looked at the Inlet neighborhood through venetian blinds, at old frame houses and empty lots, telephone poles standing alone on streets named after states and oceans. He saw homes that looked like barns with bay windows and dormers stuck on, built in a time when tourists came here in the summer and the Inlet offered rooms only a few blocks from the ocean. Step up on the Boardwalk right here and stroll down-beach for miles—the old man told Vincent, standing behind him. To Vincent the area looked as though it had been fought over in a war, house to house, and half the people had packed up and left. See? Way over there, look down the telephone poles. Those are the casinos, the old man said. Hotels with a thousand rooms and a casino you could play football inside if it didn't have a ceiling. Glass ceiling where they watch you you don't cheat. Towering shapes against the gray sky. Six P.M. near the end of March, overcast today, a high of 47 predicted. The casinos would be here soon, Mr. Bertoia said. They would force him to sell. They don't want a funeral home next to a casino. His son was going to Linwood, live in a colonial house. Mr. Bertoia didn't know where he would go. Nine, ten, eleven, twelve now, they were coming this way.

The invasion of the casino monsters, Vincent thought.

The younger Mr. Bertoia, his French cuffs turned up, said he was finished and walked out of the room. Then the old man left and Vincent was alone with Iris.

A girl they said was Iris. The face in the casket

bore a resemblance to a face he remembered, but this one was a coloring book face. The younger Mr. Bertoia had colored in reds and pinks, purple around the closed eyes, not going out of the lines but bearing down to color an Iris cartoon. For a moment it was in Vincent's mind to color the younger Mr. Bertoia. Paint him chalk white, draw black eyelashes on him, round red circles on his cheeks and a clown mouth, make the little son of a bitch smile. This couldn't be Iris. The Iris he knew was alive . . .

Except that the police Summary Report form stated in black ballpoint she was found at 1:10 A.M. in a condition that indicated no apparent signs of life. The Atlantic County Major Crime Squad's summary said dead on arrival at Shores Memorial, Somers Point, and the medical examiner's report confirmed it. She was dead, all right.

You can't go off the top floor of a high-rise condominium, hit the pavement from 18 stories up and be anything but dead.

Vincent still had his suitcase with him. A raincoat over Florida clothes. San Juan to Tampa-St. Pete to the Atlantic City airport and a taxi to Northfield, New Jersey—"offshore" they called it, inland from Atlantic City on Absecon Island—to the county facilities in Northfield where the Major Crime Squad was expecting him. Waiting to look him over, ask him questions. Vincent could feel it when he walked in. They were patient, the way cops can be patient. Courteous, too. Vincent knew what they were doing, but didn't know why.

Until a captain named Dixie Davies said, "A girl dies with a man's name and address written on an envelope that's stuck in her panties, we want to have a talk with him."

Lorendo Paz hadn't said anything about a note.

"No, we asked Puerto Rico not to mention it," Dixie said. "They told us about you and we checked you out. Still, if you hadn't come we would've invited you."

They showed it to him, his name and San Juan address, the Carmen Apartments, on a plain white number ten envelope that was creased and blood-stained.

"Folded twice in her panties. Which is all she was wearing at the time."

"Iris wrote it," Vincent said. "I'm pretty sure."

"That was our guess," Dixie said. "But why would she keep it in her panties?"

"I don't know," Vincent said.

"She trying to tell us something? Get a cop?"

"I doubt it."

"She have any friends here, from Puerto Rico?"

"Not that I know of."

"Shit, I was hoping you'd open the door for us," Dixie said.

* * *

What happened in Northfield—Vincent had the feeling it was Dixie Davies who opened a door. A few minutes with the guy, just the two of them cop to cop in a pale-green interrogation room away from phones, Vincent was back on familiar ground. He could relax with this guy, the Major Crime Squad's homicide star, and feel his confidence return. Because they were alike. Dixie was twenty pounds heavier with a weathered sandy look, big full mustache, more presentable in his brown suit than the bearded, suntanned, gunshot cop in the raincoat. But they were alike and they both knew it. They could be partners who'd worked together ten years. Dixie said, "I was hoping you'd open the door for us," and Vincent had felt himself smile because it was something he might have said. Dixie described the investigation of Iris Ruiz's death. Vincent listened, stored facts to think about later . . . now.

In the funeral home. Alone in this room since he'd arrived a few hours ago.

He would begin to go over in his mind what the county police had and what they didn't have, the holes in the case, and he would see Iris falling through dark space, alone. He could see her eyes and then see the ground coming up as she would see it, alone, trying to hold back. But he couldn't see her going off the balcony alone. Someone had been there with her. About one A.M.

There were traces of semen in her vagina.

The medical examiner couldn't tell if she'd been assaulted, sexually or physically. Blood, fingernail scrapings, tissue samples of vital organs had been sent to the state police lab in Newark. They'd wait for the report, learn the apparent cause of death before trying to determine the nature of the girl's death. Homicide, suicide . . .

"Or she could've been on something," Dixie had said. "Acid, angel dust. She might've thought she could fly. If she was dead before she hit, that's different. But if it was the fall killed her then we have to consider it might even've been accidental."

"Somebody picked her up," Vincent said, "and threw her off. Somebody who came to see her. Walked in the building, went up to her apartment."

"Except she didn't live there," Dixie said.

See? You think everything's going to fall in place . . .

"Nobody did. The place was suppose to be empty. Furnished apartment but nobody staying there. Iris was living in a rooming house on Caspian Avenue. First question, how'd she get in the apartment? There's no sign of forced entry. Next question, what was she doing there?" Dixie said, "You want my guess, based on I talked to

Puerto Rico and I know they have a sheet on her? She was turning a trick. Is it all right to say that? I'd rather I didn't have to, 'cause if the guy was a john it's gonna make my job a hundred times harder, isn't it? Who're we looking for? A guy came in on a junket? If he was staying overnight why didn't he take her to his hotel room? Or was the guy a friend? Either way, from what we've got, at least from the semen traces, we know Iris was fucking *some*body. Right?"

Vincent didn't say anything.

"She was a cocktail waitress at Spade's Boardwalk, worked days, ten A.M. to six P.M. Which doesn't mean she couldn't have been moonlighting. We talked to Personnel. They tell us she missed two days in a row, didn't call in."

"The day she died," Vincent said, "and the day before that?"

"No, one-ten in the morning they found her. Don't count that day. They mean the two days before that. She took off, didn't call in sick or anything."

Vincent nodded. He said, "You talk to Donovan?"

"He's got something like thirty-five hundred employees," Dixie said. "I don't think he keeps track of 'em all."

"Donovan hired her, personally. Brought her up from San Juan."

"Yeah?" Dixie seemed to like that. "We'll put him on the list."

"Told her she was gonna be a hostess."

"Maybe she was. We'll find out."

"If you don't, I will," Vincent said.

Dixie looked at him but let it go.

"Girl she roomed with identified the body. They only knew each other a couple weeks. Iris worked days, the other girl works nights, in the band that's staying in the same house. She says they hardly knew each other."

"How'd you find her to make the I.D.?"

"She called in a Missing. Morning of the day we found the body. Like eight hours later, nine o'clock. She called the city cops and they let us know. Her name's Linda Moon. She's with a band plays at the hotel."

Vincent worked the name around in his mind because it was familiar. After a moment he said, "Let's go back to the scene. If nobody was staying in the apartment, and none of the building tenants know anything or heard anything outside of maybe a scream . . ."

"No scream," Dixie said. "I would've screamed, I would've tried to fly."

"No scream," Vincent said. "So where are you?"

"Still talking to the doorman, old guy in a rent-a-cop outfit. We're checking on deliveries made that day. We're talking to everybody who worked with

Iris, might've known her. And we got our snitches to talk to yet."

Vincent said, "You mind if I pick through what you've got? I won't do anything without telling you first."

"I never turn down professional help," Dixie said. "Long as the chief doesn't find out."

All they knew as fact, so far:

Was that Iris had gone off the balcony of Apartment 1802 in a high-rise condominium that stood on the corner of Surrey Place and Atlantic Avenue in Ventnor.

That the apartment was owned by a manufacturing company in Trenton that made janitorial supplies, cleaning compounds. Guy with the company said as far as they knew the apartment was vacant, hadn't been leased or rented since last season. Yes, the company had contracts with several hotels in Atlantic City, including Spade's Boardwalk.

That the apartment was relatively clean and did appear to be vacant. Except that one of the beds had been slept in and remade. Though not made the same as the bed in the second bedroom, tight, with fresh sheets. The slept-in sheets were at the lab.

Vincent saw Iris in a bedroom . . .

That a black cocktail dress was hanging behind the door in the bathroom. Silver high heels on the floor. A purse with cosmetics on the back of the washbasin.

He saw Iris on a balcony . . .

That a lady's black wool double-breasted coat was hanging in the bedroom closet, the room where the bed had been used. A few pieces of costume jewelry were in the top drawer of the dresser, in the same room. Cut-glass earrings, two bracelets, a necklace. Cheap stuff.

He saw Iris falling.

A young woman wearing a raincoat entered the parlor, her gaze holding on the casket.

Late twenties. Dark hair pulled back. Pale skin, delicate features cleanly defined. No makeup, not bothering on this rainy day to make herself more attractive. Still, as he watched her, Vincent saw a glamour shot of the same girl and a name with it. *Now Appearing in the Sultan's Lounge, Linda Moon.* Then saw her in a soft blue spot that diffused her clean features, but it was this girl. It had to be. He watched her stop short of the casket.

"Why did you have it opened?"

"I wanted to see her," Vincent said. "Make sure it was Iris, not somebody else."

"It's Iris." She said, "I don't know if I can look at her again," but moved almost cautiously toward the casket to stare into it without moving. "God, whoever did her makeup . . ."

"Ought to be arrested," Vincent said.

The girl he knew was Linda Moon looked over at him, taking her time now. She said, "You're the one from Puerto Rico," with some surprise. "Iris's friend. I came in, I didn't recognize you." She turned away, walked over to the empty rows of folding chairs, hands in the pockets of her raincoat, and sat down before looking at him again. "Where's your cane?"

"I forgot it," Vincent said.

He sat down with a chair between them, the girl staring at the casket again. She said, "Isn't that pathetic? Last seen in this life in a genuine wood-veneer plastic box."

Vincent studied her face in profile, dark hair tied back, giving him a good look at her features, hollow cheeks, delicate nose, long dark lashes—a girl who knew things about him, knew Iris well enough to pay for her funeral.

He said, "You are Linda Moon." Wanting to be absolutely sure but sounding like a lawyer or a court clerk.

She said, "I didn't make too big an impression, huh? You should see my act now. I wear an orange outfit, with ruffles." Very dry. Staring at the casket.

He said, "You did a weather set 'Stormy' and then 'Sunny' . . ."

She turned to look at him.

"Then you did 'Where're the Clowns.' "

" 'Send in the Clowns.' I thought you'd left."

"I stopped at the bar for 'Send in the Clowns.' I thought you were great."

"Weren't too broken up, uh, after your talk?"

"Do you want me to tell you about Iris and me? It'll take about two minutes."

"But you're here," Linda said.

"To bury her. You beat me to it." Looking into quiet blue eyes, and those long lashes. "I didn't know you were friends."

"We met that night. We flew up together and roomed in the same house."

"But you're paying for her funeral."

She glanced around. "I didn't see anybody breaking down the door. I still owe three hundred, which I don't happen to have at the moment."

"I took care of it," Vincent said. "I'll give you a check for what you paid them."

She said, "You don't owe me anything. If you want to go halves on it, fine, I won't argue with you."

"You knew her two weeks," Vincent said.

"Yeah? How long did you know her? You say you can tell me all about it in two minutes."

"Don't get mad."

"I'm not mad. I'm in a shitty mood, that's all." Looking at the casket again. "It's pathetic, the whole thing. The little party girl, looking for excitement—she gets two people at her wake."

Vincent waited a moment. "What about Donovan? Hasn't he been here?"

"Are you kidding?"

"Have you talked to him?"

"About what, Iris? Why would I? It's an idea though. Shake him down, get him to pay his share."

"She thought she was going to be a hostess," Vincent said. "Is that an *in* joke in the casino business, a hostess?"

"She was a cocktail waitress."

"During the day," Vincent said, and paused. "What was she doing in that apartment?"

"I don't know."

"She tell you she was going?"

"You know what we talked about, the few times we saw each other? Clothes. Iris borrowed things and never returned them."

"A black wool coat," Vincent said.

Linda didn't say anything.

"You tell the cops it's yours?"

After a moment she said, "I haven't yet."

"Why not?"

He could hear the silence, the sound increasing gradually, becoming the hiss of a radiator. She was staring again at the casket. Something to hold onto.

"Linda?"

Her hands in the pockets of the raincoat, her legs crossed. She wore narrow jeans, scuffed brown boots that were creased with age and looked wet. It was still cold in the room.

"You don't need your coat?"

"They didn't mention it," Linda said, "when I talked to them. I guess they think it's hers."

"What was she doing in that apartment?"

"I don't know."

"She see much of Donovan?"

"I have no idea."

"Or talk about him?"

"I told you what we talked about."

"You mentioned," Vincent said, "I wondered why you called Iris a party girl. You said, 'The little party girl, looking for excitement.'"

Linda stared at the casket and he was aware of the radiator again, the steady hissing sound higher pitched than before. She turned to look at him and paused another moment, those nice blue eyes calm but narrowing a little. She said, "You're a sneaky mother, aren't you? I don't know why I didn't remember right away, as soon as you started asking questions . . . She talked about you on the plane. Not a lot but enough. How she was leaving this American who was so in love with her, this guy Vincent, the cop."

"In Miami Beach," Vincent said, "not here. Atlantic City I'm only a civilian." He touched her arm and said, "But, Linda? I'll bet I can help you."

She said, "Now wait a minute—"

"You don't have anybody to talk to. You need a friend," Vincent said. "Tell me if I'm wrong. And you need somebody who can get you your winter coat, before you freeze your ass. Boy, it's cold up here in New Jersey, isn't it?"

Linda said, "If you can get the coat I'd love it. Beyond that, I don't need any help."

9

PARKED ON SEASIDE, Teddy had a clear shot of Bertoia's, over there across a trashy vacant lot on Oriental Avenue. Place looked more like a neighborhood bar than a funeral home. A couple of black guys in leather coats had come past the car twice looking to find out if he was cool. He could see them without any trouble in state clothes, doing a loose shuffle across the yard. They'd be back. "Hey, brother, you got the time?" Half minute or so of bullshit and, "You looking to get high, my man?" Try and sell him some meth. This town was full of meth. Keep the suckers' eyes open to play the games.

The taxi pulled up in front of the funeral home, a half block from him, and Teddy said, "All *right*," out loud, and watched two figures in raincoats come out to the cab. He had called the funeral home and learned Iris was going to be cremated tomorrow. He'd like to see her first, what she looked like after falling eighteen stories, *splat*, but they probably wouldn't show her. He wondered if he slipped the guy some money he'd give him a peek. If he slipped him enough. Only he was almost broke, shit, and his mom had tightened up since his last visit, changed into another person. It was amazing, in seven and a half years, to see the change in her: from a sweetiepie mom who would do anything for her sonnyboy, to a selfish old broad turned mean and tight as her arteries hardened and senility crept into her brain.

He waited until the taxi was a block up the street before putting his mom's car in Drive and turning onto Oriental to follow.

Big yellow turd of a car, '77 Chevy Monte Carlo that had lost its gleam to the salt air while traveling less than 20,000 miles, 19,681 on the odometer—she'd never wear the son of a bitch out, but she wouldn't trade it in either. What he might do, run it off that low bridge to Somers Point; there were always people going off drunk into the channel. Long as he didn't get trapped in it and go down with the turd. His luck was good and bad, starting and stopping. What he needed was to get on a roll with money to spend, operate on.

Teddy followed the taxi down Pacific Avenue, then left on Pennsylvania to the Holmhurst Hotel, a half block from the Boardwalk. It was one of those big old-timey frame buildings with a porch a mile long, even a glassed-in second-floor porch, kind of place where tourists used to spend their vacation in a rocking chair. Now you could almost hear the slot machines clanging over at Resorts International, the back side of it across a couple of parking lots.

The cop went into the hotel with his suitcase and the taxi stayed there. Now what? Teddy waited, parked down the street.

Trade this big yellow turd in. He liked that Datsun he had in San Juan. Be a good car in all this traffic, getting around the goddamn tour buses. Two thousand a day they came into the city, dropped the suckers off for six hours to lose their paychecks, their Social Security in the slots and then haul them back up to Elizabeth, Newark, Jersey City, shit, Philly, Allentown. Bring some more loads back tomorrow—like the Jews in the boxcars, only they kept these folks alive with bright lights and loud music and jackpot payoffs that sounded like fire alarms. A giant hotel billboard out on the highway said their slots paid out over 68 million dollars last month. Yeah? And how much of it did the suckers put back in? They didn't say.

His mom said colored men were coming in the house and stealing things, somehow getting through the windows covered with grillwork or the triple-locked doors. He said, "Mom, there's no way anybody could bust in here, even jigs I met who spent their lives doing B and Ees, pros. What would they want, your parrot dishes?"

His mom said, in a voice shaky but snippy, "Well, they took my best ashtray, they took my sewing basket, they took all my underwear. One of them, I saw him walking down West Drive with my mattress on his head, going toward Ventnor Avenue."

Teddy said, "Mom, how could the jig steal your mattress when you're always laying on it?"

She said, "Oh, you. You think you're so smart."

The old lady had flipped, her mind out to lunch, till it came to money. Get on money she'd recite interest rates on T-bills, CDs and cash management accounts like a bank teller. "What're you gonna *do* with all your money?" he'd ask her. "You don't have time left to spend it all."

She'd say, "Never mind."

The hell kind of an answer was that? "Never mind." Then she'd be off again, worrying about a colored guy coming in and kidnapping her parrot, Buddy.

He said, " 'Ey, mom, the jigs're making a fortune working the men's rooms at the casinos. They turn the water on for the sucker going to the toilet, hand him a paper towel with a big nigger grin and the sucker gives him a *buck* for taking a leak."

His mom gave him a dirty look and said, "Where on earth do you hear language like that?"

Now the cop was coming out of the hotel. He still had the beard from San Juan, but wasn't using the cane anymore and didn't seem to limp. He got back in the taxi and they drove off.

Teddy followed them down Pacific Avenue again. This time they turned off to pull up in front of Spade's Boardwalk Casino Hotel and the girl, Linda, the friend of Iris's on the plane, got out and went inside.

Iris was right the time she said this place was bigger than Spade's down in San Juan. Man, that seemed like a long time ago. This place had the green neon spades decorating the front, but that's all it was, a front, a snazzy new hotel lobby and casino of glass and chrome, green awnings, built onto an old hotel that had been here fifty years. Look up, there was the old hotel, like a different building. There were other places just like it, wearing shiny false fronts. Put up a glittery shell over an old Howard Johnson and call it Caesar's Boardwalk Regency.

The taxi U-turned, went back to Pacific Avenue and headed south with just the cop now. Where was he going? Teddy followed. They drove along through early evening traffic to where Pacific petered out and Atlantic Avenue curved down to become the main thoroughfare, and kept going, Atlantic City to Ventnor, out of one and into the other without even knowing it, unless you were a native. Teddy was getting a feeling now that told him where the cop was going. Yeah, Surrey Place. The taxi turned off, came to a stop in front of the condo on the corner, where Iris had taken her swan dive. Teddy pulled to the curb on Atlantic Avenue. He couldn't help looking up at that top floor, way, way up there, then watched through traffic going by as the cop got out of the taxi and went in the building.

Wasn't that like a cop? Didn't trust the local fuzz, had to come here and see for himself. "Well," Teddy said out loud, "good luck."

At first Vincent believed the building security guard was at least seventy. Jimmy Dunne. Bald with a thin, clean look, alert, bright-eyed, an old man who'd never grown up. "Haven't had a drink in thirty years." Just coffee, but plenty of it. "You want some more? Here. All I gotta do is ring Norma, she'll bring me down another thermos." Sitting behind his clean desk in the lobby Jimmy Dunne lined up the clipboard registration pad exactly in front of him. He'd taken this job to be doing something. He liked people, liked to chat, but didn't get much company when he worked nights. It was a shame, that poor little girl. Captain Davies—or was it in the paper said she was from Puerto Rico? Jimmy Dunne said he was down there with the U.S. army in 19-and-19. Two years later he was playing trumpet with the Victor Herbert Band out on the Steel Pier and had been here ever since. Loved Atlantic City. Vincent revised the man's age, pushing it up from seventy to somewhere in the mid-eighties. Jimmy Dunne said they'd had him in a nursing home a few years ago over there in Somers Point, but he'd broke out with his trumpet and was now living with this woman friend of his, Norma, right here in the building. The tenants' association told him he could have this job if he promised not to play his horn anymore. Well, he had lost his lip anyway. He said, "What else can I do for you?"

They sat in black leather director's chairs Norma had bought him, drinking coffee out of thick pottery mugs, each with a big *J* baked into the glazed surface.

"Captain Davies was wondering," Vincent said, "if any of the tenants are Puerto Rican."

Jimmy Dunne said, no, mostly they were Jewish, but nice folks. He said your Puerto Ricans were all up there by the Inlet.

"You gave the captain a list of visitors."

"Yes sir, they have to sign in right here or they don't go upstairs."

"How about deliveries?"

"We gave 'em a list. Florist, dry cleaners, ones the day man saw. On nights you don't have many deliveries aside from maybe a restaurant, you know, like an order from the White House Sub Shop. There was a delivery from there. Fella had an extra cheese steak sub he gave me. Nice fella."

"Did you know him?"

"Yeah, he looked familiar. But you get a turnover, those restaurant delivery boys, they don't make a lot of money. You see 'em a couple weeks, they're gone."

"How about the night before?"

"The night before . . ." Jimmy Dunne sipped his coffee.

"The night of the day before. You give the captain a list of visitors?"

"Well, we musta talked about it."

"You're not sure if you did?"

"I guess I did, you know, if he asked."

"Were you on the night before?"

"Well, I'm always around here, you know, since I live up in two-oh-nine. That's why the tenants' association, they know they can count on me."

"Who was on the night before?"

Jimmy Dunne sipped his coffee. "The night before . . . You know when we switch off, change from days to nights, there's a time in there I'm not sure if I worked that day or that night. See, cuz I'm here seven days a week."

"Just two of you work it?"

Jimmy Dunne paused. "Well, they're substitutes, you know, like one of us gets sick."

"Maybe that night before, somebody else was working."

"Gee, I don't know . . ."

"Could you look it up? It was only a few days ago."

"Well, we don't punch in or anything . . . you know."

"Jimmy, this is pretty serious. Girl was killed . . ."

"Listen, I know it is. This town, it can happen. I love this town but . . . well, you got an influence here now you didn't have in the old days, it's different. The old days this's where you brought your son to get his first piece a ass. You know, so there was plenty of action. But you had everything. You had your classy places, lot a big money had homes here. You had your shoobies, people'd bring their lunch in a shoebox, eat on the Boardwalk or out on the beach, never spend a dime. You had, I mentioned Victor Herbert, you had Sousa, 'Stars and Stripes Forever,' you had all kinds a entertainment. Horse that dove off the pier . . . Then people stop coming, I don't know why. They're watching color TV or something. Stores're going out a business, hotels closing. So they bring in casino gambling to pick up the economy . . . Boy, people like to gamble, don't they? Twenty-four hours a day, some of 'em."

"I thought the casinos closed—what, four in the morning?"

"Four A.M. weekdays, six A.M. Saturday and Sunday, open again at ten. But this's a twenty-four-hour town. You want something, say you want a game, no matter what time a day it is. You know what I mean? You can't find it, you can arrange it."

"Yeah? . . . I bet you've got some stories."

"Make your hair stand up. Like I 'magine you could tell a few yourself."

Vincent paused. "Jimmy, I'm not with the police."

"You're not?" Wide-eyed. "But you said—"

"What I mentioned was, I talked to Captain Davies and he told me what they had. No, I'm not with Atlantic County."

"You're not?"

"I'm a good friend of the girl that was killed. No, I came up from Puerto Rico to make the funeral arrangements."

"Oh, I see."

"I talked to the cops . . . but you know how they are. They're good guys, we got along fine. But they only want facts, they're not interested in any ideas, you know, you might have. Any theories or guesses."

"Oh, I know it," Jimmy Dunne said. "Just the facts, ma'am. 'Member that show? Sergeant Friday? Yeah, I know what you mean. They don't want you playing detective on 'em."

"Just tell what you know."

"Exactly."

"See, what I'm wondering—" Vincent paused. "This is just between you and me."

"And the gatepost. I gotcha."

"I was wondering, what if she went up to that apartment the night *before* it happened and was there all day and nobody knew it? And that's why you didn't see her."

"Uh-huh." Jimmy Dunne was thinking, re-aligning his clipboard registration pad, getting it just right.

"I wouldn't want to bother the cops with it," Vincent said, "it's just, you know, an idea. But I could ask the guy that was on duty that night, see what he says."

"Uh-huh."

"For my own peace of mind more than anything else."

Jimmy Dunne stared at his clipboard.

"He says he doesn't know anything, well, at least I've tried." Vincent paused. "Guy just works once in a while, huh? . . . Jimmy?"

"Yeah, he'll come in certain times."

"Cops didn't talk to him."

"Well now, they might've. I don't know."

"But if you didn't tell 'em this guy was work-ing . . . Jimmy, this's just between you and me. You understand? I won't even tell the guy where I got his name. I give you my word on it."

"He won't tell you nothing anyway. I know."

"If he doesn't, he doesn't. But I'd sure feel better."

"See, I don't want anybody to think I was talking

behind their back. Especially this guy, he's funny."

"Kind of a tough monkey, huh?"

"Hey listen, I think I've said enough."

"Jimmy, you ever take a polygraph?"

Jimmy Dunne pushed up in his chair, looking away from Vincent and then back to him. He said, "I don't know how we got to where we are, but I'm not gonna say another word and have it come back to me, no-sir."

"It won't happen," Vincent said. "All you have to decide, Jimmy, in your present frame of mind, would you rather have the cops holding you by the nuts or me?"

Yeah, rain helped business, the cab driver told Vincent. Rainy night, wind blowing. But otherwise, say you want to go a few blocks on Pacific you hop a jitney, six bits. You want a broad? They're on the corner. Look, there's one—got everything but a sign on her. Or you call an escort service. You *walk* to the casinos, the ones up at this end. Look. Golden Nugget . . . Tropicana . . . Playboy . . . Caesar's. Then you got Bally's, the Sands, the Claridge, Spade's Boardwalk all close together . . .

What about after hours? Vincent asked him . . . After hours what, gambling? Twenty hours you don't get enough? You can find it . . . They pulled up in front of Vincent's hotel, the Holmhurst.

You're staying at a place, the driver said, the bar there, dealers go in there after work to party, unwind, five, six in the morning. Ask one of 'em where the action is after hours, they'll tell you. If you can afford it.

Vincent was allowing himself a hundred bucks a day. Thirty for the room, not bad. But another thirty or forty if he had to rent a car. Eat cheap and drink beer . . . He liked the Holmhurst. It was homey, lot of furniture and paintings in the lobby, old leather sofas, flowery carpeting. Snug little cocktail bar. His third-floor room was okay, redecorated sometime during the past thirty years. He took off his raincoat—he'd had it on since the plane landed this morning—and dialed Dixie Davies's home phone in Brigantine to ask him:

"The name Catalina mean anything to you?"

"You're not talking about the island."

"Or fashionable swimwear," Vincent said. "Guy name Ricky Catalina was the doorman, the night before."

"Oh, shit."

"What do you mean, oh shit?" There was a silence on the line. "You understand what I'm saying? Not the night Iris was killed. Ricky was on the night before."

"Who told you?"

"I'm not allowed to say."

"Jimmy Dunne."

"Jimmy's afraid you're gonna talk to him and get his name in the paper. You see any need to do that? You want Ricky, whoever Ricky is."

"He's a nephew of Salvatore Catalina. Sal the Cat, very high up. In fact, he's the boss."

"I never heard of him."

"I'll get you a Pennsylvania Crime Commission Report."

"I understand what you mean—you're talking about South Philadelphia, all those guys shooting each other to see who gets Atlantic City. I've been reading about it, *Time* magazine."

"Something like twenty-two hits, killed different ways," Dixie said, "car bombs, the usual; another half dozen attempted. It started out the young guys hitting the old guys, the mustaches, 'cause they wouldn't get off their ass, make a move on the gambling. Then the guy who sent the hitter gets hit, the macaronis are shooting each other and it's hard to tell who's on whose side."

"They should wear numbers," Vincent said.

"You telling me. Six digits on a gray shirt."

"I've read about it, but I don't know the names," Vincent said. "We got our own league in Miami. We got the wise guys, we also have the Cubans Fidel sent us."

"We got Cubans," Dixie said, "we got bikers

handle the speed concession, brew methampheta-
mines out in the Pine Barrens, have their own chem-
ical plants."

"You have any Colombians?"

"I think I could look around, scare you some
up," Dixie said. "Sal Catalina, getting back, is
South Philly. Except right now he's in Talladega
Correctional on a gun charge. They been hound-
ing the shit out of him, finally got him on that con-
victed felon with a firearm. He had a High
Standard Field King in his trunk, under the spare
tire. Sal says the feds put it there—who knows? It's
only two years, you know, but it's better than
nothing. We got a tape of Sal and Ricky, you have
to hear it. They're in a toilet somewhere, I forget,
men's room of a restaurant. Sal's giving Ricky the
Zit a lecture on table manners. Guy eats like a
fucking goat, Sal's telling him never talk with your
mouth full and chew each bite forty times, for
your digestion. Ricky the Zit says, 'I know how to
fuckin eat, I been fuckin eatin all my life.' You hear
whack. Sal slaps him across the face. You hear
Sal's voice, very calm, always, 'Ricky, listen what
I'm telling you.'"

"Ricky the Zit," Vincent said.

"He was about twenty then, had a terrible complexion. It's cleared up, but he's still a mean little
fucker. Sal, Sal thinks he's George Raft. Expensive
suits, or he's got the shirt open all the way, the

chains. Maybe just a little swishy. So he's known as Sal the Cat or he's Sally, or he's Sal 'Little Pussy' Catalina. Only you call him that to his face he'll kill you. Sal, though, you can talk to him, he's not a bad guy. Ricky's something else. Ricky the Zit. Ricky 'the Blade' Catalina. Ricky the Sickie. I wish somebody'd shoot him in this war they got going."

"You're telling me," Vincent said, "he's not ordinarily a part-time rent-a-cop, somebody's doorman."

"These guys," Dixie said, "they're into extortion, shylocking, prostitution, they take a cut from the bookies, any illegal gambling. Sal, they say, runs it from Talladega, on the phone. Ricky's suppose to be a collector. Or you're late with a payment they send Ricky."

"So if he's watching the door that night," Vincent said, "he's not upstairs collecting. Something else is going on, right? Would you say that, a party, they don't want to be disturbed?"

"A party, a card game, a sex show, some type of off-premises gambling . . ."

"After hours?"

"Yeah, or less stringent rules than in the casinos. Guy might want to gamble in his underwear eating a cheese steak sub. Or they're playing blackjack, guy might want to handle the cards. New Jersey, you can't do it in the casinos, you can't touch the cards. They got a lot more rules than out in Nevada."

"You said 'off-premises' . . ."

"Not in a casino, not regulated. They could still have the same equipment, but without all the rules."

"Would a casino operate the game?"

"Not the casino, I doubt it. Somebody *from* the casino might," Dixie said, "but you're getting out of my area. I'm Major Crimes, homicide, any kind of sudden or unattended death. The wise guys, racketeering, narcotics, they come under the Economic Crimes section. And then anything in the casinos, cheating, stealing, that's handled by the DGE, Division of Gaming Enforcement. They're state cops."

"Iris's death was fairly sudden."

"That's why I'm on it."

"So you're gonna talk to Ricky," Vincent said, "not give him to somebody else."

"No, I'm gonna talk to him first thing in the morning," Dixie said, "if he's still around. Bring along a couple of guys to hold him."

Vincent said, "Dix?" He was going to mention Linda's coat, but then hesitated. Maybe he'd better wait. "Never mind, I'll talk to you tomorrow."

After he had another talk with Linda.

She had warmed up a little in the cab, smiled a couple of times. There was hope. He liked her and had a feeling she liked him. But he also had a feeling—one of those good ones that kept you wide awake—she knew a lot more than she was telling. Most of the ride, from the funeral home to Spade's, she was very quiet.

10

WELL, SHE WAS A DIFFERENT GIRL NOW. Brought back to life in a gold-orange turban, big loop earrings, low-cut bra and layers of ruffles on her orange tango skirt open all the way up the front to show bare legs moving, doing spastic little knee-jerk trip steps to a rattling, rackety sound of bongos, congas, steel drums, now a synthesized marimba sound kicking in—*Now Featured in the Winner's Circle Lounge, LA TUNA!*—Linda Moon moving with the guys, everybody moving, caught up in the rhythm of the Caribbean funk, or was it barrio punk? There were dreadlocks gleaming up there in the stage lights, but it wasn't reggae. Vincent sipped his beer and wondered, because what was the number? "Beat It," that's what it was. "Beat It" gone to the Gulf of Mexico and converted, brought back latinized. Linda was singing it in Spanish, belting it— *"Pégale! . . . Pégale!"*—shoulders back, whacking maracas off hips cocking to one side and then the other, back and forth to the beat.

Everybody in the packed lounge loved it, clapped and whistled and stayed through the set, sitting up, moving to "La Bamba" and "Hump to the Bump" and then grinning at the quick slick lyrics of "Oh, Frank Sinatra . . . Oh, Frank Sinatra . . . Frankie my boy you don't know, you have the perfect voice to sing calypso." Followed by "Mama, Look a Boo Boo."

Linda said, "Cute, uh? Jesus."

"You look different. I'll say that."

"I have to wear this goddamn Chiquita Banana outfit four straight sets. No costume change." She glanced around. "I wouldn't mind a drink."

"I ordered you one," Vincent said. "It's coming."

"All that noise, that jungle rock—six guys, they're beating on everything but a washboard and a gutbucket. I can duplicate all that with one poly-synthesizer and a rhythm box. They're not bad guys, but they ought to go back to Nassau, play for the cruise ships . . . How do you know what I drink?"

"You kidding?" Vincent said. "With that act? I got you a Rum Sunrise."

She frowned, "What is it?"

"We'll find out."

The waitress's legs appeared, long ones in net stockings. "In a frosted glass with an umbrella,"

Vincent said, as the girl did the bunny dip to place the drink on the table without losing her breasts.

"Just what I wanted," Linda said. She sipped it. "I could kill Donovan . . . You have a cigarette?"

"I quit while I was in the hospital."

She said, "Yeah, why get cancer when you can get shot." She said, "Donovan, the big shit, he tells me I can have my own band. I get here, I've got one number I do, 'Automatic,' the Pointer Sisters? These guys, they get on their roll I don't even know what they're playing. They're spazzed out on ganja anyway, they don't give a shit, they're gone. 'No Parking on the Dance Floor,' the Midnight Star number. I'm on the synthesizer? I'm trying to keep it precise, these guys ride right over you."

"You're not happy," Vincent said.

"I don't know what I'm doing here."

"When're you through?"

"What's today? Started at eight, we're off at twelve. Weekends we're on ten to two."

"We could get something to eat after."

"I don't know—I could meet you for a drink. But not if you're gonna ask questions."

"I think Iris went up to that apartment the night before she died," Vincent said.

Linda put her drink down, started to rise.

"That wasn't a question. I didn't ask if she went up there the night before. But I think she did."

"I have to go back to work."

* * *

The bartender came down from the lounge interior to the far end of the horseshoe bar nearer the casino floor, the dark edge before the circus of lights and mechanical sounds. The bartender was smiling. He said, "Mrs. Donovan, I'm sorry, I didn't see you there."

Nancy Donovan was watching Vincent and beyond Vincent the girl in the orange tango dress walking through the tables to the bandstand. She said to the bartender, "What's her name? The singer?"

"Oh, that's Linda. Linda . . . I don't recall her last name. What can I get you, Mrs. Donovan?"

She watched Vincent get up from the table. Bearded man in a raincoat, out of his natural element. Talking to the waitress now, paying his check. Then coming this way, along the dark lounge side of the bar.

Nancy could take three steps and be standing in front of him. She thought about it. She thought of an opening line but didn't like it. She turned to the bar and said, "A glass of water, Eddie. Please."

"Nothing in it, Mrs. Donovan?"

"Ice."

The bartender said yes ma'am and moved off as Vincent passed behind her. She wasn't ready for him quite yet. But she would keep him in sight and turned to watch him as she had watched him in the lounge talking to Linda, Vincent close to Linda's bare shoulders, dark hair showing beneath the headdress, Linda not bad looking, the same Linda who was in San Juan. They seemed to be friends. She watched Vincent walk through the empty outer lounge to a railing and stand looking over the casino, at the activity, the flashing lights, the serious faces in that funhouse the size of a dozen ballrooms. She watched him turn and walk toward the stairway, the five red-carpeted steps to the casino floor.

Nancy rode a gold elevator to the fourth level. She followed the executive hallway, pale gray and silent, past suites of offices with nameplates on double doors. Casino Hosts. Administration. Payroll. Division of Gaming Enforcement. Casino Control Commission . . . turned the corner, walked past executive offices and her husband's suite of rooms to the end of the hall where she knocked on a door marked *Surveillance*.

"Mrs. Donovan—"

The woman stepped back, surprised, opening the door wide for Nancy.

"What can we do for you?" She wore a plastic-covered I.D. card pinned to her blouse that said she was *Frances Mullen, Supervisor, Casino Surveillance*.

"I think I saw somebody I know," Nancy said, "but I lost him." She led the way through a narrow hall.

Behind her, Frances Mullen said, "What's he look like?"

"Beard and a raincoat, dark hair, about forty."

"That shouldn't be too hard."

They entered a small, windowless office where a young man and woman sat before a bank of twenty monitors, rows of video screens that framed areas of the casino floor, bits of action in black and white, angles on gaming tables, aisles of people playing slot machines. Frances leaned in close to the console, between the young guy and the girl. She pressed buttons and pictures on several of the video screens changed while looking much the same as before. "Man with a beard, wearing a raincoat. What color, tan?"

"Yeah, natural," Nancy said.

The young guy looked over his shoulder and smiled at her. "Mrs. Donovan, how's it going?"

"Just fine, Roger. Thank you. Terry, you holding up?"

Now the girl glanced around, a healthy, happy face in this high-tech room. "No problem, Mrs. Donovan."

Nancy stepped in behind Roger to watch a man in a leather jacket standing at the corner of a crowded craps table, next to the player with the dice. She noticed, now, the same man on three of the monitors, presented at different angles.

"Anyone we know?"

"Guy's acting a little shifty," Roger said. "Could be a railbird, waiting to grab a few chips."

Frances looked over. "He still there? Let's check him out, see if he's in the file."

Roger turned a knob, bringing the image of the man in the leather jacket into a close shot. From the floor next to him he picked up a Polaroid camera with a scoop attachment on the front of it that was like a long square megaphone. He placed it against the screen, covering the screen, and snapped a picture.

Nancy's gaze moved to another screen. "Is that Jackie?"

Standing at a blackjack table where a single player sat facing the dealer, the player's back to the camera.

"The one and only," Frances said. "And here comes Miss Congeniality."

On the monitor a young woman with swirls of blond hair approached Jackie Garbo from behind. When she spoke to him Jackie turned his head, said something over his shoulder without looking at her.

"Poor LaDonna," Nancy said.

"Poor LaDonna my ass," Frances said. "She

begs for it. Jackie, you have to talk back to him or he'll walk all over you. She wears that pushup bra with the peasant blouse? Jackie calls her boobs her Kathryn Graysons."

"He's a lovely man," Nancy said. "Turns now . . . gives her a pat on the behind . . ."

"Means he still loves her."

Nancy could see Jackie talking now, the diamond flash on his little finger as he raised his hand to his nose, turning again to the blackjack table.

"What's he doing?"

"He's scratching," Frances said.

"It looks like a signal."

"I don't know about it if it is," Frances said, "and I worked for him in Vegas twelve years, dealer to pit boss. Jackie's always scratching, he's a nervous type a person, lives on Gelusils . . . There's Tommy. I didn't think he was around this evening."

"We had dinner in the Versailles Room," Nancy said. "I think the food's getting better."

"They saw you coming. But I hear it is better," Frances said. "That cute little Mr. Hayakawa, he's finally straightening things out. All the restaurants served from the one kitchen, that's gonna save you some money."

Nancy was watching her husband talking to Jackie Garbo: Tommy's silver crown towering over Jackie's ball of curls, Jackie talking now. Jackie almost always talking, Jackie nodding toward the blackjack player, Tommy waiting, getting a smile ready as Jackie reached over to touch the player's arm. She watched her husband in action now as he took the player's hand in both of his and poured on the macho charm, big shooter to big shooter, the player's head nodding mechanically up and down, expression deadpan.

"Do they know each other?"

"They ought to," Frances said.

"Who is he?"

"Well, he's from Colombia . . ."

"Not the one in South Carolina."

"The other one," Frances said. "Jackie has the company plane pick him up in Miami."

"Is he on file?"

"*My* file? You kidding? This guy's comped to the eyeballs, the whole shot."

The player was middle-aged, a small man, gaunt, with dark Indian-Latin features. His hair glistened. His starched shirt with the dark suit showed bright white on the monitor, with a sheen.

"I think I'd like a picture of him," Nancy said.

Frances pushed a button and a close-up of the player appeared on the monitor in front of Roger. She said to Nancy, "You could work here."

"I was at Bally's a few years."

"I know you were. You got the eye, there's no

doubt in my mind." Frances motioned to bring
Nancy away from the monitors, hand on her arm.
"I not only see things up here, Mrs. Donovan, people tell me things 'cause they trust me and they
don't know how to handle certain situations."

"What people?"

"Well, like the cashiers. Guys I've worked with
for years, we're like family. They see certain irregu-
larities taking place and they tell me about it 'cause
they want it on record. You understand? I'm talking about top management allowing certain things,
not the help. The help I'm watching twenty hours a
day."

"What's Jackie up to?" Nancy said.

"See? You know what I'm talking about."

"I have an idea."

"I work for you and Tommy, Mrs. Donovan. But
I did work for Jackie at one time. I learned everything I know from him, I mean the finer points, and
that's the only reason I'm saying this. I don't want to
see him get hurt, lose his license. It could happen—
some of the people he's hanging around with, the
hotshots. I don't mean the celebs and the legit high
rollers, he's got to take care of them and he loves it."

"So does Tommy," Nancy said. "The two of
them, they're an act . . . Wouldn't you say?"

"Well, Tommy's in a different position, he's having a good time. Why not?" Frances smiled faintly.

"We kid around. You know, about the old neighborhood, growing up on the West Side there."

"Who would've ever thought," Nancy said, "a Mick from Columbus Avenue—"

"Yeah, like that. He says to me, 'Don't go back, Fran, it's all artsy-craftsy over there now. Hurley Brothers Funeral Home, they changed the name to Death 'n' Things. The bars, you can't walk in you hit your head on the ferns in the hanging baskets. Where would our dads go for a drink?' They were subway motormen, you know. Both of 'em."

"I know," Nancy said.

"He calls me Wrong-Way Mullen 'cause I went out to Vegas, worked there fifteen years to end up in Atlantic City. Tommy says, 'You could a taken a Fugazy tour bus, been here in three hours.' "

"He's quite a guy," Nancy said.

"He's having a good time—what the heck. This place with Tommy it's like a toy, you don't mind my saying."

"Please," Nancy said.

"I'm not taking anything away from him, he's a brilliant guy, very charming. I don't have to tell you that."

"But what?" Nancy said.

"Well, Jackie—you know what he's like, all the celebrity photos in his office, the poor kid from the Bronx showing off. That's what he is, he's a show-off."

"Among other things," Nancy said.

"But he's getting mixed up with some people he shouldn't go anywhere near, and Tommy doesn't realize it. Jackie thinks, you know, he's discreet; but some of the people, you can't miss 'em."

"Like the guy from Colombia," Nancy said. "What's his name?"

"Excuse me." Terry looked over from the bank of monitors. "Here's a guy with a beard. On this one." She pointed to a screen.

Frances said, "Is that him?"

Nancy nodded, walking over, seeing Vincent Mora in profile playing a quarter slot machine, carefully inserting the coin, ritualizing it, pulling the handle and watching the drum spin . . . to come up with nothing. She heard Roger say, "I don't recognize him, do you?" And Terry say, "No, but he's kind of cute."

When Vincent walked away from the machine Nancy said, "Follow him." She moved to a telephone on the wall, touched buttons, then turned to watch Vincent appear on several monitors.

"Hi, is this Milly? . . . Mrs. Donovan. See if we have a Vincent Mora staying with us."

As she waited she saw Vincent stop to watch coins clattering into the tray of a slot machine. He said something to the woman scooping quarters into a paper cup. The woman, very serious, turned and smiled, nodding.

Nancy smiled a little, watching him. She said, "Thanks, Milly," and hung up the phone. Roger was saying, "We know this guy?"

"He looks lost," Terry said. "Came in out of the rain—wow, never saw anything like this before."

It was a long raincoat, below his knees. He stopped at a blackjack table and watched several hands among three players before taking a twenty-dollar bill from his wallet. He bought four red chips from the dealer.

Nancy watched Vincent draw a pair of aces on the deal and split them to bet two red chips on each. Then was hit with a king and queen and paid three-to-two for the naturals, sixty dollars. Roger said, "Look at the guy."

"I'd like a picture of him," Nancy said.

She watched Vincent bet the $60 and win when the dealer went over. She watched him bet $120 on eighteen and beat the dealer who had to stand on seventeen. She watched him bet $240 and win on nineteen when the dealer drew up to eighteen and stayed. She watched him bet $10 and lose, watched him gather his chips and walk away from the table.

"Let's follow him," Nancy said.

Vincent appeared on several screens, different angles. "He's gonna cash in," Frances said. After a moment she said, "Look, who's at the window ahead of him."

It was the player from Colombia, his back to the camera. Jackie Garbo stood next to him, in profile.

"I wouldn't mind a picture of this," Nancy said.

Roger said, "Guy in the raincoat? I already got him."

"The one cashing in."

"I got him too."

"Maybe we can see what he won."

"They'll give him a nice clean check," Frances said and looked at Nancy. "What I mentioned, you might say something to Tommy."

"I probably will," Nancy said, watching the monitor.

The cashier was away from the window. Jackie Garbo chatted with the man from Colombia, using his hands, smiling a lot, while the man from Colombia stood without moving.

"There was a stockholder, one of the other casinos," Frances said, "his license came up for renewal the Control Commission turned him down. He didn't do a thing. His daughter married some guy with a shady background."

When the cashier returned he pushed a form through the opening in the window for the man from Colombia to sign. The cashier then separated the copies of the form, attached a check to one of the copies and presented it with a smile. The man from Colombia turned . . .

Roger looked up from the Polaroid, the scoop attachment covering the monitor in front of him. "The guy in the raincoat's in the way."

Nancy didn't say anything. She watched Vincent, wondering, Is he?

11

VINCENT TOLD THE BARTENDER at the Holmhurst he'd won 470 bucks playing blackjack. Just like that, in about three minutes. The bartender told him he'd lose it before he was through. Vincent said, no, he was going to buy some warm clothes as soon as the stores opened. He felt good. It was a snug, knotty-pine bar, more like somebody's rec room than a saloon, and it was cold and rainy outside. He ordered another scotch and told the guy who came in and sat next to him at the bar he'd won 470 bucks at Spade's Boardwalk. Just like that, in about three minutes. The guy said, big fucking deal; you want to keep it, get out of town, fast. The guy was a blackjack dealer at Resorts International, across the street. He had been a floorman at Tropicana, but he'd tapped out a dealer for looking away from the cards and it turned out the dealer had more juice than he did, so listen to this, he got fired for doing his job. Politics, man. Who you know. You don't party with the right people, kiss your ass good-bye. It was 12:30. Linda should be here any minute. See, you got the dealer looking at the cards and the players. You got the floorman looking at the dealer. You got the pit boss looking at the floor-man. You got the shift manager looking at the pit boss. Craps, you got the boxman looking at the stickman. You got the assistant casino manager looking at the shift manager. Wait, you got the slot manager in there. No, fuck the slot manager. You got the casino manager looking at the assistant manager. You got the vice-president of casino oper-ations looking at the casino manager—

Vincent said, "Excuse me, but I have to meet somebody," and got out of there.

He waited in the lobby, pacing, looking at old paintings, about to give up when Linda arrived a little before one. Everytime he saw her she looked different: a little weird this evening, wearing her stage makeup with the raincoat and jeans. Seeing the look in her eyes he said, "What'd I do?" She didn't answer. She sat down at one end of a leather couch and lighted a cigarette.

"I won four hundred seventy bucks playing blackjack. You know how long it took?"

"I got fired," Linda said. "You know how long that took? I'm the only thing those Jamaican ya-hoos had going for 'em and I get canned."

"Why? What'd you do?"

"What do you mean, what'd I *do*?"

"Who told you?"

The kingfish—what's his name, Cedric, the head Tuna. Man, that burns me up. I should've quit, you know it? But I didn't. Jesus, get dropped out of that outfit—it doesn't do a lot for your pride. Cedric goes, 'They nothing I can do, mon. It's the monagement give me the instruction.' "

"Donovan?"

"Probably, the son of a bitch."

"But he's the head guy, chairman of the board."

Linda looked up at him. She said, "He brought Iris here, didn't he? All the way from Puerto Rico?"

Vincent had remained standing, looking at her dark hair, at her face now, her painted eyes staring at him. He said, "What do you want to drink?"

"Scotch."

"Don't move."

He got two of them, doubles over ice, and brought the drinks out of the happy, crowded little bar to the empty lobby, to the girl in her stage makeup sitting alone. He pulled a leather chair over close, wanting to watch her face.

She said, "I wasn't that bad." Quiet now, subdued.

"Bad? You were the show. They loved you."

"That's why I'm thinking there's more to it." She blew cigarette smoke past him and it smelled good.

"Maybe the head Tuna didn't like you cutting in on his act."

"No, I believe Cedric. He had nothing to do with it. He was even starting to come on to me."

"He was? . . ."

"That's why I think it's something else." She looked at him, silent for a moment. "It might have to do with you. The two of us."

Vincent didn't move, sitting forward in the deep chair. "Tell me why."

"If we were seen together. In the lounge, or maybe even at the funeral home."

"We were the only ones there."

"Somebody could've looked in."

"Who are we talking about, Donovan?"

She hesitated. "Maybe. I'm not sure."

"And if he saw us together—what?"

"You're Iris's friend. You come all the way here from Puerto Rico and who's the first person you talk to? Me."

"And that's why you were fired?"

"It's possible. To get rid of me. I can't hang around here if I'm not working."

It was getting better. "All right, say Donovan saw us together. Why would that bother him?"

"You're a cop, aren't you? For all he knows I could be telling you things I shouldn't."

Better and better. Vincent said, "Let me have one of your cigarettes." She handed him the pack. He lighted one, inhaled deeply—surprised at the sudden cold hit of menthol—and looked at the pack.

Kools. He was smoking again, just like that. He said, "Donovan, even if he saw me, doesn't know I'm a cop. I've never met the man."

She said, "Then they're afraid I might tell the other cops. I don't know—I've got this feeling I'm being watched."

"You talked to them, the police."

"They talked to me."

"Are you afraid?"

"You're damn right I am."

"Somebody advise you not to say anything?"

She shook her head. "I knew better. Once I found out what Iris was doing. She didn't tell me. It was one of the guys in the band, a Puerto Rican, the only one Iris was the least bit close to."

"He tell the cops anything?"

"Are you kidding? Those guys—they named their band La Tuna after a federal prison where they met, the whole bunch of them doing time for narcotics. The Puerto Rican, he thought I was like Iris's big sister, so he said things when he was stoned he assumed I knew about. She was telling him everything."

"What was she doing?"

Linda hesitated, on the edge of involving herself. He watched her light a cigarette and was aware of a tender feeling, looking into those painted eyes. She said, "I could be making a big mistake."

Vincent said, "She was a party girl, she entertained high rollers . . . What was she doing in that apartment?"

Linda exhaled a slow stream of cigarette smoke, almost a sigh.

"They used the apartment for illegal gambling. They set up a crap game for this particular guy who must be very important but doesn't speak much English. That's why Iris was there. The guy is from Colombia, Bogotá, which should tell you something. The Puerto Rican was dying to meet him, score some cocaine. Iris couldn't stand the guy. He made her take her clothes off, because he said a naked girl brought him luck. He'd rub the dice in her pubic hair."

For a moment Vincent wondered if the guy had won or lost. But something didn't make sense. He said, "How do you know that?"

"Iris told her friend, the Puerto Rican."

"But she stayed in the apartment . . ."

"She was there with the guy two nights in a row. She told her friend about the first night and said she had to go back, but it was okay, the guy gave her five hundred bucks. Even though he lost about a hundred thousand."

"The guy spend the night with her?"

"The first night—I don't know. She got home about five."

"The second night," Vincent said, "she stayed.

She was there all day. Let's say she was. And somebody came back to see her that night."

"Or somebody stayed with her," Linda said.

"Who was there? Who brought the Colombian?"

"Well, he had a suite at Spade's. They flew him up from Miami in their private jet, comped the room, meals, everything. If you can afford to lose a hundred grand, Vincent, it's all on the house."

"We talking about Donovan now? He set it up?"

"Or Jackie Garbo. He runs the casino. But Donovan would have to know about it, it's his hotel."

"Was Donovan at the apartment?"

"I don't know, it's possible."

"Or Jackie—what's the guy's name, Garbo?"

"Yeah, it's more likely he was there."

"Who else?"

"I don't know."

"Local people?"

"What do you mean, local people?"

"Guy by the name of Ricky Catalina?"

"Never heard of him."

Vincent eased back in the chair, finished his drink. He saw the condominium in Ventnor, the carpeted lobby, Jimmy Dunne's neat desk and wondered what Ricky looked like—wanting to picture him in that lobby. Then wondered what a loanshark collector would be doing there, acting as

doorman. The lookout. Just a guy in the ranks, one
of the soldiers. But he wouldn't be there unless
someone he worked for was upstairs. Vincent began to see a connection that made sense. The wise
guys doing business with the Colombian; he was
their supplier. They partied together when he came
to town, arranged for Donovan or Garbo to bank
an illegal game where Iris had to take her clothes
off to bring the guy luck. Vincent was thinking he
would like to try his luck with the Colombian, he
sure would. If it wasn't too late. They could disappear on you. He had known a few Colombians
who posted half-million dollar bonds and took off
in the night. It was only money. What this town
was all about, money. Nothing else.

· Linda was staring at him. She said, "There was
another girl there." Staring at him with those
painted eyes. He watched her raise her glass and
hesitate, looking off now.

Vincent waited.

"But I can't think of her name. I know who she
is, I saw her in the lounge with Jackie. She was Miss
Oklahoma about five or six years ago."

"Take your time," Vincent said.

Teddy could see his mom's scalp her curlers were
turned so tight, wound up in thin tufts of her gold-
colored hair. Coming home he'd thought it was a

wig her hair was so bright. She told him, no, she still had her crowning glory, she had to just touch it up now and then. He said to her bird face glistening with beauty cream, covers up to her chin, " 'Night, Mom. Don't let the bedbugs bite you," closed her door and went out to the living room wondering if you could taste chloral hydrate in warm milk.

Get some up in Boystown, New York Avenue, those cute guys had anything you wanted, knockout drops, percs, street ludes, all kinds of meth.

Buddy cocked his green-and-orange head and stepped sideways along his perch saying, "Magic! Magic!" his parrot voice sounding like a movie cartoon witch.

Teddy said, " 'Ey, Buddy, 'ey, Buddy boy. How's my old buddy? I bought a handicraft bird looks just like you this PR girl was suppose to deliver, but I guess she never made it. You coulda played with it, Buddy, had yourself a little playmate."

Buddy stepped sideways to the edge of the perch stained white and bluish green with parrot shit. His mom could offer Buddy a sunflower seed from her puckered mouth murmuring, "Kisser mom, kisser mom," and Buddy would peck the seed out of the red goo of her lips, crack it and eat it without thinking twice. Teddy, all he had to do was approach the stand—there in the living room on spread newspapers—even offer a peanut, and Buddy would shit and become edgy. Why?

" 'Ey, I ain't gonna eat you. Here, walk onto my hand . . . Okay, don't then. I don't care. The heck're you nervous about?" Teddy hunched down to look into Buddy's eyes as Buddy side-stepped back the other way now. It would show if Buddy saw something in *his* eyes. Did he? It was hard to tell with a parrot.

He had looked into the eyes of convicts, wondering if they saw something, and had got propositioned, proposed to and finally picked by a big colored guy, Monroe Ritchie, to be his old lady. But he had never seen the look in any con's eyes like the look he had seen in the cop's—that morning when they woke him up busting through the door and the cop held the gun in his face.

Not a look of hate exactly, it was more a look of knowing something.

Then saw the look in the cop's eyes again, on the car ferry down in Puerto Rico, this time the cop holding the curved end of a walking stick in his face. This was like confirming it, he hadn't just imagined the cop saw something that first time. No, seven and a half years later the cop still saw it.

Teddy said to Buddy, "How would you like it? Guy thinks he knows more about you than you do? Like he can look in your head and see things that make him want to blow your head right off. I mean a guy that *shows* he wants to kill you. What would you do, let him?" Teddy hunched in close to Buddy.

"I make you nervous, don't I? Huh? Would you like to peck my eyes out so I can't look at you no more? Would you? 'Ey, then you know what it feels like."

He had watched Monroe Ritchie's eyes cloud. "No, I don't see nothing." Then go milky soft. " 'Cept my sweetie."

He would lie spooned in Monroe's arms on the lower bunk in darkness, Monroe's bulk against his spine, Monroe's big arm lying dead across him, Monroe's sleepy breath on the back of his neck. "I want to kill him, Monroe." And would hear Monroe say, "Do it, honey, and hurry back." But how? Many conversations about that part. Monroe would say, "Walk up behind the man, what you do, and shoot him right here." Teddy would feel Monroe's finger poke into the groove at the base of his skull. Monroe told him where to buy a gun in Miami. Do it and throw the gun in the ocean. Told him a little .22 was all he needed.

But when Teddy saw the Colt .38 Super he couldn't resist it. That was the start of what was becoming an expensive proposition. The gun, air fare to Puerto Rico, the hotel, the car . . . now back home and his mom wouldn't give him any more money.

She actually believed he had worked for International Surveys, because he'd showed her the business cards he had printed and there was the company name and his own name with *Research*

Representative under it. So when she asked him if he was going to get a job he told her he'd probably go back with I.S., they were a good outfit, offered a generous bonus plan and other benefits. His mom said, "That's nice." He told her, not right away though, he needed to readjust himself to the world, try to put the nightmare of prison out of his mind. He told her he had met other innocent men in there, like himself, unjustly accused. His mom patted his head and said, "My fine boy, treated like a criminal . . ." But would she break into one of her CDs or Treasury Bills and give him a few dollars, just a couple hundred say? No, her mind had more locks on it than her front door when it came to discussing money. She had given him $1,200 dollars and that was all he was getting, no more. "No. No. No," his mom said. "Do you know what no means? It means no." He said to her, "I met boys in there who turned to crime for less reason. Had to." She wouldn't budge, the old bitch.

What he'd have to do now, get next to some little old lady scooping a jackpot out of a slot tray. Offer to be of help and kid around, tell her he loved her blue hair. Take her for a nice walk on the Boardwalk. One good score might make him enough. He didn't know how much time he had, how long the cop was going to hang around. He would like to walk in the cop's hotel room, wake him up with a gun in his face, just like the cop had done it. Look in his eyes and say, "What do you see?" Look in his eyes first, then tell him to roll over and stick the barrel against that little groove at the base of the skull.

Tomorrow, though, he'd have to see about getting hold of some operating cash.

12

WHEN MOOSLEH HAJIM JABARA was sixteen years old, in his second year at Southeastern High School in Detroit, he changed his name to DeLeon Johnson. So people would look at his name and know he was American.

When he first arrived in this country, still a little boy, his father's cousin's uncle by marriage, who taught in the high school, looked at him with wonder and said, "My God, boy, you know who you are? You know where you've been?" All Moosleh knew was that someone would die, first his mother and father, and he would cry and be sent someplace else to live. His father's cousin's uncle, Mr. Johnson, showed him a map and said, "Look, my God, where you were born. Ethiopia, the kingdom of Haile Selassie, Lion of Judah. You could have his blood in you from your father's side. Your mama's mama was raped by an Italian—don't you ever forget it—and your mama came from that. They say her people killed him with a spear." Mr. Johnson said, "It's all right, it's not your fault he was your granddaddy. But he was a big strong Italian fella and I see you're going to have size on you." He pointed to the map. "Now look here. You left this place called Djibouti, went up to Egypt, the land of the Pharaohs, to live in Ismailiya, love that name, and was put on the boat, little fella eight years old to come here. Look at you."

He loved Mr. Johnson and took part of his name and part of the name of the guy he read somewhere went to Florida to find the Fountain of Youth.

This DeLeon went there too from Michigan State to the Miami Dolphins, played defensive end five years till a knee and cocaine tripped him up, ruined his desire and size wasn't enough. The coke got him six months in the Dade County stockade and some community-service work, talking to kids. When Jackie Garbo offered him good money to guard his body DeLeon took it. There was nothing to the work. What he didn't care for was the way Jackie spoke about him to people right in front of him, like Jackie had bought him off a slave block. Jackie always called him the Moose; so most people thought of DeLeon as Moose Johnson, named that because of his size.

At this moment DeLeon stood at the big window in Jackie's office looking down at the Boardwalk and the Atlantic Ocean working its way in, getting mean. He was thinking about Puerto Rico, wishing he was there. He liked the people, he liked the food. He remembered the first time he went there to the casino, saw the spade dome and felt drawn to it, with the desire to go inside and pray. Some Muslim sounds still in his head from when he was a little boy. Had he stayed there in Ismailiya, man his size, he'd be loading ships 'stead of wearing a $400 sharkskin suit, pearl gray, and working for this little Hymie fool . . .

"Hey!" calling to him now.

DeLeon turned from the window to see Jackie behind his desk, his phone buzzing, Jackie picking it up and jabbing the air with his other hand, stubby finger pointing. DeLeon walked over to the glass cocktail table and picked up the phone there to listen in, like Jackie wanted. See, then Jackie would have a witness if somebody was trying to fuck him. Man had to trust somebody. So he trusted his Moose with secrets, even trusted him with his woman, like the Moose was his palace eunuch in a pearl-gray suit.

DeLeon eased down into the couch, low, laid his head back against the cushion as he heard the voice on the phone say:

"They picked up Ricky this morning, eight a'clock they come in his house, take him to Northfield."

DeLeon grinned. Beautiful. Nail his ass.

Jackie's voice on the phone and Jackie in the room said, "For what?"

"Come on, Jackie. The voice very patient. "They take him over to the green room there they want to talk to him."

Slow husky voice with that South Philly street guinea accent, that tough-guy shit they learned when they were kids. Frank Cingoro speaking. Chingo. Frankie the Ching. Frank the Wheel. Capo, or something like that, under Sal Catalina, big in the dope business.

And little Jackie trying to sound just as tough, man, saying, "Yeah? Talk to him, okay, about what? They could talk to Ricky, they could talk to him about anything went down the past *year* could a been Ricky."

DeLeon grinned. Love it. Throw the little motherfucker in the hole. Then stopped grinning as Frank Cingoro came on again.

"They talk to him about the little girl, Jackie."

There was a silence. DeLeon looked at Jackie who would be wondering all of a sudden if he should be talking like this, wondering where the Ching was calling from. Bar on Catherine Street in South Philly? He hoped to Christ not. That social club on Hutchinson? Either place could be wired. The Ching must have read Jackie's thoughts in that silence. He said, "I'm way the fuck and gone out the White Horse Pike, Jackie. Talk to me."

Jackie the Fatty was standing behind his desk now, moving like he had to go to the toilet. Jackie said, "Well, Ricky won't say nothing."

DeLeon thinking he could make him talk; make him tap-dance.

"I know Ricky won't say nothing," the Ching said. "We not talking about Ricky, we talking about the little girl. Those guys in Northfield, they're busting their ass. I want to know what they're gonna find, Jackie. Then I'll tell you why."

"How'n the fuck do I know?" Jackie said. "You think I had anything to do with it?"

"Benny says he never touched her."

Benny?

"I know he didn't," Jackie said. "I was with him every fucking night, getting him something."

Benny, DeLeon remembered now, that was what the Ching called Benavides, the cat from Bogotá, the South American grass man, that scary, snake-eyed greaseball.

"Where's he at now?"

"Left this morning. The Moose put him on the plane to Miami." DeLeon watched Jackie glance over, man's eyes wide open so he wouldn't miss anything said to him.

"Talk to me," the Ching said. "Who pushed her off?"

"You asking me for?" Jackie sounding desperate. "I didn't even know the broad was there.

Everybody cleared out, I left, it wasn't fifteen minutes after you did, Benavides went in a bedroom
there with the broad, gave her a jump, that was it.
We brought him back to the hotel." Looking up at
the mass of photographs on his wall now—all the
gold-framed celebrities, the film stars, comics, entertainers, the has-beens—like he was seeking help
or inspiration, and DeLeon had to grin at those
folks with the perfect teeth smiling back at Jackie,
like they were enjoying the Ching doing a number
on him. The Ching saying:

"Here you got a dead little girl you don't even
know what happened to her. I know she wasn't one
of our girls—"

"Tommy found her."

"Tommy, what I understand, don't know shit.
He don't watch the girl, she decides to do some
business there and gets a freak wants to ball her
hanging off the fucking balcony or some fucking
thing. You get your freaks, the girl isn't protected
she takes a chance every time she takes her pants
off. I'm not too concerned about the little girl,
Jackie, but the cops *are*. You see my point?"

Ignorant man, DeLeon thought, believed he was
wise because he wasn't dead. Man, there were some
fools in the crime business. But mean motherfuck-
ers. Some of 'em could make good ballplayers.

"The cops, say all they find out you're running a
game there, it's still your ass, Jackie."

Man will put you to sleep, DeLeon thought.

"The cops, the least they'll do is tell the DGE. Right? The DGE tells the Control Commission and they pull your license, that's what they do. You see my point? 'Cause you got careless, didn't keep track of this little girl, you could be outa business."

"Wait a minute—" Little Fatty sounding amazed now, can't believe this shit he's hearing. "Who'd I set it up for? You stick me with Benavides—I didn't want any fucking part of him!" Little frantic now.

"All I saw was you raking in those pinky-white chips," the Ching's voice said. "What'd you take off him, about two fifty?"

Jackie said, "Yeah, and I can stick it up my ass a buck at a time waiting for the fucking roof to come down on me. This is not my fault, no *way*—" Turning from the pictures on the wall and stopping right there. Jackie's voice, lower, said, "I gotta go," and there was a loud click in DeLeon's ear.

Mr. and Mrs. Donovan were in the doorway, coming in without knocking, Tommy Donovan saying, "Moose! Hey, man!" But Mrs. Donovan, carrying a manila envelope in her hand, was leading her husband and she said, "Would you excuse us?" before DeLeon could answer him.

"Yes, ma'am."

Got up and gave her a little bow, eyeing her slickness, the effortless way she was eyeing Jackie.

Nothing to it. DeLeon walked down the executive hallway in his pearl-gray suit, realizing he had glimpsed something for the first time. It was the lady had the juice around here, not her husband. She looked like she could bust any man's balls she wanted. Do it with her little finger.

They sat at the conference table in the Major Crime Squad's interrogation room, Vincent wearing his new tweed sportcoat, smoking a cigarette, halfway into the pack, Dixie Davies reading from a computer printout.

"Aggravated assault with a knife, Philadelphia, May of eighty-two. Charge dismissed. Homicide, November eighty-two, Ricky stabbed a guy to death was an official of Local Fifty-four, Bartenders' International, following an argument in Cous' Little Italy, restaurant in Philly. Copped to voluntary manslaughter, did eighteen months in Trenton. Contempt of court, refused to testify before New Jersey State Commission of Investigations on loan-shark activities, sixty days, in and out. Questioned in regard to four, five, six homicides in the past two years. Witness saw him shoot a guy in the back of the head three times, cut the guy's shlong off and stick it in his mouth. This's an inside witness agrees to flip. He disappears and we find him a couple

months later, bullet in his head, cock in his mouth.
Here's one, charged with the illegal lending of
money at interest rates as high as a hundred
seventy-five percent. Another loan-shark case they
tried to get him, guy was behind in his payments so
Ricky chopped him with a hatchet, severed his
spine. The guy's a paraplegic, never walk again, but
he won't testify against Ricky 'cause he's afraid for
his fucking life."

Vincent stubbed out his cigarette, flicked an ash
off the lapel of his new sportcoat. "You didn't get
anything at all?"

"I got almost an hour of him on tape. You want
to hear it?"

"He let you tape him?"

"Why not? He didn't say nothing. He didn't see
nothing, nobody came in or out. Unless they did
when he happened to fall asleep a couple minutes.
He took the job 'cause he needed money. Only security guard I ever heard of drives a Cadillac Eldorado."

Vincent said, "Let me just hear what he sounds
like." He got another cigarette ready while Dixie
went over to the recording machine and pushed a
button. As Ricky's voice came on Dixie said, "This's
a few minutes into it. Little prick—listen to him."

RICKY: . . . construction business, remodeling. We'd
    do rec rooms, uh, you know, or like enclose a

porch. But Sal, he got, since he got sent there to Alabama that was the end of the business.

DIXIE: You draw unemployment?

RICKY: Fuck no. I look like a jig to you?

DIXIE: I won't say what you look like. There's a nice young lady has to transcribe this shit . . . Who was up in that apartment?

RICKY: Where the broad was? It wasn't even the same night, man. That night I wasn't anywhere fucking near that place. I was up in Brigantine, at a party.

"That's good," Vincent said. He watched Dixie shut off the machine. "What would you say, I have a talk with Ricky? Ask him a few questions of my own."

"As what?" Dixie came back to the conference table. "Cop or civilian?"

"An interested party. I wouldn't show him a badge, try and bullshit him and it comes back, jams you up. But I wouldn't have to be as nice to him as you are, would I? Read him his rights, anything like that."

A smile played in Dixie's big mustache. "You wouldn't have to be nice to him at all." There was a silence in the room. "But I can't let you do it. Look at his sheet, he's crazy."

Vincent said, "I won four hundred seventy bucks last night playing blackjack. It took about three minutes. Won the money and quit, walked away."

"I admire that," Dixie said.

"I bought this sportcoat—you like it? And rented a car. Nice one, a Datsun. Tan with a brown interior."

"Match your jacket," Dixie said. "What else's new?"

"Let's see—there was a crap game in that apartment," Vincent said, "two nights in a row. Iris was there to entertain the shooter. Guy from Colombia, staying at Spade's. I don't know what his name is but I'll find out if I can talk to Ricky."

Dixie didn't say anything.

"You can ask him, he won't tell you. Why should he? He doesn't have to open his mouth. Let me ask him in a different way, see what he says."

There was a silence again. Dixie, staring at him, said, "You got to the roommate. Linda."

"Anything she can tell you is hearsay," Vincent said. "You can't use it, so why get her upset? Anybody you talk to about this who knows *any*thing," Vincent said, "isn't gonna say a word. You know why? Because the guys who were up in the apartment that night scare the shit out of people. You tell me about a witness, you find the guy shot in the head. You tell me about a guy gets whacked in the spine, paralyzed, he still won't say anything. You get a good witness—can you guarantee protection? You say you will. I've said it I don't know how many times. You get cooperation on homicides when it's mom and pop or commission of a robbery, guy comes in the store with a gun, customers in there see him, they testify. But you don't get any cooperation with these guys. I mean when they're involved—Ricky and guys like that, because they'll kill you if you come in to tell on 'em. You've seen it happen and the witnesses you might have on this one, *they* know it happens, they been reading about it. Okay, if Ricky was on the door then you know that a guy who's bigger than Ricky and probably doing business with the Colombian was upstairs with him. Guy who arranged the crap game, got him a girl, Iris—guy's entertaining his supplier who's bringing him all the good shit, making him rich. Isn't that how you see it?"

Dixie took his time; he nodded.

"But you don't do narcotics or racketeering, that's somebody else's area. You're homicide, so keep it simple as long as you can. Right?"

Dixie nodded again.

"Okay. Somebody stayed with Iris all the next day or somebody went back that night, slipped in and Jimmy Dunne missed him. I think we can take Jimmy's word he didn't see anybody," Vincent said. "So here we are. You can ask Ricky if he knows who was with Iris, or I can. And right now I'm lucky, I'm on a roll. But in order for me to talk to Ricky I'm gonna need your help."

Dixie raised his head a little higher.

"I don't want to go to his house. I'd rather catch him he's out somewhere, on the street. So you'd have to put him under surveillance and let me know where he is. I call in from time to time, you tell me he's in a bar on Pacific, such and such a place, that's all you do. Your guy clears out, 'cause you don't want to know anything about it till I make my report. How's that sound? Also—I almost forgot. You know that coat you found in the closet, the black one? You don't need it and I know somebody'd really appreciate having a warm coat, this weather. Boy, it's cold, isn't it?"

Dixie said, "The roommate. Jesus Christ."

Vincent said, "I promise you, anything she knows is hearsay and anything I find out I'll tell you, so . . ."

Dixie said, "What about?" and hesitated. "I don't know if I should ask . . ."

"When in doubt," Vincent said, "don't."

"If you brought your gun."

"Yeah, you can ask me that."

"I better not," Dixie said.

13

JACKIE SPREAD HIS ARMS OUT in welcome. He said, hey, this was a special occasion. Not only the boss, the boss's wife coming into his humble office. This was the first time, wasn't it, the two of them? And they'd been open almost a year?

"First timers," Jackie said, "I make 'em a bet. Name a major star, I mean a top attraction that's ever appeared in Vegas, Tahoe or Atlantic City. You don't see that star's photograph on the wall here, personally inscribed, I'll give you a hundred-dollar bill. Standing bet."

Nancy said, "Sit down, Jackie. Please."

Coming on like the lady of the manor, low-key, Jackie didn't like the feel of this one bit. He glanced at Tommy. What's going on? And the boob gave him a shrug, innocent, then straightened as his wife looked over at him, Nancy not missing a fucking trick. Jackie tried another approach, see if he could loosen things up, clapped his hands and said, "How 'bout a drink? Who's ready? Honor of the occasion." Tommy lit up but kept his voice in control, said hey, why not? Tommy had never turned down a drink in his fucking life. Jackie handed him a glass from the mirrored wetbar behind his desk, got a beer and the ever-ready pitcher of martinis out of the fridge . . . "Nancy?" No, she was fine, thank you. Cunt. Sitting with her knees locked together, manila envelope on her lap— something in there she was going to spring she cut out of the *Wall Street Journal* or one of those. Tommy left the glass on the edge of the desk to drink out of the can. They were a pair. Jackie took a nice big bite of the ice-cold extra-dry martini, sat back in his leather chair and felt soothed. Fuck her. What could she do to him?

Nancy said, "Is that a martini?"

A couple of answers came to mind immediately, but Jackie said, "My tastes are simple. Sure you won't have one?"

He watched her shake her head, slowly, giving him the stare. It was a shame, good-looking stylish broad—he'd lay five to one she was frigid, have to pry her legs apart to get at it. She said, "No, but go ahead, if it relaxes you . . ." She said, "You're not afraid of it becoming a problem?" With that innocent look.

Jackie said, "That's what I am, as a matter of fact, a problem drinker. Take a drink when I have a problem and it goes away."

It seemed to lighten her up, but not much. She said, "My first husband drank martinis."

And Tommy said, "Kip Burkette. You know, Burkette Investments in Philly? Used to be very big, go back a hundred years. Nancy married Kip and joined the Main Line, high society, man.

Jackie grinned, pretty sure Tommy'd already had a few this morning. He was safe now, it was past noon.

"Actually I moved *up* the Main Line," Nancy said, "from Narberth to Bryn Mawr. Not to school, I went away for that, Emerson in Boston. I thought I wanted to be an actress, but found out I wasn't very good."

"That's hard to believe," Jackie said.

Nancy shrugged. "Getting back to Kip, he was a sweet guy. Loved ducks."

"Is that right?"

"All his neckties had little ducks on them. He was quite a nice-looking man." Nancy paused. "But not very bright."

"He didn't have to be," Tommy said. "Burkette Investment Bankers, that time they were worth a couple hundred mil, easy."

"Kip liked dogs too," Nancy said. "He had one, a golden retriever named Lance. Every morning at breakfast Kip used to read market reports out loud, the closing prices of stocks he was watching. He'd pause after each quotation and look at Lance. If

Lance snarled it meant sell. If he woofed and wagged his tail, obviously it meant buy. Kip swore by Lance, even when he began to lose customers."

Jackie held his grin for several moments, waiting. He said, "You're putting me on."

"Kip was at the Merion Cricket Club one afternoon," Nancy said, "at the bar, of course, with his Beefeater martini. He was telling someone he'd just met about Lance. The man's reaction was much the same as yours. Was Kip serious? Kip said to him, 'I kid you not.' One of his favorite expressions. And fell over dead."

Jackie said, "Jesus."

"Acute alcoholism, but they called it something else. Lance died not long after. He was hit by a car."

Jackie said, "Ouuuuu."

"But not before I'd unloaded all my Burkette Investments stock," Nancy said. "Got out before it bottomed."

"You were lucky."

"Is that what you think?"

Jackie said, "You mean you saw it coming." She nodded and now he wondered if she meant watching Kip drinking himself to death or the dog getting hit by the car. What was she trying to tell him? Now Tommy was getting into it.

Tommy saying, "Right after that was when Nance went to work at Bally's, learn the business where it's the state of the art. Have some fun, too.

But this little girl's a fast study, man. She's told me a few things about the floor I never even knew."

Mistake. Jackie knew it immediately; he saw Nancy's expression tighten just a little, a hairline crack in the facade.

She said, "I wonder if I'm attracted to alcoholics," and Jackie wanted to get out of here, right now. "I don't know if I'm fascinated because I don't understand them, or it's a negative attraction, I'm looking for trouble."

Here we go, Jackie thought. He watched Tommy shift around in a deliberate, half-assed dramatic way to give his wife the look. Called, Not Taking Any Shit from the Little Woman.

"I know what attracted you to Kip," Tommy said. "Money money money. You couldn't make it as an actress—hey, but don't give me that shit you never act." He said to Jackie, "She plays the superior rich broad you're suppose to believe never takes a crap like everybody else."

Nancy said, "What attracted me to you, Tommy, your wit?"

Jackie felt he should move in. "Come on—you two're the perfect combination I ever saw one. The lady and the tiger. Nifty Nancy and Tom Terrific." Not bad.

Except Tommy wasn't listening. He was staring hard at his wife, trying to back her down with a look. Which Jackie could see wasn't working worth *shit.* Dumb schmuck. He should never've called her *"this* little girl," talked down to her like that. Now he was giving her another tune.

"While you were on the Main Line there, love, hanging around the old Cricket Club, waiting to get the poor guy's dough, I wasn't exactly working as a shoe clerk. I had a hotel-casino operation before you ever went in one."

"I know that," Nancy said. "You've worked hard."

"Bet your ass."

"And you're smart enough to hire good key people."

Jackie waited for her to look at him but she didn't. Tommy was saying, "Well, gee, thanks a bunch. I thought maybe I was a total fuckup."

"Not yet, but you're close," Nancy said. "I'm not sure if it's your drinking—I know you're not paying attention—or you're in over your head and you really don't know what's going on."

Tommy said, "Je-sus Christ," shaking his head at Jackie. "She dealt blackjack, worked the floor . . . Anything you want to know about a casino, Jackie, ask her."

All Jackie wanted to do was get out. He had a button under the desk that buzzed in the Moose's cubbyhole and would bring him running, but then what? He said, "Listen, you two want a argue, whyn't you wait till you get home? Okay? I got work to do."

Nancy said, "This concerns you, Jackie. Since you're close to losing your license."

He did tighten up, surprised, but didn't say a word because she was too cool; this wasn't an emotional thing with her, looking at Tommy now, opening the envelope, saying, "You're on the edge too, whether you know it or not." She took out a Polaroid print and handed it to him.

Tommy squinted, holding it up. "Who is it?"

"You comped him to everything but the ice-cream parlor," Nancy said. "Are you telling me you don't know him?"

Jackie didn't think he wanted to see that picture. But Tommy said, yeah, he'd met the guy once, and tossed the print on the desk and now Jackie was looking at the Colombian, Benavides, standing at a blackjack table. It was Jackie's turn to squint, try to look bewildered. "Yeah, that's . . . I can't think of his name. Frances shot that? What for?"

"I asked her to," Nancy said.

"Yeah, we comp him," Jackie said. "Has a very impressive line of credit. The hell's his name? He comes in, stays a few days."

"He was here a week," Nancy said. "Deposited a million nine, in cash."

Tommy held up hands, open, innocent. "What's

the problem? There's no law a player has to tell us where he got his money."

"Not yet," Nancy said, "but it's going to happen, soon, and you'd better be ready."

"Sweetheart," Tommy stirred in his chair, filling it with his size, getting comfortable, "there's a little more to the casino business than the play at the tables. First and foremost, we have to be objective. By that I mean this business is about money, and all money looks alike. Am I correct?"

Jackie didn't want to listen.

"A player brings in a lot of cash, hon, we have to look at it impartially, only as money, nothing else. In other words we have to keep our eye on the player's line of credit. Guy bets heavy, offers us a shot at him, we have to concentrate on taking about twenty percent of his dough if we expect to make a profit." Tommy frowned. "I explained all this once before, didn't I?"

Wrong wrong wrong. Jackie held onto the arms of his chair. She was going to kill him.

"Mr. Osvaldo Benavides, from Bogotá," Nancy said, "deposited a million nine, in cash, and left with our check for almost a million eight."

Jackie watched Tommy twist in the chair again, the schmuck finally realizing what was happening to him. He took a moment and said, "That's not twenty percent but, see, it averages out."

"Once a month," Nancy said, "you fly Mr. Benavides here in the company plane—"

"Just from Miami," Tommy said.

Jackie closed his eyes.

"He draws markers for up to two million in cash, loses five to ten percent, never more than that in the last seven months," Nancy said, "and goes home with a clean check for the balance. Mr. Benavides is laundering his money in our casino. Since you're aware of it, both of you, I have to believe you approve."

Tommy said, "Honey, Jesus Christ . . ."

Nancy waited. "Yes?"

"Hon, this's a tricky, complicated business."

Nancy waited again, Jackie watching her. Broad was a fucking shark. Gets her teeth in you and never lets go—and thought, Wait a minute. She's in the boat too, isn't she?

Jackie said, "What he means, Nancy, we got ourselves a little problem with Mr. Benavides. I say *we* 'cause you're on the board, you got a key license and you could lose it like anybody else can lose a license for associating with the wrong people, undesirables, the wise guys, if you understand what I mean, people known to be in organized crime." He was beginning to roll and felt good. Tommy had his mouth open, the schmuck, like he couldn't believe it, telling her all this. But look, she was paying attention, because she was a smart woman, calm, reasonable, even as she watched her tits getting pulled into the wringer.

She said, "Tell me about it."

"That's exactly what I'm doing," Jackie said. He stood up and felt an added advantage, able to move, use his body. "The problem with Mr. Benavides, he's got friends here who do business with him."

"Who buy his dope," Nancy said.

"Prob'ly. I never asked," Jackie said, "it's none of my business. The problem is, they also do business with *us*, indirectly. By that I mean by controlling some of our suppliers. I don't have to mention any names, I think you know what I'm talking about. Basic materials and services you need to run a hotel. Not to mention they're into a couple of unions."

"Go on," Nancy said.

"Anyway, these people who do business with Mr. Benavides would like us to extend him every courtesy."

"And launder his money," Nancy said.

Jackie held up his hand. "That's a word. We don't treat him right we got trouble with some of our key suppliers. That's a fact."

Nancy kept staring at him.

"Was Iris a comp for Mr. Benavides?"

Coming at him from another direction now.

"All I know," Jackie said, "she was on her own time. Broad like that—really, what can I tell you?" His gaze moved past Tommy—no help—to the depressing wet sky in the window, lingered as he again considered buzzing the Moose, dropped the idea and came back to Nancy, Jesus, still right there, staring at him. "Honest to God, I don't know any more what happened to Iris'n you do."

What was she going to prove staring like that? It was the *truth*.

After a moment Nancy said, "No more Mr. Benavides. We're through with him."

Jackie cocked his head at her. "Well, that's easy to say. You don't know these guys."

"Work it out," Nancy said, "or look for a job."

Tommy raised up. "You're talking to the key man in our operation—twenty-five years' experience."

"He's on his own," Nancy said. "If I ever see Benavides in the hotel again I'll report him to Gaming Enforcement, with a list of his deposits. And if I find out either of you knew Iris was in that apartment I'll tell the police about it."

Tommy said, "I'm your husband, for Christ sake!"

Jackie kept still. He knew she meant it. Telling Tommy she wasn't going to lose her license over a technicality, because they happened to be married. Her hand going into that envelope again. Tommy got up to use his size, look down at her. He said,

"We'll handle this, okay? You mind? Don't get so hot and bothered, for Christ sake." Big dumb schmuck—she wasn't the least bit hot and bothered. Look at her. Cool broad sitting on an iceberg—no emotions whatsoever Jackie could see. She dropped another Polaroid shot on the desk. Tommy's boozy face squinted in a frown.

"Who's this?"

Jackie made note of the pause, the playful look in Nancy's eyes.

"Iris's boyfriend."

Jackie looked at the photo—bearded guy in a raincoat—continued to look at it, waiting for the sharklady to strike again. He heard Tommy ask, "What's he got to do with us?" and Nancy say, "He's here." Tommy said he could see that. So what? Jackie thinking, She had his picture taken, *she knows him*. And heard Nancy say, "I'm sure he'll be coming to see you." Tommy said, for what? He didn't have anything to say to the guy. "I hope not," Nancy said. "But he'll get to see you, one way or another." *How?* Jackie thought. "And if I were you I'd be ready," Nancy said. *She knows the guy*, Jackie thought. "That means cold sober," Nancy said. Listen to her . . .

With the straight face, the tough-shit tone talking to her own husband. She knew the guy and the guy was more than just Iris's boyfriend. The guy was a threat, but not so much of a threat it worried

her, involved her. The guy looked like a narc, yes,
he did, a movie-actor narc. Jackie wondered if he
should take a shot, thought about it a few moments . . . Why not? He looked up from the photo
to the sharklady.

"He's a cop. Right?"

It zinged her, caught her by surprise and she
raised her eyebrows, stared at him.

"How do you know that?"

Even a little impressed.

"Instinct, Nancy. Experience."

"And a wild guess."

Jackie said, "Nancy, I appreciate everything
you've said here today, your concern, you want to
keep us on our toes. Good. But if I can't tell when
it's time to cover my ass—if you'll pardon the
expression—I'm in the wrong fucking business."

14

VINCENT DROVE TO LONGPORT in the rain, down-beach to the bottom of Absecon Island. Big money, big homes, but it looked barren to him; there were so few trees. He was used to the Florida coast. Here were weathered frame beach homes out of the past next to white modern ones with round corners, as different as privies and spaceships. Maybe it would have more of a seaside resort look with the sun shining. He found Donovan's address and was surprised to see one of the old, old ones, with peaks and gables and a porch sitting on brick stilts that circled the entire house.

He recognized the maid, the same one who opened the door in Isla Verde. She recognized him too, he could tell. But he said, "Remember me?"

Dominga smiled, shy, touching her chin. "Yes, by your bear' you have."

"My beard," Vincent said. "Yeah, I'm glad I kept it. It keeps my face warm. You cold?"

"Yes, I'm cole all the time I'm here."

She asked him to come in, please, and Vincent told her he wished he was down in Puerto Rico right now. She asked him if he wanted to see Mr. Donovan.

"I'd like to."

"You having a har' time to see him."

"Not home, uh? How about missus?"

Dominga shook her head. "I think you see them at the hotel today."

It was so quiet in the house. Still, it had a comfortable, lived-in look, bright colors in the living room, a gallery of paintings, a Taino Indian jar on the mantel. It was like an urn, or how he pictured an urn. This morning he had spoken to Linda on the phone. They had to decide what to do with Iris's remains. Linda said, her ashes. A stainless steel urn would be thirty-nine dollars. Or they could pay up to nine hundred for solid bronze.

He said to Dominga, "I wonder if you could do me a favor," taking a small notebook from his raincoat pocket. "Call a number for me here in Longport, Mr. Garbo's home. You know him?"

"Mr. Garbo, yes."

"Here's the number. Ask for LaDonna Padgett. The name's written there."

"Yes, I see it."

"If you could say to her, 'Mr. Mora is coming over from Mr. Donovan's house to talk to you.' Just like that. You think you could?"

"I know how to speak on the phone," Dominga said. " 'Mr. Mora is coming there from Mr. Donovan so he can talk to you.' "

"Perfect," Vincent said.

LaDonna said, "Is that what Tommy's worried about? I told Jackie—he musta asked me a hundred times, 'You sure you didn't leave anything?' I said, well, what would I have left? I didn't take any my clothes off. I guess I did take off my pumps, I always do that if I'm just sitting around. You know. But I surely wasn't gonna walk out of there without my shoes. He musta asked me a hundred times. You know, after it was in the paper and we heard what happened." LaDonna shook her head. "Boy, I'm telling you, it's scary."

She had told him to hang his coat on the door of the fronthall closet so it would dry, said he could take his shoes off if he wanted, she had hers off— leading him barefoot in a heavy fisherman's sweater that almost covered white shorts that showed about an inch of each cheek, leading him into a room of summer furniture and a wall of humid glass against the weather, a wall of gloom today, the room dim, silent.

Vincent said, "Iris was the only one took her clothes off? Nobody else?"

"I didn't go for that one bit," LaDonna said, "it

was embarrassing. I mean since I was the only other girl, you know, that was there. Iris, she could care less. She walked around stark naked, it didn't bother her at all. That age, you can get away with it, not worry about your butt looking like a bowl of cottage cheese. I do exercise—you ever try to lose weight off your butt? It's impossible. I keep telling Jackie he *has* to lose weight—you know how he eats, and he drinks way too much . . . You want another Bloody? I think I'm ready."

"Let me do it."

"No, sit still." She pushed up from the couch with an effort. "This weather, I wish I could find something to do besides watch soaps. I watch 'em with the maid but she's off today. You like my Bloodies?"

"You make a good one."

"Jackie taught me."

"I think I'll switch though, if you have scotch."

"We have everything, crème de menthe, Southern Comfort. You like that Amaretto? It's good."

"Scotch'll be fine."

LaDonna Holly Padgett, one-time Miss Oklahoma, slipped on tinted, heavy-framed glasses, a tall girl made taller with all that blond hair piled up. She stared out at the gray mass of sky and ocean, stared for several moments, then seemed to come awake. Vincent watched her cross to the elaborate bar: her bare feet in deep shag, long white legs reaching to the shapeless fisherman's sweater. Her thighs looked fine, dimple-free. She was still a great big Miss American beauty. He could see her up on the pageant stage telling how she loved democracy and small animals and believed in the fellowship of man. Vincent believed she'd had at least a couple of Bloodies before he arrived.

"Were you there both nights?"

LaDonna used a shot glass to measure exactly an ounce and a half of vodka. "I don't know what you mean." She poured it carefully into her glass, deliberated and added a quick splash from the bottle.

"At the apartment."

"Oh, you mean with Benny? Sure, well, you know Jackie had to wait on his beck and call, go everyplace with him." She put in three teaspoons of Lea & Perrins, hunched down close to the rim of the glass to shake in one, two, three drops of Tabasco.

"Tommy didn't say too much." Vincent watched her add tomato juice and stir. "I wasn't sure which night he was there."

"Who?"

"Tommy."

"You want that on the rocks?"

"Please."

She brought him a generous scotch, started toward the couch and stopped. "What do you mean, which night? Tommy wasn't there either time." She frowned, "Or was he? Now you got me confused."

Vincent sat in a deep, slipcovered chair, ashtray on the arm. He lighted a cigarette, watching as she sat down on the floor, careful of her drink, and leaned back against the couch.

"I think I'm safer here," LaDonna said. "Can't fall off, can I? I been feeling kinda fuzzy, like I'm coming down with the flu or something."

Vincent told her he was supposed to check on everyone who was at the apartment either night, make sure they hadn't left anything. Not even hotel matches. Tommy didn't want it to get back to him. LaDonna said she imagined not, it could sure put a monkey wrench in his business. Vincent said, well, let's see, there was the dealer . . . Two dealers, LaDonna said, and Benny and the other creepy guy, Ching. Actually he wasn't as creepy as the guy from Colombia. He was kind a nice. But he still scared her . . . Vincent said, Ching? LaDonna said, don't tell me you haven't met Chingo, the Wheel? Where've you been? And the Moose was there, of course. Thank goodness for the Moose. He's fun to talk to 'cause he's so cool but has a really good sense of humor too, like he says things without smiling or anything? But you know he's being funny. He's nice. Jackie doesn't laugh at him 'cause he's jealous. But, boy, he wouldn't go anywhere without him. Moose says he didn't think it was anybody in our crowd had anything to do with it, Iris getting killed. Vincent listened. Unless it was

Ricky, another one of the greasy creeps; 'cause Ricky wanted to go up there, Moose says, but Ching made him stay outside. Moose says Ricky was the only one he knew crazy enough or would do it for fun, to see her fall. Moose doesn't like Ricky at all 'cause Ricky refers to him, like he's talking to Jackie, as Jackie's pet nigger. Vincent listened. LaDonna said, if I didn't have him to talk to . . . boy, I don't know. I mean Moose. She said, hey, who's ready?

Vincent made the drinks. LaDonna rested her Bloody Mary on her chest and stared at it, her head low against the front of the couch. He asked her if she had talked to Iris much. She said Iris was the kind only talked to men. She had known girls in the pageant that way. Most of them were real friendly and sincere, but there was a few snooty ones in every pageant she had ever been in. She said it felt really weird to be back in Atlantic City. God, time went so *fast*. It seemed like only about a year ago.

"I was voted Miss Congeniality."

"I can see why," Vincent said.

"You better be congenial, try and get along with somebody like Jackie. He's so . . . God, he's so full of himself. I can't stand the way he talks, his language. Can you?"

"Why do you stay with him?"

"We're out, he talks all the time. We get home, he doesn't say a word unless he's swearing at me.

Frances says if she was me she wouldn't put up with it. I've talked to her—well, I've known her ever since Vegas. She's really smart, you know, to get where she is. Up there in the Eye in the Sky. You know what? I think she likes him and she's trying to get us to break up. She says to me, why the hell do you put up with him?"

"Why do you?"

"Well . . . Frances says he's really good at how he knows how to run a casino and all. You know, and he's funny. He can be real funny when he wants to. He used to be, when we were in Vegas he always swore a lot, use terrible language but, God, he was funny. He always had people laughing, so he must a been. Now . . . I think he's scared but he won't admit it."

"Scared of what?"

"Those guys—what do you think? See, then *I* get scared. You know what I'm scared the most of? We're having dinner at Angeloni's or one of those places and somebody comes in with a machine gun to kill one of those guys like you see in the paper? You see 'em lying on the floor with blood all over? And Jackie and I get killed because we happen to be having dinner with him. I think about it, I get petrified." Vincent said he didn't blame her. "I don't even like Italian food anymore. You just, like all you have to say is mention fettuccini with clam sauce I start to feel sick. I never even *heard* of fettuccini with clam sauce before. I never had *clams*. I mean in Tulsa. Boy, I don't know . . . I went to Wilson. I never heard of fettuccini, you probably never heard of Wilson, huh? There was a girl when I was going there, she was my very best friend in the world name Melanie Puryear? She had a really sensational way she wrote her name. So I copied it, LaDonna Holly Padgett, till my arm almost fell off. LaDonna Holly Padgett, I'd fill up sheets of paper with it. She wrote in my yearbook . . . No, my God, it was Marilyn Grove wrote in my yearbook . . . Yeah, it was Marilyn. She wrote, 'Twinkle, twinkle Wilson's star, LaDonna Padgett is going far.' See, 'cause I'd already been Miss Tulsa Raceway, you know, to present trophies. I remember one time, oh God, I thought I was gonna have to kiss this old guy had won a race? But he just shook my hand, I couldn't believe it. Then, I'll never forget, Corky Crawford grabbed me and gave me this terrific kiss square on the lips, everybody screaming and yelling . . ."

Vincent could hear the rain coming down.

She said, "Yeah, I was voted Miss Congeniality." Her eyes raised and she said, "I work my fucking butt off trying to be congenial. Look at me."

15

VINCENT FOUND THE HOUSE on Caspian where Linda was staying with the band: another wooden relic somebody had painted yellow about twenty years ago and since then said the hell with it, wait for the casinos. He was beginning to get the feel of Atlantic City and its surrounding geography and was getting to like it. At least it amazed him, held his attention, to see an old seaside resort being done over in Las Vegas plastic, given that speedline look gamblers were supposed to love. Here you are in wonderland, it told the working people getting off the tour buses, all those serious faces coming to have a good time. That was something else that didn't make sense, nobody smiled.

He walked in the front door of Linda's house and knew *some*body was having fun; the smell of reefer almost knocked him over. The La Tunas were sitting around the living room in a cloud of smoke, laid out, accepting his bearded look, at least not worried. He waited in the hall. When Linda came downstairs he said, "I thought for a minute your house was on fire. Those guys blow weed they don't fool." Outside he said, "How can you live here?"

She said, "Where'm I gonna go? I'm paid up for the month and they don't give refunds."

He said, "You could stay with me, at the Holmhurst." Not sure if he was kidding or serious.

Linda said, "I'd really be moving up, wouldn't I?"

He opened the car door for her. "I forgot, I was gonna bring it in. Look what's in back."

Her black winter coat, lying on the seat.

Standing in the rain she reached up and took his face in her hands and kissed him on the mouth. He held onto her to make it last a little longer than a thank-you kiss. She said, "Vincent, I'm going to have to start giving you some serious thought." She sounded as though she meant it.

They drove over to the funeral home on Oriental where Vincent told the younger Mr. Bertoia they had come for the ashes of Iris Ruiz. The younger Mr. Bertoia left them and returned with a stainless steel urn the size of a half-gallon milk container. Vincent looked at it. He said, "Something you might consider, put the ashes in Taino Indian pottery."

The younger Mr. Bertoia said, "Actually, what you're getting are about eight pounds of bone fragments, not ashes. A body is cremated there aren't any ashes, as such, just bones."

Vincent said, "Thank you," took the urn in one hand, Linda's arm in the other. As they reached the front door she tried to pull free, but he held onto her, got her outside and in the car.

"Why do you let him bother you, guy like that?"

She said, "You thanked him." Sounding amazed.

"What'd you want me to do?"

"Tell him off. Jesus, tell him *some*thing."

"I couldn't think of anything good."

She was silent as they pulled away from the funeral home and turned corners toward Pacific Avenue. Vincent still couldn't think of anything. Finally Linda said, "How about, 'Why don't you shove a hose up your ass, Mr. Bertoia, drain out the embalming fluid and maybe you'll act like a living person. With feelings.'"

"You want to go back?"

"You don't like it."

"I think it needs work."

"But that's the idea. See, it would be better if you could mention the embalming fluid first and end it with 'So why don't you shove a hose up your ass,' like a punch line. You know what I mean?"

"I think so."

"'You know what your trouble is, Mr. Bertoia?' . . . 'Mr. Bertoia, the trouble with you is, you have the sensitivity of a . . . ' That might work. Tell him what an insensitive nerd he is."

"You feel better?"

"Not a lot."

"Tell me what I'm gonna do with Iris. Take her back to Puerto Rico?"

"You think she cares?"

"She'd probably rather stay here."

"Even in her present condition," Linda said. "I've got her clothes, a few pieces of costume jewelry, a hand-carved parrot that's kind of nice . . ."

Linda was going to call on hotel entertainment directors and see if she could get an audition, beginning with the Golden Nugget. Vincent dropped her off. Then gave the doorman a quarter and asked him if he'd keep an eye on the car while he ran in and made a quick phone call. The doorman stared at Vincent, holding the quarter in the palm of his white glove.

He heard Dixie Davies say, "You sure you want to do this?"

Vincent said, "Let's see what happens." He sat in a phone booth off the lobby.

"Ricky's out in the rain he must be making collections today, getting their cut from the horse books and the numbers. Maybe shylock payments too, I don't know. He went in the Satellite Cafe on the Boardwalk about two minutes ago. Alone."

Vincent said, "I appreciate it, Dix." And said, "Wait. How about a guy named Ching? The Wheel?"

"Frank Cingoro," Dixie said, "the Ching. He's been here, he's one of the few older guys still around. He used to kill people. Now they say he's like an honorary consig, a counsellor, reactivated while Sal's doing his two years."

"He was at the apartment," Vincent said, "the night Ricky was on the door."

"Who told you?"

"Jackie Garbo was there too. From Spade's. You know him?"

"The name," Dixie said. "We'll bring him in, get better acquainted."

"Why don't you sit on it for the time being?" Vincent said. "It could turn into an illegal gambling conspiracy and fuck up the main issue. Then where's your homicide investigation?"

"Same place it is now," Dixie said, "nowhere."

"Satellite Cafe on the Boardwalk."

"Near St. James Place."

Vincent stood at the counter drying his face and hands with paper napkins. He could see the Board-walk through steamy glass, that wide expanse of herringboned planking, empty in the afternoon rain. He turned, wiping a napkin over his beard, nodded to an old man, the only customer at this hour, watching him from a booth. The old man looked down through his glasses at the newspaper he held folded lengthwise. The cafe was narrow, done in yellow Formica and dark wood. Two waitresses sat at the end of the counter head to head, intent in their conversation. Vincent waited. The one facing him looked up. She rose, smoothing her yellow uniform and apron. Vincent took a stool as she came down the counter with a menu.

"Just coffee. Black." He waited for her to place it in front of him and said, "I don't see the boss." The waitress stood without moving.

She said, "He's busy," and left him quickly.

Vincent smoked two cigarettes and looked at the menu for something to do before the door to the kitchen opened and the owner came out followed by Ricky. Vincent believed the older man wearing a sweater over his shirt and tie, and holding a dishtowel wrapped around his right hand, was the owner. He knew the other one as Ricky Catalina because he had studied him in four different sets of pock-marked mug shots, his black hair trimmed a little shorter in each set. As the owner and Ricky came past him, on the other side of the counter, Vincent could see the owner was in pain, holding the towel-wrapped hand tenderly, raised in front of him. The owner reached the cash register and stood frowning at it as though the keys were unfamiliar. Ricky nudged him with stiff fingers in the ribs and the old man pressed a key with his left hand. The drawer of the register opened.

Vincent got up from the stool and moved to the glass cigar counter where the register stood. He heard Ricky say, "You're still light," as the old man handed him money. Ricky was somewhat better looking than he'd appeared in his pictures, his complexion scarred but under control, a sallow color in this light. He was chunky, overweight, several inches shorter than Vincent who looked at his eyes now and saw the dumb glazed look of a guy who had conditioned himself to go through life pissed off. Vincent could see him swinging a hatchet at the man's spine while his expression remained almost deadpan, showing little effort.

Vincent laid a dollar bill on the rubber mat next to the cash register. "One coffee."

Ricky picked it up, dead eyes raising to Vincent, peering at him through heavy lids. Did he practice in front of a mirror? He added the dollar to the currency in his hand, folded the bills into a roll, twisted on a red rubber band and shoved the wad into the breast pocket of his jacket.

"Where's my change?"

"You had a coffee? It's a buck."

"The menu says fifty cents."

"It went up."

Vincent looked at the old man, saw the pain in his eyes. "What happened to your hand?"

"He had an accident," Ricky said. He moved around the counter to the front door and looked back. "I'll see you tomorrow. Right?" The old man nodded, said yes, right. With some kind of accent. Ricky stared at him and seemed about to say something else, but pushed through the door and was gone.

Vincent took a moment. Both of the waitresses were behind the counter now, coming to the old man, touching him. He was pale, perspiring and could be in shock. "What did he do to you?" Vincent asked him. But the old man didn't hear him and one of the waitresses said, "Please—" with anguish, and Vincent left.

He followed Ricky's hunched figure along Boardwalk storefronts, lights showing now in the rain mist, to the end of the block and around the corner to a stairway that descended to St. James Place, where a Cadillac Eldorado was parked at the dead end of the street.

Ricky stood at the trunk of the car getting his keys out. He looked up. Vincent was on the stairs now. Ricky paused. As Vincent came down Ricky turned and walked a short distance up the street to a bar. He paused again to look back before going in. Vincent followed.

It was dark inside. Vincent ordered scotch. He said to the bartender, where's everybody? The bartender shook his head, he said he only worked here; nobody wanted to come in, that was up to them. Ricky sat four stools away drinking a beer. Vincent studied the bottles on the back bar, trying to make out the labels, the brands. He could feel Ricky watching him. When Ricky got off the stool and walked to the back, into the men's room, Vincent said to the bartender, "You got a little knife I can borrow? Like you cut lemons with?" The bartender held up a paring knife with a serrated edge. "Yeah, lemme borrow it, I'll bring it back." The bartender watched Vincent walk out with his knife. He didn't seem to care.

Vincent knew the Eldorado's doors were locked; he tried the one on the passenger side to make sure. Then looked around, peered into dim spaces beneath the Boardwalk that were like mine shafts with supporting timbers, saw trash, empty bottles—he needed something with heft he could hold in one hand—looked around some more and saw the bulldozer, the piles of rubble, where some type of small building had been razed. Vincent went over and poked around, selected a chunk of masonry that weighed about ten pounds.

When Ricky came out of the bar Vincent was standing close to the Eldorado's rear deck, right hand inside his raincoat, his left arm covering it, folded across his chest.

Ricky came along the sidewalk, wary. "The fuck you doing?"

Vincent wondered if he was any good face to face, no gun. He wouldn't be packing today, risk doing two years for nothing.

"Get away from the car."

"Somebody smashed your window," Vincent said.

"Where?" He came in a hurry now. Vincent nodded toward the driver's side and Ricky moved past him, intent. Vincent followed, walked up next to him.

"What're you talking about? The window's okay."

Vincent looked at it, his expression curious. He brought the chunk of masonry out of his raincoat to slam it in the same motion against the tinted glass and the window shattered in fragments. He turned to Ricky and said, "No, it's broken. See?"

Ricky said, "You crazy?" With amazement. "You fucking crazy?"

Vincent liked the question and liked the way Ricky stood there in a state of some kind of shock, those dead eyes showing signs of life for the first time, wondering, What is this? His expression, his pocked face made him appear vulnerable, sad, the poor guy wanting to know what was going on here, perplexed.

Good. Vincent dropped the chunk of cement. Ricky glanced down and Vincent grabbed him by his jacket and his hair and slammed him against the car; told him to spread his legs, come on, spread 'em, and kicked his shins to make him lean, reach out. There were protests, Ricky wanting to know what the fuck Vincent thought he was doing. Vincent tightened his fist in Ricky's hair, banged his forehead against the curved edge of the car roof and said, "Anything I want, Rick." Reading it to him out of the unwritten manual. "Any fucking thing I want. Give me your keys."

Vincent handed them back when they were both inside the car, Ricky subdued, behind the wheel. He backed into the lot where the building had been torn down, came out to creep toward Pacific Avenue and began to give Vincent looks, recovering, getting the dead stare back in his eyes. Vincent brought out his gun, laid the 9-mm automatic across his lap to point at Ricky and Ricky said, "Where you want to go, Northfield?"

"Atlantic Avenue."

"You're gonna be in deep shit we get to Northfield, man. Somebody's gonna pay for my window. What'd you bust it for? You fucking crazy or what?"

"Take a right."

"That ain't the way you go."

"Take a right," Vincent said.

"Where we going, for Christ sake? Shit, I'm getting all wet."

"Watch the road," Vincent said, and listened to the beat of the windshield wipers as they followed

Atlantic Avenue out of traffic, almost to its end, turned north through the rundown Inlet section, Vincent feeling his way, looking for the right kind of isolated place. He saw it finally as they approached Gardner's Basin, entered the empty parking area that looked into the mouth of Absecon Channel. He told Ricky to keep going, right up to the breakwater and stop. There were commercial fishing boats moored in the basin, but no one around, no houses nearby or for several blocks.

"Where does that bridge go?"

Through the windshield, filmed with water and wiped clear, a distant arc that was barely visible in the rain came in and out of focus.

"Brigantine," Ricky said, "where you think?" And said, "Wait a minute—"

"What's that, way over there, a hotel?"

"Harrah's," Ricky said. "You don't even know where you're at. Who'n the hell are you? You're from Northfield, right?"

"Think about it," Vincent said. "What're we doing here?"

Ricky narrowed his eyes, glanced down at the blue-steel Smith & Wesson. "You're a cop. You got a cop gun."

"What'd you do to that old man?"

"What old man?"

"In the restaurant. Guy a slow pay, you put his hand on the grill?"

"Fuck off. You want to take me in, take me the fuck in. I don't have to talk to you."

"You got your mind made up I'm a cop," Vincent shrugged. "It doesn't matter."

"I know goddamn well you're a cop. Some new guy—you're gonna show those other assholes can't get me to say shit how it's done . . . Right?"

Vincent shook his head, taking his time.

"I'm Vincent the Avenger, Ricky."

"The *what*?"

"Just doing my job."

"Wait. How you know my name?"

"I was sent for," Vincent said.

"I never saw you before in my life. Where you come from?"

"Miami."

"You were *sent* for . . ."

"I understand you fucked up, Rick. Killed some broad and then made a deal with the cops? That it?"

"You're crazy." Amazed. "What're you talking about?"

"Threw her off a balcony, eighteen floors up?"

"What, the Puerto Rican broad? I never went near her. I was in Brigantine, I was there almost the whole fucking night, man. I can prove it."

"Hey, don't tell me," Vincent said. "You should a straightened this out with Frank. You say you got a good story, I guess he thinks it's a bunch a shit, or I wouldn't be here."

"Frank? Wait a minute—Frank who? Who we talking about?"

"What do you call him, Ching? Chingo? I barely met him. He told me where to find you, told me how he wanted it done." Vincent's left hand went into his raincoat and came out with the paring knife he'd borrowed from the bartender. "Let me ask you something . . . See, the way I ordinarily do it, I put one right here." Vincent touched the knife point to his forehead. "But Frank wants it done, you know, according to custom. I guess set an example. So I gotta ask you something."

"The fuck're you talking about?"

"My question is, do I cut your dick off and stick it in your mouth before I shoot you—"

"Hey—hey, listen to me a minute, no shit—"

"Or do I shoot you and then cut your dick off? I always wondered," Vincent said, "since I'm not up on any your quaint guinea customs you guys're into, leaving the dead rat, any a that kind a shit. I think I know which way you'd prefer . . ."

"There's a mistake," Ricky said. "Somebody's made a big fucking mistake, man."

"You're right there," Vincent said, "you should never a copped or let 'em offer you a deal. They give you immunity?"

"I never *told* 'em nothing!"

"Or you shouldn't a done that to the Puerto Rican broad, one. As I say, I don't know the whole story. They never go into detail, they say here's the name of the fink, do him."

"Man—listen to me. I can prove I never went near that broad."

"That isn't what Frank says."

"Fuck him—he never even asked me about it. What's he putting this together from? Fucking guy—he's using this, try and take me out while Sal's away. That's what it is. I don't know why the fuck I didn't see it." He looked at Vincent intently and said, "Listen to me, okay? You got nothing against me. Like you say, it's a job, it's nothing personal. It's what you do, man, you get paid. I know where you're at, man, but listen to me a minute. I didn't kill the broad. It was anybody it was that fucking Colombian, Benavides, but I didn't have nothing to do with it, man, I can prove it. There was two three other people I was with all night, five o'clock in the morning. The broad was killed like at one. See, it's got nothing to do with that or talking to the cops 'cause I never fucking said a fucking word, man. They taped it, you can listen to it, what I said. It's that fucking Ching, man. He wants my ass for some reason I don't even know, so he says I dimed out on him. Bullshit. You see what I'm saying to you? You don't give a shit one way'r the other, right? It's got nothing to do with you. Okay, then how about this? You don't care who pays you either, right? How much is the Ching giving you?"

Vincent had to think about it. It was an interesting turn, new possibilities being presented.

"Come on, gimme a number."

"Twenty-five," Vincent said.

"Bullshit. The Ching could get it done for nothing he wanted to. There guys—shit, I can name 'em, would pay *him*."

"Yeah, but he sent to Miami," Vincent said, "and here I am."

"I don't care he sent to fucking China, he's not paying you any twenty-five. I'll give you ten to get fucking lost, disappear. No, uh-unh—call him up. Tell him I wasn't there, you couldn't find me. Stall him two three days. That's all you got a do."

Vincent nodded. "Okay. Give me the money."

"I don't have it on me, for Christ sake. You think I walk around I got ten grand on me?"

"What're you gonna do, send me a check? I think I'll stay with the deal I got." Vincent raised the Smith. "Get out of the car."

"Come on, you *know*, for Christ sake, I don't have it on me. We make an arrangement. I deliver it to you the next couple days, wherever you're staying. Tell me where."

"That's some arrangement," Vincent said. "I didn't get to be thirty-nine years old, Rick, making deals like you're talking about. I want to see the money."

"I swear to God I'll pay you. I give you my fucking word of honor, man—ten big ones, how you want it, hunnerts? Whatever you say. Two three days—I gotta get it together. I meet you . . . How's the restaurant, the Satellite, on the Boardwalk? What a you say?"

"Where do you live?"

"You want a come to my house? I live on Georgia Avenue. You know where Angeloni's is? Right near there." He gave Vincent the number, Vincent watching, fascinated, as Ricky tried to get an expression of trust in his eyes.

Vincent said, "You want to show your good faith?"

"How? Tell me?"

"Gimme the money you got in your jacket."

"It's yours . . . Take it."

"Now get out of the car."

He did, but hesitantly, wary. "We got a deal?"

Vincent dropped a piece of glass out the window and moved behind the wheel. Ricky stood with his shoulders hunched against the rain, waiting. "See you the day after tomorrow," Vincent said, "four o'clock. If you're still around, in one piece."

He drove back to St. James Place, left the Eldorado where he'd found it, key in the ignition—no hard feelings. His Datsun was in a lot up the same street. But first, back to the Satellite Cafe. The waitress behind the counter recognized him.

"How's your boss?"

"He's at the hospital."

Vincent handed her the wad of bills, made her take it as she hesitated. She said, "Don't tell me anything, okay? I don't want to know."

He used the pay phone to call Northfield and said to Dixie, "Ricky didn't do it."

"You sure?"

"Ninety-nine percent."

"How do you know?"

"He told me," Vincent said. "But it's okay. You're gonna get a chance to bring him up on attempted murder. I hope attempted. Day after tomorrow it looks like he's gonna take a crack at me."

Vincent walked back to the corner, tired, till he got to the stairway, started down to St. James Place and stopped halfway, wide awake, remembering the Eldorado as he had seen it a little more than an hour ago, the same high-angle view from the stairs, Ricky standing there getting his keys out . . .

But to open the trunk, not the door!

Because today was collection day, right, according to Dixie Davies, and Ricky the bagman was making pickups from the horse books, the card-game and numbers guys, from whoever owed them a cut or a shylock payment. Vincent popped the trunk lid and there it was, the bag, a blue canvas carry-on with straps and buckles and handy pockets . . . and wads and wads of currency in the main compartment, rolled up in red rubber bands.

The bartender at the Holmhurst said, "Well, how we doing? We still a winner?"

Vincent was holding a double scotch to take upstairs with him. He lifted the blue canvas bag from the barstool.

"You wouldn't believe how much I got in here."

"I probably wouldn't," the bartender said.

16

TEDDY'S MOM SAID TO BUDDY, cocking her head the same way Buddy had his green-and-orange parrot head cocked, "He don't remember all I've done for him. What I went through at the hospital when he was born and I almost died of a hemorrhage, the blood gushing out a me like it would never stop."

Teddy said, "Aw, Mom, Jesus."

"He don't remember the times I was up the night with him when he was sick." Now she was talking to the bird in a pouty little Shirley Temple voice. "No, or he don't remember all the meals I cooked for him."

"I remember how Dad use to go out in the garage where he hid his bottles and drink," Teddy said. "I remember him leaving and never coming back. 'Ey, let's me and you stroll down mem'ry lane and see what else we can remember of our happy home."

"You love to hurt me," his mom said. "Don't you?"

All he wanted was to borrow the car. He'd already heard what it was like in Camden, New Jersey, during the Depression when his mom ate ketchup sandwiches and fried mush. She still couldn't cook for shit. Put a pork roast in the oven and every twenty minutes throw a glass of water on it. He had better chow at Raiford. When it was something he didn't like Monroe Ritchie would get him candy bars. For his sweetie's sweet tooth, Monroe'd say. It was funny, he sort of missed Monroe. He worked up his nerve and asked him one time, "Monroe? Are you a homasexyul?" And Monroe wrinkled his eyebrows and said, "Nooo, man, you pussy. I touch you with my wan' you all of a sodden a magic pussy." Really? Oh well.

What Teddy did finally, he put on his Van Halen tape with the volume turned up and David Lee Roth set him free. He had George Thorogood's "Bad to the Bone" ready to go when his mom said, "Go on, take the car. I can't listen to that no more."

She wouldn't give him any money though. He had about ten bucks left . . . Hey, and a twenty stuck down in his camera case! He'd forgot about it. His mom said, "Oh, you going out to take pictures in the rain?"

Teddy said, "It's stopped, Mom. It's gonna be a beautiful evening." He believed it, just remembering he had that twenty-dollar bill. It meant he could get back to trailing the cop and not have to bother some old lady.

*   *   *

It was close to eight o'clock when the cop came out of the Holmhurst.

Teddy had gone in, taken a chance, and asked the desk clerk if Mr. Mora was in his room. The clerk checked a file and said to dial three-ten on the house phone over there. Teddy dialed it, heard the cop's voice and hung up, got out of there, sat in his mom's big yellow turd to wait. It really surprised him when the cop got in the tan Datsun in front that he'd admired and wished was his. He believed it was a sign. He liked the idea of signs and omens: they showed you were on the right track.

He followed the Datsun's taillights into the poor section and look, another sign: the Datsun pulling up at the house on Caspian where Iris had stayed, the cop going inside.

He had followed Iris here . . .

He had followed Iris all over the place. He had tried to talk to her in the lounge, in her cute little cocktail waitress outfit and tried to get her to go out with him and even offered money he didn't have. Had twice seen her come out of the hotel with three guys, one of them a big jig, and another woman and get in the limo he followed to the condo in Ventnor. Three A.M. he walked all around the building, looking up at the windows from the other side of the street and saw where lights were on: hardly any except for half the top floor on the Atlantic Avenue side. Half past four they came out and the limo took them home. The next night she went up again, Teddy learning surveillance work was a pain in the ass. Fun in San Juan but not here. Never be a private eye. But the next morning Iris didn't come out with the three guys and the woman and Teddy perked up, wondered if this was his chance. He sat there all day. No Iris. All day thinking.

Half past eleven that evening he went in with the cheese steak subs from the White House, ran a game on the security guy telling him he'd lost the slip with the name on it, but the apartment number was eighteen-something. The security guy looked at his clipboard list with one hand on the phone. Let's see, it wouldn't be 1802, nobody was there and 1803 was out for the evening; 1804, also 1805, they went to bed early, never ordered carry-outs; he said it must be the Shipmans in 1806, he'd ring. Teddy said that was it, Shipman. The security guy still wanted to ring them. Teddy said, 'ey, how'd you like a sub? Happen to have an extra one. Mmmm, smell those onions . . . That was how he got upstairs to knock on the door to 1802.

Then he had to run a game on Iris when she opened the door, not looking very happy. He told her somebody from the hotel had sent the food over. She nodded, closed the door, didn't even offer him a tip. He ran down the stairs and opened the delivery door in back. Ran up the stairs, thought he was going to have a heart attack, caught his breath. Then rode the elevator down, stepped off in the lobby and said nighty-night to the old guy eating his cheese steak sub.

Now he entered from the rear, *walked* up the stairs this time and when Iris opened the door gave her a smile and a wink and said, "Miss me?"

It amazed him they would hire a girl with so little personality. Especially a PR.

"Don't you know how to smile?"

"I'm tired of smiling."

See? She was a grouch. She didn't seem afraid of him or even care he was here. It was something else bothering her, or her life in general that made her crabby. Sitting there pissed off in her black bra and panties.

"You staying here now?"

"If I feel like it."

He looked around the apartment. There was all kinds of booze in one of the kitchen cupboards, the cheese steak sub sitting on the counter. Teddy realized he was hungry and ate it. Even cold it was good. He fixed two rum-and-Cokes then, emptying a street-lude cap into Iris's—eighty milligrams of Valium to take off her edge—and brought their drinks out to the living room.

Of course she didn't want it; made a face. So he slapped her, hard, and when she looked up at him, startled and then scared, he said, "Drink it. Don't gimme any shit. Drink it." Then when she took a sip he eased off and said with a grin, "I'm gonna make you smile if it kills you."

She yawned instead. He acted nice with her, sympathetic, said come on, what's the matter?

She told him about this man with the eyes of a snake from Colombia who made her take her clothes off in front of everybody and then rubbed the dice in her *cocha* to bring him luck.

Teddy said, " 'Ey, yeah? Did it?"

She said it was the worst experience of her life. He was so angry when he lost he was rough with her in the bed, he was an animal and punished her with his *bicho*, the way he would push it into her and make her cry out.

Teddy said, "Yeah?" interested. He said, "I'm getting a Spanish lesson. How do you say titties?"

She said she came here to be as a hostess with gentlemen, not an *indio* who should be in a field. Teddy asked her if she felt like going to bed, her story getting him in the mood. She said no, she was too sore. He made her finish her drink and said, well, let's keep it in mind. He made them each another drink, came back in and asked her if she felt like going home to San Juan. She said, sometimes.

"You miss Vincent?"

"That guy? Why would I?"

"He'd protect you, wouldn't he?"

"If I want him to."

She was yawning and sounded sleepy, her eyes closing. Maybe he shouldn't have given her the whole street lude. He believed he'd better hurry.

" 'Ey, why don't you write Vincent a letter? Ask him to come up here and see you."

"Why would he?"

"Tell him you miss him."

"You think he do it?"

"Tell him you're in terrible danger, you need him," Teddy said, pulling her panties out and peeking in.

"Yeah? You think? . . . Man, I'm so tire."

Shit, he didn't bring any paper. He said, " 'Ey, don't go to sleep on me." There was a desk in the room. He went over to it and found a writing pad, envelopes, a pen . . . What he needed to do was pep her up. He went back to her and said, "Here, get started," putting an envelope on the cocktail table in front of her. "Write his name and address on there. I'll be right back."

Teddy took her glass out to the kitchen and poured rum in it. Maybe it would give her a kick. He should've brought meth—she needed to get *up*, not down. He'd wanted to be able to control her, but should've remembered how she moved, like it was an effort. One of those girls, his mom would say was so slow she couldn't get out of her own way.

With his help, dictating, she got the envelope addressed, but that was it. At this point Iris lay back in her chair and konked out on him. He could slap her face all he wanted, throw water in it, hold her under the shower—he could see she wasn't about to come around for the rest of the night.

Well, he wasn't coming around here either, anymore. He'd had enough of playing private eye in his mom's car staring out the window, then getting a chance like this that might not ever come again. He thought about printing a note that would say COME QUICK I NEED YOU. I AM IN DANGER and put it in the envelope. But the cop, come to think of it, would get the note and probably phone her. If he bothered at all.

When Teddy thought of how to do it he knew it would work because the cop wouldn't have a choice anymore. They'd *make* him come. It was exciting thinking about it. Jeez, he wanted to lay her on the floor right here.

He did, he pulled her out of the chair, her eyes coming open a little, but closing again when he got her stretched out on the carpet. He raised her up to unhook her bra, pulled it free and laid her down again. She would have to have her panties on . . .

Another kind of feeling came over him, that he'd

better leave them on and get out of here. What if somebody was coming upstairs this minute?

Teddy folded the addressed envelope once, twice, and slipped it into the front of her panties. He pulled her up, got underneath to let her body fall across his shoulder and carried her out to the balcony this way, into the overcast night. A wind came up as he sat her on the rail in front of him and held her tight under her arms, standing between her bare legs.

Iris moaned, cold, but didn't open her eyes.

Teddy brought his hands away slowly. Her head lowered. As her body came toward him he placed his hands against her shoulders to push her upright, to let her tilt back just a speck, there. Then took his hands away and watched her go off the balcony without a sound, her body turning over as it dropped into the night.

An eight-point-five, Teddy thought. Nice execution, but 'ey, she didn't keep her feet together.

They were coming out of the house now. The cop and a woman in a dark coat. It looked like the woman from the funeral home, Linda.

Teddy saw himself slipping the car into gear, creeping up the street silently toward the Datsun. Time it, get almost there and pop the lights on and as the cop came around to the street side of the Datsun and stood close to it as he saw the headlights coming, shoot him going by.

Except that he wasn't ready. He'd have to have his gun out, the window open on the passenger side . . . He should've thought of it sooner. Except what if the cop had a gun and had time to shoot back and hit his mom's car? How would he explain it?

No, it seemed like a good idea and it was a good place, dark and lonely. But it wasn't what he wanted. He wanted to see the cop's eyes again just before and wanted the cop to see his. Hi. Remember me?

17

TURNING ONTO ATLANTIC AVENUE Vincent said, "I've tailed cars for a living, but I've never been tailed myself, that I know of." He glanced at the rearview mirror.

Linda turned in the front seat to look back. "All I see are headlights. Are you sure?"

"When the same car turns the same corners you do, it's a good bet."

"I thought you were lost. Which one is it?"

"It's three back. Looks like a Chevy, light color, maybe yellow."

"Do you know who it is?"

"I think it's a guy who usually drives an Eldorado, but somebody broke his window so he borrowed a friend's car. Or else it's a friend of the guy who drives the Eldorado."

Linda said, "Am I supposed to know what you're talking about?"

Vincent drove straight to Spade's Boardwalk

now; he left the Datsun with the valet parking attendant. It seemed to surprise Linda. And when he brought the blue canvas carry-on into the hotel with them she said, "I thought we were just having dinner. Are we spending the night?"

Vincent smiled. It had crossed his mind. He checked the bag with the bell captain, La Tuna sounds coming from the lounge across the lobby. He asked Linda if she'd like to go in and mambo and she asked if he'd like a kick in the balls. Was she touchy or being funny? Sometimes it was hard to tell when she was serious. Up a gold elevator to a dining room of crystal chandeliers and scenes of Versailles on the walls, heavy silverware, gold linen, candlelight . . . Was she impressed? Vincent was. They drank scotch and looked at menus, silent, but it was okay; he was comfortable with her and in no hurry. He felt a glow; he believed it might be fun to have a lot of money. Linda could be wealthy, she had the right look in the navy-blue dress. The pale skin and dark hair, fine bones, a $500-an-hour model. Cosmetics, shampoo . . .

"What're you looking at?"

"Nothing."

She brought her napkin up. "Do I have lipstick on my teeth?"

"You get cleaned up you're a knockout."

She narrowed her eyes in those long lashes, said,

"Thanks," gazed at him another moment, suspicious, and returned to her menu. "What're you going to have?"

"Liver and onions. Or the Dover sole. I don't know anything about you," Vincent said. "You started playing piano when you were about nine . . ."

"Eight."

"You grew up in New York."

"New Orleans. I played trumpet in the Tulane marching band . . . I prefer the cornet."

"You fooled me. I thought you had kind of a Brooklyn accent. Just a little. You played the trumpet, huh?"

"You making conversation?"

"I'm interested."

"You know something you're not telling me. You're trying to act cute and you don't know how."

"I feel good, that's all."

"Why?"

"Well, I had a pretty good day. How was yours? You get an audition?"

"I'm pretty sure I'm in at Bally's, if I want it. But I'd have to go with a guitar and drummer they want me to use. Which is okay, I guess. At least I'll be working."

"You like it here, Atlantic City?"

"Compared to what? The Holiday Inn in Orlando? If I can play just a little of my music for an audience that listens part of the time and isn't too drunk, that's as good as it gets in a bar. Most of what I have to play, you take it out of a can and heat it over a low fire. Some of it's okay, some riffs you can have fun with, fool around. But you do the same kind of pop stuff every set, the computer music, key in a little bossa nova—I feel like an engineer, I ought to be wearing a white lab coat with a row of pencils in the pocket. Once in a while, I play with my own guys we throw the charts away and break loose, take some chances. Who's doing that and getting paid? Nobody. McCoy Tyner, Gil Evans, maybe a few other guys. Let the audience keep up if they can—why not? They can tap their toes if they want, but it's a head trip too. Where're we going—who knows? Let's find out, feel it and play it, look for an opening and break out . . . Do you know what I mean? The manager gets nasty, I go, 'Wait a minute, they came to hear me play, right?' The manager goes, 'They came to drink and be entertained, but mostly they came to drink.' And hands me a bunch of requests that read like Michael Jackson's greatest hits. So . . . What was the question?"

"I'd like to hear you play sometime," Vincent said, "doing Linda Moon instead of Carmen Miranda. I got to admit, though, I enjoyed that."

"You would," Linda said. "I'm surprised you don't wear a double-knit suit with white stitching.

Cops being known for their daring fashion statements."

"Let's have another drink."

"I'm ready." She was looking him over, his new sportcoat, white cotton shirt. "You're not a bad dresser, really."

"I'll take my tie off and open my shirt, you want me to."

"No, you won't, you're too conservative." She raised her eyes to his. "It's okay. I like a change now and then."

Driving back to Linda's rooming house Vincent said, "I never saw a skinny girl eat so much. Where do you put it?"

"I'm not that skinny," Linda said. She looked at a street sign as they passed it and said, "I think you should've turned," though didn't seem to care. "Are you a little high?"

"Just right."

"I get mellow when I drink. I mel-low."

"I'm glad to hear it."

"All the streets are named after states . . ."

"North and south."

"Except they aren't in order, they're all mixed up. North Carolina, Pennsylvania . . . Shouldn't we have turned?"

Vincent glanced at the rearview mirror, at headlights and reflections on wet pavement. "He's with us again."

Linda turned in the seat to look back. "The same car?"

"Yellow Monte Carlo . . . I don't think I should take you home. He probably saw me pick you up . . ."

She was quiet a moment. "You're saying, what, I should stay with you?"

"I think it'd be safer."

"For who? If the guy's after *you* why would it be safer for me to *be* with you?"

"You don't want to go home," Vincent said, "and I don't think you should be alone. They're bad guys."

"I think you hired somebody to follow you. Is that it, Vincent, to get me in your room?"

He said, "Let me tell you about Ricky Catalina and what a sweetheart he is." He gave her a profile, a brief one on the way to the Holmhurst, told about meeting Ricky and taking him to Gardner's Basin, but didn't go into detail or mention the blue canvas bag.

As they walked up to the hotel entrance Linda said, "He's after you because you broke his *car* window? . . . Why did you?"

They went inside. Vincent turned to look through the glass door, in time to see the yellow Chevy creep past.

"Get his respect," Vincent said. "Show him I have a violent nature."

"Is it fun," Linda asked, "being a cop?"

"Some times more than others. I've never given a traffic ticket or busted a hooker."

On the way up the stairs Linda said, "You forgot your bag, you checked at Spade's."

"I'm leaving it there for safekeeping."

She gave him her narrow look. "You're not telling me everything, are you? I won't ask what's in the bag."

"It's up to you."

"What's in it?"

"Twelve thousand eight hundred and seventy dollars."

"Oh, my God."

They walked down the third-floor hallway, silent.

"You didn't win it."

"In a way I did."

She stopped. "*That's* why he's after you."

Vincent brought her along by the arm. "He thinks I probably have it, but he's not sure."

"He's tailing you to find out."

"All he has to do is ask."

"What would you tell him?"

"I don't know what he's talking about."

"Wait—whose is it?"

"I told you, collection money. Numbers, sports

bets, card games—all illegal, the sources."

Linda said, "Wow," her voice hushed. "But you can't keep it. Can you?"

"Why not? I turn it in the state keeps it, or it goes in the Police Recreational Fund. But they're not gonna return it, we know that. And we know Ricky's not gonna go to the cops and file a complaint. So . . ."

"What're you going to do with it?"

"I've got an idea . . . But you can have some if you want."

"Jesus, Vincent—"

He got his key out, opened the door, touched Linda to go in ahead of him. He closed the door, double-locked it. When he turned Linda was close enough to touch, her coat off her shoulders, holding it, looking at the polished stainless-steel urn standing on the dresser.

She said, "Is it going to bother you?"

"What?"

"Iris being here."

His hands moved over her shoulders to take her coat, get it out from between them.

"I'll put Iris in a drawer."

Teddy opened his eyes, saw the roof interior right there over him and thought he was in Monroe Ritchie's bunk. Nope, he was parked down at the end of Pennsylvania Avenue, the windshield, the first floor lit up, the two upper floors dark except for a couple of windows. The Datsun was still parked in front. It was ten past three by the luminous dial in the dashboard. His mom had probably got up to make wee-wee and looked in his room. He'd have to have a story for her. How about— "See, I had to wait till this fella was asleep before I went up to his room and shot him." And his mom would say, "Oh, you." But there was the idea, the way it came to him just waking up, and he thought, You could look into it. You been fooling around all this time, you gonna do it or not? The woman could be there with him or she went home, took a cab. Would it matter? No, he didn't think it would. She could watch. Jesus. That idea excited him a little—the woman laying there naked, watching—the way the idea of pushing Iris naked off the balcony had excited him. Yes, he was getting excited; he could feel it.

He opened his camera case, got the Colt automatic but didn't stick it in his pants till he was out of the car. Nice evening. Morning now. Should he lock the doors? No—what if he had to leave in a hurry? Should he have the motor running then? No—what if somebody stole the car while he was in there? There was a lot to think about in a deal like this; you didn't just walk in and shoot some-

body. He smoothed down his suede jacket over his
gun and approached the hotel. The bar looked
busy. He entered the lobby. Nobody around. And
you couldn't see into the bar from here, there was a
partition.

Up to this point he believed he was going to
knock on the cop's door, say "Bellboy," if he had to
and stick the .38 in the cop's face when he opened
the door. Not foolproof at all. What was he deliver-
ing, flowers? A message that could be stuck under
the door?

But wait just a minute here—looking around the
empty lobby, looking at the desk and the room
mailboxes behind it, nobody anywhere around.
There you go. Teddy got a key to 310 and headed
for the stairs.

A light, over the parking lot across the street,
showed the window, the wall where the dresser
stood; it revealed the foot of the bed, the spread
hanging off, and reached almost to the door. In the
silence she kissed his chest, came to his beard and
whispered, "Where's your mouth? There it is,
right . . . there." Whispering, "I love your mouth. I
can kiss your mouth, Vincent, and know it's you."
Whispering, "You lied to me, Vincent, but it's all
right. I still love your mouth."

"When did I lie to you?"

"You don't have a violent nature. You have a nice one. But that's all I know about you."

"I'm rich. You know that much."

"That's right, I forgot."

"I'm conservative."

"I might've been wrong." She said, "I won't ask if you're married."

"Okay."

"Are you married?"

"I was . . . My wife died."

She said, "Oh," and was silent.

He told her he was here now, right here, nowhere else. Touching her, aware of an intense feeling of tenderness, he believed he was falling in love—not unlike the way he had fallen in love with Ginny, the nurse who removed his catheter. He told Linda he had never made love to a piano player before.

She said, good, and moved her hand over his shoulder, his chest, fingers moving lightly over his ribs, feeling each one, down to his hip, feeling him, finding out things about him, touching smooth scar tissue. Whispering, "I could play you, Vincent. Very slow . . . funky . . . bluesy. Stretch the note till you think it's going to break . . . Stretch it some more." Whispering, as her hand moved to his groin, "Ah, there it is, my instrument."

"Play it," Vincent said, "you'll get a standing ovation."

"What would you like to hear?"

He didn't answer. She seemed to feel his body tense slightly and raised her head. His finger, one finger, came to her mouth and touched it. They moved apart. She watched him roll to his stomach and reach over the side of the bed to the floor. His hand came up holding a gun, then went down and came up again, his white jockey briefs hanging from the barrel.

Teddy's hand came away from the door to 310. He'd turned the knob both ways as quietly as he could, checking; it was locked. As he got the key out of his jacket he realized it was going to take two hands: insert the key with one, turn the knob with the other. Shit—he had to stick his gun in his belt. He looked down the length of the hall toward the stairs, a long haul if you had to get there in a hurry. Then the other way, about thirty feet to the dead end of the hall and the EXIT sign lit up over the door to the back stairs.

He wished he knew which way to turn the key. He wished he knew if there was a second lock inside, a deadbolt, the kind you set at night. Would a cop use it? He didn't even know if the cop had a gun or not.

The palms of his hands were moist. Well sure. He'd knock on a door and say he was with International Surveys and his palms would be like this. It was part of it, always a little scary.

Teddy slipped the key into the lock, turned it easily with just a tiny *click* of a sound. He put his other hand on the knob. Okay, he'd open the door just barely, pull his Colt, bang in there . . . In this moment, right in front of him, so close, he heard the deadbolt released and felt the knob turn in his hand—turned by somebody right there on the other side of the door—Christ, and felt goosebumps as he jumped back, brought up the Colt with his arm extended straight out . . .

The way Linda saw it, from the offside of the bed, where Vincent had motioned her to get over there and get down:

She saw him in his undershorts with the gun held close to his shoulder, jockeys snug and compact against dark skin, a white band below his hips, sexy, really nice buns. It amazed her to think that, the way her heart was beating. He stood against the wall next to the door, reached over to slip the deadbolt, took the knob in his hand to yank the door open . . . God, and the sound was deafening, the gunshots, three in quick succession and the sound of glass breaking as the window shattered. There was an aftersound in the silence, a ringing in her ears, and she was aware of running steps in the hall and a door banging. Vincent moved into the doorway, careful rather than hesitant, the way he looked out. She heard his steps then, lighter, barefoot. By the time Linda got to the doorway and took a look, Vincent was at the end of the hall. He pushed open the EXIT door very carefully, paused to listen a moment and was gone. She looked down the hall in the other direction. It was quiet. Not a sound, not a single door opened.

Linda came back in the room, put on her coat and hugged it to her, shivering, telling herself there was nothing to be afraid of. But it was so quiet now. She stood close to the broken window to look down at the street, the light reflecting on wet pavement.

A car door slammed shut. An engine came to life, its revs increasing to a high whine, a sound of panic, and now a light-colored two-door appeared out of the dark end of the street, lights off, and shot past the hotel toward Pacific Avenue. She saw Vincent now, Vincent without a doubt: a figure in the street light in white skivvies, holding something in his hand, extending his arm . . . Then lowered it as the sound of the car faded. He walked toward the hotel. A much darker figure appeared, a man who had come out of the hotel. The man stood waiting, watched Vincent approach and spoke to him as he walked past. Vincent, coming toward the entrance now, looked back to say something, then was out of view.

Linda got back in bed, pulled the covers up against the chill in the room and watched the crack of light along the edge of the partly open door. She tried to guess what he would do. Phone someone, the police. Get dressed. Pack his bag . . .

He came in and got in bed with her making sounds to let her know he was cold, shivering, making his teeth chatter, overdoing it. She pressed her body against his, a leg between his legs and moved her hand over him. He *was* cold, his nipple hard, but he felt good. She knew his body in one night, the familiar parts. She wanted to ask him questions. She heard his voice low, close to her:

"A drunk comes out of the hotel, he sees this guy in his underwear with a gun. What does he say?"

She said, "Wait, let me think." But she couldn't wait and she couldn't think. She said, "Quit trying to be cool. Who was it? Did you see him?"

"It wasn't Ricky. Maybe a friend of his, but I don't know . . . I don't think so. The guy didn't do it right."

She said, "Vincent, somebody tries to kill you— you don't know who it is?" He didn't answer. "Did you talk to anybody? I mean from the hotel, the manager?" He told her no, only the drunk, outside. She said, "I can't believe it. All that noise, nobody even looked out in the hall."

They were silent, holding each other. Maybe

both with the same thoughts, Linda wasn't sure. Close to her Vincent said, "A drunk comes out of the hotel and sees this guy in his underwear with a gun . . ."

18

THE MOOSE, DELEON JOHNSON, would say, uh-huh; say, unh-unh; say, umh-humh; nod, nod some more. While Jackie Garbo walked back and forth in front of his desk, fat little curly-haired Hymie pleading his case.

"What's happening to me? I been paying attention. Haven't I been paying attention? I don't get out a bed in the morning I know what I got on for the day. I got the fucking printout next to my bed, I open my eyes I know whose ass I'm gonna kiss, exactly what it looks like. I know the guy's credit line to the dollar, what kind a scotch he drinks. I know if he wants one a the showgirls or he wants a midget with big tits, I know his taste. You pick me up, I come out a the house, what've I got in my hand? I got the fucking printout in my hand, right? I'm not paying attention? I grew up doing this. I can do it no-handed with my eyes closed. Our first year we're gonna gross two hundred fifty million, I guarantee—highest gross per square foot of any casino in town outside a Resorts and maybe the Nugget, this cunt infers I'm drinking I don't know what's going on. 'Oh, is that a martini?' No, it's a cream soda with a fucking olive in it. Twenty-five years I'm in Vegas, right? I think it was Johnny Carson, very dear friend of mine. He says, 'You ever drive in Vegas? It's terrible, it's unbelievable.' He says, 'I put my hand out to make a turn and somebody grabbed my martini, took it right out a my hand.' I could tell her that one she'd go, 'Yeah?' waiting for the punch line. You know what I'm saying? It's a gag, but it's *Vegas*. She doesn't comprehend that. Tommy, he doesn't know Come from Don't Come. He starts talking, using words, not knowing shit and walks right into it. Pow, she lets him have it. She's right, he's in the fucking bag half the time. I don't know for the life of me how he ever got where he is. Comes out a Fordham Law, the guy, I think what he is he's a real estate salesman happen to be at the right place the right time. He's not on the juice he can bullshit his way right into your heart, right? He sold *me*. I thought, fuck, the guy's a natural. He must a sold her too, Nancy. But now she sees, Christ, he doesn't know half a what she does. What's she need this asshole for? So she's swiping at his balls with anything she can lay her hands on"—DeLeon nodding, yeah, that's right, yeah—"and I'm standing next to the schmuck, I could lose mine in the same swipe. For what? Do I need this shit?"

"You're the man here," DeLeon said. "They don't have but a hotel, some restaurants without you."

"We're in the deli—listen to this."

DeLeon, on the couch, glanced away from Jackie to Rosemary, Jackie's secretary, fine red-headed woman, standing in the doorway waiting to cut in.

"We're in there having a quick sandwich, I'm telling him all the heat I'm getting outside, these guinea fucks want a bring all their pals in here, let us comp 'em, we don't even break even. The manager, listen to this, the manager happens to stroll by, Tommy says, 'Irv, I notice those salamis hanging over there behind the counter're wrinkled.' He's serious. Irv goes, 'Yeah? Those're aged, Mr. Donovan, that's how they look.' I'm telling him about a situation could put him out a business, he's worried about the fucking salami. You want a hear some more?"

DeLeon held up his hand, nodded toward the doorway.

"There's a gentleman in the lobby, Mr. Vincent Mora," Rosemary said. "You want to see him?"

Jackie looked at DeLeon. "What'd I tell you? They put him off on me." He said to Rosemary,

"Sure, I'm not doing nothing. Bring him in, see if he wants a drink."

DeLeon waited; Rosemary left and he said, "You want me here or where I can be reached?"

"I'll see him alone," Jackie said. "I buzz, you come in, quick. I nod, don't be polite, I want him carried oùt."

They shook hands. Mr. Garbo? Yeah. Mr. Mora? Standing, facing each other across the desk, Vincent with the blue canvas carry-on bag hanging from his shoulder. Drink? No thanks. Please, sit down. What can I do for you? Pleasant, to this point.

Vincent got comfortable, placed the canvas bag next to his chair. He said, "Let's talk about Iris Ruiz."

Now Jackie got comfortable, sat back in his leather chair.

"We could," Jackie said. "Except I don't see where I have to say one fucking word, sitting here in Atlantic City, to a cop twelve hundred miles out of his jurisdiction. Which happens to be Miami Beach. Gotcha." Jackie grinned. "Twenty-five years looking at stone-faced dealers I see just a twitch, a blink, I can tell when I caught 'em by surprise. Are we straight so far? You're a dick, or I understand you say you are, and you're a friend of Iris or you know her. Okay, and then I say I don't give a fuck who you are or what you want. Though I got a good idea what it is. What else?"

Vincent liked the way Jackie came right at him. Fat little guy with his pinky ring, his pictures of stars—wanting to sound tough, hip—with lifts in his alligator shoes. He made assumptions and liked to talk. And Vincent liked to listen. He had known many Jackie Garbos in Miami Beach; they were fun. You could act just a little naive and they'd perform for you.

He said, "The way I understand it, you were with Iris the night before."

"The night before what?"

"She died. There was also a guy there by the name of"—Vincent dug into his jacket for a slip of notepaper, opened it—"is it Benavides?"

"You asking me or telling me?"

"It looks like Benavides," Vincent said. "Anyway, he was there too. I think he stayed at this hotel."

"You're not sure?" Jackie came forward in his chair, reached for the phone. "You want to call Reservations and check? Come on, what kind a shit is this?"

"You flew him to Miami yesterday and he went out of there on Avianca, flight seven to Bogotá."

"Wait a minute," Jackie said. "You Drug Enforcement?"

Vincent shook his head. "I know some DEA

guys though." He looked at the sheet of notepaper.
"Also present was DeLeon Johnson, formerly of
the Miami Dolphins."

"And still mean and aggressive," Jackie said.
"You want to meet him?"

"I understand he works for you?"

"Guards my body, does whatever he's told. Who
else you got? Let's see where we're going here."

Vincent said, "I've got a LaDonna Padgett?"

"Very dear friend of mine."

"How about Frank Cingoro? Is he a friend too?"

Jackie didn't answer. His eyelids seemed heavier
as he stared at Vincent. He brought his hands
slowly from the desk to his lap.

Vincent said, "Frank Cingoro . . . No comment?
How about Ricky Catalina? Ricky a friend or just
one of the many assholes you associate with?"

"Maybe I been misinformed," Jackie said.
"You're with the Miami Beach Police . . ."

"You asking me or telling me?" Vincent waited a
moment, then smiled.

So did Jackie. "You're not here in any official
capacity."

"You mean, like I'm on loan to the police here?"
Vincent shook his head. "Hardly ever happens."

"So you're on your own. Is that correct?"

"You could say that."

"Okay, you come here, you're a city cop, you
know your way around. Am I correct? Back home

you got a car and a boat, nice house. Find it tough to send the kids to college? On a cop's pay . . ."

Vincent shrugged.

"It's funny," Jackie said, "I first saw you I put you down as a narc, the beard, the grubby raincoat. Now, you look very presentable. You don't look like a narc at all. You look like a blackjack counter, fucking math teacher from Minneapolis. I get 'em coming from every direction, all the hotshots think they can beat the house, make a fortune. I get the card counters, all kinds a cheats, guys that stick wires down the slots. Or they try and run a con on me, which sounds like what you're doing, my friend. All the dope traffic in Miami, you don't score enough off a that? You got to come and lean on me, for Christ sake?" Jackie placed his elbow on the desk, raised a limp hand, diamond winking, and pointed a finger at Vincent. "Lemme see if I can make the connection, okay? You got time? I'm not keeping you from any skim deals you got going?"

Vincent said, "Go ahead."

"You know Mrs. Donovan."

"I met her once."

"Made a point to meet her. Maybe score, catch her on an off day she forgot to tie her knees together. This's in San Juan. Our story has taken us down to sunny Puerto Rico. True?"

Vincent nodded. It was moving right along.

"You're there on a medical leave. Some dink shot you on the street."

It was moving faster than expected. "How'd you know that?"

"Hey, I know what you prob'ly had for breakfast. Couple beers. You kidding me? I could see you coming all the way down the fucking street. Let's get back to San Juan. You must have some cop friends there. Not incidentally the PR cops being world-class shakedown artists. You guys exchange notes? How to make it on the side? You could book Spade's Isla Verde, hold a convention, bring in cops from all over . . . So what happened, let's say the cops here notified the PR cops about little Iris, how she took the dive eighteen floors down to the street. Jesus. They're looking for next-a-kin and they tell you about it down there and you say to yourself, hey, somebody fucked up. Since you prob'ly knew the type of work Iris was into . . . How'm I doing so far?"

"Not bad."

"Not bad, your ass. That's exactly how you got onto it. They put you in touch with some PRs up here, guys that know Atlantic City, how it works, what goes on in the dead a night. You get some names, some of the bad guys. You get lucky, see Benavides hanging around and you check him out with Miami. They give you his flight home, read his sheet to you—one of your pals in the DEA. You make a few assumptions and come running into my office, see if you can make out."

Vincent listened, nodding, entertained and amazed; the guy talking about making assumptions.

"So what'd you put together?"

"You were at the apartment," Vincent said. "With Iris."

"When? Come on, gimme a date."

"The night before she was killed."

"The night *before?*" Jackie frowned. "I don't get it."

"You were there. So were these other people."

"Yeah, but how's that worth anything? The night before may as well be the year before. What's the difference? I mean even if there was a connection who're you gonna get to say we were there?"

Vincent didn't answer.

"Whoever was with her the night she was killed, that's the guy you want to shake down, for Christ sake."

"Who do you think it was?"

Jackie took a moment. He said, "I don't believe this. What do you do down in Miami, you raid bingo parties? You been at this long, or what? You come in here to rip me off, now you're asking my advice. As my dear friend Joan Rivers says, 'Can we talk?' I'll give you the word, hotshot, tell you ex-

actly where you stand here. You fuck with any
those guys on your list you may as well kiss your ass
goodbye, you're done. You fuck with me—watch, I
got this magic act I put on. You watching?"

Vincent nodded. The guy looked so small, his
round shoulders hunched behind the big desk, his
array of stars smiling down at him.

"I rub my balls and say the magic words, 'Abra-
cadabra, send in Jabara.' And who appears?"
Jackie looked toward the door to his office. "None
other than Moosleh Hajim himself. Known to all
his many fans as the Moose."

Vincent turned in his chair, starting to rise. He
recognized DeLeon Johnson from newspaper photos, television interviews, saw the smile coming toward him, the Moose much bigger in real life,
looking seven feet tall today in his nifty light-tan
suit. Vincent was standing, ready to offer his hand.
He saw the smile. He saw the forearm coming at
him and was able to turn his head but that was all,
it came at him so fast. That forearm slammed into
him and he saw pink lights popping, went over the
chair to land on his hands and knees, head ringing,
stunned. He heard Jackie say, "Get him out a
here . . . Hey, his bag too. Throw him out'n the
street." Vincent felt himself lifted, held upright. In a
few moments he was able to walk. They went
through the outer office to the hall and toward the

bank of gold elevators by the reception desk, the Moose holding the canvas bag in one hand, Vincent in the other.

As they waited for an elevator Vincent said, "I'm glad I'm not a quarterback," closing and opening his eyes, trying to focus on the door's bas-relief: a gold sunburst with a face in it. He said, "That's what it's like to get sacked, uh?"

DeLeon said, "I wouldn't know. I never been the sackee."

"Five times unassisted against the Lions, Eric Hipple. I was at that game."

DeLeon turned his head without moving his body, looked down his shoulder at Vincent, but didn't say anything. A gold door opened. DeLeon looked at him again as they got on the elevator and Vincent said, "If there was a ref in there you would've gotten fifteen yards. You know that, don't you?" Going down in the elevator Vincent asked him how his knee was. DeLeon said it was pretty good. He said, "I can't kick." Vincent said, "Good."

During his career in the NFL, defensive end for the Miami Dolphins, there were some quarterbacks DeLeon Johnson helped up after dumping them on their ass and there were some he left stretched out on the turf. The ones he helped up, some would give him a sad look as he pulled them to their feet, or shake their heads like to say, shit, why you picking on me today? There were one or two might comment with a straight face, ask him why he didn't stay in Africa, man, play with real lions. This man, Vincent Mora, was like that. In the elevator he said he never missed a Dolphin home game. It seemed he didn't take getting decked personally. They got to the lobby he said, "You know, what I planned to do was check in. But I never got to mention it."

"This hotel, you mean?"

"Yeah, do some gambling."

Right here DeLeon saw Mrs. Donovan across the lobby by the gift shop, talking to a security man with a walkie.

DeLeon said to Vincent, "Got a stake, huh? How much, twenty-five dollars?"

"Let me have the bag," Vincent said.

"You keep all your spending money in this?"

Vincent said, "Over here," going to the bell captain's counter, nobody there at the moment.

Mrs. Donovan was coming this way now and not, DeLeon believed, by chance. The executive-floor receptionist had picked up her phone as they got to the elevators; would have called somebody who got hold of the lobby security man who then told Mrs. Donovan, her network keeping her informed. Was anything she didn't know, it would surprise DeLeon.

Here he was a witness, being sure of this fact, and she walked up and surprised the hell out of him. Not when she said, "Can I be of help?" But when this man Vincent gave her a big grin and she said, "Well, how are you? It's so good to see you again." Meaning it. She didn't just know him; there was more to it:

Vincent telling her, "I've been looking for you. I drove down to your house yesterday."

She telling him, "Yeah, Dominga said you stopped by. I'm sorry we missed you." Then telling him she was terribly sorry about his friend, Iris. That was awful. Telling him she and Tommy had both spoken to the police several times and that the police didn't seem to be getting anywhere.

The man Vincent said, "I talked to them too."

She said, "Oh? You did?" Little hesitation there, like she was half-expecting him to hit her with a surprise. DeLeon caught it. Saw her maybe relax a tiny bit as the man said, "They're working on it." The woman said it was a shame, young girl like that . . . This good-looking stylish woman, top of her class, could be sympathetic; she could scare the shit out of Jackie, emasculate her hubby; and she could act sweet as could be, giving Vincent a big-eyed look now. "It's so nice to see you again. Where are you staying?"

"I was thinking of coming here . . ."

"Well, we'd love to have you."

"I don't know if it's okay."

Getting to it now. DeLeon seeing the man look at him, about to lay it on, get snippy, sarcastic, treated bad by the help. But all he said, factual, was, "I've been asked to leave."

DeLeon got ready as Mrs. Donovan gave him an executive stare, serious business, man. "What's the trouble?"

"I'm suppose to escort this gentleman out. See, but now he tells me the reason he came in, he wants to do some business with the casino."

Lady acted patient, a little cool, pulled her nice blond hair away from her face; very queenly now.

"Who asked Mr. Mora to leave?"

"Was Mr. Garbo. Just now."

The man Vincent surprised him. He said, "Somebody must've told Mr. Garbo I was coming." Said it with a little bit of a grin looking at Mrs. Donovan, like to see what she would have to say to that. Cat was sly. DeLeon liked him. Mrs. Donovan hung in, didn't change her expression, frowning some, innocent; like she was thinking, My, who could it be? The man said, "I think Mr. Garbo, somehow he got the wrong idea about me."

DeLeon thinking, Misjudged you. Ten to one that's what the little show-off Hymie did.

Mrs. Donovan saying now, "Well, let's not worry about Mr. Garbo. I'll speak to him."

Meaning—DeLeon smiled just a little—she was going to cut his curly head off.

Mrs. Donovan saying, "We'll get you checked in. Okay? And I'll see that you get a line of credit. I'm sure it can be arranged."

The man Vincent brought the canvas bag off the counter saying, "I don't need credit, I brought some money with me. Right here."

Mrs. Donovan said, "Oh," and nodded. "Fine." Very polite. The gracious lady married to the man that owned the place. "How much would you like to deposit?"

Vincent held the bag in front of him, looked in it, looked up. "I guess about twelve thousand."

Nothing to it, like he carried that much around. Beautiful. Man had style. Knew his timing, saying to the lady now, "Do I have to pay for the room or do I get comped?"

Beautiful.

And give Mrs. Donovan a hand. Cool, not blinking an eye. Coming right back to say, "For twelve thousand, Mr. Mora, you're not in a room. You have a suite."

DeLeon said, "Here, let me take your bag, my man."

19

"IT'S LIKE YOU'RE IN A HOTEL in *Star Trek*," Vincent said. "You know what I mean? It's so modern you don't know how to open anything or turn the lights on."

Dixie said, "They comped you to a suite? Come on."

"They like me," Vincent said. "Or they want to keep an eye on me."

He sat with the telephone in a corner of the gold sectional sofa, wrapped in a king-size gold towel. Dixie Davies was home in Brigantine, in the kitchen.

"Everything's either green or gold."

"The color of money. Keep you reminded."

"With white walls, means they're honest. I don't know what the paintings mean. I've got a bar, stocked. I've got a phone in the *bath*room. Three phones, one in each room. The bathtub, you could get four people in it. You walk down steps."

"I'm about to eat supper," Dixie said. "You want to know what we're having? Meatloaf."

"I got shot at," Vincent said.

There was a slight pause. "I believe it. Ricky?"

"I was hoping, but it wasn't."

"Say you got good reason to think it was and I'll get a warrant. Give me a chance to go through his house."

Vincent told him about it and said, "Does that sound like those guys? It wasn't set up right. One guy, takes a wild shot and runs. He didn't even have a driver . . . You might check stolen vehicles for a yellow Monte Carlo at least five years old."

"The hotel report it, the shooting?"

"Nobody heard a thing. I ran outside in my underwear, got my gun, I'm coming back in a drunk is standing there on the sidewalk looking at me, weaving. You know what he said?"

"Atlantic City, three o'clock in the morning," Dixie said, "Resorts International across the street, he told you don't do it, it ain't worth it. Think of your wife and kids."

"He said, 'You should a bet your underwear. You never know when your luck'll change.' I checked out, I said I want to pay for the window too. They said, what window? Miami Beach, a hundred old ladies would've called it in, seen the whole thing."

"I'd still like to pick up Ricky," Dixie said.

"You could keep an eye on him," Vincent said. "He's supposed to meet me tomorrow, but it wouldn't surprise me he's gonna go see Frank Cingoro first. You know what I mean? Call Frank up and if there's no answer he could be lying on the floor. The way those guys are doing each other—and I bet Ricky thinks he's got every reason. Would you like to see that?"

Dixie said, "Would I like to see it, I'd buy tickets. You kidding? Jesus, bring Ricky up for doing the Ching and send his ass to Trenton. I'm getting excited thinking about it."

"The thing is," Vincent said, "I'm pretty sure none of those people had anything to do with Iris."

"I have to agree with you," Dixie said. "On the one hand it's no help with the girl, but on the other . . . You never know, do you?"

"Wonderful things can happen," Vincent said, "when you plant seeds of distrust in a garden of assholes."

"Wait, I want to write that down."

"I talked to Jackie Garbo. Very entertaining guy. I think he used to get beat up a lot when he was a kid. He's on shaky ground, running games outside the casino. You can tell he's nervous and you could use it to grab him by the balls. Except he doesn't know anything. I mean about Iris. I'm pretty sure." Vincent said, "This's some town. You got a lot going."

"You ever want to work here," Dixie said, "I could probably fix it."

"Leave my suite, my phones? . . . How about the autopsy report?"

"Be another week or so."

"What's the hurry, uh?"

"You want to complain, call Newark."

"In the meantime," Vincent said, "ask Jimmy Dunne about a delivery, some sandwiches . . ."

"From the White House Sub Shop. We checked," Dixie said, "they don't have a record of it. We talked to Jimmy again, he said it must've been from some other place."

"He describe the delivery boy?"

"White male, thirties, blond hair, suede jacket. Could be anybody."

When Linda came Vincent made drinks and they got in the bathtub and played.

"You realize," he said, "you could get away with this for at least a month? Go from hotel to hotel, deposit the same twelve grand?" Linda smiling as she listened. "Soon as they find out you're not gonna spend it you move on. Do all the hotels here and then go out to Las Vegas."

"You're in the wrong business," Linda said. "You should be a crook. You *are* a crook."

"I may gamble, if I have time."

"When you're not taking baths."

She got out of the tub to make fresh drinks and

light cigarettes. Vincent watched her—waited on by a good-looking naked woman he felt at home with in a $500-a-day hotel suite. She wasn't the least bit self-conscious, looking at the bath oils and lotions on the marble vanity. She was the first woman he had ever seen without tan lines, her white skin making her appear more genuinely naked and appealing to him. He said, "What're you doing? Get back in here."

"I have to go to work soon," Linda said. "I'm opening tonight, kid, at Bally's." She threw her arms out and struck a pose. "Linda Moon, Now Appearing . . ."

"You sure are. But you didn't tell me."

She let her arms drop. "That's what I'm doing, telling you. Why're you so surprised?"

"I thought it was down the road, a couple weeks off if you got it."

"I *had* to get it. Vincent, I work, I don't sit around."

"But right now . . ." He hesitated. "Whoever it was last night, he finds out you're at Bally's . . . I don't think it's a good idea."

She stood at the edge of the recessed tub, hands on round white hips, looking down at him.

"Vincent, I spent half the day with the entertainment director . . . Where do you think I've been?"

"I knew where you were." He was having trouble, looking up, keeping his eyes on her face.

"Yeah, but did you really care?"

"What're you mad at?"

"I got the entertainment guy—I wouldn't leave his office till he said, okay, I can play anything I want, *my* music, Vincent . . . Look at me. Quit staring at my crotch. I played a rehearsal set and he loved it—as much as those guys can love anything, but he said go ahead. That's the thing, I can play what I want . . . Are you listening?"

"I'm listening."

"Well, look at me. Do you know what this means?"

"Yeah, I understand."

"I've been working my ass off for a shot like this, Bally's Park Place, *my* charts, and you want me to hide in a hotel room. You want to protect me, Vincent, then come sit in the audience."

"What time are you on?"

"Ten o'clock."

"Okay. We'll come back here after."

"And take another bath," Linda said.

The phone rang.

He met Nancy Donovan in the lounge: dark and quiet in here between sets. They'd have a drink first and then she would take him into the casino, show him around.

She told him if he didn't like his rooms he could

choose another suite. Or if there was anything at all
he wanted . . . He said no, it was fine; green and
gold were his high school colors. He liked the bathtub a lot; he said you could practically swim in it,
do all kinds of things. He said he liked the view, he
liked to watch the ocean when it was breaking in
with a high surf. They covered the weather and
beaches in New Jersey, Florida and Puerto Rico.

She was a much different type than Linda. Both
were confident, looked right at you; but Nancy
hung back, in no hurry, seemed to choose her
words, while Linda came right at you and said
what she felt. Sort of like Jackie Garbo, with class.
He said, "I had a nice chat with Mr. Garbo. He's a
pretty hip little guy, isn't he?"

"He hopes desperately you'll think he is," Nancy
said.

"You don't care for him too much."

She said, "As long as he does his job," and
shrugged her shoulders, sitting in her fashion-
model slouch. Nancy would model expensive
clothes and have the walk down—whatever way
the models were walking this year. Linda would
model lipstick, her mouth partly open. He had
wanted to bite her lower lip right off, without hurt-
ing her. They were about the same size, both slim;
but he believed their bodies would look different
side by side, naked. Linda pulled off her sweater
and there were those white beauties with the pink

tips looking right at you while her head was still in the sweater. He believed Nancy wore a bra and her breasts would be as tan as the rest of her body. He had never seen a deeply tanned ass. Just as Linda was the first woman he could remember without tan lines at all. Nancy said, "You're deciding what you want to play."

Vincent smiled. "How'd you know?"

"I'll bet you like blackjack."

"You're pretty good."

"Will you play with green chips or black?"

"Green are worth . . . twenty?"

"Twenty-five. Black a hundred."

"You ever comp anybody who just plays the slots?"

Teddy walked through Bally's, the Claridge and the Sands without seeing one lady who was his type. The girl of his dreams would be in the 58-to-65 range, not too big, with dyed hair or a wig and played the slots with a big cup full of coins and a drink on the counter in front of her. A cigarette hanging out of the corner of her mouth was a good sign, and if she was coarse in her speech, a kidder, that was the best sign of all she was the one for him. Close to eight, the casinos were filling up with the evening rush of greedy spenders and would be going strong with lights flashing and bells ringing for hours. He felt security people, with their name badges and walkie-talkies, looking him over. They weren't, but that's what he felt. Like driving and seeing a cop and getting nervous for no reason. He had reason last night to be nervous. Jesus, the way the hotel room door came open in his hand. Not expecting it—that'd scare the shit out of anybody. It was a good plan, it was just the cop had probably got up to take a leak and happened to hear the key turn. But the door had been double-locked so it wouldn't have worked anyway . . . He had in mind now another plan. Follow the cop in his car, the Datsun. Pull up next to him at a light and let the cop get a look, surprise the hell out of him. Not wave or yoo-hoo at him, he'd have to be cool, but make sure the cop saw him. Then zip ahead and let the cop follow. Take him out Longport Boulevard and over the JFK Bridge, out in the marshland and pull off the road. The cop comes over to the car, looks in the window right at him, close, eye to eye. Pow pow pow . . . Soon as he got some money. Shit, he didn't even have enough on him to buy gas.

Teddy left the Sands and headed for Spade's Boardwalk, next stop in his quest for the ideal old lady.

Leaving the lounge Nancy held onto his arm, guided him through the lobby to the familiar gold elevators. Vincent said he thought she was going to show him the casino.

"I am, but a way few people ever see it."

She brought him along the executive hall to the surveillance room: to the bank of monitors, twenty movies playing at one time: deadpan characters suspended, waiting for the turn of a card; the slot players, the "high pullers" at the dollar machines; only the crapshooters animated. Vincent said, "I could spend some time here." Nancy said, "You haven't seen anything yet." She introduced him to Frances Mullen who glanced up from a monitor off to the side. Frances said, "Be with you in a minute."

"She's watching the soft-count room," Nancy said and pointed to the dropboxes that were brought in from the tables at the end of each shift, the money taken out and counted by employees in coveralls, no pockets, then transferred to the main cage. When Frances turned to them she said, "Well, here's a familiar face. You were playing blackjack the other night—" Vincent saw her expression change as her eyes moved from him briefly and back again, a glance at Nancy close behind him shutting her up.

"I won four hundred seventy bucks," Vincent said, imagining himself on one of the screens, "and I swear I didn't cheat." He was sure Nancy had a picture of him.

She said, "They would've caught you if you tried. If the dealer or the pit boss didn't spot you Frances would. Come on, I want to show you something else."

He followed Nancy along the hall, through a door and down a metal stairway, a ship's ladder, into a dark area that resembled the rafters of a building, the crawl space above the ceiling. Except that here you could stand upright, follow a wide catwalk with handrails, and from both sides of it look down through one-way smoked glass at the casino floor: at the tables, the slot machines, the mass of players and strollers less than ten feet below.

"The Eye in the Sky," Nancy said.

Teddy had read somewhere they had over sixteen hundred slots here at Spade's. He wouldn't want to count them; though he could, moving up one row and down another, looking for the girl of his dreams. Jesus, but dollar slot made a racket, those big slugs clanging in the tray. He liked the sound of quarter-slot payoffs better; it sounded more like real money, the coins *ching*ing down on top of one another. Half-dollar payoffs were somewhere in between, a hefty sound and real too.

He'd stop and play a quarter slot every once in a while. Won four bucks, lost it, won five, moved on with his green paper cup and lo, look-it there . . . a woman playing two machines at once, her territory staked out with a drink, two cups of coins and her purse there on the counter. Look at her, no wasted motions. She'd insert a coin, give the handle a yank and step to the other machine as the first one spun. A payoff less than a big one not even making her pause to look. Back and forth feeding half-dollars like she was working on a factory line. Letting up, but only to get out a cigarette. Now there's a cute woman, Teddy thought. Right around sixty, hair a pretty henna color that went with her gray knit pants suit and pink blouse. Her glasses flashed as she looked at a big heavy woman who stopped by her and said, "Marie, we're going over the deli get a bite t'eat." Marie lit her cigarette, blew smoke at the woman and said, "Go ahead." Independent little woman, wasn't she?

Teddy said, God, let her win. She deserves it.

Vincent stood with his hands on the metal rail looking straight down through the angled pane of glass at a blackjack table where two men and a woman were playing with green chips; he could read their cards. "It's so close to everything."

"But when you're down there you don't notice it," Nancy said. "We're part of the sparkling decor. No one looks up anyway."

"Covers the whole floor?"

She nodded, indicating the length of the catwalk. "Goes all the way to the end, over to the other side of the room and comes back."

"You have people in here?"

"Sometimes, or if they spot something on the monitors, a dealer slipping a chip behind his tie. Or a player they think is cheating, like trying to double his bet after the dealer shows his cards." Nancy had moved close to him, their arms touching. "At the moment we're alone."

She stared through the glass at the floor below, letting him look at her and feel her close and get the scent of her perfume—more subtle than Linda's, more expensive. Linda would have said, "We're alone," and rolled her eyes at him or given him a vampy look as she reached for his fly; and he'd jump. But it could work either way. Nancy's method, stagey-serious, must be working because he felt a clear urge to make the next move. Grade it later, what it meant. They were fooling around, that's all, flirting a little. It didn't have anything to do with Linda. Except that Linda did appear in his mind and he had to say to her, in there, What am I doing? I'm not doing anything. It was his having been raised a good boy that was trying to hook him with guilt, ruin his chances here. Hell, Linda was a friend, her life was music . . .

Nancy said, "Tommy's down there, somewhere.

With another one of our big spenders." She gave Vincent a nudge.

"I still haven't met him."

"Do you want to?" Her voice very quiet.

He could hear a hum of sound from the floor. "It's not important. I don't think he knows anything about Iris, what happened to her."

"You're being kind," Nancy said. "He knows very little about anything that happens around here."

Vincent kept quiet.

"He's drunk most of the time."

She was telling him to make the move, it was okay.

"I've always thought I was a fairly good judge of character. At least had an eye for typecasting. But I really blew it with Tommy. I married him on impulse, much too quickly."

She was saying, come on, let's go. What're you waiting for?

"We talk about business, but it's been months . . . Well, never mind."

And you say, Vincent thought. "What has?"

"Since we've slept together."

Do it, will you? Go ahead. He couldn't think of anything to say, which was just as well. It was time, very quiet, the urge, the tender feeling there. Tender enough. He turned her face to his with his hand, gently; their mouths came together, he felt her tongue . . . and heard bells ringing, like a fire alarm, from somewhere almost directly below them. Their faces still close, her nice brown eyes smiling at him, she said, "Jackpot." Now Vincent smiled. Why not? And closed his eyes again as she closed hers, going for those slightly parted lips.

Well, Marie had quit working her two machines now with the bell ringing and those fifty-cent pieces still coming out, letting up for a few seconds then pouring out again, some spilling on the floor there were so many. Teddy grabbed an empty cup and got down there to pick them up. He set the cup next to her purse saying, " 'Ey, you won four hundred dollars. Not too shabby. I just hit two hundred bucks myself over to the Sands. It's nice, 'ey?"

Marie raised her eyebrows, proud of herself. She looked at him through smudged glasses; the frames were gray, with sequins. "Them others go and eat all the time. I tell 'em you got to *play* if you expect to win."

"That's the truth," Teddy said. "And you got to know which slots to play, the ones timed to go off."

Marie turned back to her scooping, but then looked at him over her shoulder. "I heard it pays it don't empty. They's always money in it."

"That's right," Teddy said, "but you heard of frequency modulation? See, the big jackpots are timed to pay off at certain times or frequencies, when there's lots a people around."

Marie said she never heard of such a thing.

Teddy looked at his watch. "Well, I got, let's see, about twenty-five minutes to get back to the Sands where I'm pretty sure a couple half-dollar slots're gonna pay off. I been watching 'em all day. See, I live right here."

"You wouldn't kid me," Marie said.

"Come on, you don't believe me. I been studying slots since they opened Resorts, the first one. I don't even have to work." He took a quarter out of his pocket and held it up. "See this? Got nineteen seventy-eight on it?"

Marie said, "So?"

"I been playing *this* quarter for six years. I never lost with it. I hold this quarter over the slot? I know when it's gonna pay and when it ain't."

"You expect me to believe that?"

"I still have it, don't I? . . . You coming or not?"

"I just might. Sands the next one up?"

"Take us fifteen minutes."

"I got to cash in first."

"Well, hurry up, will you?"

Act like her kid. If she had one it would seem natural to her if he was grouchy. Marie did; she had three grown sons. She had come on a bus from Harrisburg where she was a checkout girl in a supermarket; they were going home at nine. Out on

the Boardwalk Teddy told her she just had time to
win another pot. Wasn't it a beautiful night after all
that rain? He told her when he was little they used
to go under the Boardwalk and look up through the
cracks at girls in dresses. They called it stargazing.

Marie said, "You were a little dickens, weren't
you?"

Teddy said, " 'Ey, look. There a bunch a stars out
tonight."

Marie looked up.

And Teddy said, "Oh, no!" He sunk to his hands
and knees, got down close to a space between the
boards. "I dropped my lucky quarter!"

Marie bent over. "You see it?"

"It fell down underneath. I *got* a find it." He
worked his face into a frown. "God, wouldn't you
know? . . . I'm sure it's right down there, right below us." He looked at Marie. "You got a lighter,
haven't you?"

She said, "Yeah, but . . ."

"Come on, we can find it. I know we can."

20

LADONNA SAID, "You want me to barf all over the car?" Trying to tell Jackie she was petrified, getting physical about it now. "You know how I feel. How can you even ask me to do something's going to make me ill?"

With her baby-doll Tulsa drawl and then Jackie speaking in his dialect—a tribe that used to live in the Bronx—like he was suffering, and he probably was, trying to make himself understood, get her to realize the importance of this dinner. "I got a talk to the guy."

"You talk to him on the phone all the time."

"Face to face. I got a tell him this across a table. It's how he wants to do it, fine, it's how we do it."

"But I can't go *in* there."

"I got what you need, help you out," Jackie said.

Now he was pouring her a tequila and lime juice, chilled, from the limo's bar next to the little TV set.

DeLeon Johnson was catching all this from the front seat, sitting eyes-front behind the wheel; like

listening to a radio skit. He'd shift his eyes to the
mirror, see shapes, movement; but Jackie'd had him
put up the glass separating front from rear, for privacy, and DeLeon was getting headlight in his eyes
to make it worse, harder to see anything. The black
Cadillac stretch limo was parked on Fairmount Avenue, on the north side, across the street from La
Dolce Vita, "Authentic Italian Cuisine" blinking in
red neon, making the girl sick. They were supposed
to meet Frank the Ching in there for dinner and the
girl was fighting it every way she knew.

DeLeon had pushed the button to raise the glass
partition, then brought it down a couple inches
while they were talking so he could hear the skit. It
was anybody else, Jackie would want him to listen,
be a witness; didn't matter if he got dumped on or
made to look a fool by some Eye-tie. (Jackie would
call them "guinea fucks" and one time DeLeon
said, "Excuse me, my granddaddy was Italian,"
and had to listen to Jackie explain he meant these
wise-guy schmucks, not your real Eyetalians.) But
Jackie didn't want a witness when he was talking to
LaDonna, who had these hysterical seizures and little Jackie didn't know shit how to bring her down.

She said, "*You* go in. What do you need me for?
I'll wait here."

DeLeon grinned at the mirror. Tell him, girl.

He'd be at the house talking to LaDonna, giving
her advice how to maintain cool—that is, the abil-

ity to respect yourself while taking a minimum of shit—and Jackie would come bust in the room like he meant to catch them making it. The fool. There were all kinds of times and places DeLeon knew he could take LaDonna up in the sky; but it would be a glide, it would be to say, yeah, I ride this one-time beauty queen runner-up. It would be a score, was all. It wouldn't be anything like some little bitty Puerto Rican chicks he knew could take him up laughing all the way and do loop-the-loops, man, get him light-headed with the pleasure of their being there. He wished he was back in Puerto Rico instead of here listening to Jackie saying, no, he didn't *need* her, he wanted her at the table because the Ching would behave himself. "Not stick a fork through my hand he doesn't like what I'm telling him."

"It's going to happen," LaDonna said. "I know it is."

"That's in the movies they do that. *The Godfather*."

"It's in the paper, it's on TV. I *see* it."

"That's in South Philly. Come on, it's after eight. Christ, twenty after."

"Why can't I get you to understand?" LaDonna said. "That fella works for Tommy, he's the only one of you is the least bit sympathetic. I tell him I can't eat with those people, he says, 'I don't blame you, I couldn't either.' "

DeLeon raised his eyes to the mirror as Jackie said, "What guy works for Tommy?"

"The one, you know, with the beard. He's nice."

DeLeon heard Jackie say, "Jesus Christ, you *talked* to him?" Then Jackie was rapping on the glass partition. "Go in and tell Ching we're gonna be a couple minutes—I got a phone call. Buy him a drink." DeLeon got out of the car hearing Jackie say to LaDonna, "Okay, when'd you talk to the guy?"

Ricky Catalina had decided, first, he couldn't use any of his own people. A family deal, it was best to get outside help, scummers with no personal interest, muscle you hired by the pound.

Late afternoon he cruised Boystown till he ran into a couple of heavyweight bikers. They were in Snake Alley selling homemade killer weed, parsley flakes sprinkled with PCP, telling a gay couple in jogging suits and headbands how the dust would stretch their minds, their bodies, grow actual fucking wings on them, man. The scummers were dressed sleeveless now that it was fifty degrees out, showing their muscle, their tattoos, their chapter insignia, Hagar the Horrible from the funnies. Ricky got them aside in a bar, gave them the deal with sleepy eyes and they said yeah right away. Anything crazy or destructive, they said, yeah, babe.

One of the pair, called Bad Isham, had been burned when his lab blew up, out in the Barrens; one side of his face was shiny scar tissue and he was missing an ear. The other scummer, Weldon Arden Webster, was known for making explosive devices. He said to Ricky, "You have a diversion, I could blow you a car out front a the place."

Ricky said, "Yeah, but I don't want the guy I want to run out—he hears any kind a big explosion."

Weldon said, "Shit, you want it done right, I wire the *guy's* car."

"*I* want to do it," Ricky said.

"Yeah, give you a remote control box."

"I want him to *see* me do it. It's the kind a deal this is, it's between me and him."

Weldon said, "You people got queer notions how you have to settle things."

Bad Isham said, "The guy ain't the only one gonna see you, Ricky. Lemme think on it."

The trouble with getting scummers to help, they sat with their big shoulders hunched over the table making muscles jump in their arms, drinking their schnapps and beer chasers, and pretty soon the deal was their idea, how it should be done. Ricky had to give one, then the other, his sleepy eyes. You through? You through?

"That place, all they get now are tourists," Ricky

said, "the way their prices are. Except in the bar
there, guys still hang out in the bar; they lay some
heavy sport bets. Weldon gets in a fight with some
guy, anybody. Make some noise, bust a few bottles.
The help comes out from the restaurant part, see
what's going on. Reno, the guy's driver comes out.
You know Reno? _. . Okay, you belt Reno, be sure.
I walk up to the guy"—Ricky wouldn't say his
name—"I come in that entrance from the parking
lot, cap him and walk back out. The car's over on
the side street. Isham, you pick up a car. You drive,
that's all." Wasn't that simple enough, even for a
couple of spazzed-out bikers?

Bad Isham said, "Other way around. Weldon
drives, I bust up the bar."

Weldon said, "Bull*shit!*"

Ricky finished his glass of red while they argued
who was meaner, dirtier, who'd stomped more
civilians, hit more cops, got brought up more on
charges. Ricky listened, wondering what made
scummers the way they were. All that muscle shit.
They could come at him with their tire irons, their
chains, their big bare arms, he'd say, you guys
crazy? And blow holes in them. There was no way
to understand people like this. If they asked him to
judge which of them was scummier it would be a
tie. So he said, "Hey." He said, "Hey! Goddamn
it!" When they looked at him he was settled back.

"We leave the car on the side street. You guys want to fight so bad, both a you go in there, fight each other."

At eight P.M. they were sitting in the bar at La Dolce Vita, schnapps and beers in front of them. They'd start out swinging like a movie fight, coldcock some guy close by and start a free-for-all if they could. But when Weldon turned and threw his beer in Bad Isham's scarred face it surprised Isham. It seemed a pussy way to get things going. So he faked a backhand fist and came under it with a body punch that sent Weldon and the civilian next to him off their stools. Isham lunged off his, sweeping the bar of bottles and glasses . . .

The noise caused the people in the dining room to look toward the archway with the red neon sign over it that said BAR.

Ricky moved along the coatrack in the side-door vestibule to the cashier's counter. He took a mint from a dish sitting there and put it in his mouth as he looked over the room: white stucco walls decorated with paintings of northern Italian landscapes and Venetian canals. Six tables occupied that he could see—no one he knew. Frank Cingoro sat alone at a table-for-four in an alcove, semiprivate, an antipasto tray and a bottle of red on the table.

Frank was eating peppers and shrimp, taking a big sip of wine. He didn't look up until Ricky was standing at the table, his back to the room.

"You can't bet on the fight, forget it. Hey, Frank?"

"Some clowns," the Ching said, looking over his black-framed glasses. "Who cares? How you doing, Ricky? You getting much?"

"You don't look surprised to see me."

"You want me to?" The Ching used a toothpick to dip a shrimp in the sauce, put it in his mouth. "You can sit down you want, till Jackie and his broad come. He goes to the toilet I'm gonna jump her, that LaDonna."

"You got a cool fucking way about you, Frank. I got a say that. You old guys."

"How old am I, Ricky?"

"You're sixty-something, sixty-three?"

"How old?"

"What're you, sixty-two?"

"How old?"

"Okay, how old are you, sixty? Jesus."

"How old, Ricky?"

"Sixty, you got a be."

"I'm fifty-eight, you fuck."

Ricky said, "Well, you're not gonna get any older, Frank." He put his hand in the side pocket of his leather jacket.

The Ching had a shrimp on a toothpick close to his mouth. He hesitated, held it there and said, "Ricky, what're you doing here?"

"What?" Ricky said. "I can't hear you, Frank. I'm up'n Brigantine, man, I been there all night."

He brought a .38 Special out of his jacket, the revolver covered in toilet paper from grip to two-inch barrel, a tissue-wrapped present he extended in both hands, pushed his index finger through the flimsy paper covering the trigger guard and aimed at the shrimp on the toothpick. He shot Frank five times, the toilet paper catching fire; he had to tear it from the grip fast, then held the wad of paper up and let the revolver unwrap to fall on the white tablecloth.

DeLeon saw it, saw Frank go down behind the table, saw Ricky turn and come this way bunching scorched toilet paper in his hand. Tidy little dude, looking away from the tables toward the BAR sign where he could still hear sounds in there like people beating each other up, breaking things. The people out here all with their heads sticking up not knowing shit what was going on.

DeLeon stepped back against the coats hanging in the rack, no way to hide in there head and shoulders above it; but he stood not moving a muscle. And here came Ricky, Ricky coming along cool, looking up now and a little surprised. DeLeon stepped out and let him have that forearm with mostly elbow in it, hunched and threw it hard at Ricky's face but caught him a speck low and heard bone crack. DeLeon took him by the jacket quick and let him follow his buckled knees to the floor. The boy looked awake but in some pain. Little Ricky the Blade. Shit. DeLeon raised a size fourteen boot to bring it down on Ricky's knee, render him immobile, tell him wait, help was on the way. But paused. Got a crazy idea in that moment—part of an idea anyway—pulled Ricky to his feet, took hold of him under one arm, Ricky moaning, "My shoulder, my shoulder," walking on tiptoes as DeLeon brought him out the side door and up to the corner of Fairmount Avenue. DeLeon told Ricky to behave himself or he'd throw him in front of a car. Traffic passed, he took Ricky across the street. Now they came up behind the stretch limo. DeLeon opened the trunk, got Ricky inside, and gently closed the lid.

Jackie didn't know shit behind his smoked glass windows, sitting on the edge of his seat to look over at the restaurant, at people running out of the bar. DeLeon got in. Before Jackie could ask him anything he said, "You want to watch the police arrive or leave right now?"

* * *

At dinner Nancy talked and Vincent listened. He smiled once in a while. Last night in the same glittery room he had listened to Linda talk about music, playing lounges, and had smiled a lot because he could feel what she was feeling and had wondered what living with her would be like, or even being married to her, committed. Tonight he smiled to be polite, not feeling a thing, listening to Nancy describe how she'd doze off as this sweet guy Kip, her first husband, sipping martinis, told long drawn-out stories about dogs with human characteristics, a golden retriever that listened to stock market reports at breakfast . . . Vincent nodding, thinking, The poor fucking dog. Nancy said, "After Kip died, what was I going to do in Bryn Mawr, play tennis the rest of my life? Join The Gardeners? Hell, no. I came here and got a job." Vincent nodded in admiration. Nodded in sympathy as she told him about Tommy's drinking, his macho jock attitude, his high blood pressure. Tommy sounded like a fairly regular guy. She said, "Tommy wanted to have dinner with us, but he's very busy." Pause. "I think he's playing video games on his computer. He loves Donkey Kong." Listening, nodding, it finally occurred to Vincent that he was going to get seriously propositioned before too long. Nancy was giving him her specs. She had money, position, a line to the Main Line; she had poise, style, outstanding looks. What else? She tended to overkiss, but it wasn't bad. She was getting ready to dump her husband. There was only one thing wrong . . .

She brought Vincent to the top-floor Penthouse Lounge, reserved for high rollers and their guests, quiet this evening, almost empty, the room dark in low lamplight, enclosed in glass. She brought him to the top of Atlantic City and said over cognac, "I could make you rich."

He said, "It's what I've always wanted."

She hesitated, giving him a serious look. "I mean it."

So he said, "Why?" It was more important to him than "how."

"I think it would be fun."

"Work for you?"

"Work for Spade's."

"I don't know anything about it."

"Neither do half the people at the very top in this business. They were something else before, that's all. You were a police detective."

"I still am."

"How did you get hold of twelve thousand dollars wrapped in rubber bands?"

"I was lucky."

"So am I. That's why I know you'd be good at this." She looked at him over the rim of her glass. "You have no intention of gambling, do you?"

"Listen, I feel like I can't lose."

"You're a crafty guy, Vincent. Easy to misjudge.

But I think I know you and my hunches are almost always right." She sipped her cognac. "I could make you an actor, Vincent, get you a decent part in a film within six months, I guarantee. That's why I know this would work. I can use you, Vincent."

That's what he was afraid of.

"You'll love it here."

"Why me?"

"Don't be coy."

"I'm serious, I'm a cop."

"No, you're one step away from being a senior vice-president in charge of . . . I don't know yet, but I'll think of something. Start you at, say, a hundred and fifty thousand. How does that sound?"

"Do I get a car?"

"Of course."

"I have to wear a regular suit?"

"I'll help you pick some out." Giving him her nice smile.

"Where do I live?"

"Wherever you want. Longport's nice. We'll find you something."

"You're not gonna keep me in an apartment?"

She wasn't smiling now. "That's uncalled for."

"How many times a week do I have to go to bed with you?"

He thought she was going to throw her cognac at him, or try; but she didn't. She placed the glass on

the table and got up, the lights of Atlantic City behind her. As she started to leave he said, "Nancy?"

She stood for a moment turned away, taking her
time before coming around enough to look back at
him.

"What?"

"Do I still get comped for the suite?"

That wasn't nice. He could have said it in a different way. A simple no-thank-you wouldn't have
been too bad.

Except that he didn't feel his remark was any
more out of line than her offer. There was no way
she was going to make him a casino vice-president
based on some gift she had of sniffing out latent
ability. On the other hand, how could he assume
she was after his body, considering all the slick guys
with haircuts and shiny suits hanging around? Unless she wanted to make one of her own out of raw
material, use him as a stud kit. He might have made
a mistake. Not in his refusal, but in assuming what
she wanted.

Vincent went down to his suite to change shirts,
get out of the white one he'd worn two nights in a
row, put on a blue workshirt—yeah, it ought to
look nice with his new sportcoat—and pick up his
gun. It was 9:30 and Linda was Now Appearing at

Bally's at 10. He paused to look at the urn resting on the dresser, Iris in stainless steel without diamonds or whatever she had come here for . . .

The phone rang.

It would be an assistant manager with a cool tone telling him his time was up.

But it was Dixie Davies telling him he'd called it right and should be one of the first to know: "Frank Cingoro was shot and killed an hour ago, in an Italian restaurant on Fairmount Avenue. You'd think those guys'd learn to eat some other kind of food. Heavyset guy with dark hair, leather jacket, walked in and walked out. Nobody saw his face good, but who does it sound like? We sent a car to Ricky's house, he's not home."

"He was in Brigantine at the time," Vincent said. "With about eight witnesses."

"Where I should be," Dixie said, "home watching TV. I got this one, I got another one came in I have to see about soon as I finish here. Elderly woman they found underneath the Boardwalk at Kentucky Avenue. Bum went in there, tripped over her body. She's from Harrisburg, it looks like. So we got to check the tour buses, see if she was with a group, who saw her last, all that."

Vincent was thinking about Ricky and Frank Cingoro, but he said, "What happened to her?"

"She was beaten to death, robbed, it looks like, and probably raped, her pants pulled off."

Ricky and the Ching vanished and a name came into Vincent's mind without thinking, as a free-association reflex, nothing more. But there it was and he said the name to himself and then out loud, "Teddy Magyk."

21

POLICE-CAR HEADLIGHTS illuminated the scene, showed the understructure of the Boardwalk, figures standing in the timbered sections at the dead end of Kentucky Avenue. Flashlight beams moved in the dark, deep beneath the structure and at the outer edges of the scene. Close to Vincent waiting sounds popped on and off, radio voices from squad cars and walkies. Then silence and he would listen and hear the ocean, still out there. He waited among the police cars and ran Teddy Magyk facts through his mind, what he could remember, wanting to place him here or close by. It might be a long shot but that didn't matter, because Teddy's first conviction had been in New Jersey and his mother had come from New Jersey for his trial in Miami, and Vincent was running on a gut feeling that had him moving, smoking cigarettes. The odds made no difference.

He could see Teddy clearly in San Juan, in the Datsun. Teddy at the beach. Coming in a taxi, then in the rental car. He could see Teddy at his trial almost eight years before, and a stout woman with blond hair in the first row. Vincent did tell himself he was dealing with a remote possibility at best. Because if Teddy's presence seemed so logical now, why hadn't he thought of Teddy before this? And his gut feeling would say, Never mind that. He's here.

Dixie came out of the lights and said, "Only good thing about it, it just happened. Usually it's days before a body's found under there. Like when you get a floater, you don't know where to start."

"You could close both before morning," Vincent said, trying to sound calm, offhand. "You could luck out. Pick up Ricky, you know you have Ricky."

"I know it was Ricky, yeah, but I never heard of this other guy. Teddy?"

"Magyk. He did time in Yardville, for rape."

"Where's he live?"

"I don't know where he lives, but you could call it in, have 'em turn on the computer. Punch five keys and see if it's your lucky night. The guy's a known felon. Miami Beach he raped an old woman, almost beat her to death."

"Where'd he commit the offense he went to Yardville for?"

"I don't know that either, but he was from Camden originally. Look up his mother. He came down to San Juan—listen, he's right out of the can he's got money for a hotel and a car. Maybe his mommy gave it to him."

Dixie was facing the lights, frowning; he turned his head to look at Vincent. "This is the guy you're telling me about has the hard-on for you?"

"This might even be the guy tried to pop me the other night. From what I saw of him, it was dark, but it could be the guy I'm talking about. The description of the delivery boy Jimmy Dunne gave you, the cheese steak subs, *that* could be the same guy."

"Wait a minute," Dixie said, "just a minute. I thought we're talking about this one right here, the woman."

"We could be, it's what the guy does," Vincent said. "Look, you tell me about it on the phone and it's like you say hot and I say cold. You know what I mean? You say an old lady was raped, beaten to death, and I say Teddy Magyk. The first thing that comes into my mind. But there's more to it than this one, this case. All this did was make me think of him."

"More to it like what?"

"He knew Iris. He saw her with me."

Dixie touched his mustache, began to twist one end, idly. "He did?"

"Teddy left San Juan the same day she did.

Check Eastern, see if they were on the same flight.
Find out his destination. If you don't, I will. But
you can do it a lot quicker."

Dixie seemed to agree, nodding, giving it some
thought. Then stopped. "How come, you're so sure
it's this guy . . ."

"I'm not sure. My gut is, and I listen to it."

"Okay, how come your gut's so sure you never
mentioned him before this?"

"Because we start out, all we see are heavy hit-
ters, all your suspects. It's got to be one of them.
Teddy, he ever walked in the same room with
Ricky, the Colombian, Jackie, any of those guys,
you'd never notice him. He looks like a guy rings a
little bell and sells ice cream. He walks down the
street, you wouldn't give him a second look. You'd
never think to hassle him, you know, like you do
with assholes, give 'em a hard time. Never. This guy
looks absolutely harmless. And that's the worst
kind."

It got Dixie nodding again. "All right, we'll
check him out."

"When?"

"Soon as we can. I'll give you a call. Where you
gonna be, in your suite, taking a bath?"

Vincent hesitated. "Yeah, I'll be there."

* * *

He unlocked the door to the suite thinking about Linda. She was going to kill him for not showing up . . . Started to push the door open and stopped. Lights were on. His hand went inside his coat to his hip. A voice he recognized, DeLeon's, said, "It's cool, come on in. Nobody's gonna hurt you."

He saw DeLeon in a streamlined gold easy chair with a drink, legs extended, feet resting on the glass cocktail table. He saw LaDonna on the sofa, in front of the window wall reflecting the room in lamplight. LaDonna sat turned, to look at him over the low back of the sofa, her expression—it was hard to tell—solemn? Vacant? She raised her drink in both hands, her eyes not leaving him.

"Yeah, you had the lights off, didn't you?" DeLeon relaxed, at home. "That's right, it was dark we came in."

"There's a notice over by the bar," Vincent said, "a little card. It says please turn the lights off when you're not in the room. To conserve energy. They've got, what, about a thousand lights on downstairs all the time."

"At least," DeLeon said. "Yeah, it's a crazy place to be." He brought his polished boots off the table, rose without placing his hands on the chair. "What can I fix you?"

"Scotch," Vincent said, looking at LaDonna, moving toward her now. "What's the matter?"

"She's all shook up," DeLeon said. "Like Elvis use to say."

"I was almost killed," LaDonna said.

DeLeon looked over from the bar. "Now, now, don't lie to him, girl. Tell the truth."

"Well, I could've been," LaDonna said. "It was just like I kept thinking it was gonna happen. Remember?" She held her drink on the back of the sofa now, her body turned as she looked up at Vincent and he looked down the front of her purple dress. She seemed too healthy to be sad.

"I remember," Vincent said.

"Well, it happened."

Vincent looked at her face, her eyes. She had been crying—that's what it was. He realized what she was telling him and said, "You were there, with Ching? You and Jackie?"

"She was al*most* there," DeLeon said. "Hey, you heard already?" He handed Vincent his drink, stood close to look down at him, without expression now. "So you in with the police, they tell you things . . . Well, I guess that's okay. Sit down, my man, we got something to discuss . . . LaBaby, you go on in the bedroom and rest. Be good for you."

"God," LaDonna said, "I keep seeing it."

"Girl, you didn't see nothing. Go on in there, close your pretty eyes. We look in on you, see you're all right."

She left her shoes on the floor, came around the sofa with her mournful look, barely moving. Vincent gave her a pat on the shoulder. She looked at him with her poor-me eyes, trying to smile. What was sad, she was too big and well built to be a baby doll. DeLeon followed her to the bedroom, told her yeah, leave the light on if you want; no, I won't close the door all the way. Coming back he said to Vincent, "My, but that's a fine titsy young woman, ain't it?"

"She needs help," Vincent said. Maybe he could talk to her. He came around to the sofa as DeLeon got in his chair. "What're you, about six-five?"

"And a half, in my socks."

"And you weigh about two fifty."

"If I take off some excess."

Vincent leaned forward to place his drink on the glass table, reached under his coat then and drew the Smith automatic from his hip. He laid it on the cushion next to him, hand remaining on the grip.

"Now I'm bigger than you are," Vincent said. "I can ask why you think you can walk in here and make yourself at home. And if I don't like what you say, or even your tone of voice, I can throw your ass out and complain to the management." There, he had to say that. But then had to add, "Even though I'm curious. Even though you've got my full attention."

DeLeon smiled. "You're my man. I knew it. I knew soon as you scammed your way in here, got the free ride. I said to myself, here's the thinking man's policeman. Let me apologize to you, all right? One, for decking you the way I did, I am truly sorry. And two, for coming in here. See, I had to look after LaBaby. Was suppose to take her home, all the way down to Longport. But I had to see you right away on something can't wait. Otherwise—I would never walk in without you invite me otherwise."

Vincent said, "That's not bad," brought his hand away from the gun and picked up his drink.

"It gets better," DeLeon said. "Cops told you about the Ching shot dead, huh?"

"As a courtesy," Vincent said. "But you must know more about it than they do. You say you were almost there, you must've been close by. Is that right?"

"I wasn't almost, I *was*. I was there. You understand me? I saw it. LaBaby and Jackie, they're in the car having a fight 'cause she don't want to go in. So Jackie send me in the restaurant, tell the Ching they be in directly. I'm there, I see little Ricky big as life walk up and shoot him. Man. I never seen anything like that before."

"Not like in the movies," Vincent said.

"Not anything like it."

"So you got out a there."

"Wait and let me tell it, all right?"

"I'm sorry. Go on."

"I see Ricky do it." DeLeon paused. "But Ricky don't see me. You know what I'm saying? I'm over behind the coats hanging up, by the hall to the side door there. Ricky comes over, he's going out. Left the gun on the table. He still don't see me till he's right like here in front of me. I step out, I give him one. Drop him like a sack of shit."

Vincent raised his eyebrows. "That must be where it comes from, sack the quarterback."

DeLeon's expression became thoughtful. "Hey, I believe you right. Yeah, drop him like a sack . . ."

"But Ricky wasn't there when the cops arrived."

"Uh-unh. You know why? I took him with me. Jackie don't know it; LaBaby, she don't either. I brought him out, hid him in the trunk of the car."

Vincent said, "You took him with you."

"In pain. I give him a little more elbow than arm. See, and I went low to compensate for him being short as he is. You understand me? Little motherfucker's built to the ground. I believe I cracked his jaw, I might also've separated his shoulder or broke it. He was in pain."

"He still in the trunk?"

"No, I moved him, I put him in a storage room down it's by the garage. He can't get out, but to make sure I got the La Tunas to keep an eye on him."

"The band?"

"Yeah, see, three of those La Tunas, they're Rastafarians. You know what I'm saying? From Jamaica, wear the dreadlocks, how they do their hair?"

Vincent was nodding.

"They believe Haile Selassie, man use to be king of Ethiopia? Was God. Don't ask me why but they do. They find out I'm from over there originally, born there, they want to build an altar, man, set me up on it and blow ganja at me. They think I'm Jesus."

"You're bigger," Vincent said.

"They all fucked up with weed, but they nice boys."

Vincent said, "Can I ask you something? Why you brought Ricky here?"

DeLeon straightened in his chair. "You don't understand? You don't see the possibility looking at you?"

Vincent shook his head. "Not right off."

"I brought him for *you*, man. Make it up to you for what I did, for hitting you just 'cause that fatso told me. I shouldn't have done that."

"You've giving him to me?"

DeLeon seemed surprised now. "You're looking for who killed your friend Iris, right? Well, here's Ricky, man. Talk to him. Ask him things while he's

in terrible pain, he'll tell you. You understand me?
If he didn't do it he'll tell you who did. There isn't
anybody else could know but Ricky. Man, I'm giving you this. Take it, you don't owe me nothing."

"I appreciate it," Vincent said. "But I already
talked to him."

"You did?"

"He doesn't know anything."

"Wait now, he's got the desire. I mean he's crazy
enough."

"I know that."

"I *saw* him kill a man, the Ching."

"I might've given him the idea," Vincent said.
"But he didn't do Iris. No, I had a long talk with
him."

The room was quiet. Vincent got up, he took
their glasses to the bar and poured scotch over ice.
DeLeon said, "You way ahead of me, huh? You
know things I don't." Vincent told him about his
talk with Ricky, sitting in Ricky's car in the rain.
DeLeon grinned. But wait now. What was he going
to do with Ricky? Vincent said, drop him off at a
hospital, the cops would find him. DeLeon said he
could step on Ricky's knee first, so he wouldn't
walk out on his own. Vincent said, "I wouldn't."

DeLeon said, "You way, *way* ahead of me, ahead
of Jackie, ahead of everybody. He shook his head
saying, "All this hip shit. You understand what I
mean? The casino business, all this razzle-dazzle.

All the people thinking they know everything. Now you, I see you go about quietly doing your business, I know I been exposed to Jackie too long."

"He's fun to watch," Vincent said.

"Yeah, he's fun to watch, but he tires you out you with him for a while. I would like to get out of here. You know what I'm saying? Man, I'm a free agent. Why not? Go some place nice, like Puerto Rico."

"I could live there," Vincent said.

"Set us up a kidnapping business."

They sipped their drinks and had another one while Vincent told him about Teddy Magyk. DeLeon sat without moving or interrupting, finally nodding to say he liked it, the possibility. "Like he put your name in Iris's panties to bring you up here," DeLeon said.

And Vincent nodded. "I can see him doing it." But what was in Teddy's head, if he did?

"Making you his career," DeLeon said.

"That's what I mean. Why am I so important to him?" He wanted an opinion and said to DeLeon, "You did time on the drug bust, didn't you?"

"Six months in Dade, then a halfway house. I wasn't there long enough to get crazy. Or I was lucky, I knew I fucked up good. Let myself get taken in by the dudes, the sporty jock freaks with the boats, the cute blond-haired ladies, the private clubs. You know what I'm saying? Got myself into all that deep shit till the only way out was through the county. You understand? You asking me what's in those people's heads in there, doing time, or what's in this Teddy's head. Who knows? Ask them, they lie to you from jump street, don't know how else to talk."

"Lay the blame somewhere else."

"*Any*where else. I couldn't do it. My mother come to visit me—she not my mother but like my mother. This little woman come to visit, I'm in the stockade there, you know the place. She look me in the eye, I could no more lie to her I could to a polygraph. They repossessed her house, was in my name. She never mentioned a word about it. Only thing matter to her, this little boy had lied to himself. You understand me?" Thoughtful. "I got her another house now, in Miami. Send her money every month."

"My mother lives in North Miami," Vincent said. "She sells real estate, lost her second husband last year . . . I'm older than my dad. You ever hear of that?"

"I know what you mean," DeLeon said. "Me too. I never even met my daddy."

"I didn't either. I've only seen pictures of him."

"Now my mother," DeLeon said, "the lady I call my mother, she like to grow things, she in the yard all day."

"I'm wondering about Teddy's mom," Vincent said, "if she's been supporting him." He told DeLeon he was waiting to hear from the county police, find out if they'd got a lead on Teddy or where his mother lived.

DeLeon said, "You look in the phone book?"

22

THERE WAS HIS MOM'S FACE right on top of him. Teddy tried to push back away from her into the pillow. He thought, opening his eyes, she was going to kiss him on the mouth and it scared him. It was the middle of the night and the ceiling light was on in his bedroom. His mom's stale breath came over his face as she whispered, "There some men here to see you."

"What men?" Scowling at her. Wanting her to get away from him.

"They're policemen, they showed me. Sonny? . . ."

"What?" Why didn't she get away? All eyes and hair curlers.

"Why do they want to see you?"

"*I* don't know." Crabby. Feeling crabby. "Would you mind?" Jesus. She straightened finally, picked up his Japanese robe, and held it open.

"Here. So you don't catch cold."

Teddy walked into the living room, hands in his

sleeves. The two detectives were looking at Buddy,
one of them crooking a finger at Buddy's beak and
pulling it away. He looked up and Buddy bit his finger, good, as the other one said, "Mr. Magyk?" and
introduced himself and the detective sucking his finger, both of them heavyset and serious, as all cops
were. He asked Teddy if he'd mind riding just over
to Northfield with them to MCS headquarters—
cops loved initials—like Northfield was only a couple minutes away.

Teddy said, "Why, what's the matter?" Wide
eyed. Look at how innocent he was. Polite too.

The detective told him he didn't have to talk to
them if he didn't want to. Teddy said, well, if they
would tell him what it was about . . . The detective
said he could agree to come with them or they
could go to Municipal Court and get a warrant, if
Teddy wanted to give them a hard time. What hard
time? They became deadpan, immobile, giving him
a brick wall to butt his head against. There was no
way to win if they felt like being mean. It made him
mad though.

"You want to stick me in a line-up, don't you?"

One of the detectives said, "Why would we want
to do that?"

"I know you guys."

"Is that right, Teddy? How do you know us?"

Teddy said, "I been here all night."

His mom said, "He's been right here with me."

The detectives said, "You coming, Teddy?"

Shit. He got dressed and went with them, the two cops in front speaking once in a while in low tones, a woman's voice coming over the radio now and then but not making any sense; otherwise it was dark and quiet out on that lonely Margate-Northfield road across the islands, no other cars. The one driving flicked his lighter and held it to his cigarette.

Marie would flick her Bic down underneath the Boardwalk, stooped over in the trash and weeds. She'd say, "I don't see it nowhere." Looking for his lucky quarter. "I don't see it . . . Listen, I got to go." He hit her with an old beer bottle he'd picked up, brought it down on the back of her head. She dropped the lighter making a funny sound like a yelp, surprised. He struck again, in the dark now, and realized she had her hands up on her head. She yelled louder and he felt her right up against him, facing him, saying, "Oh, help me, oh," not realizing he was the one had hit her. He hit her again but couldn't see what he was doing. He grabbed the front of her suit as she tried to take hold of him for protection it seemed like, putting her arms around him and was so close he'd chop at her but wasn't able to get anything behind his swing, to put her away. She was moaning, oh or no or oh no, as he hit her. Then headlights came on up Kentucky Avenue about a half block up the street and it gave him enough light to see her, catch glimpses of her cut face, her glasses gone. He was able to push her away, see what he was doing now, and give her a good one over the head with the bottle. It wouldn't break, darn it. He hit it against a support timber, it still wouldn't break. He shoved Marie against the timber, banged her head against it good a few times and that seemed to do the job. He had learned trying to shoot somebody in a hotel room didn't work spur of the moment; and he had learned a beer bottle was no good for knocking a person out quick. The trouble was, he didn't like the sound of it hitting the person's head. What might've happened, he held back just a little each time instead of swinging through, not wanting to hear that mooshy sound of the bottle doing its job. So it took longer, finally beating her senseless against the timber. Once that was done it was quiet under here and even a little cozy in that faint headlight beam up the street. He cleared trash away and got down with Marie in the damp sandy dirt. God. All alone with this woman he could do anything he wanted to. Get some of her clothes off, feel her body all over. Ouuuu, it was mooshy. He wanted to look at parts of her too. He got her clothes undone, pulled off her pants and her big panties, big as his mom's hanging in the bathroom. Then got out hotel matches, lit and held each one as long as he could, getting a good close look at her. He had not planned on making love to Marie, but was getting the urge staring at her puss, wondering how long it had been for her. Tickle, tickle, tickle. It looked worn or moth-eaten, strange. Oh well . . .

In that ride to Northfield, across the channels and marshy islands, Teddy was thinking next time what he might do, try to keep the woman awake or semi-out till he started making love to her. Be doing it to her and then, right at the right moment, hit her over the head. But not with a beer bottle. He'd never use one again. He ought to have checked with certain people while he was at Raiford. Sit around in a circle on folding chairs and have a group session. He'd tell them when it was his turn: Rule number one, Put the money away first, before you start having fun. Else you could get carried away and forget it. He almost did.

Cedric, the head La Tuna, was waiting in the cement hallway back of the casino. He unlocked the storage room and there was Ricky on the floor between rows of slot machines, sitting with his head down, holding his arms to his body. He looked up slowly, his dead-eyed expression in place—until he saw Vincent.

DeLeon said, "Try to open his mouth, mmmm, it hurts him. Be cool, Ricky, we gonna take you to the hospital."

Ricky kept staring at Vincent, trying to say something, find out what the hell was going on, and still look mean.

Vincent feeling just a little sorry for him, thinking, They work so hard at it. He said, "I bet Frank was surprised, huh? The cops ask why you did it, tell them it was a mistake."

"Tell them somebody messed with your head," DeLeon said, and looked at Vincent. "He's gonna have a time even to give his name."

"Maybe he should write it down," Vincent said. "To whom it may concern. How I did the Ching."

Ricky groaned something, a word, trying not to move his mouth.

Vincent said, "What was that, Rick? Speak up. Sounded like he said, 'Bull*shit.*'"

DeLeon said, "He can write it or I can fix it he has knee surgery while they wire his jaw."

Vincent left them, walking out past Cedric with his aura of reefer, his sheen of serenity, Cedric calling DeLeon "Mon," saying he was a joy, he was so fine . . .

Well, he wasn't bad. A good one to have along. Vincent got on the elevator and pressed his floor and then held the button to make the door close and said, "Come on, let's go." It was almost 2:30 but seemed much earlier. He still hadn't heard from Dixie. He'd give him a call and if Dix didn't know where Teddy's mom lived he'd tell him. In Margate.

You believe it? Marvin Gardens, less than five miles away. The only Magyk in the book.

Linda stood in the doorway to the bedroom. She turned as he came in but didn't say a word. She seemed calm enough, patient, and he had nothing to hide. Nancy Donovan came into his mind, a glimpse of her, lips parted; but he got rid of it, no trouble, in and out.

"You're wondering what Miss Oklahoma's doing in our bed, aren't you?" He could fool around, play with it, free of guilt, glad to see her. "I'll tell you," Vincent said. "But first, how'd it go?"

Linda said, no, she'd like to hear about Miss Oklahoma first. So he told her about LaDonna's fear, her recent experience, what was going on, and Linda raised her eyebrows a few times as she listened, interested but not overdoing it. What a girl. Maybe she could have given it just a little more; but he was satisfied. Linda didn't act until she got on the stage. "So, how'd it go?"

"I was a smash."

"They liked you."

"Vincent, they loved it. We're doing two weeks to start. The guys are great, better than I ever expected. We start moving and it's so full. It's so . . . well, it's just so *full*. Three of us, just—it was great. We're gonna play some music."

Vincent said, "You were good, uh?"

"Not bad. I'm gonna take a bath. What do you say? You feel dirty?"

"Filthy. Soon as I make a phone call."

He spoke to a male voice at Northfield who told him Captain Davies was in conference and would have to return his call when he was free. Vincent asked if they had located Teddy Magyk. The voice said he had no information about that. Vincent hung up and sat looking at the name he had printed on the hotel memo pad in block letters, MAGYK, the number written beneath it. He picked up the phone, pressed nine for an outside line . . .

Someone was at the door: the sound of three quick knocks and then silence. Too soon for DeLeon to be back . . . Vincent crossed the room, opened the door.

It was Nancy Donovan.

Dressed casually now in a navy jacket and slacks. She said, "Are you going to invite me in?" Her voice softer than he had ever heard it, giving him a movie-star look with her eyes.

Vincent had to think about it a moment. He said, "Sure. Why not?"

Nancy hesitated now. "I'm not disturbing you?"

"No, come on in. Sit down, I'll fix you a drink."

"Could I have a small cognac?" She was in now, moving to the couch. Vincent told her she could have anything she wanted and poured a couple of good ones. This was getting to be some night. He handed her the snifter glass and she said, "I want to say I'm sorry . . ."

"You don't have to apologize."

"I'm *not*." Letting him have it, but immediately drawing in again, passive. "I was going to say, I'm sorry if there was a misunderstanding. Sorry you got the wrong idea. You had no reason, Vincent, to say what you did."

She was at the end of the sofa, tailored and trim. Vincent eased into DeLeon's chair to sit at a close angle to her, their knees almost touching.

"I shouldn't have said that. I'm sorry."

She waited a moment, her clear stare turning wistful. "Can we be friends?"

"I don't see why not."

"Start over?" When he nodded and said you bet, she smiled. "Did I frighten you? Just a little, maybe?" He gave that one a nice shrug and she said, "I thought about it after. I can understand how you might've gotten the idea I was, well, sort of coming at you. But I meant well, honest." Nancy gave him the look over the rim of the glass, head lowered slightly, one he remembered from the Penthouse Lounge, upstairs. She sipped her cognac, swirled it lazily in the snifter bowl and looked at him again. "When we were alone earlier, spying on the casino, we seemed so"—she hunched her shoulders, becoming tiny—"at ease with one another, and yet so aware. It was as if in that moment, Vincent, I knew you and I knew I was right, what I'd felt from that first time." He said, That first time? . . . And Nancy said, "In San Juan, when you came to my house. I knew then—"

"God," LaDonna said, coming out of the bedroom, her white legs coming out of a shorty robe Vincent didn't recognize, "how long did I sleep?" The robe, or beach cover, would have to be Linda's. He glanced at Nancy, sitting up to look over the back of the sofa, turned away from him.

LaDonna said, "Oh, hi. Can somebody tell me what time it is?" The sleepy girl stretching now, reaching out, the cotton robe rising on her milky thighs.

"Two forty-five," Nancy said. "I think it's time for me to go." She said to Vincent, "Sorry."

He had to pull his eyes away from LaDonna to look at Nancy, not sounding anything like the voice from a moment ago. Amazing—no longer tiny in that navy-blue outfit but standing tall, shoving her hands in the pockets now to get back a casual effect, indifference.

It didn't last.

Not with Linda coming out of the bathroom now doing a funky drag step nude, with subtle hip moves, doing things with a towel as part of the vocal number, a rendition of "Automatic" in the Pointer Sisters' style, a low gutty voice telling them all of her systems were down down down . . .

Till she saw her audience.

Vincent was proud of her, the way she did a turn without missing a beat, wrapped the towel around her, even tucking the end in, said, "Well, what do you think?" and threw her arms out to strike a pose. "This, or the banana outfit?"

Vincent imagined telling his friend Buck Torres about this night. Or Lorendo Paz in San Juan. Yes? And then what happened.

Then Nancy Donovan left. Yes, of course. How was she going to compete? She was cool though, she took her time. Looked at everybody, said, "I think I'd better say goodnight," and walked out. Yes? Then Linda and LaDonna started talking. Both of them on the sofa in shorty robes, sitting on their legs having a private talk that I could hear. Linda saying, Look at you. You realize the advantages you have? LaDonna saying, I know. Linda saying, You're not only a beauty, you're congenial, you're thoughtful, you're a very nice person. LaDonna saying, I try to be. Linda telling her to quit moping and get off her ass, *do* something, quit the booze, and so on. That Linda, you could put all your money on her . . . Then DeLeon came in, back from dropping Ricky at the hospital, said hands taped and a note pinned to his jacket; shoved him out of the car at the security cop on the door. Then the phone rang, finally, almost four o'clock in the morning.

Dixie Davies said, "You know where we found your guy?" . . . He said, "We pulled in the net, got all the sexual assault stars available, including your guy. We put every one of 'em in a lineup for this group from Harrisburg. Nothing. We brought Jimmy Dunne in, let him take a good look at Teddy. Maybe, maybe not. He can tell you all about playing trumpet with Victor Herbert, but not what happened last week. Teddy says he was home all night. His mom says he was home, the parrot says he was home. The fucking parrot bit one of my guys. I got no reason even to offer him a polygraph."

Vincent said, "What about the car?"

"You might have something there . . ."

"It was him," Vincent said. "Jesus Christ, it was him, wasn't it?"

"Yellow '77 Monte Carlo, in his mom's name."

"I don't care whose name. I don't care what else you say. It was *him*."

"We checked Eastern . . ."

"And they came on the same flight."

"Looks like it."

"Get a warrant," Vincent said, "go through his house."

"What am I looking for?"

"You'll know it when you find it. Come on, I don't have to tell you that."

"I lay the warrant in front of the judge, is that what I tell him? They don't do it like that here. I got to show cause the guy's a suspect and I'm looking for hard evidence. I don't even think he did the woman, and I got no reason to hold him for anything else."

Vincent hesitated. "You still have him?"

"He's sitting in the green room. Very polite young man. Says he wishes he could help us."

"Keep him another hour. Can you do that?"

"For what?"

"I want to talk to his mom."

23

THROUGH THE PEEPHOLE in the front door Verna May Magyk saw a white man with a beard, hippy-looking, and the biggest colored man she had ever seen in her life. It made her shiver and feel goose-bumps up the back of her neck. She said, "Oh, my Lord," and jumped as the chimes rang again. The porch light was on, she could see them good. As they stepped apart, looking at the house, she saw the black car parked in front. A real long one, shiny even in the dark. An undertaker's car, that's what it was. Teddy's mom was relieved, though not much. She said through the door, "You have the wrong house. There's nobody dead in here."

Then realized she'd made a mistake as the hippy one with the beard said, "Mrs. Magyk? We'd like to talk to you for a minute. Would you open the door, please? Sounding just like the detectives that had come for Teddy.

She said, "Where's my son?" and saw them look at one another.

"He's fine, he'll be home pretty soon. Could we come in and talk to you, please?"

She told them just a minute and took about that long to get the door unlocked and then unfasten the catch on the storm door. They were as polite as the others. They came in, the big colored man looking around, the man with the beard going over to Buddy's perch and saying he understood Buddy bit one of the detectives. It made Buddy nervous; he edged away.

Teddy's mom said he did no such thing. Buddy was a good li'l birdie boy. Arn'cha, huh? Arn'cha? She said, "Pretty bird, pretty bird," and Buddy said, "Hello, May. Want a drink?" Wasn't he a li'l cutie? Teddy's mom let Buddy peck a sunflower seed from her mouth, prompting him with, "Kisser mom, kisser mom," and holding her kimono closed so the men couldn't look down it. "There. Did he bite me?"

"That's a beautiful bird," the colored man said.

Close to Buddy Teddy's mom said, "He has to have his li'l beak shaved so he don't hurt hisself, huh? Huh, Buddy? I'm taking him for his appointment at ten o'clock. Yes, I am."

"Did Buddy, I mean Teddy get Buddy for you in Puerto Rico?" It was the man with the beard. He said, "I was down there one time myself."

Teddy's mom told him no, Buddy had been in the family twelve years; but Teddy had sent her a beautiful handcarved parrot that was supposed to have been delivered but never was.

"That's interesting," the man with the beard said. "I wonder what happened to it."

Teddy's mom didn't think it was so interesting; she didn't believe Teddy had even sent it. He liked to fib. Then he'd get that guilty look. He'd be mean to Buddy and there would be the look. Police questioned him about different things and there was the look again. She believed it was his guilty look that had got him sent to jail those times. All it was, he was self-conscious. She said to the big colored man looking all around the living room, "What is it he was suppose to've done this time?"

The big colored man said, "Who's that, ma'am?"

"My son, Teddy."

"Oh, they just want to talk to him is all. See what he thinks." He said, looking around again, "My, but you got parrot things. Must be a valuable collection."

She was a judge of character and liked the looks of this colored man. He was polite, he wore a suit and tie—which the other one did not—and he appeared to be clean. She said to him, "Do you like parrots?"

"Love 'em." He was looking at the display of china parrots on the mantel. "I wouldn't mind you showed me all the different parrot things you got."

Teddy's mom said, "Well, let's see . . ."

Then the one with the beard asked if he could use the bathroom.

The overhead light was on in Teddy's room: a young boy's room with scarred bird's-eye maple furniture, a single bed, slept in, unmade. A water-color print of a parrot in a jungle setting, on the wall above the bed. But no posters, no records, hi-fi or radio, books. Vincent changed his mind: not a young boy's room, a guest room. Teddy was here but had not moved in. Vincent went through the dresser, each drawer, feeling beneath the clothes; stepped into the closet to feel Teddy's trousers and jackets, sweaters. He found the Colt .38 automatic in the camera case, looked at the gun in the over-head light without touching it and put the case back on the closet shelf. A new leather-bound pho-tograph album was on the desk, its pages empty. In the drawer were envelopes of prints, several from a Fast Foto shop in San Juan. Vincent began to look at pictures of familiar places. He saw the beach at Escambron in a dozen or more shots of Iris and himself. There was his rattan cane hanging from the chair. Iris talking to him as he tried to read. Walking with her. Eating pineapple. Like pictures taken by a friend but not posed. He slipped one of the prints into his jacket and looked through another envelope quickly. Shots of San Juan land-marks, those familiar buildings, narrow streets, monuments, flower beds, trees, old ones, trees high in the clouds . . .

Vincent stopped.

He turned the desk lamp on, hunched over to look at a print. Then another one. The two almost identical. The same figure in both pictures in the same pose. It was the background that was famil-iar. Remembered from another time, a different person in the picture. But a background that would never change. Vincent could see it with his eyes open or closed.

It was light out by the time Teddy got home. He waved to the unmarked light-tan Fairmont pulling away. Assholes. His mom was still up, waiting to tell him about the hippy and the huge colored man who'd been here while he was gone. Sure, Mom. What'd they take, the refrigerator or just the TV? She said they didn't take nothing; this was a very nice colored man, a great big one, his head almost touched the ceiling. Teddy said that's how they grew them these days; the big ones played basket-ball and the skinny ones became millionaires selling you paper towels in the men's rooms. Teddy's mom kept going on about the colored man, how he was polite and clean. Sure, Mom. Her old arteries controlling her mind. Weird. A lack of blood in her head bringing colored guys into the house to steal things.

"They must a taken *some*thing."

"Well, they didn't. Police don't rob you. Don't you know nothing?"

"You're saying they're cops?" This was a new one. "They show you their I.D.?"

"They said you'd be home soon, the others just wanted to talk to you."

"Get my opinion on world affairs. They look around the house?"

His mom said she kept an eye on the colored man because you never know. But they were both polite. Even the hippy one with the beard, "He asked could he use the bathroom and said please."

Teddy said, "Je-sus Christ," and ran into his bedroom.

His gun was still in the camera case. Whew, that was a relief. He'd better either hide it good or get rid of it. Then thought, why? He'd shot at the cop with it, but so what? He'd only actually killed one person with it and they couldn't do nothing about that here. Except cops were sneaky and he could get two years just for having the thing in his possession. Teddy looked in his drawers; his clothes seemed in order. He went over to the desk. If the one with the beard was the cop Vincent, who was the big jig his mom thought was so polite? Man, they were sneaky.

He had marked the print envelopes and put them in numerical order in the drawer to trap his mom, be able to tell if she looked through his things.

Well, they weren't in order now. He began to feel a little tense looking through the Escambron beach shots. They seemed all here. Then counted the ones of the cop and Iris. He believed there were twenty of them . . . But there weren't. He counted them twice and got nineteen each time. Well, nineteen or twenty, he'd better get rid of them—anything that linked him to Iris—just to be on the safe side. Teddy went through the rest of the envelopes looking at his postcard shots of sunny Puerto Rico . . . There was the liquor store in the Carmen Apartments. That couldn't screw him up, could it? Naw. What else. More postcard stuff . . . Wait a minute. He went through every print in one of the envelopes, expecting the shot he was looking for to come up next. Two, there were two he was looking for. He went through all the envelopes, just to make sure. But the two prints were missing. Both of them. Jesus Christ. Unless he had thrown them away himself. Now he couldn't remember; it seemed so long ago he was down there.

But those pictures wouldn't mean anything to the cop. How could they?

* * *

At 8 A.M. Vincent called the Bureau of Criminal Affairs in Hato Rey, Puerto Rico, asked for Lorendo Paz and waited, hearing voices in Spanish.

Linda was in bed. DeLeon had left with LaDonna rubbing her eyes, to take her home, get in a few hours sleep and come back. Vincent waited with a silver coffee pot and two photographs on the desk next to him, sunlight in the window, the remains of drinks the morning after on the glass table. He stubbed out the cigarette he had lit as he placed the call. He'd quit again, soon. He needed to sit in the sun and read. He would like to sit in the sun with Linda and read, but that was a hard one to picture, Linda on Condado Beach doing nothing . . .

Lorendo said, "Vincent!" and began asking questions about Iris. Vincent told him to wait, he wasn't asking the right ones.

"You had an investigation going," Vincent said, "the body you found in the rain forest, El Yunque . . ."

"Yes, the taxi driver, Isidro Manosduros. The man left a family."

"How're you doing?"

"We identified him, that's all. Four days we believe he drove the same man around, an American.

But we don't know his name, who he is. Isidro was an independent, he didn't keep a record."

"You know what he looks like, the American?"

"Only what Isidro's wife told us. A rich one, of course. They're all rich to some people. Not young, but not an old man. Staying in a hotel, but she doesn't remember which one. Isidro told her this guy was a prize, very generous, bought presents for his mother. But he was strange, too. She said she told Isidro to be careful of him."

"She did? Why?"

"Who knows? She's from Loíza. One thing, yes, Isidro told her the American has a tattoo on his arm, up by the shoulder."

"Does it say Mr. Magic?"

There was a silence before Lorendo said with awe, "Oh, Vincent, I don't believe it. How do you know this? Please, tell me."

"Wait. What's Isidro look like? Is he dark?"

"Very dark, black. Thin, medium size, heavy bones. Not very good teeth. A little gray in his hair. Vincent—"

"I've got a picture of him," Vincent said, "taken up in the rain forest, I think right above where you found him. He's standing at the edge of a cliff, where you look out at the view."

"On El Yunque, you're sure."

"Positive."

"You visit there, you know the place."

"No, I didn't make it. I told you, I don't know if you remember, I wanted to see Roosevelt Roads, where my dad was stationed during the war . . ."

"Yes, I remember."

"And I wanted to see El Yunque. My dad had his picture taken there, a long time ago."

"Vincent—"

"Wait. I don't have the picture with me but I can see it, almost every detail. I used to study it when I was little. This was my dad and I'd never really met him. Salty young guy in a sailor suit, up on the mountain. You see the ground, some trees but there's hardly anything behind him but clouds. Mountains way off."

"Yes, rain clouds. It rains every day there."

"The picture I have of a Puerto Rican with very dark skin, smiling but not really smiling, was taken in exactly the same place."

"Send it to me, quick as you can."

"It's Isidro," Vincent said. "There's not a doubt in my mind."

"Okay, now the guy that took the picture—"

"Teddy Magyk. He lives about five miles from here."

"Ahhh, Magic. It's his name."

"You don't remember him."

"No. I should?"

"We had him," Vincent said. "The ex-con I

wanted to scare and you said take him out on the Loíza ferry."

"Yes, yes, *Teddy*. I remember, sure."

"I might not've mentioned his last name. At the time it didn't mean anything."

"Okay, listen," Lorendo said. "I have to do something about him quickly . . . Wait. How did you get the picture of Isidro?"

"I stole it."

"Oh, I believe that, Vincent. Listen, I want to hear it, but don't tell me now. I have to get the machinery moving. First, I have to request Atlantic City to pick him up as a fleeing felon. What do you think? Do it that way, uh? Before he leaves and we can't find him. Then I get the extradition performed and I come and get him."

"That could take you a couple of weeks," Vincent said, "if you're lucky. Get the court down there and the one up here to agree. Meanwhile he's got a lawyer dragging his feet. It'll take you months. Even then you won't be sure of getting him."

"I don't know—but send me the picture, all right?"

"I've got an idea might be better," Vincent said. "Why don't I fly down with the picture?"

"Yes, wonderful."

"And bring Teddy along with it."

24

TEDDY'S MOM WOKE HIM UP to tell him she was taking Buddy to the pet shop to get his little beak shaved so he wouldn't hurt hisself. She said, "Were you 'sleep?"

"I was trying to. Jeez."

"I thought I smelled smoke a while ago. Were you burning something in the fireplace?"

"Just some old stuff I don't need no more. I cleaned out my drawers."

"Well, I'll be. You're a lazybones, but you've always been neat about your things."

" 'Ey, Mom—"

"Li'l sleepyhead," his Mom said, and left with Buddy in a cage.

No sooner the Chevy backed out of the drive and pulled away—peace at last—the front-door chimes rang. He was positive it was the cops, a couple of day-shift guys this time; they'd take him over to Northfield and go through the routine again. You were in Spade's casino last night? Yes sir, I was.

What time was that? I was at Bally's, the Claridge
and the Sands too. Who keeps track of time when
you're gambling and having fun? You win? I did all
right. They loved to hassle you. Put you in a lineup
with drunks and cops, lights in your eyes. He'd go
with them today and make a statement: I've an-
swered your questions. What you are doing now is
called harassment. Any further questions will have
to be directed at my attorney. That sounded good.

The front-door chimes kept ringing.

Have his mom get him a lawyer, not the court.
They didn't have anything on him anyway. They
couldn't.

The damn chimes, that double ding-dong re-
peated over and over and—shit—over until the irri-
tation of it pulled him out of bed in his black bikini
briefs to the front door for a peek through the peephole. Not three feet away from him on the porch
was a giant colored guy. He should have stopped to
think, kept quiet, but the sight of the guy startled
him and Teddy said, "What do you want?"

The giant colored guy said, "You, baby. Open
the door."

It wasn't the way a cop addressed you. Teddy
stepped over to the window, peeked through the
grillwork and saw the black limo parked in the
drive . . . Like the limo Iris had got in with those
people to go to the apartment. And there had been a
big colored guy in that party. Now he was good and

confused. If this was the giant colored guy his mom had talked to, where was the bearded guy who had used the bathroom? If the bearded guy was the Miami cop, Vincent, what was he doing with the spade from Spade's? Man, it was confusing.

Teddy ran through the hall to the kitchen and looked out back. Nobody in the yard. Now the giant colored guy was banging on the door, shaking the house almost, calling "Teddy? Open up, man. I'm a frien'." The dumbest thing he ever did was ask what the guy wanted. He wondered if he should call the real police. That would be something, wouldn't it? But decided, no, play a lone hand. Mr. Magic. Now you see him, now you don't. He got dressed fast and packed a canvas bag, a couple of knit shirts, undies, extra pair of jeans. He slipped on a pair of blue Nikes. The money Marie had given him was in his wallet. Shit, the camera case—he got it, hung it over his shoulder. What else?

He got one of his mom's VISA cards out of her dresser, then slipped quietly out the side door into the empty garage. Buddy would have to have his appointment today. If his mom was here she'd do something. He'd go through backyards to East Drive and up to Ventnor. Teddy opened the door to the yard and stuck his head out to look one way, across the back of the house, then the other . . .

The cop, Vincent, said, "Hi, Teddy, you all

packed?" Taking the bag and the camera case.
"Good."

Teddy had to go back inside and open the front
door. He watched the cop, Vincent, take the Colt
out of the camera case and hand it to the giant colored guy. He was even bigger close. The cop headed
through the living room then. Teddy knew where
he was going and couldn't help but call after him
" 'Ey, good luck."

Teddy began to hum George Thorogood's "Bad
to the Bone"; see if the giant colored guy knew it
and would say anything. But the giant colored guy
was studying the Colt automatic, looking it over
good. Teddy said, "Careful with that if you don't
know nothing about firearms."

The giant colored guy looked up, aimed the gun
right at him and said, "You remind me. I remember
seeing a cartoon, this poor little skinny bum is
standing behind this big heavy-set rich cat holding
a gun in his back? The little bum is saying to him,
'Stick 'em up, this is a water pistol, I mean a
holdup.' Little bum, you know he ain't ever gonna
make it. You remind me of him."

Teddy said, "Come on, don't fool around, 'ey?"

The cop, Vincent, came back in empty-handed,
of course. Teddy said, "Didn't find what you were
looking for? That's too bad."

"You got rid of everything," Vincent said.

"You mean the pictures? Oh, they got burnt up

in a fire. Yeah, all my PR memories. Like I wasn't even there."

"I'm glad I saved a couple," Vincent said, taking two prints out of his coat pocket to hold them up. "Didn't you miss them? Or'd you just burn everything without looking?"

Teddy said, " 'Ey, wait a minute . . ."

The cop was holding up the two shots of Isidro, the cab driver, and it didn't make any sense. What did the cab driver have to do with Iris, here? Was the cop trying to confuse him or what? Then the cop was saying he hoped he'd packed his resort clothes and Teddy said again, " 'Ey, wait a minute . . ."

Rosemary comes in his office with some letters for him to sign. She stops dead, can't believe her eyes. "Mr. Garbo, what are you doing up there?" And he says to her, "I'm tap-dancing on the fucking desk. What's it look like I'm doing?"

That was how the day began in his mind, Jackie getting out of bed. What should be one of the happiest days of his life: Frank Cingoro dead, Ricky Catalina in custody, the undesirables off his back. But his vibes were bothering him. Something was going on. He'd stayed at the hotel last night because he couldn't find the Moose; he'd called LaDonna at home three times this morning and got no answer. Now the narky-looking cop from Miami was sitting in his office and he was trying very hard to be cordial, in light of the guy's twelve grand deposited with the cashier.

"The Moose says I made a mistake. I should offer you an apology."

"No need to," Vincent said. "But there is something you could do for me."

Jackie's mind telling him, Get him a broad, get him tickets to the show, autographs, take him backstage . . . and said, "You've noticed the personally inscribed photographs I have here on the wall? Every one of 'em major showroom attractions." Jackie moved toward the display, pointing. "Like my very dear friend Lee, wearing the jacket there cost him a hundred and fifty grand. Or the inimitable Engelbert, right here. You name me somebody of their statue, as my pal Norm Crosby would say, and if the star you name isn't up on that wall—mister, I'll give you a brand-new hundred-dollar bill."

Vincent took a moment. He said, "Joe Cocker."

Jackie said, "Joe *Cocker?* You putting me on?" He looked over to see DeLeon standing in the doorway. "You decide to make an appearance?" Jackie shook his head. Look at him, going for the sofa. "Where'n the hell you been?"

"Doing chores, Mr. Garbo, sir."

"We're gonna have a talk, my friend, soon as I'm

through here." He turned to Vincent, sitting in a chair by the desk. "What's the guy's name again?"

"Joe Cocker."

"You got to be kidding." Jackie looked over at DeLeon. "You ever hear of him?"

"Yeah, Joe Cocker, man."

Now the Miami cop said, "He had a big hit, 'With a Little Help From My Friends.' You remind me of it. I don't know if we're exactly friends, but since I helped you out, you might say, I thought you might want to do something for me."

Jackie leaned on his desk and nodded, like he was giving it some thought. "You helped me out . . ." He checked with DeLeon. "You know what he's talking about?"

"Listen to the man," DeLeon said.

"He helped me out—is he kidding? Guy walks in, gets the management in an uproar, the Donovans, Dick and Jane at the fucking seashore, I can't turn around I'm tripping over one of 'em trying to fuck me up, the broad dying to. I got them on one side, I got La Cosa Nostra on the other, I got more people trying to dick me than if I turned tricks for a living—this guy says he helped me out."

"You not listening," DeLeon said, "you talking."

Jackie said, "Hey, Moose, you got nothing to do? Go polish the fucking car'r something. Jesus, the help you get these days, I'm telling you. I start out this morning I was feeling pretty good, my stomach, no heartburn, no indigestion . . ."

Vincent said, "That's because you missed the dinner with the Ching. You were pretty lucky."

"You think so, huh? I'll tell you something," Jackie said. "There're three things I attribute to what's made me a success in life. One, I don't worry about anything happened in the past I can't change. Two, I don't hold a grudge. Revenge is for losers, guys that got nothing else to do. And three, most important of all, I watch my ass so nothing unexpected comes up behind me. And the closer I watch it, my friend, the luckier I get."

DeLeon said, "Shit," with a grin. Which Jackie took to mean appreciation, until DeLeon said, "Was this gentleman here *saved* your ass."

Jackie said, "Oh, is that right? This gentleman, all I've seen this gentleman do is come in here, stumble around and almost knock over the whole shithouse. If that's called saving my ass . . ."

The Miami cop was looking at his watch.

"I don't want to hold you up," Jackie said, "you have to be somewhere."

"Pretty soon. I want to tell you," Vincent said, "you have a point. I went after the wrong guys and it could've got you in a lot of trouble . . . from what I understand of how things work here. I mean if it ever came out in testimony you've been operat-

ing outside the casino. Like for that Colombian
gent. Also your associations with Frank Cingoro
and the wise guys. But so far it's turned out in your
favor. Good, you might say, has come of it. Frank's
dead and Ricky should get twenty-five years . . .
unless he cops and makes a deal, tells 'em things
they'd like to hear. So what my stumbling around
did, when you look at it, get all the facts, was put
you in the clear. Not all the way, but you won't be
getting it from both sides now. That ought to be
worth something to you."

Jackie said to DeLeon. "You hear this guy?"

"Man saying you owe him something."

Jackie looked at Vincent again. What would a
thirty-grand-a-year cop go for? Cop on the take
who comes here, wants to be treated like a high
roller? "What would you like, a six-foot showgirl?
Or how 'bout a broad with hair under her arms and
a mustache? More like what you're used to. Name
it, my friend."

"All I'd like you to do," Vincent said, "is fly
three of us down to San Juan in the company plane.
Maybe four, but no more than that. You won't have
to serve us lunch or anything. Couple of drinks,
that's all. How's that sound?"

Jackie said to DeLeon, "You hear this guy?"

"Ask him what happens you don't do it."

"You think I should?"

"Might be interesting."

"Don't think of it as what happens if you don't," Vincent said. "Be positive. Think of it as insurance. You'll be doing it so nobody'll testify against you before the Control Commission. Tell about all the deals you've been into and you lose your license. Yeah, what it is, it's license insurance."

"Wait," Jackie said. He touched his ear. "Hum it for me again, that's a familiar tune. I think it's the same one you played yesterday. Yeah. What's changed? You're still trying to shake me down, for Christ sake. I knew you were on the fucking take the minute you walked in. You still are."

"No, it's different now," Vincent said. "I got a witness that can put the stuff all over you."

"This should be interesting," Jackie said, "Who?"

"Him," Vincent said, hooking a thumb toward DeLeon on the sofa. "Now get the plane gassed up."

He had to watch Jackie switch roles, from tough guy to tragic figure, the little casino manager sinking into his high-backed chair, lost, staring with a pained expression at DeLeon.

"No, not the Moose, I don't believe it. You're not gonna tell me after all we been through, these many years, you'd all of a sudden betray me."

DeLeon said, "Be*tray* you?"

"That's what he said. I heard him," Vincent said, looking at Jackie behind his big desk, not as entertaining in his new role. Vincent said to him, "We're using leverage on you, Jackie, that's all. You're sitting in a spot where you don't want to make a lot of noise. You want things to quietly pass over. So what you do, you call the airport and make arrangements. Okay? Think of your secrets of success. You don't worry about anything you can't change or waste time thinking about getting even. Those are good ones. As for watching your ass, well, so you missed one. You're still lucky."

"*Him,*" Jackie said, extending his arm to point at DeLeon, showing them a gold cuff link. "My betrayer."

"Man likes that word," DeLeon said.

Vincent said to Jackie, "Look, you don't want to think ill of DeLeon, okay, I'll use Ricky. I can arrange for Ricky to tell stories about you thinking he's gonna get a plea deal. Which he won't, but the cops would find out about you and they'd tell Gaming Enforcement—you know how cops are, like to help each other—and there you are. So what's the difference? We're talking about leverage."

"Prick," Jackie said.

"He's feeling better," Vincent said to DeLeon. Then turned to Jackie again. "But what this is all about, what you tend to lose sight of because of your personal problems, is Iris. You remember Iris?"

"I never made her do a thing she didn't want to," Jackie said. "She knew exactly what the deal was."

"All I asked was, do you remember Iris?"

Jackie paused. "Yeah, I remember her. So? What do you want me to say?"

Vincent thought about it, looking at Jackie behind his executive desk; Jackie, if he was thinking about her at all, remembering some little broad who'd worked for him at one time.

"Maybe you better not say anything," Vincent said.

A quarter to twelve Vincent came away from the cashier's window with the twelve thousand dollars in the blue canvas bag. Somebody's twelve thousand; he was still reasoning his right to it. If he couldn't return it to Ricky and if he felt no obligation to give it to the State of New Jersey, who was left? He had never pocketed a dime of confiscated money or accepted a bribe in his life. When he had lunch at Wolfie's on Collins Avenue he went along with them charging him only half price. But he tipped on the full amount. He was an honest cop and this was a unique situation. He could tell himself he was using the twelve grand in the line of duty, sort of.

From the casino, Vincent cut through the lounge toward the lobby. He noticed Tommy Donovan behind the bar talking to the barman. It caused Vincent to hesitate. He thought, why not? And walked over to the bar to stand a couple of stools away. Tommy was talking very intently about something. The barman saw Vincent, but didn't want to interrupt his boss. Finally he said something and Tommy turned as the barman came over.

"A draft," Vincent said.

Now Tommy stepped over extending his hand. "Tommy Donovan. How are you this morning?"

"Not too bad," Vincent said.

"I was just saying to Eddie, I don't think I've ever seen a blue mixed drink. Have you?"

"I don't think so," Vincent said. "I don't think I'd want to either. Drinks should be sort of a gold color. Amber. Some are no color at all, they're okay. But I prefer the amber ones."

"You're my kind a guy," Tommy said. "What'll you have? It's on the house."

The barman placed the beer in front of him. "This's fine," Vincent said. "I never drink hard stuff till the evening or I'm finished work."

"I don't either," Tommy said. "I think I'll have

one with you." He looked at the barman who moved off to draw another. "You have to be careful, especially mixing business with pleasure here. On the one hand I have to socialize. On the other I have to know what's going on. You understand my position."

Vincent said, "Are you *the* Tommy Donovan?"

"Well, I'm the only one around here, anyway."

"You own the place."

"I work at it."

"Behind the bar?"

"I know what's going on in every area of this operation. To me, the bar is as important as the casino. I don't want to see any skimping on drinks or indifference to patrons. Eddie here"—the barman placed a draft beer in front of Tommy—"we were just discussing different kinds of drinks, seeing if we could come up with a new one, something unusual."

"It must be interesting work," Vincent said, "running a place like this."

"Well, it keeps you out of trouble." Tommy drank off part of his beer and touched a napkin to his mouth. "You just come in?"

"No, I'm checking out."

"I'm sorry to hear that. How'd you do?"

"Not bad. I got what I came for." Vincent raised the canvas bag, placed it on the bar and zipped it open. "Take a look."

Tommy leaned close in the timeless semidark. He said, "Jesus Christ, I hope you didn't win all that here. On the other hand if you did, well, that's how it goes. How much you win?"

"Twelve grand."

"Well, yeah, you know I thought you looked familiar."

"You comped me," Vincent said.

"Sure, I remember. You were pointed out to me."

"I'm on my way now to San Juan. Try my luck there."

"Well, hey, you're gonna stay at Spade's, aren't you? I insist. Sure, we'll comp you exactly the same as you got here. It's on the computer, we just punch it down there." Tommy grinned. "Give us a chance to get even. Yeah, your face is very familiar, I just haven't been able to put a name to it."

"Vincent Mora."

Tommy began to nod. "That's right, sure. Mora, you came down from Boston, didn't you?"

"I came up from Miami."

"Yeah Miami. Listen, I got a tell you, I have a little trouble with names, Vinnie. But faces, I never forget a face. Actually, once I have a drink with a guest I never forget his name either. Next time I see you I'll know. Vinnie Mora, from Boston."

Tommy, Jackie, Ricky, Teddy, Eddie . . . Vinnie. It was time to get out of here. Vincent finished his beer, offered his hand. "It was a pleasure, Tommy."

He stared away from the bar and looked back. "Hey, and say hi to your wife for me."

Vincent left him standing there.

He eased down to sit on the edge of the bed, not wanting to wake her, not yet; but saw her eyes open in the moment before he kissed her and felt her arms come around him and strain to hold him, keep him here. Linda said, "I'm not going to let you go."

"Come with me." Raising up on his arms to look at her.

She didn't say anything. Their eyes held in the dim light, the bedroom draperies closed, her eyes changing now. It wasn't the look he wanted to take with him. There were good ones he already had stored away. This one was solemn, almost sad; it meant she cared about him, but it was not the one he would look at when he thought of her. He said, "I wouldn't ask you to leave your job."

"My gig." Trying to smile.

"Chiquita Banana. You are some entertainer."

She said, "I don't have a name for you, not yet. But I'll think of one." She said, "You have to go, don't you?"

"DeLeon's putting Teddy in the car, the limo. You might as well use mine as long as you're here. It's on a card and I'm rich. Right? The keys are on the desk . . . They'll probably ask you to leave . . ."

"I'll get a place. Don't worry." Looking at him with sad eyes again. She said, "Vincent?" and hesitated.

"What?"

"Is it going to work? What you're doing?"

He felt she was going to say something else and changed her mind. "It has to. I don't see any other way."

She said, "Vincent?"

Her hands moved over his shoulders, bringing him to her. They held onto each other as long as they could, until he whispered to her, "I have to go."

She missed him with the sound of the door closing, in the silence now. She saw him in darkness in his white jockeys holding the gun upright against his shoulder and saw him—looking out the window of Room 310 of the Holmhurst—in the street light, out in the cold mist in his skivvies. He had never told her what the man coming out of the hotel said, the drunk, seeing him like that. They had made love. A man fired shots into their room and they made love after, under the covers, the room cold because of the broken window. He had not told her what the man said and there were things she hadn't told him. They should have told each other things. Maybe they didn't have to, but there were things that were good to hear. She got up and went into the living room.

The car keys were on the desk, lying on a hotel envelope addressed to CHIQUITA. Inside were twenty one-hundred dollar bills and a note that said:

Dear Chiquita,

This is scale, the going rate for getting shot at and being part of all this. I hope it is only the first part and we will have a lot more parts to come, but I have to leave it up to you. I'll be at Spade's Isla Verde. Maybe even comped.

Vincent the Avenger

Vincent came off the elevator, hesitated and turned left toward the casino instead of the other way, into the lobby. Twelve-thirty in the afternoon the room was alive with players, with flashing lights and bells going off. He was beginning to feel at home here. He dropped a quarter into the first free slot machine he came to and pulled down on the handle. The drum, illustrated with bars, cherries, bells and oranges, rolled, jolted to a stop. Nothing. He dropped in another quarter, pulled the handle down, watched the drum spin and stop. Silence. He slipped his last quarter into the machine, yanked on the handle and walked away, indifferent, but ready to hunch his shoulders against the sound of clanging coins, jackpot bells . . .

Well, there were all kinds of ways to gamble in San Juan.

25

MODESTA MANOSDUROS, ISIDRO'S WIFE, told them she could describe the man, yes, and identify him if she saw him. An American with light hair, a narrow nose, skin so pale you could see his bones and the color of his veins . . . They told her to wait please, not yet. They brought her into the dark end of a room where five men stood at the other end with lights shining on them. They asked her if she saw the man she believed had been with her husband. She said, yes, that one, and pointed to Teddy Magyk. They dismissed the five men and asked her where she had seen this man before.

"I never saw him the way you think," Modesta said.

The policemen looked at each other. "Then how can you identify him?"

"I don't see him with my eyes." She touched her forehead with one finger. "I see him here."

They brought her into another room, an office,

asked her to please sit down and showed her a photograph.

"My husband when he visited El Yunque with the American."

"Have you seen this picture before?"

"No, never."

"How do you know this is El Yunque?"

"I know El Yunque."

"Did you know your husband was going there with the man you identified?"

"I know he did," the woman said, "because this is my husband and this is El Yunque."

The policemen looked at each other again. They asked her to remain seated in a chair that was uncomfortable and gave her coffee that was weak, like water. After talking to them for more than an hour, repeating everything Isidro had said to her about the man who was his prize, she was hungry and told them she wanted to go home.

An American who wore a beard offered to drive her in his car from Hato Rey to her house in Puerta de Tierra. He told her his name and said he was sorry about her husband. He drove slowly, making other cars blow their horns and pass them. Her husband's car, when he owned it, was much larger and more comfortable. This car, the road was right there in front of them and the seat was small. She was thinking of her husband's Chevrolet, which she had sold for 2,500 dollars, when the American asked her if she had enough money to live.

She looked at him now, to see into his bearded face, and told him yes, she had money. She had bought a color television and new clothes for the children.

He drove so slow . . .

"Why did you tell your husband to be careful of that man, Teddy?"

"Because he's call Mr. Magic."

"That's only his name."

"Yes, what he is."

"But he isn't magic, it's his name. It sounds like magic."

Yes, well? She said, "Let me ask you what you think they are going to do to him?"

"They'll take him to Superior Court and put him on trial for murder."

"Yes?"

"As soon as the district attorney has proof to show in court."

"Yes?"

"And then, well, I think they'll send him to Oso Blanco for life."

"Tha's what you think?"

She was wrong. This one didn't know any more than the policemen. She was disappointed. But he was rich, he gave her money when they stopped in front of the house. Five one hundred-dollar bills and then five more when the children came out to see the car. He was generous, kind to her; so she said, "I'll tell you something. You don't think he's magic?"

He shook his head at her. "No."

"Then why are they going to let him go free?"

This time the Criminal Affairs investigators having lunch at El Cidreño would look over at the table—see, the same one, with the beard, still on medical leave but without his cane—and know what he was discussing with Lorendo Paz. Lorendo looking immaculate, as usual, and the bearded guy looking the same as before. Some of the investigators were discussing the same thing as Lorendo and the American detective: the fact that Teddy Magyk had killed the taxi driver, there was little doubt of it, but would be walking up Franklin Delano Roosevelt Avenue by six o'clock this evening. "We had him, on the Loíza ferry," Herbey Maldonado told the man seated at the table with him, "and we let him go." The American detective, look, had hardly touched his dinner. "I know how he feels," Herbey said. The American detective was drinking whiskey and smoking cigarettes today.

*   *   *

"You have to understand the influence of the district attorney in our system, in our preparing a case."

"The clout," Vincent said.

"Yes, the clout; that's good."

"He doesn't want to try a case if there's a chance he might lose."

Lorendo shook his head. "No, he doesn't want to see a defendant get off on a technicality, so he makes himself very objective looking at evidence. He doesn't try this guy he'll try somebody else, what's the difference? This one, he sees more holes the guy can use to walk out than ways to keep him in . . . Come on, you know what I'm talking about. What else is new, man? . . . Even if we can show he took the picture, yes, at a place directly above where the body was found, how do we prove it was taken the day of the murder? What day was the murder? There's no date on the print. The Fast Foto place, they say maybe they have his name somewhere, they'll look. But it won't prove nothing anyway. Okay, witnesses that can put Teddy with Isidro—"

"Me," Vincent said.

"I have you. You saw them at a beach, not on a mountain. I have a doorman at the DuPont Plaza, he maybe saw them together once or twice. The only person I have who can positively identify Teddy is the victim's wife, and she never saw the guy before today. You like to hear her testify?"

"She knows he's getting off."

"We should know it too, right away. Why didn't we?"

Vincent didn't answer.

"You say he bought a handcarved parrot at the rain forest gift shop and gave it to Iris. Oh, he did? What day?"

"Teddy's gun," Vincent said.

"We say is the murder weapon," Lorendo said, "but we don't find any bullets in the victim. Shot twice, only one exit wound, I thought we would have a slug for comparison." Lorendo shook his head. "He was badly decomposed, two weeks or more out there, some of him eaten by animals. I don't know what happen to it. But it's the only chance we got to prove anything, if we find that slug. So I'm sending a crew out there again, have them go over the ground with their toothbrushes."

"Can you hold him in the meantime? Lock him up?"

"No way. I can't even hold him for the gun. You brought it, he didn't. His lawyer would say, who are you? You have no jurisdiction. Teddy says it's not his gun, he never saw it before, so . . . All I can do, tell him he can't leave Puerto Rico until we finish the investigation. Put some men at the airport to make sure. Then stretch it out, uh? Maybe think of some other way. I don't know, Vincent, it look good when we looked at it. We should know better, not get excited too early."

"He did it," Vincent said.

"You don't have to tell me, I believe it. But we both been here before."

"Too many times," Vincent said.

"You had the feeling he wouldn't be extradited, you said so. You had a feeling all along. So you bring him, maybe we'll run him through, shut the door on him."

"Maybe," Vincent said.

"But it doesn't work like that, here or Miami or Atlantic City, it's the same, the bad guys have the advantage. I ask him if he like to plead. You know what he said?"

"I know he's killed three people in the past three weeks," Vincent said.

"Yes."

They sipped their drinks, a silence between them within the clatter and voices in the restaurant. Lorendo looked over at a table and back to Vincent.

"You know Herbey Maldonado . . ."

"On the Loíza ferry."

"Yes. Herbey says take him out there again and don't bring him back. Is he kidding or not? Some of these guys—you know them yourself in Miami, they wouldn't think twice about it, and they're good guys."

Vincent didn't say anything.

"I hope," Lorendo said, "you don't have something like that in your mind. Not you, Vincent. Okay?"

Vincent didn't say anything.

"Come on—you worry me. Please. Where are you?"

Here but not here. His dinner barely touched. Cigarette stubs in the tin ashtray. He raised his eyes to Lorendo.

"Never worry about anything that's already done or you have no control over."

"I believe that too, yes."

"Never seek revenge . . ."

"Don't even think about it, no."

"It's for losers . . ."

"Yes, because they can't win."

"But that's what this is all about. He wants to pay me back. The cab driver learned something and he killed him. He killed Iris to bring me up there. He killed and raped a woman because he needed money or that's what he likes to do and before that he did try to kill me."

"Because you sent him to prison."

"Because he's crazy. Because he has nothing better to do. Who knows? I think I'll ask him and find out. Have a talk with him."

"Vincent . . ."

Again there was a silence between them, within the sounds of the restaurant.

"Let's wait and see what we find," Lorendo said.

"It would be self-defense."

"No, it wouldn't," Lorendo said. "Not the way you're thinking."

He drove out of that downtown Hato Rey business world to the tourist world of beaches and high-rise hotels, to Isla Verde and the resort that resembled a mosque.

"I go in there," DeLeon said, "I feel I should have a prayer rug with me. You know what I'm saying? Kneel down in the lobby facing Mecca, which would be . . . that way."

"That's Miami," Vincent said.

"Well, then over there somewhere. Where I used to live it was a hop to Mecca, though I never went there. Right here, this could be Egypt, except there're toilets."

Vincent sat sideways on a plastic lounge chair facing DeLeon stretched out on one, dark brown and white in white bathing trunks, looking toward the spade-shaped dome of the gambling casino. There were few people still at the pool. The sun, nearly through for the day, laid a flat light on the cement and on the ocean beyond the beach. They would talk about Teddy, leave him and come back, always with something to say.

"It's a bitch, ain't it?"

"He's getting smirky," Vincent said.

"Acting up?"

Teddy had told the cops if they were going to make him stay here against his will they'd have to pay his hotel expenses. So the cops offered him an apartment that was in a tenement behind police headquarters, all the people living there on food stamps. Teddy looked at it—Vincent was told—held his nose and had them drive him to the DuPont Plaza; he'd use a card.

"He's gonna sue us," DeLeon said.

"He might."

"Should bring him out here," DeLeon said.

"I was thinking of that. How to work it."

"See if we can figure some accident might happen to him. Trip and fall down an elevator shaft."

They had arrived two days ago in the late afternoon and handed Teddy over to Lorendo Paz at the airport. DeLeon had introduced Vincent at Spade's Isla Verde as a special guest—"Check the computer, man"—and here they were, until the computer told the manager to throw them out.

"Kidnappers Incorporated," DeLeon said, "resting up between gigs, hoping to shit they don't get arrested just yet. What's the man's name, Herbie?"

"Herbey."

"I think he's got the idea. One of those boys, they prob'ly do it for you. Take the motherfucker deep in the woods, man, lose his ass."

"That's not bad," Vincent said. "If I knew where I was going—that's an idea."

"Be too easy just shoot him." DeLeon raised up on his elbow to look at Vincent closely. "You know what you saying to me? You want to kill him, but you want to do it a way you can tell yourself you didn't. What kind a shit is that?"

"I don't want to kill him."

"Mean you don't want to come out and say it."

"No. I've done it." Vincent shaking his head back and forth. "I didn't want to and I don't want to do it again. I mean it."

"I respect you, man, but what you doing you running a game on yourself."

"Uh-unh, I did not want to shoot the guy."

"I'm not referring to that one, I mean here, right now. I think, as you see it, you want Teddy to do it, expose himself, make a move on you. Then you can shoot his ass off not wanting to, swear to it, but still shoot his ass off."

"I've thought of that."

"But you make it hard on yourself, don't you? Got to do it by some book. I never been this close to a good policeman, see how he thinks. You people strap guns, I always believe you like to use them. You don't, what other way you see is there?"

"Scare him enough," Vincent said.

There it was, the Mora theory of saving lives, and Buck Torres asks how you were supposed to know when it was working or not, in that moment before you shoot and save your own life or don't shoot and maybe lose it.

"Get him scared enough to quit. Maybe even confess."

DeLeon said, "You serious?" He said, "Shit. How you gonna scare him? Police up there, police down here, they try all kinds of ways to nail his ass and they can't do it. Man must believe by now he's got fairy dust on him. Isn't *nothing* can touch him."

"Mr. Magic," Vincent said.

"He don't look like but a reject, but he must have something going for him. Little homicidal mother-fucker. The sneaky ones, man, are the worst."

Vincent asked him what he was doing this eve-ning. DeLeon said going to Old San Juan and do loop-the-loops. Vincent asked him if he'd make a stop on the way. "I'd like you to meet Modesta, the cab driver's wife. See what you think."

"Love to," DeLeon said. "She a cute woman?"

Well, for a little round two-hundred-pounder smelling of laundry, her dress barely reaching her knees because of her size. Skinny legs with strange knots on her shins. A black-black African black woman, a silhouette in the doorway looking out to the street. She said, "Come. Please."

It was a relief to turn around and go back outside, get out of the hot-grease smell of the place and the noise: the washing machine working, the electric fan blowing hot air, the television turned way up. Her kids were watching "Love Connection," wanting to see if the young lady contestant had picked the computer programmer dude, the bartender dude or the car salesman . . .

Or none of them, DeLeon thinking, following Vincent and the woman outside into light once more, across the hardpack junky yard to the street, the woman saying, "I understan' it now."

"What's that?" Vincent asked her.

"I dream of riding in a carriage without no horses, a black one," she said, approaching DeLeon's limousine. "I sit in it as you speak to me. If you would turn on the radio music, please, and the air condition . . ."

DeLeon looked at Vincent who gave him a look in return as she waved to neighbors and got in the back seat, Vincent following her in. She rolled the window down and waved some more as Vincent asked her how she knew Teddy was going to be released. She stopped waving and seemed surprised at the question.

"Because he's Mr. Magic. I told you that."

"That's why he's free. But how did you know it? How did it come to you? In a dream?"

"I come in my head. Also the police tell me."

Vincent said, "Oh."

DeLeon, half-turned behind the wheel, taking all this in, saw Vincent look at him—no expression but disappointed. What did the man expect? Vincent must have been hopeful though. He said to the woman then, "Do you know what's going to happen to him now? I mean now that he's free?"

"I don' know that unless I see him." The woman raised a hand to her neighbors. "If I see him, maybe I can tell you. I don't know." She turned from the window to look closely at Vincent. "But be careful of him."

When Vincent looked at him again and nodded, DeLeon picked up the blue canvas bag from the front seat and handed it back to him. He watched Vincent take out the stainless steel urn.

"Do you know what this is?"

The woman reached out to touch the urn with the tips of her fingers. She began to stroke it, gently. DeLeon saw her eyes close.

She said, "I see a girl . . . falling from the sky."

DeLeon felt chills and thrills and saw Vincent's eyes, alive, come at him again.

*   *   *

The house was in the same neighborhood where Iris had lived, an upstairs flat like hers with paint peeling from the shutters and dirty walls. A weak light was on in the ceiling of the living room where two women and a skinny PR guy in an undershirt were watching "Love Connection." One of Teddy's favorite programs.

Teddy was in the kitchen doing business with another skinny PR guy who wore a snappy little straw down on his eyes and a dirty T-shirt. The kitchen was separated from the living room by a counter, so Teddy could hear "Love Connection" even when he wasn't looking at it. At the same time he was telling the PR guy in the kitchen no, he couldn't use a whole baggie, all he needed were a few joints. When the PR guy heard this he acted impatient, like Teddy was wasting his time.

He had given a busboy at the DuPont Plaza ten bucks to recommend this house. Get anything you want there. Anything? Anything.

Teddy believed the girl was nuts to have picked the car salesman, a show-off type with long sideburns in this day and age. They'd had their date and were now telling Chuck Woolery, the "Love Connection" host, all about it. How the car salesman'd had car trouble, Jesus, and was two hours late to start with. Then had taken the girl to a Japanese place where the girl said she was totally turned off by all that yukky stuff. The audience liked it when she said raw fish and hot wine were not her cup of tea. Then Chuck Woolery gave the audience his innocent look and asked the asshole car salesman if the evening got any better, if there was any romance. The asshole car salesman, backstage, but on a screen there on the show, said, well, he had given her a pretty good kiss goodnight . . .

As Teddy was saying to the PR guy in the snappy straw, "See, I don't know how long I'm gonna be here. Maybe just a couple days and I can't take weed home on the plane with me. Can I? Why don't you roll me five joints? I bet you roll 'em they're like tailor-made." The PR guy got out a shoebox . . .

Teddy could see himself on that program talking to Chuck Woolery. Chuck asking if the date was a success and him saying, well, she didn't go for the raw fish too much, Chuck, but she sure raved when I put the meat to her. See what old Chuck'd say to that.

The women and the skinny PR guy in the living room were discussing the date in Spanish, arguing, yelling at each other. While the PR with the snappy straw had his shoebox open and was showing him other products would be good for a short stay. Cocaine, percs, ludes . . . It was time to make his move. What he'd come for.

Teddy looked up from the box and said, "No, I

don't think so. I'll tell you what, though." He took 200 dollars worth of folded twenties out of his pocket and got set to peel them off one at a time. "I bet you got a gun you could sell me. A *pistola*. Am I right or wrong?"

26

VINCENT WALKED PAST the open-air front of the restaurant, along the boxed hedge. The blue canvas bag hung from his shoulder. He spotted Teddy right away. Teddy wearing a red knit shirt, in there among the hanging plants and green oilcloth-covered tables. Tourist with camera case, head lowered, ordering a late breakfast from the placemat menu. Vincent continued along Ashford Avenue to Walgreen's and dialed the number DeLeon had given him.

"This better be important."

"I wonder if you'd do me a favor."

"Your house could be on fire, but I'd never tell from your voice, would I?"

"Pick up the cab driver's wife and drop her off at Consulado. You know where it is?"

"Everybody knows where Consulado is."

"Teddy's there."

"Hmmm, I like to see that."

"Better hang back. We don't want to gang up on him."

"Just shake him some if you can. Scare him?"

"You never know."

"You don't know what you interrupted here."

"You have to rest sometime."

"I do?"

Teddy was eating pancakes with one hand, holding onto his plastic glass of Coke with the other. Vincent wasn't sure if he could watch him: Teddy cutting a big wedge out of the stack, shoving it into his wide-open mouth, then taking a sip of the Coke before he began to chew. Vincent sat down at the table-for-four across the aisle, hung the canvas bag from the back of his chair.

Teddy, hunched over his plate, turned his head to look past his shoulder. " 'Ey, we got a stop meeting like this."

Was he honestly off the wall or pretending to be? Playing the nerd. Eyes with a watery glaze this morning. Hungover? Maybe. He didn't seem on guard or the least concerned. Vincent could be someone from back home . . . An old pal thinking how simple it would be reach into the back of his pants beneath his jacket, pull out the old Smith and put him away. One shot. There. Tell the waitress, let's see, I think I'll have the eggs over easy.

"What're you following me for? It won't do you no good."

"I'm not following you."

"What've you been doing all morning? I saw you go by here."

"You used to follow me," Vincent said, "take pictures . . . What were the pictures for? You mind if I ask you?"

"What've you got, a wire on you?"

"Come on, you're off the hook, you know it. I'm not trying anything. I'm curious, that's all."

"Why'd I take pictures? I'll tell you," Teddy said, his mouth full. He paused to take a drink of Coke, work his tongue around in his mouth. "I wanted to look at your face."

"Why?"

"See how you look at people." Teddy squared around to face Vincent directly. "See if you look at them the same way you look at me."

"How do I look at you? I don't understand what you mean."

"Tough shit. That's all I'm saying on that particular subject at this time. It may come up again, but we don't know for sure or when . . . Now you want to talk, it looks like. On the airplane, when you were so sure my ass was going to jail, you didn't have a word to say, did you? No, you and that big jigaboo sat there laughing with each other—oh boy, are we having fun, taking Mr. Magic to jail. I thought sure you'd want to ask me some questions then."

"Can I be honest with you?" Vincent said.

"Well, please do."

"I was afraid if you said anything I might open the door and throw you right out of the fucking plane. But I got over that."

Teddy moved his shoulders, acting cute. "Oh, you're not mad at me no more?"

"What can I do?" Vincent said. "I've been a policeman fifteen years. I know when I bring the state attorney, the prosecutor, evidence and he says it's not enough, okay, that's it. I'm not gonna go around the law just because I think the guy's guilty."

"What about getting me out on that ferry? That wasn't nice."

"Well, that was different. I was trying to keep you from doing something dumb. You know what I mean? I was trying to scare you, get you thinking straight."

"I got lost," Teddy said, "took me two hours, easy, get back to the hotel. First those two PRs take me out there, not knowing where'n the hell I am. Then you step out of that other car . . . You think I wasn't scared?"

"But not enough," Vincent said. He eased back

in his chair, looking down at the placemat menu. "Well, it doesn't matter now anyway, does it?"

"What doesn't matter?"

"I thought you could take a fall on any of three homicides, no problem. But, I was wrong."

"Wait a minute. What three?"

"The cab driver—I know you did him. But that's neither here nor there. The woman and Iris."

"What woman?"

"The one underneath the Boardwalk. Beaten to death, raped. That sounds like our Teddy."

"Her name was Marie, I believe."

"Anna Marie Hoffman."

"Yeah? That her name?"

"And there was Iris. But I don't think now you did Iris."

"Yeah? Why not?"

"I think it was some other creep. You're not the only creep in the world, Ted. There could be millions."

Teddy said, "Is that right?" Face drawn tight as he picked up his camera case from the table and came over. "You think it was some creep, 'ey?" He pulled the chair out across from Vincent and sat down, the camera case in his lap now, looking right at Vincent, Vincent lying back, waiting, Vincent very happy with the way it was going. "I hear she did a double back flip off that balcony," Teddy said. "I hear it wasn't a bad dive, but she only scored an eight-point-five. You know why? She didn't keep her feet together."

Vincent had to wait a moment. He picked up his glass of water and took a sip. He had to let himself ease back down.

"I understand she didn't scream," Vincent said. "I wonder why."

Teddy shrugged his shoulders, staring at Vincent. "Maybe she was dead or close to it. Can't they tell things like that? Do some tests?"

"It takes time," Vincent said.

"Or maybe she was on something, you know, like ludes, and had passed out."

"Iris didn't do that kind of stuff."

"She didn't? Maybe somebody talked her into it. Take that bitchy edge off her. But maybe she was worn out and it got to her quick. You know? Can't you figure things out? Speculate on it? Hell, I'm the one ought a be the dick. I'll tell you something though. You can keep surveillance. I don't want any parts of surveillance work. Other than following some stove-up cripple walks with a cane." Teddy grinned. "That's different."

"What about the woman?"

"Who, Marie?"

"Yeah, what happened to her?"

"What *ha*ppened? She got taken, it looks like.

That kind of talkative woman, she picks up with a friendly stranger and she happens to have something he wants, there you are."

"Like financial assistance."

"Could be."

"But why rape her?"

"Why did he . . . do what he did to her? I don't know. Maybe it seemed like a good idea. Maybe she wanted him to."

"She was already dead."

"Well, a woman like her can't be too choosy as to *when* she gets it. You know what I mean? I bet she hadn't had any dick in years and years. Judging from the type of woman she was and her age. Old women don't get a lot a dick. You don't know—she might a died with a smile on her face knowing it was coming."

Vincent had to wait a few moments. "You think so?"

"I understand it was dark under there. Who knows, 'ey? You think you know things and you get in trouble. You think I popped that cab driver and shoved him over the cliff, so you haul my ass down here . . . Well, least it was a free ride and I don't mind being back. I think somebody ought a pay my hotel though. I mean it's not my fault I'm here."

"It's never your fault," Vincent said. "You're probably sick, but you still know what you're doing. You're a weird fucking guy, Teddy. I've never met anybody like you before in my life."

"You better believe it," Teddy said and grinned. "You're finding out the hard way they don't call me Mr. Magic for nothing."

"Who's *they?* I never heard anybody call you that."

"Guys."

"What guys? Guys at Raiford? All the winners? I wouldn't call doing time exactly a magic act."

"I got along fine."

"And came out with some great ideas."

Teddy squinted at him. "I can see that look again, man. There it is. Like you think you know something."

"I know you ought to be taken off the street."

"Don't look away—look at me!"

He wanted to—Teddy was coming out, exposing himself—but Vincent's gaze had moved beyond Teddy to pick up the round black woman in a shiny print, shades of red, coming through the opening in the hedge; the cab driver's wife out of Africa looking around the open-air restaurant now, a big straw sunhat shading her face, worn over a red bandana.

Vincent did look at Teddy for a moment, at wide-open eyes with worry in them, something wrong, Teddy's expression not matching his tone sounding mean, telling Vincent, "You don't know shit, but you're talking about me, arn'cha? Saying things that aren't true." Calling Vincent dumb and stupid, telling Vincent, "Look at me with your eyes!" And then, "Where you going?"

Vincent said, "I want you to meet somebody," rising as the round black woman in the shiny print, the big straw hat, came to the table.

Vincent helped her into a chair saying their names, Modesta Manosduros . . . Teddy Magyk. A waitress came to pour water and Vincent watched Teddy looking the woman over without looking directly at her. Teddy sitting straight, his hands on his camera case. The waitress left them and Teddy eased back in his metal chair, picked up his glass of water, starting to grin and trying not to—his old self again.

"This your date?" Getting a smirky look.

"Isidro's wife," Vincent said.

"I know him," the woman said. "Is the one kill my husband."

Teddy kept his eyes straight ahead, on Vincent. "She never saw me before in her life."

"You still the one kill my husband." She looked at Vincent and he nodded.

"You told your husband to be careful of him."

"Yes, but he don' listen to me."

"You told me to be careful, too."

"So maybe you listen and nothing happen to you."

"You two have fun," Teddy said, "I'm leaving." He gripped his camera case, put a hand on the arm of his chair.

"Look at him," Vincent said. "Take a good look."

"Yes?" the woman said.

"Is he magic?"

"Mr. Magic," the woman said. "No police can catch him."

Teddy grinned at Vincent. "You hear that?"

"What do you see? What's gonna happen to him?"

"To Mr. Magic?"

Vincent nodded. "Look at him and tell me what you see." He watched Teddy waiting now, Teddy getting that smirky expression again.

"Is hard to see him," the woman said, half-closing her eyes.

"Now you see me," Teddy said, "now you don't."

"He is inside something," the woman said, raising her hands to hold them a few inches apart. "But is only this big." She held the palm of one hand about a foot above the table. "And, I believe, this high. Like an *olla*. You say a pot, or a pitcher?" She closed her eyes. "I see him but I don't see him."

"The hell she talking about?" Teddy said.

Vincent was reaching around for the blue canvas bag hanging from his chair, Teddy watching him. Vincent placed the bag on his lap, zipped it open and brought out the stainless steel urn. "Is it like this, what you see him in?"

"Yes, like that," the woman said. "That thing, made of metal."

"You're sure," Vincent said, placing the urn carefully in the middle of the table, seeing Teddy's frown as he studied it. The woman said, yes, it was the same thing. Teddy looked up.

"You mind my asking what you got in there?"

"Iris," Vincent said.

"Jesus Christ," Teddy said, "you're kidding me," staring at the urn again, his expression changing as he relaxed and seemed to grin. "No shit, Iris is in there? What, her ashes?"

"All that's left of her."

"Jesus. I never saw one of those before. Did you look in it? 'Ey, I wouldn't mind, if you can get it open."

Vincent said, "You're a creepy guy, Ted."

Teddy said, "Yeah? Well, so are you. Carrying that thing around."

"I'm taking it to her family in Mayaguez," Vincent said, "unless you want to. You could tell them Iris's last words."

"Boy, you're really funny." Teddy lifted his camera case onto the table. "This whole setup—trying to mess with my head, like this's the voodoo woman and she can see into the future. I know you told her what to say. You're dumber and stupider'n I even thought, try and pull this kind a shit. You got to realize it man, you're dealing with Mr. Magic."

"I see you—" Modesta began.

But Teddy, getting up, cut her off. "Not if I see you first, Mama."

Vincent said, "Wait, listen to her."

"She ain't through her routine yet?"

"I see him with a woman," Modesta said.

Teddy paused. "Well, that ain't all bad."

Vincent was watching the black woman's face, her eyes closed in the shade of the sunhat.

"I see him dancing, it look like. Close to somebody."

"Yeah? Then what happens?"

"You run away."

"You don't see me or her in the sack?"

"I don't see you no more. You gone."

"That's fine with me." Teddy slung the camera case over his shoulder and looked at Vincent. "Now you see me, now you don't. Maybe you'll see me again . . . and maybe you won't."

Jesus Christ, Vincent thought.

Teddy, grinning his smirky grin, raised and lowered his eyebrows, twice. He said, "Have a nice day," turned and walked off.

Jesus Christ, Vincent thought, feeling strangely self-conscious, as though people at the other tables were staring at him, associating him with Teddy.

Look at the freak, crossing the street now in shorts, wearing white *shorts*, camera case hanging, the freak raising his hand with a flat palm toward approaching traffic, the freak looking straight ahead, ignoring the cars blowing their horns at him. Teddy on stage, showing off. Something a kid in junior high might do. The guy who murdered three people in the past three weeks. Look. Moving off with a jaunty stride, on the other side of the street now, with a bounce to his step that seemed to lift him up on his toes.

This isn't what you do, Vincent thought. Play games with weird kids. You can't do it. You have to get out.

Still, he continued to watch Teddy, who had killed three people in the past three weeks, until he was out of sight and Modesta Manosduros said, "I think I am hungry."

Vincent turned to her. "When you looked at him, did you really see him dancing?"

"With a woman, I think," Modesta said. "But is hard to see it because is dark in that place." She said, "I wonder if I could have an 'amburgesa."

* * *

He was aware of himself winding down, worn out.

They drove Modesta home in the limo, music and cool air turned up. Then turned them down to quiet sounds to drive out of the city toward Isla Verde; a nice ride, DeLeon relaxed, Vincent trying not to think.

"I'm going home."

"Can't fake your injury no more?"

"Can't play his game."

"How 'bout I put him on the ground and you drop something heavy on him?"

"I'm tired."

"Doesn't matter or not he still wants you?"

"He does, he'll have to come to Miami Beach."

"This living on comps and good looks is gonna arrive at a screechy halt anyway, anytime now. Nothing is free, is it? Shit," DeLeon said, "I'm gonna have to get a job."

They came to the mosque on the beach. A gambler's mecca—was that the connection? Vincent still wasn't sure. They left the car at the main entrance . . . Vincent winding down finally to reach bottom after days of dead ends, tired to death of thinking.

Then starting up again gradually, not yet aware of it, as he said, "Let's have a few in the lounge, while I can still sign." The idea picking him up a little but not much. The black doorman in cape and turban grinned with teeth like old piano keys, giv-

ing it all he had. And it picked Vincent up some
more. The put-on. The man making a living, playing his part. And DeLeon playing with him, saying,
"Allah is God, my brother." The doorman grinning
his ivory grin back, "And Jackie Garbo is his
prophet. Say tell you he's in the lounge. Anxious to
see you two."

It stopped DeLeon. "Uh-oh."

But lifted Vincent even higher, the prospect of
seeing Jackie again, the idea of buying him a drink.
"Come on." Amazing, though maybe not so amazing. Because Jackie was real and good or bad you
could read him and be entertained. Jackie was
Jackie . . . Who was Teddy? You couldn't say
Teddy was Teddy . . . Teddy in and out of Vincent's
mind, never completely gone, as he walked through
the lobby with DeLeon and into the lounge. Dark,
but there he was, at the bar.

A half-grown bear in a silk suit, raising his glass,
white cuff gleaming, pinky ring winking . . . Vincent walked toward him. He would shake his hand,
slap him on the shoulder, get him off stride and listen to his assumptions and raw asides and enjoy it.
He heard a cord struck softly on the piano, another
and another . . .

Jackie was looking this way, Jackie saying, "It
works. Somebody sent in the fucking clowns.
Where you going?"

To the bandstand—was he kidding? Through the

tables to the small stage, one step up and across to the piano where Linda stopped playing as she saw him. Was she sad or smiling? Or both. He wasn't sure. He said, "You're here . . ."

And she said, "I missed you, Vincent. Boy, did I miss you."

27

AS LONG AS HE COULD LOOK at Linda Moon, close enough to touch, he could be patient and courteous and listen to Jackie, at least while the champagne lasted. Vincent's whole outlook had changed. He sensed there was even something different about Jackie. Listen.

"When you know you're getting it up the kazoo but you allow it, then it's not what you ordinarily call forcible entry. You know what I'm saying?"

Sort of.

"I was hurt. Lemme tell you something, ladies and gentlemen, I can't remember in my experience ever being more deeply hurt . . ."

Actually on stage. He stood at the edge directly above them, a dead mike in his hand as a prop, his audience two light faces and one dark face in the gloom of the nearly empty noontime lounge: Linda, Vincent, DeLeon seated with Jackie's offering, the bottle of champagne, Jackie the good guy continuing:

". . . I couldn't believe it. Here's this honest cop, supposedly, using what he calls leverage, holding my old sidekick, my confidant, the Moose, over my head as a threat. When all he had to say was, 'Mr. Garbo, you mind if we use your company plane? It's very important.' I mean that's all you had to do, ask." Jackie paused, lowered his head, raised it slowly. "Moose, am I a reasonable guy? Relatively you'd say easy to get along with?"

"Kindest man I know," DeLeon said, back in his old job under new conditions, a favorable location.

"Thank you."

"He's a peach," Linda Moon, Now Appearing in the Sultan's Lounge, said. "Has a great ear for music." And looked at Vincent. His turn.

But he couldn't think of anything to add until DeLeon said, "Man's wise, too. Knows when to bail out," and Jackie hooked the mike onto the stand and stepped down to the table.

"He's an entertainer at heart," Vincent said. "Should have a stage in his office."

Sitting down with them Jackie said, "I wanted to I could work this room right here, get a routine together. It's a gift, you got it or you don't. Confidence, presence . . ." Turning to DeLeon. "But I didn't bail out up there, the inference being I ran out on the Donovans . . ."

"Uh-unh," DeLeon said, "I know you wouldn't do that."

"What I did, I excused myself," Jackie said. "Left Dick and Jane playing cutthroat with each other. She is, he's thinking up catchy names for the sandwiches in the deli or he's playing with his Wang. Hey, they want to run the casino *and* the hotel, good luck, they're principal stockholders. I'll run the show here from now on, that's the understanding. Some morning four A.M. I'll get a frantic call, hop back up there and straighten things out. Otherwise I'm here and I love it."

"There's something different about you," Vincent said.

"You notice 'cause you got an eye, you don't miss anything."

"What is it?"

"I'm gonna pay you the highest form a compliment," Jackie said. "You came in my office when we met, sat down, didn't say much . . ."

"Got carried out."

"That was your own fault. You should a stated your business, not led me on like that. But I should a paid more attention to you at the time, your style, the way you handle yourself. You know why? 'Cause I thought about it later. I realized something. I said to myself, this guy's got nice easy moves, never pushes, he listens and he learns things. Which is how you found out all you did, right? I said to myself, that's the way to do it. Don't get excited, lay back. But listen, that's the key to it I learned from you. Listen and don't talk so fucking much. See, guy like you, you prob'ly think you don't have any effect on people. Well, don't sell yourself short, my friend, you got a very nice way about you. Stay with it, you'll do okay."

"Thanks," Vincent said.

In the lobby he said, "I'm not gonna be able to keep my hands off you." She said, "I hope not." In the elevator he said, "I can't wait," and she said, "I can't either." So they took hold of each other and began, their mouths not able to get enough, and didn't come apart when the door opened. They went all the way to the top and had to come down to Vincent's floor to hurry through the hall and into his room, no words between them now, nothing in the way of "I can't wait I can't either" once she stepped out of her pants and raised her dress as he shoved down his jeans and they joined together across the bed, not a moment too soon, breathing into each other until it was done and with immense relief they could again smile, speak.

Teddy was worried he'd have trouble staying on Vincent's tail in this automatic Chevette he'd rented. Some piece of equipment—it took about twenty minutes for the son of a bitch to lug out of

low gear and get moving. When he saw Vincent
also had a Chevette he had to laugh. Here they
were playing a deadly game in a couple of kiddie
cars. The red one following the white one from Isla
Verde through the busy Condado Beach section
and across the bridge to Vincent's old neighborhood. In fact, it looked like he and Linda—wherever the hell she had come from—were going into
the same place where he'd stayed before. The Carmen Apartments above the liquor store. The cop
sure had a lot of class, didn't he? Moving in, it
looked like, both of them with suitcases. Well,
wasn't that cute?

What he'd do, work something like the idea he
had in Atlantic City but never got to use. Follow
Vincent to get Vincent to follow him. Come up next
to him at a light. Let him see you. Maybe make
some remark to the girl, or to Vincent about the
girl—she wasn't bad looking—and then lead them
out in the country somewhere. Have a place picked
out. Stop off the road in some trees and wait for
Vincent to come up to the car to chat or whatever—
look up in his police rule book to see what he could
do and what he couldn't, as dumb and stupid as he
was. Time it, pull out the new stainless steel Smith
& Wesson .38 they said was a military weapon,
stolen from the army depot; it was okay, nothing
fancy. Mr. Magic would do a job with it—pop the
cop between the eyes looking in the car at him and

then give old Linda a pop, hey, give her two pops for one, both at the same time, Jesus—and bid adieu to sunny Puerto Rico on the first plane out. Get back to Atlantic City and see what was cooking.

His mom had said on the phone nothing was. She said the police had not stopped by or called, not even that nice colored man who had admired her parrot stuff so much. He'd told her, "Mom, the jig ain't a cop he's a goddamn kidnapper." His mom said, "You didn't learn language like that in my house." He asked her to send him a check on account of lawyers didn't take VISA and he was going to sue the ass off the police here for persecuting him. His mom said, "What? I can't hear you so good, this connection . . ." Teddy said, "Sure, Mom. All I can say is, you got a pretty shitty attitude for a mom." His mom said, "What? What'd you say?"

Parked across the street and down a bit toward the Hilton, Teddy looked up at the Carmen Apartments, three floors of windows and tiny balconies, an old building on a street named after an Indian, Calle Geronimo. Which didn't make much sense. He didn't believe Geronimo had been a PR. He wondered what apartment they were in . . . And just like that stopped wondering, as Linda appeared on a second-floor balcony, right above the liquor store.

* * *

Vincent didn't mention Miami Beach, that it was
time for him to go home, past time; he would set it
aside for a while. They were together now, closer
because they had been apart. They sat in the sun at
Escambron beneath that clean sky and talked
about things as they thought of them, Teddy already out of the way as a topic, done to death.

"I can't play with him anymore."

"Good. But it makes you mad."

"More than that."

"You have to forget about him."

He was trying. They watched the sleek young
bodies in skimpy stringy bathing suits, the vendors
cooking, selling, the families on blankets, and
looked out at the low barrier of rock a hundred
yards offshore and imagined it, squinting, a rusting
snip's hull, a long brown submarine . . . And a red
Chevette behind them. Parked back in the shade of
Australian pines. He didn't imagine the car, it was
there, and felt someone inside it watching them—
trying to forget Teddy but feeling his presence.

Linda had said, "I missed you, Vincent. Boy, did
I miss you." And it was true, he believed it. But
then learned another truth. An executive at Bally's
had forced a keyboard player on Linda. "A guy
who used to arrange for Jerry Vale—I'm not kidding, he actually did, and he brought his charts,

very tight with the exec, you understand, had worked for him before and I was supposed to play his music, this high romantic drama or cute little happy Italian numbers . . ."

"So you didn't leave there—" Vincent began.

"Wait. I had to get out, Vincent, it's true, I won't lie to you. But I missed you—I mean I really missed you, and that's truer. I could've gone to Orlando, I had an offer . . ."

"You got a ride with Jackie . . ."

"I went to see Tommy about a job and ran into Jackie as he was getting ready to leave. He said the building was starting to shake and things were coming loose. He said he needed somebody to talk to, preferably a woman."

"He sounds different."

"Don't you know why? Wait. First I find out Miss Congeniality left him."

"She didn't."

"LaDonna went back to Tulsa. Jackie said after all he did for her. Could've made her a star. Then, I find out, he had a long session with the cops, I guess about Ricky and the guy Ricky shot."

Vincent said, "That was it," with a grin. Jackie had got out before they connected him with the bad guys; no other reason. "He's the same Jackie but he sounds different."

"That's it exactly. He was more nervous than usual—I mean when I went to see him. But he came onto me without wasting a minute. 'You want to work, kid? You're just what I need down at Isla Verde, make you a star within eight weeks, guaranteed.' The hotshot from Vegas. On the plane he starts telling me about all the celebrities he knows, his very dear friends, all the personally signed photographs in his office and how he makes a bet with everybody who comes in . . ."

Vincent nodding, "I know."

". . . he'll give 'em a hundred bucks if they can name a major fucking entertainer who isn't on that wall. Well, I bet him a hundred bucks he couldn't go the whole trip, from wherever we were at the time all the way to San Juan without saying 'fuck' in one form or another at least once."

"He lost."

"He could barely speak. He'd start to say something and there'd be a long pause, like he was learning a foreign language. Finally he said, 'Fuck it,' and handed me a hundred-dollar bill and said he was going to do it on his own."

"That's what it was," Vincent said, "I noticed in the lounge. It isn't that he listens any more than he ever did. But he didn't use the word, I don't think even once."

"He did use it once, I remember," Linda said, "but for Jackie that's fucking remarkable."

*   *   *

As they dressed to go to dinner Linda watched Vincent slip the blue-steel automatic in the waist of his trousers, at the small of his back, and glance at his profile in the dresser mirror, his linen sportcoat hanging open, limp.

"You saw him," Linda said.

"I think so."

"He knows where we are?"

"I think so."

"What're you going to do?"

"Nothing."

"You're shutting me out," Linda said.

No, he was detached; he was a policeman, he knew how to get outside of himself, look at something without letting his feelings get in the way. Teddy might be back but he was not between them. He told her that at dinner in the Spanish restaurant, Torreblanca. He told her Teddy would have to wait, and maybe he would get tired of it and go home. He told her he wasn't worried about Teddy, as long as he sat facing the door. Linda said, "I've never even seen him."

Vincent said, "Would you like to?"

They came out of the restaurant, waited as the parking attendant brought them the white Chevette, backing it up the entrance drive from the street. "He's about halfway down the block," Vincent said, "to the left."

Ready to tail them. Magdalena one-way east and

Vincent would have to turn to the right leaving the drive.

But he didn't. He turned left, no cars coming in the moments it took to coast quietly toward the red Chevette, head on, to hear tree frogs shrilling and see Teddy raise his hand in the headlight beam—there he was. Linda saying, "That's Teddy?" as Vincent cut around the car and picked up speed. He turned off Magdalena at the end of the block.

"That's Teddy."

In the night traffic on Ashford Avenue, the young Puerto Ricans cruising the Condado section, he appeared behind them again. Vincent kept track of him in his mirror. Linda turned in her seat to look back.

"He *waved*. Did you see him?"

Vincent didn't answer.

The red Chevette's headlights moved out of the rearview mirror. Vincent glanced over. Teddy was coming up gradually on their right. They stopped at a light and Teddy pulled up next to them, close.

Linda said it again. "That's Teddy?"

Vincent watched him, Teddy looking straight ahead, drumming lightly on the steering wheel to the music coming from the car radio. The light changed. Teddy looked over and gave them his smirky grin.

Linda said, "You haven't even laid a hand on him? I don't believe it."

"If I started," Vincent said, "I don't think I could stop."

"Why would you want to?" Linda said.

The white Chevette and the red Chevette crept along in traffic side by side, came to a stop at the light in front of the Holiday Inn.

Teddy looked over. He said, "This your new girl-friend? . . . Nice-looking babe." He waited, staring, Linda staring back at him. " 'Ey, arn'cha talking to me no more?"

Vincent kept quiet; he believed he'd better.

Linda turned to him. She said, "Vincent?" But didn't say anything after that.

Teddy said, "She as good as our PR pussy was?"

The light changed.

Vincent was watching it and the white Chevette moved off the light ahead of the red Chevette, coming to the end of Condado Beach now, out of the rows of hotels and shops, to cross the low bridge that was like a section of causeway over the inlet and pointed one-way in the direction of Old San Juan.

Vincent pushed the white Chevette to forty-five watching the mirror to see the red Chevette gaining, coming up again in the lane on Linda's side. He eased back slightly on the accelerator. The red Chevette came up, pulled even, close to them, Vincent thinking, Give him a nudge, just enough. Teddy was yelling in the wind, through his open window and into their car, " 'Ey, stupid! Catch me if you can!"

Now, Vincent was thinking, ready to crank the wheel, when Linda beat him to it—Jesus, with the same thought, the same urge—grabbed the top of the steering wheel with both hands, gave it a quick hard yank to the right as she yelled, "Fuck you, Ted!" Even the proper name he would have used, amazing. And saw the guy's eyes go wild in the moment the white Chevette tore into the side of the red Chevette, metal scraping ripping metal, forcing the red one to veer off and jump the sidewalk, out of control. The white one slowed down, Vincent and Linda looking back at the sounds of horns and brakes; the red one last seen, a glimpse of it, plowing along the guardrail, metal scraping cement till it ground to a stop.

He told her in the night he wasn't going to lose her. Not now, after all this. She told him he couldn't lose her if he tried.

They could tell each other in different ways they were in love and couldn't live without each other and become analytical and say it wasn't just physical either, the hots. Was it? It *was* physical, you bet it was, not able to get enough of each other, but it was even more than that. Wasn't it? Yes, of course, it was. It was real. They could talk in the night about love, with feeling, using familiar words, and it sounded wonderful, natural, no other way to say it.

But he had to go home.

Tomorrow they'd go to Mayaguez and the day after that, in the afternoon, he'd leave for Miami.

She understood. She had an eight-week engagement and would do part of it, a couple of weeks, then follow him to Miami and find work.

She said, "You can't follow me around, doing what you do, and you're more important to me than playing a piano, Vincent. But I wish I could make you stay a while. I wish you had just come here on your leave and I had just started playing . . . I play better when I know you're close by . . . And we'd have all day together and almost all night and nothing to think about but us. Wouldn't that be neat?"

"That would be neat," Vincent said.

Later on in the night, waking up, he walked to the balcony and stood for several minutes looking down at the empty street.

Teddy got up during the night to go to the bathroom. "Go potty," his mom called it; woman her age. She'd even say to Buddy, poop all over his stand, "Buddy go potty?" Tub a lard trying to be cute. He had actually been inside her and almost killed her, she said, coming out at birth. Well, excu-uuse me. It could still be arranged. She's sleeping, hold a pillow over her face so as not to have to look at her. Lay on top of it till she finally quit bucking and breathing and he would never have to hear her say "Kisser mom" or "Buddy go potty" again. He shouldn't think things like that. He said to the bathroom mirror, "Would you do that to your mom?" Then had to grin at himself, turning his head to look at the grin from different angles.

"Hi."

"Hi, yourself."

"Haven't I seen you someplace before?"

"Now you do, now you don't."

"Wait."

He stared at himself in silence, not grinning now.

"When you gonna do it?"

"What?"

"You know what."

He stared at himself in silence.

"Tomorrow. Didn't I tell you?"

28

IN MAYAGUEZ, in a barrio called Dulces Labios, they found Iris's grandmother living in a house made of scrap lumber painted light blue. The grandmother sent for relatives to come and Vincent and Linda waited, standing by the white Chevette with red scrape marks on its side. They were tired from the drive. It had rained on the way here from San Juan. They didn't look forward to the hours it would take them to drive back, or the road or the leisurely traffic. At least they were together; they had been together in this from the beginning and it was part of the feeling between them. When the women came Vincent presented the stainless steel urn to the grandmother. She hesitated before taking it and passed it on quickly as she saw her reflection in the polished metal. Each woman in turn looked away to avoid seeing herself in the urn, passing it on and making the sign of the cross. Vincent told them Iris's death was an accident; one night she fell from the balcony of an apartment. He said he was very sorry to have to tell them this; he said Iris's friends loved her and would miss her. The women nodded. None of them asked him how it happened that she fell. She fell; they accepted it or didn't wish to know how or why or if anyone was with her.

It was done. They were relieved but remained silent until they were out of the barrio called Sweet Lips, past the docks of the port and finally in the country, out in the island. They let the wind blow into their open windows, the sun fading behind them.

"You've done this before," Linda said.

"I've never delivered ashes."

"I mean told people someone was dead, the relatives."

"Too many times."

"You do it so well. You show you care."

He turned the radio on to static and turned it off.

"I'm glad I didn't say anything at the funeral home. Remember?"

"To young Mr. Bertoia?"

"It would've been dumb."

"There was no need to."

"You have a nice calming effect on me, Vincent." After a moment she said, "Except when we're in bed."

It was full dark by the time they got back to the Carmen Apartments and pulled into the parking area, the courtyard by the liquor store.

* * *

Teddy said out loud, "Well, it's about time. Where'n the hell you been, sightseeing? Shit, keeping me waiting."

He watched them from across the street, sitting in the dark-gray Dodge Aries he'd got when he turned the Chevette in as defective. He'd watched the two PRs that worked for Hertz walk around the car running their hands over it, waiting for them to ask what happened. Was he in a wreck? Was it reported to the police? He told them he'd left the car parked on the street and this was how he found it. Somebody must a sideswiped it. They said, on both sides at once? On this side, yes. See, white paint? But on the other side—what did it, a building? Getting smart with him. He didn't have to explain nothing. He told them to get another car for him, fast, or he wouldn't give them any more of his business. They had sure taken their time about it.

Vincent and his girlfriend Linda were out of the white Chevette, walking away from it arm in arm. Wasn't that sweet? They stopped like they were going to go into the liquor store. Nope, decided not to, kept going and went in the apartment entrance.

Teddy slid down some in his seat so he could look up at their balcony now, second floor, directly above the liquor store. He waited for lights to come on . . . There.

"Now make yourselves a couple of drinks," Teddy said. He told them they were thirsty from all that sightseeing. He told them to get comfortable and bring their drinks out on the balcony, get some fresh air. Sitting down or standing up, it didn't matter to him. Or whether he looked in the cop's eyes or not. The hell with it. Teddy had made up his mind he was going to get it done. Soon as they appeared—walk out into the street like he was crossing, stop, aim his .38 up there and give 'em each three rounds, Vincent first and foremost, Vincent more than three if it was necessary. A woman you could go up there and kill all different ways. Have some fun.

It looked like only one light was on up there. What were they doing? Teddy said, " 'Ey, you can screw her anytime. Come on out on the balcony." He waited. Shit.

A figure appeared, moving the curtain aside.

There was nothing attractive about the street in daylight, a turnoff to the Caribe Hilton at the end of the block. In darkness now the street showed moments of life, cars occasionally moving past, reflecting the liquor store's lights on painted metal. The ocean, a long block away, lay hidden, with only a faint trace of its scent in the night air. Linda breathed it in and out: Linda on the balcony in the

short light wrap LaDonna had worn, Linda seeing
the Hilton lights and thinking of LaDonna, who
had walked away from the noise, the neon dazzle.
No, LaDonna had backed away, still bewildered . . .
soon to appear at shopping-mall openings and say
or sing whatever she was told. It would happen because LaDonna wanted to be seen and LaDonna
would strike a glamor pose and shine in the glitter
of commercial lighting. You had to have talent and
style to turn on your own lights and perform for an
audience that listened and knew what you were doing and if they didn't, okay, you played for yourself,
and your husband, your lover. How about in a
beachhouse on Key Largo? Linda sipped chablis
from a water glass, let the curtains fall in place as
she heard Vincent.

"It's all yours."

Vincent stood in the living room in his white
briefs, buttoning his shirt.

"You have great legs."

"So do you."

"As good as LaDonna's?"

"Who's LaDonna?"

She held up the glass. "We could use some more
of this."

"It's on the list. You think of anything else?"

"Bread?"

"We've got the rolls. *Empanadillas* for appetiz-
ers, a mixed salad, *alcapurrias*, what else? DeLeon's

friend's bringing the *piononos*. Wine, coffee, I'll get some booze . . ."

"Vincent? Am I going to have to learn to cook Puerto Rican?"

"You'll love it."

He was going back into the bedroom and she raised her voice. "That's not an answer."

She heard him say, "You need cigarettes?"

"Yes. Please."

"What else?"

"That's all. What time are they coming?"

"I have to give the Moose a call." There was a silence. She finished the wine in her glass. Vincent appeared in the living room again, dressed now in his blue shirt and faded khakis. "I didn't know what time we'd be back."

"Don't forget to call the hotel."

"I won't. I'll tell them you've got the trots. Puerto Rican food will do it to you."

"Vincent?"

"What?"

"This is our last night."

"Our last one here." He walked to the door and opened it. "We can do a lot better than this. Be right back."

He was going out as she said, "Can we live on the ocean?" The door closed.

* * *

Teddy had six .38 rounds in the revolver, he had six more in his right-hand pants pocket and six in the left. If he couldn't do the job with—what'd that make?—eighteen shots, he oughtn't to be here. The gun was so shiny he'd have to keep it in his pants till he was out in the street, no cars coming. Linda had appeared up there, looking cute in her shorty outfit. But no Vincent. Shit. Teddy said, "Come on, Vincent, you son of a bitch," lowered his gaze to the street and, Jesus Christ, there he was, coming along the side of the building past the cars, coming out of darkness to the liquor store. Look at him, right there across the street. Going in for a six-pack or something. In his shirtsleeves. No place to hide a gun, no way. Teddy wiped the palms of his hands on his pants. He picked up the .38 from the seat close to him.

Walk over there like he had his arms folded. Get behind one of those cars by the building. Wait. Get him coming out of the store.

Linda was pinning up her hair, the shower running, when she thought of it and said, "Cheese" to the bathroom mirror, caught her own smile and was out of there, slipping on the wrap as she hurried through the living room to the balcony, to catch Vincent before he got inside the store—tell him to get cheese and crackers and potato chips, some gringo snacks to go with the *empanadillas*—and looked over the rail straight down. Too late, missed him.

She looked up to see Teddy in the middle of the street.

Even before the car passed and he continued across and she recognized him she knew it was Teddy coming. Teddy concentrating on the liquor store, cautious, keeping beyond the edge of light on the pavement, walking in a peculiar way. People didn't walk with their arms folded. She saw his arms unfold as it was in her mind and saw the glint of bright metal and wanted to call out—gripping the balcony rail as hard as she could. Yell for help, yell at Teddy, yell at Vincent the moment he came out—and it could be a moment too late. She saw the gun in Teddy's hand, Teddy moving toward the cars parked in the courtyard. Linda let go of the rail, aware that she had to run but remain calm, hurry without losing her head and do something dumb.

Vincent's gun was on the dresser.

It was heavy and her hand was wet. There were catches and strange little knobs, numbers and names etched in the metal. She saw someone in a movie, in a hundred movies, slide the top part of the barrel back and she did it and jumped as a cartridge ejected and the slide clicked back into place. Vincent would keep the safety on. The catch, she hoped to God, by her thumb as she gripped the gun. Push it up . . .

Vincent saw it coming and thought, Not again.

Carrying the groceries reminded him of that other time. Hearty Burgundy, prune juice and spaghetti sauce. This time chablis, J&B scotch, Puerto Rican rum and a family-size bottle of Coca-Cola, carrying the sack in front of him, both arms around it. That other time he thought he might have seen the guy before, in a holding cell. This time he knew the guy quite well and knew the guy was not going to tell him to drop the groceries and hand over his wallet. This guy's only intention was to shoot him dead. What had he learned that other time that might help him now? Absolutely nothing. This time he had learned, so far, never go to the store without your gun. But even if he had it . . .

Teddy said, "Well well well," coming out of the dark to smirk at him, holding the bright-metal piece low, elbow tight against his side.

Vincent looked him in the eye, trying for an expression that would show honest surprise. What's going on? What is this? He didn't want to look threatening. He didn't want Teddy to take anything the wrong way and all of a sudden empty the gun. He wanted to reason with Teddy, at least try. The trouble was, Vincent had to concentrate so hard on appearing harmless, surprised—while hiding the fact he was scared to death—he couldn't think of anything to say. *Drop it, motherfucker, or I'll blow your fucking head off* kept coming to mind. It was a good line, but not one that would work here. Blow his head off with what?

Teddy said, "I want to be looking in your eyes as I pull the trigger."

"Why, Ted?"

"I'm not Ted, I'm Teddy."

Shit. "Okay. Would you tell me—see, I don't understand—why you want to do that?"

"You don't know what I feel or anything about me. You *think* you do."

"I give you that impression?"

"Cut the bullshit. Time you busted me seven and a half years ago, I could tell. Like you thought you could see inside me. Well, you can't."

"No, I'd be the first to admit that. I think what we have here is a misunderstanding . . ." Jesus Christ, did they.

Vincent was about to stumble on, think of something, anything, when he saw a figure in white, beyond Teddy's right shoulder, run from the building entrance to the cars parked in the courtyard, and he said, "What we should do is clear it up."

"What else you gonna say, I got a fucking gun aimed at your gut?"

The figure was beyond Teddy's left shoulder

now, among the cars, coming out toward them. Linda, Jesus, in her skimpy white robe.

"You don't want to be in the position, get brought up for murder—you know, that's pretty serious—and find out you were wrong. I don't mean *wrong*, I mean you misinterpreted, made an honest mistake of what you thought I was thinking."

Hearing himself but seeing Linda, Jesus, holding his police gun out in front of her in both hands, sneaking up hunched over, maybe twenty feet away and closing in. Teddy was saying "Bullshit!" repeating it with feeling, with everything he had, working himself up. Teddy saying, "Look at me! Look at me in the eye, goddamn it!" Vincent wanted to. He raised his eyebrows to stretch his eyes open wide, felt like an idiot and didn't care, wanting with all his heart to tell Linda about the safety at the back end of the slide on a Smith & Wesson Model 39 parabellum. If it was on and she tried to fire and Teddy heard her . . . Wait. Or if it was off and she did fire a steel-jacketed nine-millimeter round right at Teddy right in front of him . . .

Teddy was saying, "Open 'em wide! Come on, wider!" Showing the whites of his own wild eyes, Teddy right at the edge . . .

As Linda stretched both arms all the way out, braced herself and fired.

And Vincent closed and opened his eyes, saw her

juggle the gun and drop it as Teddy slammed into him and Teddy's gun went off between them into the grocery sack of bottles, went off again and went off again, the bottles gone now as Vincent tried to grab hold of Teddy clinging to him and put him down, step on his gun. But something was wrong. Shit, he knew what it was. It wasn't pain, not yet, it was his strength going. He had been shot somewhere and the rug-burn pain would come once his adrenaline drained off. He had learned that the other time. He had to find Teddy's gunhand right now, Teddy holding on like dead weight. He got hold of Teddy's arm and took a step and threw him as hard as he could, but it wasn't enough. Teddy reeled off, staggering, but stayed on his feet. Vincent started after him and his legs lost their purpose, wouldn't work. It was Vincent who went down and had to crawl in the dark toward Linda's white bare feet on the pavement—where his gun was supposed to be and wasn't—Linda saying something, mad or urgent. He couldn't tell or stop to look up at her and listen, not now, or explain what he had in mind. But she knew. She came down to him on her knees holding the Smith and put it in his hand, grip into the palm. She knew. He turned with one hand on the ground, gun extended in the other and put it on Teddy. Vincent paused to say "Drop it." Gave him that option.

Teddy looked wobbly, drunk, weaving as he

aimed the bright-metal piece right at them, at one or the other, from less than twenty feet. So Vincent shot him. Put one dead center through Teddy's solar plexus and killed the poor wimp who thought he was magic and couldn't be scared.

29

VINCENT MADE A TRIP through the Ashford Medical Center from Emergency to Surgery to Intensive Care without seeing much of it. In the morning they moved him to a private room on the second floor of the old hospital's newer wing. Through the window at an angle he could see the high-rise top of Howard Johnson's Motor Lodge against blue sky. A good sign.

He believed he was on safe ground legally. Even after the guy had shot him, attempting to commit murder, he had offered the guy the option of staying alive, for an indeterminate period of time, or dying then and there. He had not read the fine print to him, but that was what "Drop it" amounted to.

He believed he was reasonably okay physically, though his chart would indicate some kind of trauma inside, an insulted organ maybe; he did have a couple of tubes in him and a key question to ask somebody. He knew the pain he felt could be relieved. If his condition were serious he'd be in a room full of monitors and not looking at Howard Johnson's Motor Lodge.

They had given him good dope. He opened his eyes to see Linda in the hall talking to DeLeon and Lorendo Paz, Linda the one he wanted to see.

When she came to him she looked so sad and then felt so good, close, and smelled so good, kissing him, touching his face, asking him if he was all right, if he needed anything. He asked her if she would go close the door.

She smiled—he was all right—closed it, came back to him and he asked her where he was shot, touching the sheet below his waist, close to his groin.

"I think it's right here. But what I don't know—did I lose anything important?"

"About six inches of bowel. You can't eat Puerto Rican food anymore. The bullet lodged in your gluteus maximus," Linda said, "your ass."

"I know where my gluteus maximus is."

"Can I look?"

"You want to?"

She pulled the sheet down carefully, lifted his gray hospital gown. "You've got stitches in your groin, like you had your appendix out."

"Nothing's missing?"

"No, it's there. Awww, look at it. Poor little guy."

He said, "Linda? Pull the catheter out, will you? I don't need it."

"Should I?"

He could tell she wanted to and he would love her forever if she did. She knew what was good for him, how to make him happy. She pulled the tube out so gently, slowly. What a touch. His eyes filled. He wanted to tell her how much he needed her and wanted to be with her . . .

But she was kissing him again, brushing his mouth with her lips, murmuring then, close to him, "Vincent, there's something I have to tell you." He waited and she said, "You know the bullet they took out of your butt?"

He said, "Oh no, you better not tell me."

"I have to," Linda said. "It was from your gun, not Teddy's. I guess it went right through him."

He took a moment, breathed in and out, settled. "It will do that."

"I shot you, Vincent."

"You didn't mean to."

"No, but I shot you. I want you to understand, it wasn't to get you to stay."

Vincent said, "Oh." He said, "Are you sure?"

Coming Up . . .

A sneak preview of

TISHOMINGO BLUES

by Elmore Leonard

DENNIS LENAHAN THE HIGH DIVER would tell people that if you put a fifty-cent piece on the floor and looked down at it, that's what the tank looked like from the top of that eighty-foot steel ladder. The tank itself was twenty-two feet across and the water in it never more than nine feet deep. Dennis said from that high up you want to come out of your dive to enter the water feet first, your hands at the last moment protecting your privates and your butt squeezed tight, or it was like getting a 40,000-gallon enema.

When he told this to girls who hung out at amusement parks they'd put a cute look of pain on their faces and say what he did was awesome. But wasn't it like really dangerous? Dennis would tell them you could break your back if you didn't kill yourself, but the rush you got was worth it. These summertime girls loved daredevils, even ones twice their age. It kept

Dennis going off that perch eighty feet in the air and going out for beers after to tell stories. Once in a while he'd fall in love for the summer, or part of it.

The past few years Dennis had been putting on one-man shows during the week. Then for Saturday and Sunday he'd bring in a couple of young divers when he could to join him in a repertoire of comedy dives they called "dillies," the three of them acting nutty as they went off from different levels and hit the water at the same time. It meant dirt-cheap motel rooms during the summer and sleeping in the setup truck between gigs, a way of life Dennis the high diver had to accept if he wanted to perform. What he couldn't take anymore, finally, were the amusement parks, the tiresome pizzazz, the smells, the colored lights, rides going round and round to that calliope sound forever.

What he did as a plan of escape was call resort hotels in South Florida and tell whoever would listen he was Dennis Lenahan, a professional exhibition diver who had performed in major diving shows all over the world, including the cliffs of Acapulco. What he proposed was that he'd dive into their swimming pool from the top of the hotel or off his eighty-foot ladder twice a day as a special attraction.

They'd say, "Leave your number" and never call back.

They'd say, "Yeah, right" and hang up.

One of them told him, "The pool's only five feet deep," and Dennis said, no problem, he knew a guy in New Orleans went off from twenty-nine feet into twelve inches of water. A pool five feet deep? Dennis was sure they could work something out.

No, they couldn't.

He happened to see a brochure that advertised Tunica, Mississippi, as "The Casino Capital of the South" with photos of the hotels located along the Mississippi River. One of them caught his eye, the Tishomingo Lodge & Casino. Dennis recognized the manager's name, Billy Darwin, and made the call.

"Mr. Darwin, this is Dennis Lenahan, world champion high diver. We met one time in Atlantic City."

Billy Darwin said, "We did?"

"I remember I thought at first you were Robert Redford, only you're a lot younger. You were running the sports book at Spade's." Dennis waited. When there was no response he said, "How high is your hotel?"

This Billy Darwin was quick. He said, "You want to dive off the roof?"

"Into your swimming pool," Dennis said, "twice a day as a special attraction."

"We go up seven floors."

"That sounds just right."

"But the pool's about a hundred feet away. You'd have to take a good running start, wouldn't you?"

Right there, Dennis knew he could work something out with this Billy Darwin. "I could set my tank right next to the hotel, dive from the roof into nine feet of water. Do a matinee performance and one at night with spotlights on me, seven days a week."

"How much you want?"

Dennis spoke right up, talking to a man who dealt with high rollers. "Five hundred a day."

"How long a run?"

"The rest of the season. Say eight weeks."

"You're worth twenty-eight grand?"

That quick, off the top of his head.

"I have setup expenses—hire a rigger and put in a system to filter the water in the tank. It stands more than a few days it gets scummy."

"You don't perform all year?"

"If I can work six months I'm doing good."

"Then what?"

"I've been a ski instructor, a bartender . . ."

Billy Darwin's quiet voice asked him, "Where are you?"

In a room at the Fiesta Motel, Panama City, Florida, Dennis told him, performing every evening at the Miracle Strip amusement park. "My contract'll keep me here till the end of the month," Dennis said, "but that's it. I've reached the point . . . Actually I don't think I can do another amusement park all summer."

There was a silence on the line, Billy Darwin maybe wondering why but not curious enough to ask.

"Mr. Darwin?"

He said, "Can you get away before you finish up there?"

"If I can get back the same night, before showtime."

Something the man would like to hear.

He said, "Fly into Memphis. Take Sixty-one due south and in thirty minutes you're in Tunica, Mississippi."

Dennis said, "Is it a nice town?"

But got no answer. The man had hung up.

This trip Dennis never did see Tunica or even the Mighty Mississippi. He came south through farmland until he began to spot hotels in the distance rising out of fields of soybeans. He came to signs at crossroads pointing off to Harrah's, Bally's, Sam's Town, the Isle of Capri. A serious-looking Indian on a billboard aimed his bow and arrow down a road that took Dennis to the Tishomingo Lodge & Casino. It featured a tepee-like structure rising a good three stories above the entrance, a precast, concrete tepee with neon tubes running up and around it. Or was it a wig-wam?

The place wasn't open yet. They were still landscaping the grounds, putting in shrubs, lay-ing sod on both sides of a stream that ran to a mound of boulders and became a waterfall. Den-nis parked his rental among trucks loaded with plants and young trees, got out, and spotted Billy Darwin right away talking to a contractor. Den-nis recognized the Robert Redford hair that made him appear younger than his forty or so years, about the same age as Dennis, the same slight build, tan and trim, a couple of cool guys in their sunglasses. One difference, Dennis's hair was dark and longer, almost to his shoulders. Darwin was turning, starting his way as Dennis said, "Mr. Darwin?"

He paused, but only a moment. "You're the diver."

"Yes sir, Dennis Lenahan."

Darwin said, "You've been at it a while, uh?" with sort of a smile, Dennis wasn't sure.

"I turned pro in '79," Dennis said. "The next

year I won the world cliff-diving championship in Switzerland, a place called Ticino. You go off from eighty-five feet into the river."

The man didn't seem impressed or in any hurry.

"You ever get hurt?"

"You can crash, enter the water just a speck out of line, it can hurt like hell. The audience thinks it was a rip, perfect."

"You carry insurance?"

"I sign a release. I break my neck it won't cost you anything. I've only been injured, I mean where I needed attention, was my first time at Acapulco. I broke my nose."

Dennis felt Billy Darwin studying him, showing just a faint smile as he said, "You like to live on the edge, uh?"

"Some of the teams I've performed with I was always the edge guy," Dennis said, feeling he could talk to this man. "I've got eighty dives from different heights and most of 'em I can do hungover, like a flying reverse somersault, your standard high dive. But I don't know what I'm gonna do till I'm up there. It depends on the crowd, how the show's going. But I'll tell you something, you stand on the perch looking down eighty feet to the water, you know you're alive."

Darwin was nodding. "The girls watching you . . ."

"That's part of it. The crowd holding its breath."

"Come out of the water with your hair slicked back . . ."

Where was he going with this?

"I can see why you do it. But for how long? What will you do after to show off?"

Billy Darwin the man here, confident, saying anything he wanted.

Dennis said, "You think I worry about it?"

"You're not desperate," Darwin said, "but I'll bet you're looking around." He turned saying, "Come on."

Dennis followed him into the hotel, through the lobby where they were laying carpet, and into the casino, gaming tables on one side of the main aisle, a couple of thousand slot machines on the other, like every casino Dennis had ever been in. He said to Darwin's back, "I went to dealer's school in Atlantic City. Got a job at Spade's the same time you were there." It didn't draw a comment. "I didn't like how I had to dress," Dennis said, "so I quit."

Darwin paused, turning enough to look at Dennis.

"But you like to gamble."

"Now and then."

"There's a fella works here as a host," Darwin said. "Charlie Hoke. Chickasaw Charlie, he claims to be part Indian. Spent eighteen years in organized baseball, pitched for Detroit in the '84 World Series. I told Charlie about your call and he said, 'Sign him up.' He said a man that likes high risk is gonna leave his paycheck on one of these tables."

Dennis said, "Chickasaw Charlie, huh? Never heard of him."

They came out back of the hotel to the patio bar and swimming pool landscaped to look like a pond sitting there among big leafy plants and boulders. Dennis looked up at the hotel, balconies on every floor to the top, saying as his gaze came to the sky, "You're right, I'd have to get shot out of a cannon." He looked at the pool again. "It's not deep enough anyway. What I can do, place the tank fairly close to the building and dive straight down."

Now Darwin looked up at the hotel. "You'd want to miss the balconies."

"I'd go off there at the corner."

"What's the tank look like?"

"The Fourth of July, it's white with red and blue stars. What I could do," Dennis said, deadpan, "paint the tank to look like birchbark and hang animal skins around the rim."

Darwin gave him a look and swung his gaze out across the sweep of lawn that reached to the Mississippi, the river out of sight beyond a low rise. He didn't say anything staring out there, so Dennis prompted him.

"That's the spot for an eighty-foot ladder. Plenty of room for the guy wires. You rig four to every ten-foot section of ladder. It still sways a little when you're up there." He waited for Darwin.

"Thirty-two wires?"

"Nobody's looking at the wires. They're a twelve-gauge soft wire. You barely notice them."

"You bring everything yourself, the tank, the ladder?"

"Everything. I got a Chevy truck with a big van body and a hundred and twenty thousand miles on it."

"How long's it take you to set up?"

"Three days or so, if I can find a rigger."

Dennis told him how you put the tank together first, steel rods connecting the sections, Dennis said, the way you hang a door. Once the tank's put together you wrap a cable around it, tight. Next you spread ten or so bales of hay on the ground inside for a soft floor, then tape your plastic liner to the walls and add water. The water holds the liner in place. Dennis said he'd pump it out of the river. "May as well, it's right there."

Darwin asked him where he was from.

"New Orleans, originally. Some family and my ex-wife's still there. Virginia. We got married too young and I was away most of the time." It was how he always told it. "We're still friends though . . . sorta."

Dennis waited. No more questions, so he continued explaining how you set up. How you put up your ladder, fit the ten-foot sections on to one another and tie each one off with the guy wires as you go up. You use what's called a gin pole you hook on, it's rigged with a pulley and that's how you haul up the sections one after another. Fit them on to each other and tie off with the guy wires before you do the next one.

"What do you call what you dive off from?"

"You mean the perch."

"It's at the top of the highest ladder?"

"It hooks on the fifth rung of the ladder, so you have something to hang on to."

"Then you're actually going off from seventy-five feet," Darwin said, "not eighty."

"But when you're standing on the perch,"

Dennis said, "your head's above eighty feet, and that's where you are, believe me, in your head. You're no longer thinking about the girl in the thong bikini you were talking to, you're thinking of nothing but the dive. You want to see it in your head before you go off, so you don't have to think and make adjustments when you're dropping thirty-two feet a second."

A breeze came up and Darwin turned to face it, running his hand through his thick hair. Dennis let his blow.

"Do you hit the bottom?"

"Your entry," Dennis said, "is the critical point of the dive. You want your body in the correct attitude, what we call a scoop position, like you're sitting down with your legs extended and it levels you off. Do it clean, that's a rip entry." Dennis was going to add color but saw Darwin about to speak.

"I'll give you two hundred a day for two weeks guaranteed and we'll see how it goes. I'll pay your rigger and the cost of setting up. How's that sound?"

Dennis dug into the pocket of his jeans for the Kennedy half-dollar he kept there and dropped it on the polished brick surface of the patio. Darwin looked down at it and Dennis said, "That's what the tank looks like from the top of an eighty-foot ladder." He told the rest of it, up to what you did to avoid the 40,000-gallon enema, and said, "How about three hundred a day for the two weeks' trial?"

Billy Darwin, finally raising his gaze from the half-dollar shining in the sun, gave Dennis a nod and said, "Why not."

Nearly two months went by before Dennis got back and had his show set up.

He had to finish the gig in Florida. He had to take the ladder and tank apart, load all the equipment just right to fit in the truck. He had to stop off in Birmingham, Alabama, to pick up another 1,800 feet of soft wire. And when the goddamn truck broke down as he was getting on the Interstate, Dennis had to wait there over a week while they sent for parts and finally did the job. He said to Billy Darwin the last time he called him from the road, "You know it's major work when they have to pull the head off the engine."

Darwin didn't ask what was wrong with it. All he said was "So the life of a daredevil isn't all cute girls and getting laid."

Sounding like a nice guy while putting you in your place, looking down at what you did for a living.

Dennis had never said anything about getting laid. What he should do was ask Billy Darwin if he'd like to climb the ladder. See if he had the nerve to look down from up there.